MW01363914

BELLA COMBE JOURNAL

BELLA COMBE JOURNAL

BILL GASTON

Second printing, September, 1996

The publisher gratefully acknowledges the support of the Canada Council and the Ontario Arts Council.

Earlier versions of chapters of this book appeared as "Big Animals" in *Exile,* and "Lying Lights" in *The New Quarterly.* Both subsequently appeared in *North of Jesus' Beans* (Cormorant).

The author would like to thank, for their help with earlier, more painful, versions of this book, Jerry Newman, François Bonneville, Joan MacLeod, Jennifer Glossop, Dede Gaston, Beverly Endersby, and Jan Geddes.

Cover design by Thomas Pritchard,

Artcetera Graphics, Dunvegan, Ontario.

Author photo © Fish Doctor.

Printed and bound in Canada.

Cormorant Books Inc.
RR 1
Dunvegan, Ontario
Canada K0C 1J0

Canadian Cataloguing in Publication Data

Gaston, Bill, 1953-
Bella Combe journal

ISBN 0-920953-94-8

I. Title.

PS8563.A76B44 1996 C813'.54 C96-900178-9
PR9199.3.G373B44 1996

For Lise, Vaughn, and Connor.
Wisdom, Humour, and Compassion.

January 14th

I am an exile. A fisherman. I live alone. And I am marked, *Keeper at the Gates of Heaven and Hell.*

Grandiose enough for you, Annie?

I start, but was hard to convince. I explained to her that to sit down to an autobiography is the truest waste of time. I added, quite cleverly I thought: words are a net trying to catch a river. But then Annie (she can't resist throwing me back my own metaphors, extended) said, "Well, you should know how water-heavy a net can get."

Then she gave me her typewriter, said she didn't need it anymore. Limped it down the beach, into the cabin, and dropped it onto my table, saying, "Here." Shrugging as if to say that now it would be easy to type down a lifetime, as if the typewriter had been the hard part.

It's electric. To get Tom Moe's generator I had to trade my beautiful little Evinrude. I hope to get it back at the end of this. Annie prodded my moaning, pointing out that Ivan never used an outboard, never. He rowed his nets out until the day he disappeared. ("It was my most romantic sight. This old man with this bronze bald head, rowing against the waves. No one but Ivan could hold his head like that. While he rowed through waves and spray. As if chaos found focus in his bald head.")

"So who am I writing this for?"

"Me," Annie answers. "Tell your life to an old friend."

The cabin is so changed now, bright at night with electric light. It hums with this machine here, this machine at the end of my fingers. Whap-whap-whaps as I type. The raccoons have left their nest under the floor. I bought myself an old kettle too, and a radio, and last week I listened to a hockey game for the first time in twenty years. All this just as I was getting used to a non-electric life. But that's typical Annie-timing: keep me stirred up, topsy, on that *ticklin'* edge, as a friend used to call it.

I still wasn't convinced. I told her: it's hard enough seeing the present puzzle, but to root back into mud and nose up a past, a past sunk so deep, is an incredible waste of energy. At my age I think of what I can do in a day. Chop wood. Go fish. Keep it simple. Time at my age is like the fat part of a string of pearls.

Why, I persisted, should I write about a childhood I simply cannot remember?

"Write it," she said, "and I promise you it will be true."

I told her I didn't want to complicate my life — simplicity being perhaps my one achievement. But then she whispered, "Ahhh!" and it was her tone that convinced enough of me. She said, "You are already so complicated, by your past. You're a heap of rusty nuts and bolts in the bilge. The past's where your start is, it's where you can be fixed. This story must begin in mythology, then gather in memory, then explode into your present. Only then can you" — she shrugged as if all this were only obvious — "heal."

Well, I'm alive today because I believe most of Annie's words.

So.

Vaughn-Vaughn

A night in January 1925, Beauséjour, Manitoba. Like a cold stone rolling out of a warm hand, Vaughn Hardy Collin fell into life. No shock or outrage when light first hit his face, no screams, no lusty bloody baby. Only a small slap on the wet pad. One cough. Quiet breathing. "One thinks," said the midwife, Mrs. MacIntyre, to her sister that evening, "one thinks the little laddie were ready. One thinks he knew what he was about."

The Collin family was too drunk with baby-fever to notice anything odd. Poised in his tux at the closed bedroom door, Mr. Collin heard from within the announcement, "A boy!" Then with family, friends, and servants watching, he gestured with his palm towards the door and bowed humbly, acknowledging tribute to a masterpiece unveiled. The latest in the line of Mr. Collins. Each in turn — family, friends, servants — lined up to stare at the quiet surprise being cooed at by its mother. Her eyes aflood with fantasy, she whispered to him. "Vaughn? Hello, Vaughn-Vaughn."

White and blue: prairie winters are stark. A thin crust of snow pretends to be the solid world, and an ice-blue sky resembles the place dreams should go. The only real thing is the cold. A cold so solid it makes houses unsure of themselves; so solid, dreams cannot go very far. Dreams and the people who have them keep behind snow-buttressed walls, beside black stoves. There is nothing much to do in the prairie winter. So it is the time, even out of this frigid blue and white ground, when stories grow, like winter weeds.

A number of rumours started. Such rumours, common enough after a birth or death, faded normally when the gossips had finished with them. But the rumour that began with Vaughn-Vaughn's birth was to last, in one form or another, for twenty years. The Vaughn-stories grew from two seeds. A farmer who had been at the Collins' claimed the child had the eyes of a hundred-year-old man. What's more, he was certain as May snow the child's stare was that of his own dead grandfather, whom he knew to be the devil himself. The Métis had a different version: someone said the babe's face revealed a soul that was the stunted fruit of a dead marriage. Embellishing the stories as they talked, the gossips persisted (it being a very cold winter), and yet good though these stories were, they began to fade.

It was only after Vaughn-Vaughn's first birthday party that they were given a second chance. This time the rumourweeds leapt out and bloomed fire. Tales of the young Collin burned then exploded into a mythology that grew, in the mind's eye, more real than the Beauséjour Bank.

It was perhaps strange that at first the Collins themselves failed to notice Vaughn-Vaughn's difference. But there were reasons.

In 1924, postwar Beauséjour was enjoying a modest boom period, the nation having reweighed the importance of bread. Like other prairie towns Beauséjour sat there like bread boxes in the middle of miles and miles of wheat.

Mr. Collin had become a successful lawyer, who, as he himself put it, was "friend of all, enemy to none". His success was due to his representing, courageously, the plight of the farmers versus the grain company or, for a larger fee, the grain company versus the farmers. This business of legal mediating was new to the area; Mr. Collin was a necessary middleman, an innocent.

Over the past few years Mr. Collin had spent little time at home, preferring instead to sit with farmers in meeting halls, or with businessmen in their Winnipeg offices, where he would "confide with those in need of advice". Most winter nights he watched hockey games. The age or ability of those he watched didn't matter. He'd choose sides based on a team's colours and then stand behind the opponent's net to harass the goalie. In any case, a new birth in the family was nothing new, certainly not enough to keep him home.

Mr. Collin already had a son, Hughie, ten now, and knew the early years well: those first cute wide eyes, the first feed-me whimpers, the first almost-words. He knew babies, he could wait until this new one was old enough before he'd step in and teach him anything important. A pair of skates when he was three.

Mrs. Collin was similarly blind to the new baby, but for different reasons. Since this was their last child (she didn't know exactly why or how, but her husband assured her that this was so), she fell into motherhood with an urgency. Hughie had been much-loved, of course, but if Vaughn was to be her last, he was going to be perfect.

Vaughn-Vaughn's actual strangeness gave her fantasy an edge of delight. She would watch over him lying wide-eyed and unmoving in his crib and say to herself, "Here's my little thinker. Here's the *smart* little Collin." She would see him clutch and stare at a twig, a button, a piece of blue ribbon, and say, "There's my poet." Holding him, rocking him, brushing baby-kisses onto his cheek while he held to her limply, functionally, like someone else's child, she would whisper, "My naughty Vaughn-Vaughn. My hard-to-getter Vaughnie."

Sometimes she would get mad. Her fantasy called for a warm baby, not this indifferent thing. When she began at last to see through the baby-blue haze, when she began to see the child the way he was really, her descent into reality felt like a fall onto sharp rocks. Now whenever she was with him she could not shake the feeling that she was confronting some strange creature. One night, holding Vaughn on her knee, Mrs. Collin found herself in a staring contest. Tightening her grip on him, she put on a wide smile and bobbed her head this way and that, singing, "Vaughnie! Vaughn-Vaughn!" Her son's eyes were deep and blue. No hint of response or feeling. But fixed on her. Mrs. Collin suddenly felt very small, and dirty. *"Vaughnie."* Her cry was hoarse, and a flood of sobs came.

Vaughn-Vaughn, and the problem, was six months old before Mrs. Collin approached her husband. What was important to him was seldom important to her, and so it stood the other way around.

To pull her husband out of the evening paper Mrs. Collin used her series of sighs. The first rang of whim, the second and third held a note of growing frustration, and the fourth had that full-throated sound of giving up, and the threat of dark moods.

"What is it?" Mr. Collin turned his face in her direction, while keeping his eyes to his paper.

"Well, it's our little Vaughn-Vaughn. Duncan? Duncan, listen. I think our little boy is sick."

"Sick! Then for goodness sakes why don't you call Dr. Watt? Goodness knows he owes us. That bit with the Horchuk girl? The advice I gave him's — Christ, four evenings over a month."

"No, Duncan. No. Duncan? It's not that, I don't think. He's just sick . . . *all* the time." She began to mumble and sob.

"Well, now, what do you really mean, dear?"

" — he doesn't *smile,* he doesn't *play,* he's always so *quiet,* he's just never *happy* . . . "

"Well?"

"Duncan, he just stares at me. He doesn't *love* me." When she dropped her teacup with a clatter and burst out crying, Mr. Collin quickly skimmed the headlines of articles he had yet to read, then rose with a grunt. He wondered if he'd have to call Dr. Watt after all — for his wife. What was bothering her? He'd ask Mrs. Delacourt about it.

"Oh Dunc, that is not my baby." She pressed the clumsy

hand that cupped her breast, a pose they relied on at times like this.

"It's the heat, dear, it's just the heat. Poor lad's suffocating up in that room. I'll have Mrs. Delacourt open a window."

"Duncan? Do you know that Vaughn-Vaughn's never *cried?*"

"Well, dear, it can't be all that bad then, can it?"

The streamers, holly wreaths, and ornamental candles were to stay; the tree and anything else Christian was to come down. Mrs. Delacourt was relieved by this. She hated being called on to perform any task that called for even the slightest creative responsibility. She would sweat instantly, and soon feel like breaking something.

But the decorations were easy. Then there was the birthday cake (she smelled it baking, reminding her) that Mrs. Collin had asked her to "fix up". When asked for more detailed instructions her employer had told her, "'Happy Birthday Vaughn' would be nice." No fancy pictures. She could take care of it.

Tip-toe on a chair, Mrs. Delacourt stretched and plucked the angel from off the treetop. With a word of caution she bent and handed it to her six-year-old daughter, Lise.

"It's Jesus! It's Jesus!" cried the little girl, who placed the ornament on her head and began to spin like a top.

"Lise!"

The girl stopped twirling only when dizziness toppled her, and as she fell she protected the angel with the rest of her body. Looking up at her mother, Lise's eyes — too bold for a daughter and too crafty for one so young — shone through coarse, tar-coloured hair. Lise would not be pretty. She was likely the only child in Beauséjour who had never once been called adorable or cute. And, a mother's pride at odds with honesty, Mrs. Delacourt saw in Lise's face only "a strong character".

"Can I have him, Mother? Can I keep Jesus in my room till next Christmas-time? He likes it in my room, he *told* me."

"Lise — "

The grand door to the living-room swung open to a purposeful Mr. Collin, who pretended to be a guest arriving. He appraised the room with a sweeping squint.

"Very good, Mrs. Delacourt," he concluded. "Vaughn will have fun today. And how's the young lad on his first, eh? How's the lad been?"

"Very well, sir. Like a horse he eats, like a canal horse."

"So says the Missus," he said, adjusting his tie at the buffet mirror.

So says the Missus! The maid wondered when Mrs. Collin had last seen the boy. How long? A week? A month?

"Mrs. Delacourt, you will greet the guests. Change your dress. The gifts are to go on this table, here, or under it, here. You will serve the lunch at two. I will send down to you for liquor when needed. You and Lise will be in the kitchen between times, I assume?"

"Yes, sir, if you wish. The kitchen." She hated using this tone. It was no wonder Lise treated her more as a friend than a mother. It was just no good for a daughter to grow up watching her mother obey orders all day long.

"Would it be all right, sir, for my Lise to come up for the gift giving? It would please her, sir, and she would like to give your son a present. Lise?" Embarrassed, the daughter plunged her face into the couch cushions and made beeping sounds.

"It's a gift, a necklace, my father gave to me to give to a son. I'll have no sons, sir" — she paused — "now that Mr. Delacourt is gone. It's Ojibwa, sir. Indian. I hope that is fine with you?"

Mr. Collin only half heard. He stared down at the maid's sturdy white shoes, scuffed grey at the toes, and recalled the husband — Joe Delacourt — and his drunken death six years ago. "Tragic" was the failsafe word most used to describe a man who happened to die on the night his wife gave birth to their only child. Lise. "Weird" was another word, whispered back and forth across the usual backyard fences, sometimes whispered through a slight smile. For if stories of men's sympathetic labour pains deserved a snicker, what face was proper for a man's sympathetic death? Métis men were rarely slapstick, but Joe Delacourt's timing had hung a vaudevillian's red nose onto an otherwise typical, sordid, lost battle with the bottle.

"Fine . . . yes, of course. Indian. Yes, fine."

Down the hall, safe in her bedroom, Mrs. Collin sat before the mirror, cuddling one of Lise's dolls. How should she hold her son? Should she, could she, appear a placid mother-with-child? Should she tickle and stroke, whisper endearments?

Alicia Collin had in the past months grown steadily more afraid of Vaughn-Vaughn. The birth had built, in the back of her mind, a kind of unassailable window-box — sturdy, weatherproof, and full of richly scented soil. Possibilities, fantasies had taken root there. The warm body of a baby in her hands had sent up pale green shoots. She saw these perfect growths become thick, leafy, soon promising seeds of their own. Vaughn-Vaughn wasn't long in changing all this. He had frozen the window-box earth to a hard grey. The plants had quietly withered, died.

Still, Alicia waited, hoping Vaughn-Vaughn would change, hoping that somehow love would descend on him and fill him with proper helplessness, and the wonderful eye-brimming heat a good baby sends back to the eyes of its good mother. For months she made a ritual of holding him for at least five minutes daily, on the chance that he had come to himself and needed her. Each time she came away with her hopes pared yet closer, scraping bone. He would never need her.

Still she watched him, but with the detachment usually given to someone else's child. She watched as he lay in his crib, staring at nothing sensible, his head pivoting smoothly as a cat's. He rarely blinked. She noted his routine: Stares at the ribs of his crib. Rolls to stare at the ceiling. Turns to the crib's inner wall, stares at the painted man on his horse, at the calf at the end of the lasso, at the rope in between. What was weighing on his mind so? Alicia wondered. She had never heard this question applied to a baby. Babies did not have things that weighed on the mind.

She gave Lise's porcelain doll a dull tickle under the chin. Should she even try? She'd fool no one. She was no more a mother to Vaughn-Vaughn than she was mother to this doll. When was the last time she had gone to his room? Six weeks now. And after that time she had kept to her bed, wanting to die. Alicia flicked the doll's eyelids down and held them. Something in them — no, something *not* in them — reminded her too much of Vaughn-Vaughn. She remembered that last night.

It had been late, perhaps the middle of the night. Watching him sleep, bending down to hear the soft breathing, had often helped steady her. He always slept in the same position: on his side, with his back to the room. And so he was this night, curled near the head of the crib, facing the inner wall, his tiny arm stretched out, touching it. A normal, sleeping baby boy. Her sleeping son. And there — he moved his hand in his sleep. Hoping to catch some hint of a dream on his face Alicia went to the head of the crib to see him in the dim light. A scream caught in her throat. The boy's eyes were wide, intent on the cowboy's rope. His finger traced the rope's path from the cowboy's hand to the calf's throat, then, gently, the curve of the noose.

Relatives arrived, one by one or in couples, and their gifts to

Vaughn-Vaughn added colour to an already gaudy room. Mr. Crother came in a decorated sleigh with two teenaged sons — a weekend pass from boarding-school, so soon after Christmas, was for them an unbelievable treat. Another weekend skating on the river, shooting rabbits. Hughie Collin greeted his worldly cousins at the door with expectant awe. They might give him more swear words from the city.

Beauséjour guests filed in, gave up their gifts and their coats, accepted drinks. Traces of the Collin Christmas party, held two weeks earlier, were evident not only in the room but also in people's faces, which betrayed a dullness resulting from familiarity. More than one guest found himself sitting in the same chair he'd spent time in two weeks ago. Sensing this lack of party impetus, Mr. Collin began pouring strong drinks, "loud drinks" he called them, and told Mrs. Delacourt to go down for some of the French brandy.

They made up the best of Beauséjour society. Mr. Collin's mother, Beatrice, whose bulk centred the couch and made it a private chair, was shouting off relatives on her fingers. In a corner, discussing bank loans, sat Mr. Collin's sister Ruth, her husband the bank manager, and the son, a teller with a future. Alicia's unmarried sister, Melody Cowan, a schoolteacher, sat alone beside the gift table, waiting for a chance to tell Mrs. Delacourt how very smart, in that native way, some of her Métis students were. By the door the school principal, bald Mr. Maddy, questioned the two teenaged Collin cousins about the strategies of private schools. Hughie made puke faces behind his back, but could not get his cousins to laugh.

Other guests had a domestic rather than social right to be there. Mrs. MacIntyre, the midwife, had come, of course, along with her husband, and they sat on either side of the empty cradle, she looking restless but regal, he looking drunk but bored. Bob, the farmer who tended the Collins' cows and small sugarbeet farm, suffered alone in a far corner of the room, standing angled as though stiff visiting clothes were what propped him up. One eye crossed slightly, and he looked to be dreaming of his spring vegetables.

A few people applauded as Mrs. Collin made her entrance, but something in her face stopped them. With Vaughn-Vaughn invisible in her arms, Alicia strode through the crowd and unceremoniously deposited the child in the crib. As a rush of inquisitive women gathered, she appeared grateful to be nudged into the background. Grateful too when questions thrown her way were handled by her husband. "Yes, growing like a tree. Growing tall before he grows fat." Was he talking? "No need for talk, not with this lot of chatterbrains about, eh?"

Someone asked if the boy was walking yet. Mr. Collin paused, glanced at Alicia. Alicia opened her mouth to speak, jerked her head in a spasm towards Mrs. Delacourt, and then dropped her eyes to the floor.

"No, no . . . I — " she said.

"Actually, Mrs. Collin," spoke Mrs. Delacourt, "Vaughn-Vaughn was tryin' for steps today, just like we saw him do the day before."

Mr. Collin added, eyes gleaming, "The boy is obviously a defenceman. I am an expert on this: one, he decides to grow like a bull. Two, he shows a reluctance to walk, or skate. Adds up to a monstrous blueliner. I wager the beet farm." His words tailed off into laughter, and now the men peered over the women's shoulders for a look at the boy. Mrs. Collin found a chair with her hand and sat heavily.

The party grew loud. Drinks were poured, Vaughn-Vaughn's gifts opened and passed around. Each gift was handed down to the child to hold, and Vaughn-Vaughn's intent appraisal of each item invited jokes.

"Your puzzle game has the boy stumped. Give him a clue, someone."

"One thinks he's stricken by your socks, Mary!"

"Well, what defenceman wears red socks?"

Mrs. Delacourt rolled in lunch on a double-shelved tray and was assaulted with greetings which rang like shots; drunken, eager eyes left the baby to fix on food. Lise handed out small plates and serviettes, on which the guests piled meat pies, perogies, pickles, bread-cake, cheese.

Now Lise crept to the crib, checking people's faces along the way for any hint of disapproval. She took the necklace from her pocket and handed it down to Vaughn-Vaughn, who took it immediately. Dangling it above his face, he stared at it. Lise, with two fingers in her mouth, her feet pointed together at the toes and her stomach protruding, stared at him.

"He is your son now, Lise." Mrs. Delacourt had paused by her daughter, stooping to whisper this in her ear. Lise continued to stare at the boy, her eyes wide.

Sedated by food, people settled into their chairs and made quiet talk. Melody Cowan managed to corner Mrs. Delacourt at last, and told her about her bright Métis kids, bright in that native way, and how she had high hopes for them. She was sure, she said, that many of them were capable of taking jobs when the time came. Mrs. Delacourt had always hated Melody Cowan, who reminded her of perfume and cobwebs, but at this moment she hated more the role she herself had to play for this *bête noire*. To her horror she found herself answering only "Thank you" when Melody had done talking.

The room grew hot. Guests slumped in their seats, some sleepy-drunk. Signs of a party breaking up. Mr. Collin had his wife open one of the sundeck window-doors. Icy air swirled into the stuffiness, the smells and the smoke.

"Well! We'll try the boy's legs!" shouted Mr. Collin. He walked with purpose to the crib and with his arms indicated the large space he wanted cleared. "Give him room and he'll walk!"

Held under the armpits, Vaughn-Vaughn was lowered to the carpet on unsteady legs.

"All right, Vaughnie, go!" Mr. Collin released the child, who fell at once. His father repeated the procedure. Vaughn-Vaughn fell again. Mrs. Collin sat in her chair, sweating.

Six guests formed a wall five feet from Vaughn-Vaughn. They shouted for him, they slapped their thighs.

"Vaughn-Vaughn! Vaughn-Vaughn!"

"Left-right, like a soldier!"

"Come on, little man, come to Melody!"

Mr. Collin assured the crowd that his son could walk. He said, "One more time, dear" to Alicia, who had been pleading shyly to please put the boy back in his crib. He had Mrs. Delacourt open the deck door wider, explaining to the party that if anything was going to make the lad walk it would be the winter on his backside. Condensation rolled in like a ghostly tide moving through people's legs. In the falling afternoon light the room had become dim, and the mist added something strange.

The father let go of Vaughn-Vaughn, and again he fell. The cold air had imposed a silence on everyone except Mr. Collin.

"*Once* more!" he promised, saying, "Here, Vaughn-Vaughn, do it for your father on your birthday."

This time, to everyone's loud delight, Vaughn stood. The child looked down at his shaking legs, then moved his gaze up the floor at the wall of people.

"Vaughn-Vaughn!" "Like a soldier!" "To Melody!"

Vaughn's legs continued to quake. His eyes rolled this way and that, and his mouth contorted. Suddenly he barked, the sound of a tiny, frustrated dog. He whirled his upper body around in the opposite direction, away from the wall of shouters, then fell to the floor. But he caught himself on his palms and, pushing himself back up, he managed to bring his legs around. On stiff legs he began to run towards the open door. With each chugging step he grunted and gained speed.

"Guuugh . . . guugh . . . guhh . . . guh! guh! guh! guh! guh!"

Brushing past Alicia, who screamed but made no attempt to stop him, Vaughn-Vaughn ran through the door and out onto the deck. His grunting breaths made little puffs in the air. He hesitated at the railing, then squeezed between two posts. He balanced himself on the eavestrough. His bare feet not breaking the hard-crusted snow, he trod slowly and deliberately to the corner of the roof. Behind, from a crowded sundeck, people screamed.

Out there on the eavestrough, what went on in Vaughn Hardy Collin's one-year-old mind? Was it creating its own world, his mind a sparkler emitting coloured light? Or is baby-mind a mirror, adding nothing to a world perfectly seen?

Let's say Vaughn's first birthday party ended like this:

He stood where he was. No distress. His world had not changed much. There were, simply, different things to look at. The deep blue afternoon sky. The smooth snowbank eight feet below. The glittering foot-pocked field of the yard. A prairie oak stood at the side of the house just beyond reach. In the icy air its branches looked ready to snap. The tree's black bark ran jagged with blacker furrows droning with a darker world inside. A tiny cold bird watched him from an upper branch.

In front of his face, white puffs followed each breath. They moved out and away, tumbling on themselves, then disappeared.

The cold was not distressing in itself. But the skin became different. Strange the wetness freezing in the nose, fingers going dumb, hard to move. A headache growing at the temples. Through pyjamas, the skin burning, then numbing. But that deep sky. It was not like a ceiling or a crib wall.

It went so far.

All those people, screaming for a ladder, made no sense.

January 18th

Three days of sitting typing with new little muscles, and no complaints except my back — which the cold Pacific will take care of in a hurry. It makes *everything* ache.

This past three days Annie has dragged her old whore's body over with a knapsack full of dinner, at sundown precisely. My reward. She watches me eat, even watches the way I chew my food I think, and then heads off into the dark again. I get the feeling this story is more her project than mine. My backache resents her.

Tonight after dinner she read the first chapter. I asked how it went. How true she thought it was.

"Great. Good. Maybe a bit poetic for my taste." She went on to say that, to her, babies meant one day of blood and then a few years of noise, and that, for her, the prairies inspired geometry, not poetry.

"I am trying to capture," I explained, "the flavour of the era."

Annie did not respond, so I asked the real question.

"But how true was it?" I knew what in my story was basic fact. The run-out-to-the-eavestrough actually happened, somewhere in my first couple of years. But I wanted to know about details. I asked Annie if I'd gotten my mother right. I told her my depiction of mother-and-child reminded me of something out of *Rosemary's Baby*.

"Well, there's something a bit sinister backstage of all suckling kids. Some mothers feel it."

Playing the reporter I tapped a pad of paper with my pen. In fact I was peeved. What was the use of doing this at all unless I was getting it right? "Was it that sinister? Was I *that* different? Is it true my mother — "

"You don't think 'sinister' is common in the world?" she said, and her interruption told me my line of questioning would get no further tonight. "Do you know how the Carriers got their name?"

What's left of the Carrier band lives up past Bella Coola. The remnants of one of the more shamanistic tribes on the coast.

"The Carriers," Annie told me, "got their name from their delightful custom of making all widows carry the charred bones of their dead husbands on their backs." She paused for effect. "In a bag. How's that for sinister. And it shows feminism isn't indigenous to the West Coast."

Still in a mood I told her, sure, maybe it was sinister to lug your dead boss's bones around in a bag. But how could either of us know what a wife felt about that?

Annie ignored my dig and instead fell to a silence and stared at the floor. I knew exactly what had overcome her, and wanted to take back the part about her not knowing marriage. With my own silence I told her I understood. She looked up.

"I *would* carry Ivan's bones. If they were ever found. I'd *eat* them. I'd swallow the skull whole."

It was my turn to look down.

"But that's not my meaning." She raised her brows and her eyes were bright with — sinister light. "Pardon me, Mr. Collin, but you carry a nice old bone-bag yourself." She flicked her finger up at my tattoo.

Gentle cruelty. A mix Annie blends well, a bit of honey to ease a lesson in.

We talked a little longer, and when we heard the loon Annie went out to the porch to call back to it. Eagerly, like a child with a new trick. Annie's range. Before she left she poked her head back in, praised my story again, and told me to keep at it.

"Don't worry about 'true'."

I recall something Connor Peake said once when we were on about books. I liked Hemingway and Peake didn't. "Too blunt," Peake said. "I want flora and fauna. What's this realism potato anyway? It's lies anyway, and if lies is all you get, make mine rococo." Something like that. Good old Peake.

Annie descended the steps carefully, wary of ice.

It's so strange to be pondering "Vaughn-Vaughn's disease" again. What people thought, what I thought. One doctor had said epilepsy, and in my teens I went out and read all the Dostoevsky I could find. But mine was not epilepsy, not Dostoevsky's brand anyway. There was no imminent explosion, no tension of the lit fuse, no *glow* as I stared — and wouldn't it be impossible to be always on the verge of an attack with the attack never coming?

Another doctor, when I was an adult, just a chat with him, said autism. Some of the symptoms were right: the unsociability, the spacing-out. But he admitted some of the symptoms didn't fit at all and suggested something else entirely. I like the word though — autism. Sounds like "automatic". What I had, what I was, should be called *automatic*. I was one of nature's simpler types. A lidless eyeball at the end of a tree branch. Or a penis that's always erect, eager at everything, no discrimination whatsoever. A visual hard-on, nothing less, nothing more. I like that, it seems to fit.

The Dog

After the birthday party Alicia Collin took to her bed. Hughie had broken his ankle falling off the roof trying to save his little brother. Vaughn-Vaughn was in bed too, with a cold.

Mr. Collin cancelled all business appointments. He talked with local doctors, demanding answers to questions he could not get straight in his head. He'd had strong words with Alicia, who shyly told all, and her year of deception made him angrier still. Everyone in town avoided him — Vaughn's party had turned Beauséjour into a town of ghosts. Mr. Collin swore he'd "get to the bottom of this". But get to the bottom of what? Was anything really wrong with the boy?

Outside, the worst blizzard of the year rushed and thudded, framing in tumult the always utter quiet of the boy's room, where Mr. Collin sat long hours watching his son watch him. If the look in the troubled father's eyes was steady, the look in the baby's was steadier, for they held no question. When the eyes shifted focus — from crib wall, to rattling window, to feather floating near his nose — they changed only in their narrowing of pupils, a function so smooth Mr. Collin found it sly.

"This will take some doing," he thought.

Mrs. Delacourt stood by the door, waiting on his questions. These she answered with a shy, protective voice. Had he always been this way? "Yes, sir. At times he seems contented, sir." Never cries, then? "Not really, sir. Perhaps he is contented, sir?" During the past months she had discovered a strange split in her affections. The mothering she gave her Lise was simple, natural, but that given to Vaughn-Vaughn was desperately tender, the kind reserved for wounded birds.

Mr. Collin's visits took the form of examinations. His methods were crude, as if he were a farmer faced with an unknown disease stunting his early wheat: hours spent clipping samples, staring at withered leaves, taking notes (but of what?), and talking to other farmers. Hours spent trying to see past the feeble light his own knowledge cast.

A schedule was set. Several times a day Mr. Collin, Alicia, and Mrs. Delacourt entered Vaughn-Vaughn's room. (Forced by her husband to attend, Alicia took a chair in the corner. As for her peculiar grudge against the boy, he had no time for that now.) Mrs. Delacourt was his assistant. He'd hand her the clipboard and tell her what to write, under what column. At his direction the maid made notes beneath the headings *Food, Sleep, Toys, Sounds,* and *What He Likes.*

Two weeks in, Mr. Collin sat by the fire, warmed a brandy in one hand and puzzled over the notes on his lap. Dr. Watt had been sent copies and his conclusions were expected at any time. But Mr. Collin would reach his own conclusions first, not wanting to risk being bullied into believing anything by a man who by his professional guise managed to bully others. Modern medicine, he knew, was little more than an elaborate guessing game which followed rules as elastic as those of law. What's more, a doctor whose inconstancy of will allowed him to chase young girls could not be expected to know about the steady wilfulness of babies.

If anything, Vaughn-Vaughn was consistent. Under *Food*, the details showed he fed on virtually anything, in healthy quantities. *Toys* gave no clues either: he would grasp whatever was given and wrap it in an identical gaze. It was the same with *What He Likes*, for he reacted no differently to the caress of a warm hand than to the rap of a stick. And it made no difference whether he was held by father, maid, or stranger. At first it appeared the *Sleep* column might reveal something. Several times, when Mr. Collin checked on Vaughn-Vaughn in the night, he found him open-eyed, awake. At other times, though, he looked quite asleep. Mr. Collin was excited by this, but when he consulted Dr. Watt he was told that babies often wake at night to be fed. Usually they cried. Vaughn-Vaughn waited.

One day Mr. Collin had tried a variation on a *What He Likes* test. Frustrated by the boy's utter sameness, his refusal to cough up some clue, Mr. Collin had reached out suddenly and pinched Vaughn-Vaughn hard, twisting the tender flab of an upper arm. He persisted, even when Mrs. Delacourt asked him to please stop and tugged at his coat sleeve. Mr. Collin didn't stop. Vaughn-Vaughn's pinched arm cringed and jerked. The child's gaze, though, merely shifted, calmly, to the rigid fingers on his own flailing arm. Horrified, his father withdrew his hand.

"Damn!" he shouted, both at himself and at the boy, who was now calmly watching a red and white welt grow. When he saw Alicia smiling knowingly at the floor, he felt for the first time in his life close to striking her.

Vaughn was to be sent to Winnipeg. Dr. Watt was to the point.

"It's not a medicine problem, Duncan," said the doctor, accepting brandy. "It's a head problem. Out of my jurisdiction."

"Absurd," countered Mr. Collin. "Impossible. He's . . . " But he found no words and could only stand in a flushing squirm, like a boy who had been caught in a lie.

"Duncan, it's this way. He never cries? Doesn't crawl around, won't try to walk?" The doctor paused, but Mr. Collin said nothing. "Duncan, consider. Vaughn is pushing a year and a half. At the same age, a dog knows to whine for food, knows who to come to for a pat on the head, knows how to run from a kick — " Mr. Collin wheeled away to stare at nothing out the window. Dr. Watt continued. "You *could* keep him here. But there's a doctor in Winnipeg who — "

"Let me guess. Who would train him to whine for food. My son is not a dog. No."

Finishing the lawyer's good brandy, Dr. Watt did not insist on the matter too strongly, for he sensed that in truth Mr. Collin would be relieved (even while not admitting it to himself) to be rid of this growing mess. Because mentally defective sons did not remain simply that they gave birth to a mentally defective family, house, yard. Kids on a Saturday-night dare would knock on the front door and run. And business? An odd son reflects an odd father. Dr. Watt could read these fears in his friend's face, but Mr. Collin's selfishness didn't shock him. He'd been doctoring in small towns long enough to know the social side of sickness.

While Mr. Collin spent the next month leaving the boy alone, letting him develop whichever way he would and so, in a sense, decide his own fate, Mrs. Delacourt took a different course. The thought of losing Vaughnie to Winnipeg strangers took her close to panic.

A week before Mr. Collin was to announce his Winnipeg decision, she contacted a sister who had never left the reserve at Lac du Bonnet. A Métis baby, she wrote, had been stricken with a fever and, though conscious, would respond to nothing. Then Vaughn's symptoms were described in more detail. A week later a package arrived. That night, as the household slept, she prepared the treatment. At her side was Lise, allowed to watch if she asked no questions.

Into a tub of hot water she emptied the wallet of crumbly brown bark. ("Sister: the chokecherry bark water must not enter nose or mouth. Poison.") Next, emptying the other two wallets into jars, she added vinegar to the dark green herb, and salted water to the yellow powder. ("Enough liquid to make porridge.") She bound Vaughn-Vaughn at the ankles and wrists with towels. The boy accepted bondage like he did everything else. Mrs. Delacourt ladled the green mud onto his stomach and wrapped it in place with gauze. She spread the yellow mud on his forehead and into the slight pockets of his temples and bound it also. Then she lowered Vaughn-Vaughn into his chokecherry bath, its bitter steam. When she dipped her nose to sniff its strength her head kicked back like a whip. Wiping her eyes, Mrs. Delacourt picked up the rattle. ("The strange rattle? By it, the boy he will stay awake while he soaks. Such is its loud Ojibwa magic.")

After ten minutes it looked like he was cooking. Sweat ran freely and his eyes, bulging out of red rims, traced long, quick arcs, as if the room had filled with wildly swirling birds. Mrs. Delacourt was frightened.

The required hour passed, and she too was drenched in sweat. Vaughn-Vaughn was cleaned off and put to bed, where

Mrs. Delacourt continued to sit over him. The boy seemed still to be in his bath: he sweated and his eyes watched the flight of the invisible birds. The fever continued into the next day. Mrs. Delacourt grew anxious, and when Mr. Collin asked after the boy, she said he seemed to have caught a flu.

Dr. Watt was called and said the child was "on the hind end of a spring fever. No reason to worry." And so it was. The next day his fever broke, and to Mrs. Delacourt's relief — and disappointment — Vaughn-Vaughn fell back into his staring, and silence. But Mr. Collin took the fever to be a sign. "Vaughn is worsening," he proclaimed, a little eagerly, and everyone understood: the boy was going to Winnipeg.

The School of Psychological Medicine at the University of Manitoba consisted of one man only, Dr. Sam Sara, who had brazen buck teeth and the pale, pimply face of a boy. Mrs. Delacourt had never seen a man like him. He talked and talked, covering everything with words, as though words cured all, as though they might fill up a quiet baby boy.

Standing behind his desk, Dr. Sara addressed an audience of two. Through the window in front of which he stood, nothing could be seen but miles of decaying stubble, miles of barren ground without a fence.

"We have been examining Vaughn for a week now, and while we have yet to encounter anything approximate to what could indeed be termed *improvement,* we hold to the opinion that such a direction is, indeed, possible." He smiled, waiting for an answer, but Mrs. Delacourt had no idea how to respond. It was the first time she'd heard a "royal we". Mouthing a silent song, Lise looked him straight in the face. The doctor cleared his throat.

"How to achieve this. Well, we will employ a method, one with which we are most pleased, and most confident. We call it the 'wooden spoon'. But — as Dr. Watt has told the boy's father — we offer no certainty as to the boy's . . . cure.

None." Again he waited. Mrs. Delacourt blinked. Lise sang.

Mrs. Delacourt was more than happy with her new responsibility, almost as happy as she'd been upon hearing she was to come with Vaughn to Winnipeg. "Of course you're going," Mr. Collin had told her. "You will take a room. Your duties will be the same as here. Remuneration the same. The three of you will be crowded, but it's not for too long. Are you willing?"

The train ride was a strangely happy time for her, packed tightly onto the wooden bench, gloriously squeezed by her little family. Here was Lise, and here was Vaughn-Vaughn, her wounded bird who was now her rejected bird, and now more hers than ever. During the hour trip she fed them nearly one pound of candy.

"On one level, this spoon can be taken as a symbol for Mother," said Dr. Sara. He held Vaughn down on the desk, and with his other hand rapped the air with a large wooden spoon. Mrs. Delacourt was writing notes on a pad, as she'd been told to do.

"When things go as they should, this spoon is what feeds him." Dr. Sara spooned invisible baby food into an invisible mouth. He paused, smirked, and spooned invisible dribble off the invisible chin.

"But when things don't go well, when baby is bad, this spoon is also what *hits* him." Pulling a padded sock over the spoon, he rapped the desk with it, sharply. Vaughn-Vaughn turned his head to find the sound, and stare.

"That is what will help Vaughn-Vaughn . . . to be better?" asked Mrs. Delacourt.

Dr. Sara took off his glasses, eased a cloth from his pocket, and began to polish the lenses. With glasses off he looked so bewildered that the woman was startled. He polished with swift, mechanical strokes while he talked.

"Have you never struck a child, Mrs. Delacourt? Lise, perhaps?"

She glanced quickly at her daughter, who hadn't reacted. "Well, I . . . n — " Mrs. Delacourt was so bothered by the motives behind such a question that she wasn't even trying to remember.

"Surely. When she's angered you?"

"Once or twice, but when she breaks Mrs. Collin's — "

"Exactly. Mrs. Delacourt, our technique is new, but only as an abstracted technique, as a scientific method. Actually it has been used by mothers since animals began. Have you ever watched mother cat keeping her litter in line? Or, Mrs. Delacourt, a mother spanking her child? We believe that mothers spank out of love. But, and of course you'll agree, this 'love' is simply instinct, and has a purpose. When a child steps out of line it triggers a mother's anger. Her anger embodies an instinctive training-to-fit. It sculpts that behaviour necessary to survival. The mother, having survived, models this success."

"It *fell,*" said Lise.

Dr. Sara replaced his glasses and confronted Mrs. Delacourt with his eyes huge once more.

"It may look like science" — *Bang.* The spoon hit the desk. — "but, here, we like to call it 'love'."

Dr. Sara smiled, which made his eyes even larger, the pupils like black grapes under liquid.

"Vaughn has not yet discovered *who* his mother is. So he needs a surrogate mother, a mother who is very simple, very direct. I refer, of course, to our spoon."

"I see," said the maid, voice itching with concern.

She was afraid when she brought Vaughn-Vaughn in for his first spoon-session, but as the weeks went by, she grew puzzled. The treatments were so simple. She kept expecting a next stage, some scientific cleverness that would see Vaughn-Vaughn tricked into being a normal baby boy. But "this spoon thing", as she called it in letters home, never changed. All that had changed was her view of doctors. One letter said: "When he feeds him he makes baby talk and coo-coo. When he hits him he talks about what he did, like a man."

Dr. Sara focused his first efforts on getting Vaughn-Vaughn to walk and talk. Vaughn was held up, pointed at Mrs. Delacourt, and released. When he fell, and he always fell, he would be rapped on the shoulder with the spoon. To get him to talk, the doctor spoke loud words in his ear. If Vaughn attempted to mimic, or made any sound at all, he was to be fed. If he stayed silent he was struck. He was always struck.

The doctor adjusted his expectations downward and decided on the simplest possible task. Vaughn-Vaughn was to be kept in a state of hunger, and Mrs. Delacourt was instructed to give him no food save for a single evening meal. The rest of his diet would come from the spoon.

Three balls, yellow, red, and blue, were placed in front of Vaughn on the floor. If he reached for the blue, he was fed; if he went for the red or yellow, he was struck. As feared, Vaughn-Vaughn showed no talent for getting past randomness: even after being struck two thousand times, and fed one thousand times, he still chose the blue only a third of the time.

Dr. Sara was perplexed. "Even amoebae," he said, "have instinct." Vaughn-Vaughn was always ravenous, and in fact was getting thinner, but he never cried for food or even seemed to want it. It was only when the spooned pabulum had gotten to the back of his mouth that his hidden hunger showed. It was a little shocking, especially for Mrs. Delacourt, to watch his throat muscles struggle and jerk and swallow like some frantic animal, an animal concealed by the boy's motionless arms, tucked feet, and perfectly placid face.

Three months passed and no one was happy, least of all Mrs. Delacourt. Only the boy's father, his letters a naïve and encouraging voice from afar, seemed at all pleased with the situation. He sent money to her and explained that these things took some doing.

But in Mrs. Delacourt's eyes the doctor had been stripped of any power his white uniform and his talk had given him, and now something she'd heard Lise say undermined her respect even more. The previous night she'd come upon Lise hovering over Vaughn-Vaughn, clawing the air and making chirping noises. When asked, Lise said she was playing "labertory rat", and that she had heard "doctor say on the phone that Vaughn was dumber than a labertory rat."

The next day in the corridor Mrs. Delacourt confronted Sara with a speech.

"Poor Vaughn-Vaughn is always hungry. Because of you he does not grow like he should. He has a shoulder black and blue. I know why you do this, but I don't care. Sometimes I look at my boy, and I cry, and I curse you. I curse you and I curse his father. And now you call him worse than a rat! I . . . I will leave and *take-him-home.*" Mrs. Delacourt folded her arms on her chest.

"My Lise told me what you said."

"You must understand." He paused, waiting for her to soften, but the maid held her stubborn pose.

"All right, Mrs. Delacourt. First of all, Vaughn is staying. Mr. Collin has made himself very clear." Dr. Sara watched the maid stiffen. "And as for this rat matter, perhaps I should apologize, but first I will explain. What was said, rude though it sounded, is quite true."

Mrs. Delacourt gasped, and gave him her worst eyes.

"We have been successful in using this method to train many animals, including rats. And I'll simply say that in all cases rats have learned this game in days, often hours — this same game Vaughn has failed at for months." Dr. Sara's voice rose as he edged closer, leaning at her. "Mrs. Delacourt, it is theoretically possible to teach a rat to play the entire *Symphony of the Air* if one could keep it in perpetual appetite.

This boy, Mrs. Delacourt, has not learned one single note."

"You hurt him again I will *take-him-away!*"

"Both of us know he is not yours to take. I'll advise — "

"If you try once more to hit him — "

Loud cries erupted from inside the office. They rushed in. On the floor, in the middle of the room, Vaughn-Vaughn sat wailing. It was because of Lise. The girl squatted before him squealing like a rat, randomly striking him and spooning food into his howling mouth. She moved wildly, feeding and hitting, hitting and feeding. Because he could not swallow fast enough, his crying was stalling by fits of choking. Orange food ran down his face. His flailing arms tried hard to imitate a bird, to get his body up and away. He groped for the blue ball, took it up, and thrust it at his assailant. It didn't stop Lise and her mad spoon. Pounding the blue ball into her shoulder didn't stop her. Pushing it into her mouth didn't stop her. Lise at her end of the spoon was hysterical and howled now too, the blue ball bubbling at the back of her throat.

What most shocked Mrs. Delacourt — before she could subdue Lise, before she could pacify Vaughn — was the strange sound of his crying. It was the first time she had heard Vaughn-Vaughn cry. The sound of a baby being born.

Vaughn learned quickly. Many months passed before he lost his fear of Lise. Dr. Sara used this unexpected new tool to its best advantage. It entailed a simple modification of method: the spoon was exchanged for a girl.

February 8th

Can I stop now Annie? Am I fixed yet?

Who would have believed what drags our bodies become? Typing has kept me from my healthy habits. The scrounging for wood, the drumbeat chopping. Setting the nets, then hauling them in heavy with hope. After just a week of sitting, this body feels like it's had years of desk jobs and pizza.

Actually I do like the feeling of these pages piling up, not unlike that of fresh split wood stacking up against the cabin.

But my stomach leaps whenever a salmon shows a tail out there on the sound. I have to stop myself from watching the water. And my supplies are low. God knows I admire Annie and her subsistence life, her contented partaking of a few seeds at the foot of the bodhi tree, but I'm not sure I want to copy her there.

She nudges the project along. Sometimes she even hangs over my shoulder when I type. (She is now.) It's slower this way — her watching makes each word nervous. Normally I can push the letters out, whack them there final — but her silent judgement on each one turns them into shy little babies and Dad wants an eraser. (There, she left.)

In the evenings, reading it over, Annie tells me changes I must make, tells me when I've strayed too far into fiction; she sighs, leans forward in her chair, knuckles her forehead, stares vacantly at my tattoo (making me blush), and tries to remember how it really went. She'll toss out adjectives and anecdotes: Alicia was "fragile", Alicia "looked like a chipmunk", or "Remember her laugh? It was like a little bell. A little bell out of control." I absorb these, hoping to add likeness to this word-carving I'm doing.

I'm proud when she reads sometimes an entire section and says "Okay". It means I've guessed right, made the connections, shone light into the shadow world. As when I go out to set net, I work with two things only: a sense of the unseen underwater terrain, and my experience with what I call the "common salmon". How deep it goes on hot days, what tides excite it to feed, how long it will hang in the channel before it heads who knows where. It's often only a *feeling*. But when my net does get heavy, when the silver surprises lie fat in the bilge, I know I've guessed right. Seen the unseen. And so it is here, catching the past in my net.

("No, not the past," says Annie, who just read this. "Mythology. It's just as good.")

She's back from the village where she midwifed a birth. An alcoholic mother, and a little girl born shaking. Black forehead hair almost down to her eyes. Annie joked about how bad to be born with a hangover. But she's deeply hurt. She's talked all day, which is the wall she builds to keep back her brooding.

She wants to hike the mountain tomorrow and camp a few nights. I hope she invites me. I need a break. From this chair, this room. This incessant sick-boy story of mine. Most of all, though, I need Annie. A night with her means a night of the best part of my life. I admit that. I am not being pathetic. And I know you will read this.

Next Day

It's raining hard, which lets me feel almost relieved at being left behind while she goes up the mountain. Miserable up there today, I tell myself. Sitting here typing by the fire is the sensible thing to do. And Annie has given me a strict "It's for your own good."

She borrowed my spare pot and a few waterproof matches — this, of course, told me I wasn't going. My disappointment must have showed because at the door she stopped and said: "You know how we never get enough?"

I more or less hold this to be true. I nodded.

"So one of the things we can do is treat hunger like the selfish brat it is: Tame it. Slap it. Open its eyes. Slap the glutton." She sliced a hard backhand through the air. I could picture the creature she was striking. A kind of Buddhist ghost, which she's described: a pale being with spindly legs, a monstrous belly, a wire-thin neck, and a mouth the size of a pea.

Hands go a mile a minute shoving in as much food as possible. But it can never get enough.

"You want to come for two reasons. For my company, which you seem to crave like a boy these days — very flattering — and to escape your project there." I glanced at the pile of pages beside the typewriter. They bored me.

"I don't *love* being alone in the bush, you know. I want you there too. Your voice. Your axe. Grizzlies! Wolverines!" Neither of us has ever seen a wolverine, and grizzlies were well inland now. But I understood her meaning.

"I don't *like* the woods. I never have. But it helps me." She paused, with a significant look. "Some of us have to practise being alone."

This was for me, of course. A warning. She's always doing that, like she's going to drop dead any second and I'll be alone and shivering in my pathetic cabin.

She turned to go, but then didn't. What she did was very dramatic, though I don't know that it was meant to be. What she did was turn back to me, lifting her head slowly, so that the elongated shadows beneath her cheekbones shortened. She looked up, her face shining — there, Annie's look. I am disarmed. The only way I can describe it, is that it is like a sunrise. A look of hope, and sadness, but also the look of a taskmaster. Time is fresh; do something before it is gone. Each time, her look affects me differently. This time, her eyes yielded such recognition that I knew she was sharing guts with me. Truly seeing me, and giving me the chance to truly see her. I think I did. I saw her fear. It felt like both of us were caught on hot ground beside the same Sisyphean stone.

"We have to keep working, Vaughn." She rustled her poncho to her chest and went out the door. On the beach, she began whistling something perfectly inane. I sat still a minute, feeling acutely Annie-eyed. Sometimes it takes a while to get over it.

When I reflect on her argument though, I wonder if she

wasn't overdoing it. And I wonder — a paranoid twinge — if she was only petting away my pout, getting herself off the hook and out the door. Because my so-called gluttony is so small here. I just wanted to go on a hike.

But then I think: small, reasonable desire, maybe, yet isn't it all a part of the huge one?

The starving stomach. The tiny mouth.

Meantime, I'll continue. Writing the Winnipeg stuff was fun. Fanciful. When I think of the name "Vaughnie" I have to laugh. It's an optimistic, prim name, and had little to do with the real creature. Smarter parents would have called me Quasimodo. I think of the scene of my birth, a prototype for many bad movies to come: "Little did pretty mother know that she had given birth to a beast, sheathed in a carapace of ancient leather, strange purpose coursing its blood. And she called him *Vaughn.*" The reality of my birth was something like that. As, perhaps, are all births.

And — yes! — Winnipeg contains my first memory. So distinct, I see it still: The doctor wore ridiculously thick glasses. While he watched me, his face right up to mine, I could see my face in them.

The Boy

The years that Vaughn-Vaughn, Lise, and Mrs. Delacourt spent in Winnipeg were rich years, both inside and outside the School of Psychological Medicine. The Great Depression had ended and the young men of North America found jobs again, deluded, for a little while, by security. At the end of the five years Mrs. Delacourt died, baffled, of pneumonia, but during these years Vaughn-Vaughn had become Vaughn and had learned to walk, talk, read, and skate. During this time, too, Lise had become Vaughn's teacher for life.

His memory surprised them all: it seemed he had only to

do a thing once to learn it. But Dr. Sara was in no way eager to explore this. "Your mother will be expecting a presentable boy," the doctor said as he showed him once more how to grind his inner ear with a cloth, how to use knife and fork on the meat made of putty, how to wipe his penis tip with a tissue after he peed. And, every afternoon, even if Vaughn didn't have to "poo", the doctor had Lise follow him into the bathroom to wipe his bottom. Though secretly Lise had taught Vaughn to do this by himself at home, it was not until Vaughn was six that the doctor had him close the door behind him and try it alone.

Lise did a lot with Vaughn in secret. It had long been her mother's habit to read to her before bed, and this was Lise's favourite thing in life. When her mother fell sick, was it premonition that led her to begin teaching Vaughn to read, so as to never be without a reader?

Her classroom was the warm heart of her bed, under thick blankets, the desk lamp smuggled in to the length of its cord. Here under creamy light she conducted her classes in whispers. Perfect. She could hold her student's arm, stroke it while she read, or squeeze it when she taught him something true. She could read softly into his ear. She could kiss him if she liked.

Perhaps because she lacked any ideas about what a four-year-old boy could or couldn't do, Lise proved a good teacher. Her method was simple: she opened a book and started at the first word. She'd show Vaughn the word "house", pronounce it, explain it or draw it, and have Vaughn say it himself. Words like "under" she could show with her hands. She would sneak Vaughn out to see what a "curbstone" was. Words like "the" and "but" and "try" were impossible to explain, but she had him read them out anyway, so she could lie back and be read to. By the time Vaughn was seven and Lise thirteen, they had read — in their warm classroom, in whispers — *Little Women, Tess of the D'Urbervilles,* and most of the Bible.

When Mrs. Delacourt died, Vaughn and Lise were returned to Beauséjour. In a dramatically sparse letter to Mr. Collin the doctor announced that, though Vaughn had "tendencies" not common in boys his age, he was in his opinion ready for school. The doctor was understandably proud.

The train arrived at night. Duncan and Alicia Collin waited in a station smelling of grain dust and sweat. Alicia said nothing. Her face was pinched, more so than he'd seen in months. When the power went out, leaving them in darkness, Mr. Collin sat still for a moment, and then laughed tentatively. Her silence and the sudden darkness left Mr. Collin feeling that his wife's foul squat was somehow influencing things here.

But she seemed normal enough. She had, after all, agreed to come and greet the children (though she didn't, as he did, wave hello into the glare of the train light); and she did prepare a good snack for them back home (though she kept mum throughout). And as the weeks passed, Mr. Collin saw that she did still, at least, act good enough for company.

As for himself, Mr. Collin didn't quite know how to take to the boy. He'd be glad for now that Vaughn was going to school. And it was a treat when Lise told him Vaughn could already skate like the wind. Hearing this, Mr. Collin calculated aloud that Vaughn was old enough to join the Playground C league.

"Would you like that, Vaughn? Playing hockey with the other boys?" his father asked. Vaughn looked over to Lise, who nodded.

"Yes," Vaughn said to his father, "if someone will please teach me how."

Mr. Collin too looked at Lise, quizzically, and met eyes remarkably like Mrs. Delacourt's: an eagle's look, and the unspoken threat to take-Vaughn-away.

Vaughn was back. Alicia began again to sulk and hide. Mr. Collin trod lightly, wary of both wife and child. Elder son Hughie, sixteen, worked at being an older brother to the boy, but when all he got for his effort was a polite, tin stare, Hughie fled gratefully to his boarding-school in Selkirk. So everyone within the Collin household, except for one, had strong feelings about Vaughn's return. To Vaughn himself, the move meant nothing.

The seven-year-old Vaughn was hollow, and in more ways than this identical to a telescope. Nothing much matters to a telescope. Given light, it will sit and take in the world forever. Let it watch a pink room for five years, then whisk it out and prop it up in a blue room — the telescope won't worry, full of the new blueness. Kill off its nursemaid, replace her with a Métis child; snatch it from a city, lay it in a wheat field; wrest it from the myopic care of behaviourist dabbling doctors, sit it down to supper with a loud man called Father and a quiet woman called Mother — a telescope does not care. The world changed to tickle Vaughn, but it never really touched.

School meant a room full of raw farm boys and spiteful, giggling girls. It meant leaving, for seven hours a day, Lise's intimate care. "You have fifteen new friends," his father put in. Vaughn had up till then no notion that there were others in the world who needed teaching. Fifteen new friends, and his new teacher, Miss Horn.

Miss Horn was a short woman, her body a battleground between youth and age. It was as if a girlish figure had sprouted a wrinkling face which had in turn (age moving only upwards) suffered blooms of crinkly white hair. The transition zone, her neck, was specially marked: just off centre, pushing her head down and her right shoulder up, was a hump.

She had come to Beauséjour from Winnipeg with a will to tame the country lawlessness out of the farm kids. Her lessons she conducted with her arms, as though to hold together an unruly sing-along, and the children gauged their successes and failures by her repertoire of arcs, slashes, and stabs. She was in her own mind an excellent teacher, and graded without self-doubt her farm kids' ability to sing in tune with As, Bs, Cs, and, for special cases, Ds.

It didn't take Vaughn long to discover that he was not like his new friends. On the one hand, he was way ahead. At age seven he had attained a mastery of learning by rote; he could spell, he could speak, and he had read about loves and lives and lands unheard of in this room called Grade One. On the other hand, the others lived in a world unknown to him as well. And this difference between them was the kind that keeps the shed-shaped peg out of the silo-shaped hole, the kind that would keep Vaughn Hardy Collin a marked man for his entire life.

One morning during Vaughn's second week at school, a bright girl, Dorothy Dinnots (Dorothy Doughnuts, at recess), was lorded to the front of the class. Miss Horn announced that because of her good work Dorothy was skipping a grade and entering Grade Two this morning. With Miss Horn leading the little girl towards the door, Dorothy Dinnots began to cry. The nearer she got to the door and Grade Two, the worse her crying got. Miss Horn had to drag her out screaming. Later, after a half-hour arithmetic lesson, Miss Horn asked if there were any questions. Out of the class's silence came a new voice, a funny, croaking little thing. It was the first time Vaughn had spoken in class.

"Why was our friend crying?"

"Oh, you mean Dorothy!" responded Miss Horn, her face cracking an extracurricular smile for an off-the-subject question. "Well, Vaughn, I suppose she was crying because she did not want to leave us."

"Why did not she want to leave us?"

"Well" — Miss Horn frowned, then smiled over-wide

again — "because, Vaughn, now she has to make new friends."

Vaughn thought a moment but couldn't arrive at how Grade Two friends would be so different from these in Grade One that it made someone scream. Nor could he begin to penetrate what "making" friends might entail. He tried another question.

"What do you keep in your hump?" This question was followed quickly by "Why are the boys laughing?" as Miss Horn strode the aisle at him, her yardstick over her head like a sword. Vaughn didn't ask why he was being hit about the head and shoulders — hitting had been a big part of teaching in Winnipeg — but he did wonder what exactly he had done wrong.

A week went by before Vaughn asked more questions. He had learned to be cautious, but still his questions were not quite right: "Why are there twenty-six letters but only ten numbers?" "Why do girls wear dresses?" "Why do we always have new things to learn about?" Miss Horn no longer hit him, but it hadn't taken her long to identify Vaughn as a special case, one which demanded Ds. There was something about Vaughn which disgusted her. His mind was the epitome of tunelessness, a one-boy chorus of frenzied bad music, of jazz. While the rest of the class could sing along, more or less correctly, Vaughn would sit there all day, straight as a prairie dog. He would watch her calmly, but with all that ugly discord behind his eyes. Even Bob Beamer, the tall stupid one who spit whether she was looking or not, was somehow less disgusting than Vaughn Collin. Vaughn's behaviour demonstrated both impertinent daydreaming and the worst kind of maliciousness — an evil humour shocking in a seven-year-old. She had heard the rumours, knew the stories — born with the eyes of a devilish grandfather, he'd been taken away for treatment by a doctor for the insane.

How was she to know that this boy was as incapable of

humour as he was of evil? Or that, in his careful watch over endless classroom details, he was just as unable to daydream?

Vaughn's school manner was finally set right by Miss Horn — via Mr. Collin, via Lise, who was able to explain things properly. "Pay attention to the lessons. That's all. That's what you talk about in school. Ask me about the other stuff."

School went well for a while, for Vaughn no longer asked questions. The lessons were simple enough. The bulk of the day could be spent studying everything else: a shoulder flinch, the polka-dots of a shirt lifting as the arm shot up; the whispers behind him, and their waft of lunch-breath; the spider under the radiator waiting quietly, like him; the weak bird tweets penetrating the frosted windows; the chalk dust ignoring gravity as it floated through light.

During his years of school, Vaughn was failed twice and skipped three. This incredible yo-yoing of ability was a mystery, but Principal Maddy, whose guiding hand each year either led Vaughn to a new room or kept him in an old one, didn't attribute the contradiction to the varied powers of insight of Vaughn's teachers; rather, like Miss Horn, he blamed it on a baby sent to Winnipeg, a baby born — his memory told him — with the eyes of an Indian devil.

Vaughn remembered — though the notion was so huge and deep it was more a part of his personality than memory — that the doctor, with his spoon, had told him again and again that it was his duty, his only goal, to "please your mother and father". He saw now that pleasing parents was not like choosing balls, or memorizing words. But before long he had two tricks, one for his father and one for his mother. His trick for Alicia had not been hard to learn. She was happiest when he came home, said hello, and then stayed out of her sight. Pleasing his father was only slightly harder. First, tell him nothing about school, or lie if he asked. Second, play hockey, learn defence, and learn it well.

These tricks made sense to Vaughn, especially the first one, where nobody had to pretend. And the lying made sense in a funny way too, because everyone else did it. They lied, he saw, when they met on the street and smiled and said "How are you?" "Just grand." Husbands and wives did it, he could see, when they went for walks, and held hands without knowing it, and the husband talked of gas-powered tractors and the wife told him about her new shoes; all the kids did it when they talked to the teacher; and he could see it even in Lise's eyes when she read for hours those books of hers.

Pleasing his father with his other trick, the game of hockey, was not hard for Vaughn. The rules of the game could be learned like any rules, like those of being polite. More difficult was knowing how to be a teammate. These rules were hidden, and had to do with shouting at the right time, and going to other teammates' houses. Though Vaughn learned about this too over the years, he never got good at it. He did much better with the easier game, on ice.

The rink in Beauséjour stayed a simple miracle for him, because it never failed to produce the same feelings. Nighttime, cold, he would stand at the open gate, the strange bright ice giving his stomach the hollowness a deep lake did before he dared jump. All so sharp a sight. Bright white, the rink at his feet. The rest of the world — the night above which stretched for miles and miles — was black. Simple black and white. Thin, cold air to breathe. Vaughn could tell right way that here was a place where you were supposed to do fast things.

He'd launch himself and it would begin: the frantic jerking of arms and legs that felt new and stupid again; the short, daring thrusts to gain speed, to bring a wind fast then burning on the face, making tears. After small lurches for balance, the start of a long glide, skates steady, pointing straight, bumping hard on ice chips, an amazing glide that changed his twitching, bug-like body into a graceful, skating boy who can't fall down simply because he is so smooth and so fast.

When Vaughn discovered how to glide the rest came easily. The secret to skating wasn't at all like his father told him, it wasn't in his ankles. It was in his stomach. In the middle of a glide he saw that everything — his thoughts, his eyes, his ears — was less important than his stomach. He learned to let his stomach take him where it wanted. It didn't have eyes but it saw better, somehow.

Vaughn would always remember learning to skate. Equally vivid was his memory of his first organized game, and the ice-fire. For years, whenever he thought of hockey, whether as a boy on a Beauséjour rink or as an old man in a nostalgic, cabin-bound brood, Vaughn would forever connect hockey and fire.

It seems life does provide symbols, which at times are almost impish. One such symbol, perhaps more ominous than impish, chose to stage itself at centre ice during Vaughn's first game.

Vaughn was nine and playing for the Beauséjour SugarBeeters. They opened their season in Portage, a poor town which, though they boasted the only indoor rink in the league — actually a cadaverous old barn — they couldn't afford to light it electrically, and made do with kerosene lanterns hung from low rafters. The smoke-orange light suited a modern cocktail bar more than a hockey rink.

The puck dropped, the game began, and from the bench Vaughn was startled at how his favourite game changed. For some reason, kids from Beauséjour suddenly hated kids from Portage: they slashed, punched, tripped, swore. Vaughn had seen this in playground games, true, but here it was more. Was it the team sweaters? Like red ants meeting black ants in a sandbox.

During Vaughn's first shift on the ice he was attacked by a small, squinting, red-haired boy. He'd poked the boy's rear by mistake and the redhead turned on him, dropped his gloves, and swung out with wild punches. Vaughn just stood where he was, too stunned to shield his face. After a few moments the flurry stopped: the redhead breathed hard, his fists still up, teeth clenched. Whatever the look on Vaughn's face, it seemed to have startled the redhead. By now the ref had gotten between them, and as they were ushered to the penalty box the smaller boy lunged at Vaughn once more and hissed, "Suck!"

In the penalty box a man sat between them. As play resumed, Vaughn leaned forward past the man to ask the redheaded boy questions.

"Hi," said Vaughn, shyly.

"Suck!" The boy's face was the colour of a bursting pimple.

"Hush now, Ross. You won the fight," the man said, smiling. He was a Portage man. A weight in his voice was aimed at Vaughn like an invisible fist. Both man and boy now ignored him.

The ice-fire started as Vaughn stepped on for his second shift. Two perfectly timed sticks slashed at the puck, sending it up hard to rafter height. It knocked a bent nail precisely. A kerosene lantern fell and spread into a ten-foot circle of orange fire. Everyone fled in time except one Portage player, who skated away making the sound of a crow, one skate fuel-soaked and burning.

He's taking some *with* him, Vaughn thought as he watched the boy skate the length of the ice *so fast,* one foot a fiery pendulum, to crash into the end boards, where he was smothered by parents and farmers who — in their eyes and wild arms and shouting — had been ignited by an invisible fire themselves.

Vaughn would never forget that fire at centre ice, or the boy's flaming foot. An old man in a cabin can call such events symbols, but to a young boy, free of many words yet, "symbols" bypassed thought and rode a truer line from eyes to stomach. In hockey he saw a hot heart: fire burned invisibly under white ice, cold air, and fast bodies, fire that was ready to show itself but rarely did. And as the years passed Vaughn saw something more, that behind not only hockey games but all occasions where people got together and spoke with sticks or mouths or bodies, there burned an invisible fire. Because of it, people did the oddest things. The older Vaughn got the more he wondered why no one mentioned this fire. For they all did odd, flinching things because of its heat. So why no mention? The fire was invisible, true, but so wasn't the wind?

Though Vaughn knew the stomach secret, felt the ice-fire, and over the years scored lots of goals, he remained baffled by the bigger game. The "Yay" he tried to shout after scoring sounded nothing like the strangled scream the others made. Neither could he brag, or show the pride that comes, he saw, when someone wins a trophy or is told by a dad just how darn good he is. He remained similarly dumb as to the right smile to answer with when his father told him, on his fourteenth birthday, about the Chicago scout who wanted to sign him, for money, to a youth contract. It was as though everyone — his dad, teammates, people on the street who stopped him and grabbed his shoulder — thought it was *him* scoring all the goals. Him. Not his stomach. Not the fire.

February 18th

Annie has been away two nights now, and despite her knowhow at being a tough old bird in the bush, I find myself worrying.

What can harm her though? Even if she died up there she'd be the first to say, "Death? At my age? Who cares?" She'd probably see death in the bush as the best of last stands.

Not like the shuffle of papers that puts you from rest home to hospital, the horror on your almost-old children's faces as they watch to see what withers first, your body or their wallets.

She'd say: death in the bush is a chance for ultimate alertness: the cliff-edge plunge, the slap of a bear. Whatever it is, if you're lucky, the killing cause will blow you, all senses afire, to the Last Hurrah, to Heaven (or Hell) Hotel, whatever comes next. She once said that if you're utterly ready, a quick death can get you, conscious, beyond the "first veil".

But she'll return, tomorrow. Any worrying I do, like all worrying, is selfish. It's not for her but for me, for me who would have to continue on alone. I have no right to worry about her — even if she is stranded, broken apart and suffering under a deadfall, crows and wasps pecking and stinging her, nostrils plugged with bark and mud, ten teeth smashed in with nerves naked in the cold air — still *my* worrying would have nothing to do with *her*. (Unless. Unless worrying is a form of prayer, and prayer travels.)

But such a mess would be her glory. She'd milk it for all she could get, she'd keep an eye open to see the stab of the first beak. The past twenty years has grown her a psychological hair shirt. She'd love it if her limp was helped out by a salmon bone in her boot.

All this nervous joking has offered up a reasonable answer: Annie likely did stay an extra night to "take advantage" of the rain. To see beyond the chill and gloom of it. (Sorry Annie. Not beyond. *Into*. I remember.) But I'll haul out some brandy and have a good fire going when she does come. Still likes her little reward after a bout of self-denial.

The writing goes slow. Recording the babyhood was fun and fanciful. But memories I have of my boyhood offer up little excitement — nothing properly gaudy, only broad beige tones. Events, big and small, came and went, but none of them hit the boy's heart. No attacks of cupid, no suicidal angst brought on by acne.

She anticipated this problem and instructed me with typical Annie-emphasis. "You've lived a long time," she said, "and most of that past is boring. Record only the change-makers. The lows, the highs. The foot that kicked you into the next room. Look longest at what is painful to see."

With this in mind I continue my plodding boyhood. But first things first: Lise. If my early days had a kicking foot — or a spoon! — it belonged to darling, limping Lise. And what better time, with Annie gone, to write about Lise?

Mark, O soul, yon swelling in my nether zone.

Lise

No one asked why he wanted a mirror for his birthday, or why he installed it above his bedroom desk.

Watching his face, making it move, guiding muscles to capture expressions. He'd tried them all, at least those that told an obvious story: awe, rage, terror. Good as he was at sculpting these words onto his face, the feelings never fell in with them. He'd known for years that his way of doing it was ass-backwards: that feelings came first, that terror kicked the eyes open, that awe made the mouth drop. But he kept trying this way anyway, hoping that the finished face might give him a hint, at least, at the first feelings.

Vaughn quivered his chin and made his cheek meat bunch up, which half-closed his eyes but brought on no tears.

He wound a belt around his school books. His eyes went to the other books on his desktop. He wished he could take them to school instead. Thick books, books that went "thunk" when you shut them, heavy with knowledge. The desk looked proud holding them up. There was the Plato, leather-bound, a huge earth-brown book. The sayings were like equations. There the green Shakespeare, with ideas so prettied up, and pinched in the end by blood revenge. There the black bible, where kings and peasants alike talked something like Dukhobors, and where Jesus said things so strange that they must certainly be true.

Books bound up, boots on. Coat and lunch waiting downstairs with Lise. What had she made them for lunch? The breakfast mush had stopped swelling in his stomach, which would soon want more. It was hungrier at lunch after a big breakfast in the morning. Mush always did that. There — the saliva was already going again.

Vaughn and Lise stepped down the shovelled walk. The morning was crisp, windless, and the sun sat small and fierce in the south — but for all its burning it couldn't penetrate the edge of cold, and its dazzle coming off the snow made the day colder still. Vaughn had heard his mother's rustlings as he passed her bedroom door on the way out. Alicia Collin had become expert at keeping out of sight while at the same time making her presence felt.

Their boots broke the thin crust; behind them, dry snow fell in from the edges of the holes they'd made. With her limp, Lise was instinctively careful on icy spots. Vaughn took Lise's books and transferred them to his own. They joined their free hands. Through the thick mitts they felt no warmth, only pressure. Back when Vaughn was seven, and leaving with Lise for his first day of school, Mr. Collin had told him that, like a gentleman, he was to carry her books and hold her hand.

"I have two things to tell you today," said Vaughn, turning to look at her. Lise's two black braids were crowned with a green toque, and in the middle of her square face her nose had already turned red. Lise: her squat body, her limp, her red nose.

"Your one thing yesterday was boring, you know," said Lise. "Three goals you get, and your daddy buys you a stick. That happens every week — I'm surprised you even told me. Do better today or I'll stop listening." Lise squeezed

Vaughn's mitt.

"Well. I'll try. The first thing. They're moving me up to Grade Nine today. Mrs. Darmansky's class. *Daddy* gave me money for the new books."

"Finally!" Lise groaned at the sky. "Caught up with your age. You're becoming a horribly normal boy, Mr. Collin. The big new books!" She laughed sarcastically. Vaughn had read the Grade Nine books, and the Grade Ten books, two years ago. She'd stolen them from the library herself, returning them, dog-eared and food-stained, several months later.

"The second thing," Vaughn continued, monotone. "I think it might be funny to you. I saw Mother naked in the bathroom last night. She was rising from her bath. I didn't hear her until I was in the door. She screamed."

Lise whooped then clamped her mitt on her mouth.

"It was a new thing for me. She had all the hair that you said was there. And I think I began to *feel* quite strange. I was staring at her, I know that. She was quiet at first and then she screamed. I walked out. I still do . . . feel strange." His face dull, Vaughn watched his feet crunch the snow. Lise was finding it hard to contain the small shrieks escaping her mitt.

"Very good work! It *is* funny. And you: have you got any . . . *hair* there?" More muffled squealing, and tears in her eyes.

"Well, yes. And no. The hair that was always there is a little longer and darker now. But it wasn't like Mother's. At all. I understand a fourteen-year-old should have it. But it looks like it's beginning. I do have some finished ones — in my armpits. They look curled on a ruler edge. Have you . . . ?"

Lise shouted "Ho!" But then became serious.

"Yes. Very black. Curly, curly. Like your mother's, but probably darker. And — probably more!" She laughed again, and as usual Vaughn had no idea why. He nodded while Lise continued.

"Had it for years. Since I was thirteen. Would you like to see it?" Lise laughed, slyly.

"And the bleeding cycles?"

"It's all there. A girl's clockwork."

"Well. I will see it if you like. But I don't know if I like the feeling."

"Vaughnie, Vaughnie, Vaughnie. Boys like it. Boys are nice to girls. They love it. They get married."

"I know that," Vaughn said.

"In the city, they pay money to see it."

"I know that too."

Tiny sparrows, feathers puffed, clung to branches in the black trees lining the road. Underneath, Lise started onto a laughing, bawdy story and Vaughn stayed silent throughout. They moved slowly, a little stiffly, Lise's limping cruch CRUCH cruch CRUCH working with Vaughn's steadier rhythm. When they reached Lise's work, the Public Library door at the side of the City Hall building, Vaughn handed Lise her books and walked to school, Grade Nine.

It was true that Lise was grateful for her job. Grateful not because she was Métis, but grateful in the way anyone would be if handed the perfect job. Lise read a lot of books — Victorian novels — two, sometimes three a week, and over the years had leached from their prim detail the sort of grace, manners, vocabulary, and feminine inscrutability that allowed her to get high marks, graduate, and succeed as a model Métis girl in rural Manitoba.

To kids her age, adolescent Lise was a gopher. Or, in modern politesse, "not pretty". The dominant genes of her paternal great-grandfather, a lettuce farmer from Toulon, were shortness and squatness, and these lived in Lise now. From her mother's side Lise had inherited the broad shoulders and waistlessness common to Indian women. That, plus a plain round face, a pug Gallic nose, and the hint — as with most female peasantry from the south of France — of a moustache.

By itself Lise's appearance wouldn't have caused much commotion. Her limp made the difference. When she was four the polio had "passed in the night and taken a bite". At ten she became self-conscious of her short left leg, and by lowering and twisting her right hip she could walk with almost no limp. Two months of these pinching steps burned both hip joints and put her in bed for a week. She decided that limping was better than not walking at all, but it was this limp, added to her dark dwarfishness, that gave boys in Beauséjour a favourite target.

Lise grew a major contradiction in her personality: though she breathed a fanciful Victorian air, she loved to fight. She often fought because she was a Métis living with a white family in a racist town, she often fought because she was almost ugly, but she usually fought because of Vaughn. Anyone who called Vaughn Collin a name could expect a visit from the barrel-bodied Métis girl.

But a boy who accepted protection from a girl only needed more bullying. And, for her part, to link herself so strongly with a child-oddity made her more freakish still. To other Métis children, witnessing her rage on behalf of a well-to-do white boy, Lise was an Aunt Tom. So she sometimes fought the Métis as well.

Once, word reached Mr. Collin that Lise had broken a young boy's arm. (He'd chanted Vaughn's name as he passed, changing "Hardy" to "Retardy".) Mr. Collin didn't lecture her. Being a lawyer, if anyone knew justice, he did. Besides giving his son a pair of boxing gloves for Christmas, he dropped the matter there.

It was not just because of Lise that schoolyard kids quit picking on Vaughn. It was really because Vaughn, though he could be beaten up a hundred times, never acted beaten up; though he did punch back and though he cried, his punches were somehow not mad enough, and his crying was over too soon, as if he really didn't mean it. Also, by age fourteen his reputation as a hockey player had earned him respect. Several times teammates fought for him before Lise had a chance.

Vaughn gave no thought to Lise's lack of beauty. He simply knew her face like nothing else. He'd had years to watch the push of her cheekbones, the falcon swoop of her brow. And her skin: in a climate that scraped a face as dry as the prairie itself, Lise's skin stayed moist, creamy with colour and scent. Her lips, too, held constant promise — fleshy, lively lips that could blow open any time and let loose a great laugh. If an older Vaughn Collin was to select one image that focused his early years, it would be Lise's startling mouth, as it laughed.

At nineteen, Lise still lived at the Collins' and her duty was still with Vaughn. Officially the maid, in truth Vaughn's teacher. "Help Vaughn find his way," Mr. Collin had told her, years ago. She was allowed her library job only because, with Vaughn in school, her days were free. After work, after school, Lise's real job and Vaughn's real school would begin.

Victorian novels. Something in their wit, their elegance, their courtly but panic-stricken sexuality drew this orphaned, homely girl. There was something so fitting to have the exploits of Tess, or *Vanity Fair*'s Becky read to her coolly at bedside by a smooth-cheeked boy whose voice had not yet begun to break. A boy who knew the meaning of no more than two-thirds of the words he read, and who understood probably none of the almost-raciness, or the secret behind the heroine's hot flush. Sometimes, at certain parts of certain books, Lise's hand would be under the covers, a hidden, bobbing bird. Vaughn paid no attention to the older girl's persistent itch.

The laughter with which Lise greeted news of Vaughn skipping a grade was the same laughter that greeted news of his failures. Their school was not her school. Lise never doubted that this living, incomplete tapestry called Vaughn Collin was hers by legacy, and hers alone. Her duty was to finish the weave, and begin the fancy embroidery.

Lise taught many things. Early on, for instance, there had been a problem with frostbite. It wasn't quite that Vaughn forgot his clothes, but more that he forgot to predict the future.

He liked skating alone on the Brokenhead River, and one warm afternoon he'd worn only a sweater. Oh, how like the smooth, head-up lope of a hare to just skate, free of a fenced-in rink, free to shoosh this narrow river, pump hard on straight stretches, worm low around corners. It went on forever. But soon it got hard to see. And so cold when he stopped to turn around. It was almost midnight when, perhaps near death, he thumped home. Everything was numb and wouldn't work, and he'd had to pound on the door with his head.

"You make plans," Lise told him over his bath. "You pick up your winter coat even when you're warm inside the house, and put it on inside the door. If you don't plan things out, you might die, they might find you stuck to the river like a twig." You plan lunch, you plan parties, you plan your life, she told him.

For Vaughn, such a proposition meant tearing his eyes off whatever face or toy or wallpaper flower, and leaping into a world where things were not really there. But he saw that, like Lise said, others did it all the time. Farmers planted in spring for a harvest in the fall. Lise put spoons and plates in a hope chest for a marriage to a boy she didn't know yet. His father talked about a special spot in the bank where he kept money for his own funeral. And yesterday his brother, Hughie, legs apart and acting old, had announced that he was maybe going to France to fight so that Hitler wouldn't come to Manitoba. Still, Vaughn resisted the notion. "Ollie Bey," he reminded Lise, "worked at sweeping grist all summer to buy new skates. His father took the money somewhere for three days and spent it."

Like many large, prim houses which both inside and out tried to lord the best of everything over the rest of the community, the real family inside was a broken web, a lame duck, a mess. One proof of its messiness was that no one ever stopped to think how bad it was.

Vaughn and Lise's partnership was strange, but it was the only one the house held. His mother's suffocating decline had continued and was almost complete. Friends and neighbours were aware of her change now, the womenfolk agreeing that she had reached the age, poor thing.

Poor Duncan Collin, too, they tittered, when someone suggested as fact that Mrs. Collin's bedroom door was shut to him. How long it had been shut was anyone's guess, and none came close. Vaughn was fourteen years old now.

Mr. Collin bore his wife's behaviour with a creeping, boyish impatience. One night, drunk, he raved at Dr. Watt, "She may be mad at me or at the world. But she's still my wife and she damn better act it!" The two friends had an argument, one which never really healed, over the doctor's refusal to try to cure Alicia. Dr. Watt's final advice, "She's older now, Duncan. Let her be," seemed to Mr. Collin an incredible thing for a supposed healer to say, and it refired his distrust of medicine in general. It didn't help that his son Vaughn, though looking good, though admired by pro scouts, was *really* not much changed at all. He was the team's best player by far, and yet he hadn't been named captain. The best player was always captain. Unless — unless he was unpopular and a freak.

"My youngest son," he mumbled sloppily into the fireplace, as the doctor rose angrily to leave, "my last son . . . who you sent to Winnipeg . . . is a . . . *door*knob, *doc*tor. And my wife . . . my wife, *doc*tor, could sit a day in the cellar and dry up the apples. *Doctor.*"

Lise hated being in such a house and so whenever possible would incite the passive Vaughn to long walks. Over the seasons their explorations had taken them farther and farther from Beauséjour, spiralling out into new fields, across new ditches and beside new stands of bush where rabbits scattered in the face of a boy who stayed silent and a loud girl who limped.

Lise chose peculiar rest stops. "Secret spots" she called them, and she would never agree to sit and unwrap their sandwiches until they found one. Secret spots were sheltered from sun and wind, and they were somehow walled and dark. They were found where prairie earth dipped: beneath a trestle, in the pit of an ancient sod hut, in the elbow of a drainage ditch, or in the scooped hollow of tree roots. In such places the ground was always moist, and the air hinting at caves.

They'd eat in silence, business-like as farmers. If there was no log or wall to rest against, they'd lean back to back. After, Lise would whirl herself around to face him, and talk. If she talked about her books, which she usually did, she sat up straighter, and even her voice changed. Instead of, "Whyunt we chuck some rocks, eh?" it was "Why *don't* we discuss *Vanity Fair*?"

In these secret spots Lise would open her special world to him, a world so foreign to Vaughn it seemed magic that she could find her way back to it each day. Speaking, her face became magical too. Her face muscles would slacken and hang, her eyes would fix on the front of his shirt and grow wide, the pupils shining madly, like the black light hidden in the middle of a raisin. And then her words would come, filling the secret spot like faint birds, twisting, shadowy.

Her wonderful face. A "half-breed". Looking at her, Vaughn couldn't get the word to fit. "Half-breed" hinted at something only half there. Lise should have been called a "double-breed", there was so much of her. Watching her, Vaughn saw the joining of races, her face the sum of historical arithmetic. He let his eyes float along the planes of her wide bones, the gentle people of the deer, which then pinched to the features of hot lands and shouting, her sharp eyebrows gesticulating like arms. The sleepy head-tilt of an Italian madonna. The pug nose. And the perfect tawny skin, holding all in. Something else too — in her voice, the correct ways of the English.

His eyes on her, lunch finished, Lise would enter her world and talk about the past and future. The past always centred around books, around "what it used to be like". She expanded on characters' lives, adding such colour and spark that Vaughn forgot she was speaking about people out of books he'd read himself. How did he always miss so much?

"Becky," she told him, "was really a lonely girl. She was a good girl, and was only looking for a man who knew her. Inside and out. A man good enough for her, who could be her father, her brother, her . . . lover . . . all at once. There aren't many men *like* this." Here Lise would pause, and Vaughn feel accused of something. And here he was supposed to think of something to say.

"Why didn't William Thackeray write in a man who was *like* this?" Vaughn's questions were usually not quite right.

"Because Thackeray didn't know Becky either. He wasn't her kind of man. He didn't know what she wanted. And that's why she stays angry."

When Lise talked of the future a strange smile would take over her face. Her eyes, still fixed on Vaughn's shirt, and wide, did not seem to know the smile was there.

"When you turn eighteen," Lise would announce, "you will travel someplace far from Beau, farther away than Winnipeg, and find a girl."

"How do you know?" Vaughn would ask, as always forgetting to plan for the impatience this question always brought.

"Because that's what *happens*," she would say, stamping her foot like an English girl. "And me, some man will travel from far away to find me."

"And you'll go away with him? And sleep together?"

"After the proper time."

"Will it be Bernard LaPierre?"

"It will *not* be Bernard LaPierre." She took a soft swing at him. "Whyunt you listen, eh?"

Vaughn Collin had other teachers beside Lise. School gave him lists of numbers, the categories of nature, the men and dates of history. Hockey had grown a fastness in his muscles. Church whispered its mysteries to him, hoping to find a slash in the skin that years had hardened around a boy's soft centre.

Adolescence had brought Vaughn no closer to fathoming people. His odd retardation loomed large in a world where people talk, love, and joke. Vaughn knew his lack and saw that others knew it too. So he withdrew and studied people from a distance. He read farmers' and housewives' faces with the fervour of an introvert stamp collector reading his stamps. Like stamps, the faces Vaughn studied stayed two-dimensional, their grins and tears painful hints of huge realms within. Certain people were more generous with their hints: Bert Flute's face was a circus.

Beauséjour abutted the main railway and had seasonal farm work, so the town saw its fair share of bums. Only a handful got jobs, and the town saw to it that the rest moved on: it was the one time when Beauséjour boys were allowed to throw rocks.

Old Bert Flute somehow managed to stay for five summers running. He rarely ventured into town itself, and as far as anyone knew he didn't steal laundry or garden crops. Some supposed he had a woman on the reserve. ("But we know that's not true," Lise whispered to Vaughn.)

It happened that their secret spots were Bert Flute's as well: under trestles or in dry ditches Bert Flute would unfurl his bedroll, make a tripod and fire for his spaghetti pot, and say to himself, "Home." When Vaughn first met him, Bert Flute had a shelter made out of old sandbags below the floodbank of the Brokenhead River. The riverbank was a bazaar of paper and muddy trash, a mile of spring-flood jetsam caught on twigs. The air hung rich with the smell of river mud, and as Bert Flute greeted them that first time, Lise whispered to Vaughn, "I think that man's been pooping near here."

He was short, bald, with a small yellow face. Though it was May and almost hot he wore a long "bum's coat", the sleeves hanging down so far they hid his hands. He stood before them and bowed low, and then stuck out his left hand to be shook.

"Most pleased, most pleased. Bert Flute, my tads, Bert Flute," he chirped in a high singing accent as he took their hands in turn. He smiled so squeezed and wrinkly a smile Vaughn couldn't tell if he was joyful or wretched. He watched for tears.

After such an elegant introduction all three of them fell silent. An old bum, a young Métis woman, a staring boy. Bert Flute saw Lise's wrinkled sneer as she sniffed the dank air.

"Springtime, eh?" He jerked his head up and looked about quickly, sniffing too. "Weddin' time! Water, mud, weeds — ol' damn earth fulla *fock!*" He shot his small fist into the air, and laughed. When Bert Flute moved it was always out of stillness — then a quick, exaggerated jerk, like a startled prairie dog.

"Fulla *fock!*" he yelled again, and up went the quick fist. Then he stared at Lise's young sugarbeet breasts.

"*You* know well the spring, eh, my miss?" he said, and before Lise had time to shout or slap, his left hand reached out, brushed her breast, and produced a penny. With no break in movement he gave the cent to Vaughn.

Bert Flute's sleight-of-hand kept Vaughn in awe and Lise smiling over summer days to come, as did his one-handed cat's cradles of muddy river string, his crudely carved birds, and his funny, springtime voice. But what struck Vaughn the most was what blazed behind the man's quickness, and what mesmerized even when he was still. It blazed — half-hidden, hissing colours — mostly in his face, especially when he shouted or cried, and he did both often. He spoke of his "fightin' friends", and laughed; he shouted about "civ'lizzation", then cried; he laughed about "you beauteous children", then went still, and tears started. Vaughn could see that whatever it was that made Bert Flute cry was also what made him laugh. A blazing. He reminded Vaughn of a jackrabbit he'd seen whose side got torn under a plough.

It had to do with his chicken hand.

Bert Flute always kept his right hand hidden up his sleeve, and didn't show Vaughn and Lise the hand until the end of that first summer. He was telling them another of his stories, a long one concerning "a fresh tad" from the old country who came to the U.S. of A., then Mexico, Vancouver, then Winnipeg; was refused jobs, laughed at by children, screamed at by "flowerin' girls". The man moved on, "saw men die and gov'ments burn", worked at odd jobs, but always in back rooms or at night. All of this because of "a wee problem".

"A wee problem," Bert Flute whispered, quietly eyeing Vaughn and Lise, nearing the ghost-story surprise.

"A wee problem," he said again. "The man — were his poor mom accursed by toads? Were his dad's own tool off-centred? — the man came into the wide world . . . *draggin' this.*" He popped his right hand out of its sleeve. Shrunken. Pale blue, gnarled claws, the nails black, cracked, overlong.

A chicken hand.

Bert Flute held it out in front of them, squeezed up his face, and laughed wildly. And then cried just as hard, his inner blaze shifting only in colour, not in heat.

Once that first summer, Vaughn's slowness made him ask for a better look. Lise shushed him, but the old man smiled, calmly produced the hand, and let Vaughn prod it and pull the fingers, which fell limp when he let them go.

"No, it can't move for me," Bert Flute whispered, and as Vaughn continued to play, his face darkened and tears started.

"Can you write, lad?" he asked softly. Vaughn nodded. "I be fifty-two, and not one letter from these fingers. My folks," he grew instantly enraged, "would not have a left-handed boy, would not add strange onto strange . . . *fifty-two!*" He began to cry in earnest, flinging his head back for full-throated donkey-brays.

Another time they arrived at Bert Flute's home — two blankets hung under a creek bridge — to see him off down-stream, standing rigidly with feet apart, screaming and flapping his chicken hand at something distant — maybe at the fields and trees, or maybe at bright cities with their bosses and flowerin' girls.

Just what Vaughn learned from Bert Flute is not clear. Perhaps, compared with the stoic farmers and their silly children, of all people Vaughn had yet met the hobo showed him best the shaggy span of emotions humans were bedevilled by. Or perhaps Bert Flute was best at revealing Vaughn's own stupidity to him. Next to Lise, he seemed to understand Vaughn the most.

That first summer, Bert Flute told them how he'd "learnt himself flyin'".

"It's like this," he said, slit-eyed and sly as when he told any story. "First you pretend a bit, boy. Can you pretend?" Lise nodded yes, he could pretend. (Vaughn wasn't so sure.)

"Pretend that your eyes be the horizon, be stretched out

there, hangin' onto land's end with little eyeball claws . . . "

"Horizontal," said Lise to Vaughn, showing him with a finger. She always translated this way for him, scientific whenever people grew whimsical.

"So," the man continued, "the eyes be as a blanket to cover the whole prairie." He pretended to smooth down a blanket which led out from his eyes. "With eyesight so, your nose pretends to be as a tree, standin' here in front of your head."

"Vertical," said Lise.

"You now have the crosshairs of a rifle!" Bert Flute was excited and punched the air. "You're pretendin', mind you, but you *got* crosshairs whatever they say." Bert Flute watched Lise and Vaughn stare at the horizon, aiming with their noses.

"Crosshairs. Rifle," he repeated. "Now, what do you shoot? Great bullets?" Vaughn and Lise said nothing.

"No! You shoot — your*self!* It's a *brain*ride!" he screeched triumphantly. "You fly, you fly far, over the farms and fields, out to a cosy hot spot in the air, you zither like a dragonfly out there in midcentre-point!"

Vaughn tried to shoot himself and fly, but failed, as he always did with imagination. But he did remember something, and spoke up.

"When I was small. I never really flew as a dragonfly, but I could look far. Way off over all the snow. And not think."

The old man looked at Vaughn curiously, and after a moment said, "Yes, yes. 'And not think'. You be givin' old Flute a lesson, boy. 'Not think' — that should be step one to my tellin' of flyin'."

"When I was younger," Vaughn added; "not so much now."

"That's all he could do, is stare," Lise said, nodding.

Bert Flute often performed his penny-from-Lise's-breast trick for them, and Vaughn never tired of it. Each time it happened, Lise did a kind of trick herself. As soon as he touched her she took control of everything, of Bert Flute himself, by acting queenly as a Grade-Twelver when asked to the harvest dance by a scared farm boy. Odd how, whenever the old man touched her, Lise could become pretty, and as if by magic turn Bert Flute into a silly boy who always removed his hand. When he asked how she did it, walking home one day after Bert Flute had tried to touch both her breasts at once, she shushed him, and told him not to tell anybody anything or they'd all be in trouble.

Vaughn was fifteen when, while on one of their winter walks, Lise's teachings took a sudden turn. Perhaps it was innocent, perhaps not. But Vaughn, at least, hadn't expected it.

A Sunday walk in early March. The night's wind had moulded six-foot drifts under the eaves of houses and against barn walls. With snow so deep, secret spots were hard to find. So Vaughn and Lise would make their own: tunnelling into the larger drifts, they discovered what Eskimos knew, that snow houses are warm enough inside to sit down and take a coat off.

It took ten minutes to dig a tunnel, and ten more to hollow out a "bedroom". Then they'd glove away enough ceiling to allow some light in through a foot-thick snow roof. They'd be sweating from the work.

On this Sunday their bedroom was smaller and warmer than usual. They had tunnelled hard to get here, laughing as they went, dog-digging snow in each other's faces. They rested, flushed red with fun. All that linked them with the outside world was a yellow ceiling glow which made the room seem more secret than usual, the snow lens over their heads allowing in only the softest part of the sun.

They'd finished lunch, were propped back-to-back, and Lise talked. Once more, about love. This time, to Vaughn's amazement, she knew exactly how "He" would look. She described his hawk-like nose, his green eyes, blond hair, one crooked tooth. He would be tall and slim, without much hair on his body. Lise paused at this point, and stared up to the lemon-lit ceiling. Vaughn tried for something good to say.

"I have thirteen pubic hairs now," he said, his tone almost apologetic, as if he had too much hair for her, "and my dinger, I think, is almost a man's."

"So!" she said, and giggled. "Let me see them!"

The bedroom was just high enough for Vaughn to kneel in front of her. He undid his fasteners and moved his pants and underwear down to the snow, in shadows. He began to count.

"One, two, three . . . there's a small one . . . four, five, six . . . "

"Let me," said Lise. She crouched lower, her face a foot away from his groin; she pushed his hands away.

"Okay. Seven, eight . . . nine, ten, eleven . . . there's twelve . . . there's thirteen. And there's fourteen. And another small one — fifteen."

"Some must have grown."

"I think I feel some more here," Lise said, "on your *tests*." She smoothed her hands over his testicles, which had been high and hard, but now they softened in the warmth of Lise's cupped hands and eased slowly down. Vaughn felt his penis lift.

"There," he whispered quickly, "there. That's what happens in the morning." He pointed past her face at his erection. Lise laughed gently.

"Don't you ever think about girls?" she asked, her voice deepening.

"Well . . . no. Yes: I think about you, and Mother — "

"This is what lovers do," she whispered. Extending her tongue but keeping the point of it soft, she smoothed it along and around Vaughn's scant pubic hair.

The light, which barely brought out colour on Lise's check-shirted back, began to pulsate with Vaughn's heartbeat. He could feel Lise's tongue more and more as his eyes and ears and thoughts themselves moved down to swell in his stomach, and then in his groin. His body seemed huge, all parts magnified.

"This feels strange . . . hot." His voice was a whisper now that stood out and shook in the smooth light of their bedroom.

"This tickles my tongue," Lise whispered back.

"Your tongue . . . feels like . . . a very polite dog," Vaughn said, which made Lise groan, and then bark softly, and then laugh like a child.

March 2nd

The rain has eased into the normal west-coast winter stuff, rain so light your face hardly feels it. All it does is bead on your hair and cool your ears. You walk through this thickened air forgetting it's raining at all, until you hear the hissing in the trees or on the water. Ferns and pine needles are luminescent during rain like this, green's hidden power. The forest becomes exhilarated, glows, gives off steam, but people become ghosts. Rain-coast winter: hard edges softened, formless. It's funny, but the reason this time of year is so distinct is because it's so *in*distinct. It's like living in a giant cigarette filter. Purgatory, what else can you call it?

Hard not to feel like an invader here. With so few man-made structures it's easy to picture the land as it was before, when it was nature's lush accident. We who live here occupy a slash. Garlic and sapphires, a discord. But people have to live somewhere. Ironic — it's these sparsely settled places which reveal the rupture most. Cities are a world apart, a nesting gone mad. Cement-framed parks are cartoons of what was. Probably Vancouver once looked a lot like Bella Combe.

Here the bush still threatens: blackberry, bamboo, and insatiable saplings of all kinds close in like a giant spiky mould. Vedder's store, wharf, the Tyee Hotel and Bar, a fishing resort and maybe forty houses scattered in trees. Mostly plank-wood shacks, like mine. No road in or out. Purgatory.

Lise in the snow. Well, so went an exciting segment in my life. Quite a scene: writing it gave me an erection! The power of words. I don't think reality itself has made me erect in weeks. The setting sun of sex.

I wonder how accurate I've gotten this "first time with Lise". Annie will no doubt have something to say about it when she gets back, but I suspect it happened much the way I put it down. What better of life's mileposts than virginity's sweet death-cry to bring out your truest memory. (Biggest lie?)

Fooled myself last night. After typing for hours I was in a jittery state and by nine o'clock the feeling of Annie being overdue grew so strong it got impossible to sit still any longer, worried and useless. By the time I was on the beach and halfway to the Tyee I had convinced myself that the only reason I was going to the bar was to raise concern about Annie, maybe roust up some kind of search party. Posse.

But when I got there, pushed in the Tyee's double-doors, smelled the smoke and fish-hands and beer, and heard the rumbling laughter, I knew it was the Tyee and not concern over Annie that had pulled me out of the cabin.

I admit it: I was there for the beer. And beef jerky, and beernuts, and bullshit. I hadn't been there in — How long? Who knows, maybe a year, maybe two. In any case, though I got the expected odd looks, the bullshit was nice. I remember last time I was in it was killer-whale stories (lies: Don Moe said he saw a pod of "fifty at least"). I recall before that it was a plague of dogfish (lies: Billy Moe said he caught three on one treble hook). Last night, ten seconds in the door told me that this night's bullshit was: "where is all the herring?"

Herring are dull to begin with, so it was good I sat down with the lying Moe brothers and I might hear that it was the anchovies' fault, that the anchovies were on the warpath and were head-butting all the herring out to sea.

On my way to the Moes I passed a table of strangers ("Strangers"! God, I should put on a cowboy hat) who gave me the real once-over, not even bothering to hide their stares or cupped-hand comments. Just when I get to the point of almost forgetting about it, someone goes and. . . . I tried to walk past with nonchalance, but nonchalance isn't what I felt. Sorry, Annie, but when I found myself faking yet another smile to get me past yet another table of stares, I cursed your advice and decided to grow my hair long again and cover the thing for good. (And that's what I'm doing. Even as I type, waiting for you, the hair's up there right now, growing.)

"Holy shit, lookit this, it's Collin. Hey Collin — so where's all the jesus fuckin herring?"

Ah, Moe brothers and beer. Easy medicine.

The World

> "What about your man who's coming?"
> "I am breaking no positive engagement."
> "If your affections have been withdrawn from me and given to someone else, I should feel no right to assert a claim on you."
> "If you are not absolutely pledged to . . . someone . . . we are neither of us bound."
>
> — *The Mill on the Floss*

Bernard LaPierre had claims on Lise. First, he was Métis. Second, being an apprentice barber, he was a career man. And third: though nothing to look at himself, he knew he was Lise's better half so far as looks went. Bernard's crewcut always sat just right, and his hairline (though incriminatingly low on his forehead) was so straight it could have been traced on with a ruler. Besides, Lise Delacourt was almost twenty-three, almost an old maid. She'd be grateful for Bernard LaPierre.

If he needed to, Bernard could always dangle a nugget. An aunt had been a secret mistress of Louis Riel. The story claimed she'd been allowed to throw the first rose into the hanged rebel's grave. Bernard had kept this tasty secret hidden ever since his early boasts were laughed at by friends (they called him Bernard LaRiel for a while), but he knew the scandal was perfect to use on a girl he planned to marry.

So Bernard was dynamite around Lise. Unshakeable confidence. Knowing he as good as had her let the real Bernard LaPierre shine through his clothes, let him bob his head, tell jokes with flair. No shyness around this homely librarian. While normally he thick-creamed his pimples, Bernard found he could visit the library uncovered and glaring, and tease Lise till the cows came home. It would be impossible for this quiet librarian, this servant girl with the limp, the doghouse body, and pumpkin face, to refuse him. For the first time since he had started running after girls, he had found one with whom he could do what he liked.

When Bernard discovered he was wrong, he couldn't believe it. Then came the gut panic that refused to answer the question: If she won't have me, who will?

He grew frantic. He thought of Lise constantly and, alternately adoring and cursing her, the image of her he flipped around in his head was a final coin toss in a high-stakes game: heads, she was Lise, blood kin, a true mate who would one day see the light and love him; tails, she was that ugly bitch librarian who sat guarding useless books for white men. The very day after he had whispered a shaky "I love you, Lise," he strode in drunk to confront the same girl at the same desk by snatching the "shitbook" from her hand and throwing it across the room.

Lise caught herself admiring Bernard for his latest act of rage, because the book he threw was *Vanity Fair*, her favourite, and his passion had seemed appropriate to the chapter she was on. But she didn't tell him, he wouldn't have understood. It wasn't hard for him to understand what she did tell him:

"Whyunt you get lost you half-breed bum and don't get found."

How could she explain that he wasn't He-who-was-coming-for-her? Good god, he pronounced her place of employment the *libary*. How could she explain that the wife of a Métis barber fell nowhere near the kind of life she knew she was fated for? And, most of all, how could he understand that, in the meantime, her affections — and a kind of love even — were fixed on a strange, wide-eyed, dull-as-porridge boy six years younger than her?

Neither could Vaughn fathom her affections. In secret spots, the hockey shack, anywhere, the act of lovemaking amazed him, how it fired his body, a body that knew how to find such pleasure in itself. But lately Lise had been confusing things, spoiling things. With her talk.

Mr. Collin caught them once in her bedroom. Vaughn would often answer her soft middle-of-the-night knock and follow her across the hall. After, when Lise was asleep, a vision of his parents' faces would help him make his dutiful way back to his own room. But on this particular night Lise wouldn't let him stop and he was exhausted. The cold room and howling winter wind, mixed with Lise's embrace and soft breathing, kept Vaughn from seeing the faces, or his duty. He fell asleep. In the morning he barely heard Mr. Collin's pounding on his own bedroom door across the hall. But at the sound of his father's calling, Vaughn leapt from Lise's bed and tried to pull on his pants, which tangled. Lise's door opened, and there was his father's real face.

"Lise, where's . . . Oh." Mr. Collin closed the door, stood behind it a while, then announced, "Vaughn, downstairs."

The lecture took place at the breakfast table, over eggs and mush. Father and son, alone. At Vaughn's entrance Mr. Collin explained to his wife that, Dear, he had to speak with his son, that there were some things a mother could not — But Alicia was already up and out, the door clicking softly behind her.

Not knowing whether to eat the food in front of him, Vaughn listened to his father begin his monotone argument. It sounded serious. Mr. Collin wiped his egg spoon clean and tapped the table with it to make final certain points. He explained to his son about hired help. He explained about racial barriers, about embarrassing complications. He said Lise would have to be "let go". He paused to watch Vaughn, whose face showed him nothing at all. Then he reddened, and a sad grin wavered at the corners of his mouth.

"Do you . . . sleep in her bed . . . often?" He bowed his head, chuckled, and began to eat his eggs again.

"No," answered Vaughn, truthfully enough. For they usually did their love-dancing, as they called it, in his bed after school, or outside during good weather. He'd never slept in her bed before.

His father seemed satisfied. But his next question puzzled Vaughn.

"So she likes hockey players, does she?" Mr. Collin laughed and shook his head, then began spooning his mush in huge gulps.

Something told Vaughn it was best not to mention how she'd been talking to him lately, strangely, about love. Instead, copying his father, he chuckled too and began to eat.

"Before I met your mother, son, in Winnipeg . . . there were girls . . . by God, girls who — " He stopped there, seeing Vaughn. His son held his spoon, full of egg, an inch from his mouth. Vaughn's eyes were fixed on him, eyes clear but uncomprehending.

Mr. Collin began to sweat. He fumbled for his pocketwatch, studied the time. He glanced up to Vaughn again, saw the eyes still on him. For the first time in long, cold years, Mr. Collin found himself feeling sorry for his wife.

The day after his father's discovery, Vaughn found a note from Lise tucked in his lunch bag, asking if he felt like "tunnel-dancing" before hockey practice. Yes, thought Vaughn. He could imagine no other answer. Meeting Lise meant skipping dinner, but then his stomach never wanted much to do with hockey after food. Lise and hockey: he wanted both. Food was only fuel.

They met outside the library in early darkness. Out in the northern pitch a budding line of green-gold borealis hung hissing. A wind gusted, and stung their cheeks with ice crystals.

"A tunnel's nicer when it's so windy," said Lise as they poked about for an old tunnel by the rink, "especially when you can hear it blowing. It's so cosy then. In the snow." Vaughn thought he could see what she meant, so he agreed.

"So what did your dad say to you?" Lise asked.

"When?"

"Yesterday, dumb boy, after he saw us in my bed."

"I was out of the bed."

"Well he knew you were just *in* the bed. *Jesus*. So what did he say?" Lise's stick had found the drifted-over entrance to their tunnel. As she hunched like a digging dog, the snow shot at an angry speed from between her legs. Vaughn had to step aside.

"He said I had to be careful because you were Métis, because you are our servant girl, and — "

"But was he mad!"

"No, I don't think so. He said you were 'let go', but his

face said he was lying. He said a lot of things. He asked if you liked hockey players."

"You aren't going to be punished?"

"I don't think so. Why?"

Lise was smoothing the edges of the hole she'd uncovered. Her shoulders sagged as she sighed her "English girl's sigh", as Vaughn called it.

"Isn't that good he wasn't mad?" Vaughn asked.

"Did you bring the candle? Give it to me. And the matches."

"Here. But isn't it good?"

"Christ almighty! *Jesus!*" Lise crossed herself and mumbled something. "Whyunt you just come in, okay? We'll talk about it."

The last thing Vaughn wanted was more talk about it. It had been hard enough yesterday, listening to his father. And now Lise: week after week she was getting harder to understand.

She had changed so much in the past year, since their first "dance", and Vaughn could not begin to see the reasons. She was still Lise but . . . something was missing, and something was getting bigger. It was at least a year since she'd sneaked into the bathroom where, giggling, she'd bent him over to wipe him clean, saying, "Just like I used to, dirty dumb boy, do you remember?" It was a year ago that she'd stopped telling funny stories about the love disasters of old schoolgirl friends. And, lately, she no longer teased him about his goat-clumsy performance as they danced in their shadowy secret spots. These days she seemed disappointed, her sighs off-key as she demanded more from him, saying testily, "No, men do it *this* way."

Something had been added. A lie. Vaughn knew the lie came from the books she read, and from the movies the Rialto was showing. The magic light that lit her eyes when she told him about the books, about the movies, about her future —

that same magical light he once thought was her delight and her wisdom — he now saw to be the light of a lie. He saw it often: a dream, a lie, in the air around her face. It sparkled there, a halo of fantasy.

Did she know she lied? Vaughn knew he was far from understanding her. But, he thought now, following on all fours her bear-like bum into the tunnel, he was nowhere near understanding lots of things. All he knew — and here he pictured her bum being led by a face that radiated a magical, lying light which lit the darkness of the snow bedroom — all he knew was that he didn't like being lied to.

He would rather just dance with her, here in the tunnel. He would rather just dance than have to pretend he was a lord who had asked her, a countess, to tea. He would rather just call her Lise than Maude or Becky. Or Tess. He especially hated Tess, for then he had to be Angel Clare, who Lise knew everything about — how he kissed, what he said, how his religious eyes looked at sex — and so she always found fault with Vaughn's performance.

No, Vaughn would rather just tunnel-dance, rather just enjoy the difference of a woman's body, a difference — if she stood a certain way, with breasts and curves just so — that made a woman's body reach out and nudge everything in a room, whereas a man's body just sat inside whatever he was wearing.

But now, in their snow bedroom, Lise wanted more talk. Vaughn was already tickling her under her pants, but she seemed bored. She told him she was glad he hadn't been punished, but it was "well . . . too bad" that Mr. Collin wasn't angry with them.

"Why?" asked Vaughn, for this went against all he'd been told about duty to parents. He withdrew his hand, puzzled, but Lise caught it and put it back in place.

"Well, it would have made it . . . this . . . better ."

"Oh."

"But your father thinks it's okay."

"I don't know what he thinks."

"Well it makes me feel like a *whore!*" Lise crossed herself and whispered something again. Vaughn still didn't know what to say, but thought it might be a good time for a joke. He wasn't at all sure with jokes, so he made himself chuckle first — to tell her a joke was coming — and then tried it:

"A whore who likes hockey players!"

Lise screamed and pushed his hand away. She looked at him fearfully, as if she'd never seen him before. Then she started crying, and cried for a long while.

Her sobs made the room so different than before. It was usually such a *quick* place, where a candle flickered, where they danced, and Lise moaned and laughed, and both their bodies shook. Now, with Lise's whimpers a small thing coming from a distant corner, the room was made quiet and vast. The candle flickered weakly, and seemed embarrassed.

Lise was lying again, this time to herself only, and this time more than ever. Huddled in the snow, she rocked and groaned. An act, yet an act so good she was truly in pain. Why?

Vaughn recalled their last meeting with Bert Flute that past spring. The old hobo had been nervous; he laughed and jerked constantly and punched the air many times, yelling, "The air's fulla *fock!*" He'd begun touching Lise, laughing, and then groping at her, crying. When Lise grew queenly he got mad and began to shake, and turned his back to them. When he pivoted to face them again he had his penis out, resting limply on his chicken hand.

"Here!" he cried, "Look at Flute, see what be hangin' off his soul!"

Vaughn looked at the penis, smooth and blind and stupid, like something that grew out of a lake bed, a clam tongue. Standing there, watching it, Vaughn knew its twofold purpose. Bert Flute's penis knew too, for it had begun to grow hard. Lise took Vaughn off by the hand.

In the flickering snow room, Vaughn waited calmly beside Lise. When he heard the first faint shouts, and the echoing clatter of pucks and sticks on the distant rink boards, he knew practice had begun, and that their tunnel-dance had failed and was over. He tapped Lise on the shoulder, but she only grunted and shrugged his hand away.

Vaughn settled back and listened to the rink noises, the precise clicks mixed with dull, ghostly booms. He heard a whistle blow; the noise stopped. He looked down at Lise and moved to touch her again but withdrew, unsure. Then a clear thought came: if only this *love* was like hockey. Hockey, with its rules, goals, off-sides. Teams that shook hands.

Love might be like that too, if you took the lies out of it. But both things, love and hockey, were ruined by people who couldn't keep things straight. Because hockey was ruined too. Not the game, the game was okay. The people weren't.

The distant whistle shrieked again and Vaughn's body jumped in response. Listening to the shouts and clicks, he managed a picture of himself playing. So fast and right, the skating, shooting, passing. His body could taste it. Only when a goal was scored and play stopped, only when he went to the bench for a rest, did the trouble start. There he didn't fit in at all.

On the bench the others managed to stay *in* the game. They shouted, swore, jerked about, followed the puck with eyes that seemed stuck to it. But to Vaughn the bench meant only . . . well, the bench. He could jerk about like the others, but what for? Why lie?

When he first started playing he'd been told that the bench was for "catching your breath". Easy enough to understand: on the ice he got tired. But to this day, years later, "catching his breath" was all Vaughn could get himself to do on the bench. Not only could he see no reason in jumping and shouting, but catching up to his lost breath occupied him entirely. For it was a spectacular thing: here was his body, so hungry for air that it was panicking. It convulsed and sucked at the whole expanse of air around and above it. Its fighting for breath reminded Vaughn of a pig at its trough, so greedy in its spasm for food that its legs quivered.

So Vaughn would be on the bench, not noticing the game going on over the boards. He'd gulp air, and think how air was like food, and think how his pig-body's snout was forever plugged into the endless trough out there. And how inside of him he carried an empty bag that was always filling up and emptying, filling up, emptying, on and on, even while he slept: for a lifetime he would be plugged into this invisible pig's-food. He was a pig that never got enough to eat. And he would think how, if he was really supposed to join in and talk to his teammates, that instead of complaining, between breaths, how dirty number three was, or how Donny Beamer was a puck-hog, he'd much rather talk with them about how exciting it was, wasn't it, to watch their own, small, panicking bags of air having such a hard time of it catching up to the grand steadiness of air above the lights of the hockey rink. He often wanted to poke someone in the ribs, like the other boys did to each other, and tell him about it. But he knew what the reaction would be. And, besides, something would always happen, someone would score and, knowing what was expected of him, Vaughn would have to cheer and pound somebody's back. An easy act. Easy to lie, to show breathless joy, when breathless is what you already are.

The candle danced fitfully, on the verge of going out. Vaughn couldn't help but watch his shadow jump on the snow wall beside him, going black grey black grey in rhythm with the leaping flame. The sight almost made him sick: his stomach couldn't understand how this room, so silent, could at the same time be so jerky. But Lise had stopped crying at last. An

English-girl sigh told him that things had settled again, that the lie, anyway, was back to normal. Vaughn moved in closer, grunting softly as he did, and slid his hand back into her pants.

"Jesus!" Lise slapped his hand away hard. She scooped up a wedge of snow and flung it in his face. Jumping to her knees, with contorted, whirlwind arms she clawed a blizzard of snow chunks at him. At first Vaughn protected himself. Then, wondering if this might not be a game after all, grunting and giggling he flailed away and pelted Lise in return.

In the middle of the flurry Lise stopped, and Vaughn's last chunk burst on her face. With snow caught in her hair, and a ridge of snow that rode her lower lip, hesitated, then began to melt, Lise stared at Vaughn. Vaughn's smile dropped. Breathing hard, they stared at each other. Vaughn watched a quiver in Lise's chin work up to her mouth, become a contorted, hideous smile which, still moving up, made her cheeks tighten, forced her eyes to shut and tears to start. As she cried she brought both hands to her pants to do up her zipper. She struggled with it, wriggling her hips this way and that, but her fingers were numb and stupid, and there was snow in the zipper teeth. Her fight to close it became more frantic until finally she screamed, and jumped to her feet, and in doing so punched her head through the snow ceiling.

It was an odd sight for Vaughn. As soon as Lise's head disappeared up through the snow she stopped moving — except her hands, which fell away from her zipper to her sides. There she stood, as if she was calm, as if she had no head, as if her head was completely hidden in a layer of cloud. Not wanting to upset her again, Vaughn did nothing, but after a silent minute had passed between him and this headless girl he felt forced to speak. And her pants were falling down her thighs.

"Lise?"

"Shut up. Get out." Coming from outside the room, Lise's voice was muted, ghostly.

"What are you doing? Isn't it time to go?"

"*You* go."

Vaughn sat still for another minute. Then he tried again. "Lise?"

"Get out. I never want to talk to you again."

Vaughn did up his coat and started crawling out the tunnel-way. He wondered what he was going to do: his hockey practice was probably almost over. Emerging from the tunnel, he stood, turned, and was surprised by the disembodied head sitting upright on the snow eight feet away. Lise was staring up at the wide black dome of prairie sky. He heard her whisper to herself, in her English-girl voice, "It seems I have such great white shoulders. . . ." Her mouth hung a little slack, and her eyes moved from east to west in a slow, slow arc. Her head was framed by a circle of faint yellow light, flickering from below.

"Lise, should I put out the candle?"

"Go away."

Vaughn chose to walk home over the farmers' fields. The night was growing colder, and his boots crunched through the crust that had formed on the snow. He felt how the air burned as he pulled it through his nostrils, how it burned less in his throat, and how it felt neither warm nor cold as it filled his chest. He watched the snow fields around him bounce as he walked, watched the smooth plane of snow approach him, heard and felt his boots crush through it. Strange, though, with all this to see and feel, how often a vision of Lise's head burst in and confused what was really there.

Years passed, Vaughn turned nineteen, spring came again, and neither Beauséjour nor its people, in 1944, had changed much. Some had died of war and others of age. Others had simply left town and that, to Vaughn, was no different. Usually, those who left were young. Their parents would be angry and confused, and in the barber shop they'd shake their heads and wonder who was left to work the farm, wonder why anyone would want to leave now that things were so easy, what with better machines and all.

"They're young" was all the barber would say, the barber being Billy Maddy, whom the townspeople thought smart. For he was the brother of the late Mr. Maddy, school principal, whose death had somehow made Billy smarter in people's eyes. In any case, fathers were satisfied, if only for the time it took to clip, trim, and pomade, with his answer: they're young.

And Lise was still young, sort of, so Vaughn was not too surprised when she left town too — with Bernard LaPierre.

It was a scandal, even though they were Métis. They hadn't married first and they stole old LaPierre's truck to run with, a near-new Ford the man had worked three poor harvests to buy. People who knew said the librarian had goaded Bernard into all of it. This was Billy Maddy's story anyway, and what else would explain it? Bernard had settled nicely during his four years of apprentice barbering, had seemed more than happy with his room upstairs.

Vaughn had a hundred questions, but the person who had given him answers for nineteen years was the person who was gone. His questions had been piling up for a while. Ever since the night in the snow cave, Lise hadn't spoken to him much about what they both knew was important. And when she did, what she told him were lies.

Lise left Beauséjour the morning after Vaughn's mother died. Vaughn did not witness the death itself, but he heard lots about it once the rumours leapt the backyard fences. His mother's death from cancer was expected, but the last moments had been shocking. Dr. Watt himself seemed surprised when he announced that she had died from a broken neck.

Dr. Watt's report had it that, at the moment of death, Alicia had suffered violent convulsions, one of which snapped her neck. In private the doctor spoke of it in awe, saying, "It was like her life had a hard time leaving her body on the bed. It was like she was sticky dough and a huge unseen hand was trying to flick it off." Old Mrs. MacIntyre's version went like this: "One could see her tryin' and tryin' not to look up to that ceiling. Poor thing, her strainin' not to look up, and then, one could *see* it, somethin' just *tore* her head up towards the ceilin'. One could see she had somethin' to repent, and did not. It was plain *Who* she saw, at her end." Another person, who wasn't there, said the room had filled with light, and that those close enough had seen Alicia Collin's nude spirit rise up to be embraced by an angel — but that none had dared mention this to Mr. Collin, who was crying in a corner, for fear of embarrassing him.

Apparently his mother's death marked the end of Vaughn's childhood. Mr. Collin himself told him, "Your mother is gone, son. You are now a man." If Vaughn failed to understand how these two statements connected, he made less sense of what his father said next. "Don't ever forget your mother, Vaughn," he said, "but there is no need to grieve." For the faces at the wake wore an identical expression of grief. Old women seemed swollen with it. Mrs. MacIntyre, doing runaway Lise's job for her, had to add a stack of hankies to the tea dolly each time she wheeled it round. The men showed their inner strength while at the same time showing, by the way they chewed the insides of their lips and hung their heads, how difficult this was. Alicia's last years of twisted silence had lost her any close friend she'd had, but it was clear that these people had come to grieve.

Vaughn knew they expected grief from him as well. And willing as he was to go into whatever fit of mourning required, he was simply unable. Strangest of all was that his mother wanted him to grieve too. What else could explain her change: a relapse, after almost twenty years, into affection. Alicia came out of her shell only once in the time Vaughn knew her, and this was on her deathbed, the morning of the day she died.

Vaughn had been summoned to her room at dawn. Alicia's bedroom was dull, as if the light came off the dirty snow in the yard before coming in the window. Vaughn entered to find his mother's smile already huge, her eyes already on him. He wondered how long she had been watching the door like that. For the first time in his life, the hairs on the back of his neck stood up.

Alicia had been shrinking faster than a baby grows. There were other changes too. It looked as if all the bones in her face had swelled, but Vaughn knew her disease had simply taken her cheek meat away. And her eyes were so round, so wide. He tried to remember if she'd ever let him look into them like this — maybe that explained how new they looked. And there was something about the way she was just lying there on the bed. Her arms, stretched out before her, seemed impossibly relaxed, already dead, forgotten by her. They were forgotten all the way to the fingers, which Vaughn thought looked nicely long and white. It was good to see a mother's hands looking so content.

Her eyes beckoned him to the bedside and sat him down. Her eyes were even more startling closer up. Though greasy, her hair was still blonde and lush, and in the hollow of the pillow it formed a fluffy, buoyant nest for her skull, which was glossy and egg-tight. His mother's head reminded Vaughn of an Easter basket: one big shiny egg surrounded by coloured fluff.

"You're my own boy, Vaughn-Vaughnie, do you know that?"

"Yes."

"Vaughn's mother loves him very much."

"Yes."

He watched her. Love. This distant word remained a distant word. Vaughn felt it recede, actually, because he realized that to fail at love beside a child-eyed, dying mother's bed is probably to fail at love for ever. Vaughn made his face go kind, and he tried to do it well.

But something happened, Annie, as Vaughn sat there watching his mother. Something happened as she stroked his hand, called him "Vaughn-Vaughnie", and praised him with baby-talk, the kind of mothering music Vaughn was sure he'd never heard, and yet faintly, faintly remembered.

Annie, something changed as he watched her blue eyes. What happened had nothing to do with love, but understanding. Watching those eyes, Vaughn saw that their love-light rode the surface stupidly, a glaze. Behind the light, in the depths, there was nothing much. He saw that this love of hers, reborn, was only what animals had, was the dying bloom of a flower around its seeds. He saw, *I* saw, that my mother could not help it. Her dumb instincts had risen violently, and had left her more stricken with mad love than with her cancer, which is a calmer disease.

So she died, and so I was born and came to understand a little more of the world. Or at least the people in it. And this is the point in my story, Annie, where "he" becomes "I" — where I can clearly recall being the Vaughn Collin beside his mother's bed, and so on for the rest of my life up until now. It's strange that it is Mother's death that bears me out of my myopia of half-truth into a life that can be relived properly. I'm tired of inventing what may or may not have been.

Perhaps this birth of memory coincides with the first break in my own "disease". For it was at Mother's deathbed that I also first felt the spark of what everyone else had suffered always, day by day, always: emotion. As emotions go it wasn't much, if I remember clearly. Today I'd call the feeling "slight excitement", but it was excitement nonetheless, and belonged to an exotic world. It was as though an idea, a thought, had descended into my stomach and then pulled hard, and kept pulling. If thoughts are blood, emotions are muscles. My first emotion, Annie! I was pulled into it so cleanly, pulled by that simple, bewildered, emotional mechanism there on the bed — my mother, grasping at last straws. It was her eyes that excited me. I was excited to see that nobody anywhere knows his own face, that any stranger on the street can see it better. I was excited to find out that nobody older and wiser had much control, really, over what they said or did, that my father was helpless to escape the maze of being a fool, that hockey players had little say over how fast they skated or who they punched, that Bert Flute was lost, completely lost, in the agony of his chicken hand, that it was the chicken hand in control, and not Bert Flute. And most of all I was excited to find out that Lise hadn't fled to Lac du Bonnet with Bernard LaPierre because she wanted to, but had been shooed there by a gang of lunatic phantoms, the cruelest of which was a spectral lover who had been wearing, in her dreams, my face.

March 5th

Why did I think she wasn't coming back?

This morning from this desk I watched her, a wet, limping bush-rat, slog up the beach. Something had happened out there to make her smile — from fifty yards I could see it through her mess of rat's hair and poncho hood.

"Built a lean-to, didn't even use the damn tent" was the first thing she said, and her smile was a defiant child's. If ever there was an old-age Lolita, Annie's it.

"Getting cocky, are we?" She was ripe for teasing.

I didn't tell her about the Tyee posse I'd almost formed. (I didn't want her to think her favourite misanthrope had become a frivolous socialite.) She said she'd actually wanted to give it a day or two more on the mountainside, but then she remembered Becky Charlie was in her last week. Becky could have taken the free helicopter to Bella Coola and had her baby there, but Annie promised her months ago she'd do it herself. And Annie needs the money. She says Becky's going to have twins, two boys. Annie'll get a bonus of some sort: a deer haunch, an axe, a bottle of scotch, something practical. No baubles here in Purgatory.

I let Annie wash, eat, and wax romantic about the bush before announcing I'd come to the end of my Beauséjour story, that I was twenty now and free. That if my life had sections, I had reached the end of part one. Her sudden reverence surprised me. She ignored her wet hair, dropped the towel, and grabbed up the new pages.

While she read I walked around aimlessly, fixed this and fooled with that, whistled, pretended boredom, warmed up a couple of brandies. Through the side of my eye I watched her flip pages, looking for something. At certain spots she'd study hard then whisper, "Well . . . okay," or "Nope."

"Nope, what?" I asked. She kept reading, torturing me with more "okays" and an "ugh."

"Ugh, *what?*" I felt like a patient whose x-rays were being ughed at by a doctor.

"Not important" was all she said, torture of a subtler kind.

When she finished I sat beside her and held out a steaming brandy, the one without cinnamon in it. I knew she could smell the spice and waited for her to mock as she always does when I catsup my meat, lemon my salmon, curry my rice, or mix something or other into my booze. But she just sat still and tapped my pages on her knee.

"So," she said at last, "it does look like you're finished part one."

I noted nothing of celebration in her voice, so I said, "But I guess there's stuff to change?" I wonder if she sensed from the size of my next swallow of brandy that I was ready to yell if she told me that indeed there was.

"No, I don't think so." She looked at me. "You got a lot wrong, but the important things you got right, I think."

"What parts are wrong? I'll fix them." I couldn't believe I said that.

"Well, your mother is too invisible, and your father you've made a simple simon. He was quite an intelligent man."

I reminded Annie that it was my life I was on about, not theirs, and what did I know about Alicia except she avoided me like a disease, and that my father had always thought *me* simple and so used only simon-talk on me, that I didn't have a lot of patience with this damn thing and that it had been her idea in the first place. I was about to get, to get — the way I used to get. A fissure opening up behind me. Almost a clanging of bells, bad bells.

We both sat quietly after my outburst. I was embarrassed and Annie seemed sad. I felt I'd ruined her camping-trip afterglow. But then I guessed what might be wrong.

"Well so how do you think Lise turned out?"

Now it was Annie who looked embarrassed as she looked away and said, "You made her into a kooky *girl.*"

"Then I got her right!" I grabbed Annie around the neck. We wrestled, and when I egged her on by groping her breasts, she kicked over my brandy on purpose, shouting *"Cinnamon."* Pleading when I started to nibble her stomach through her T-shirt, she got me to stop. We flopped back, breathing hard. Two old pig-bodies gulping the smoky cabin air.

She groaned and shook her head. "It was so long ago."

"It gets worse."

"I know it does." She shook her head. "'Whyunt.' Jesus Christ."

"Girls," I said, "will be girls."

"Whyunt you get lost and not get found?"

"Right." I laughed, satisfied. With my cleverness, with

our wit. For the moment, even with my life.

"Tomorrow you start part two?"

Her question, her leap into the serious, caught me off guard. I'd been preparing to declare that I was going to take a break. There was a lot to be done around the place: the garden needed turning, the roof had a few sick shingles, the boat hull wanted its barnacles scraped. Lots of things.

Annie said I shouldn't stop, not even for a day. We argued, and she won by using that rational-Annie tone I'm so helpless against. She won by saying she'd do all my work that needed doing, and by saying that if I quit now it might ruin everything. I accused her of melodrama, that this story wasn't "everything", but she didn't budge.

"One bit of advice though," she said, standing, packing her few things up to leave. "Remember how you say, in that last bit, that now you remember everything, and so this is where 'he becomes I'? That part?"

"Yeah?"

"Don't."

"What?"

"Don't."

"Don't what."

"Don't switch to 'I'. Stay 'he'."

"Why?"

"Perspective. Distance. Seeing. It's about who you were, not who you are."

"I know that."

"How you *became.*"

"I *know.*"

"Just think: you're done with the novel-writing stuff and all that's left is what really happened. Memory. That should be easy."

I figured she had it backwards, and was about to say so when she flipped it for me, on her way out the door: "But memory has little to do with you *then* and everything to do with you *now*. Watch your words, Collin." And she was gone again.

Within one second Annie my playmate becomes Annie my guide. In that one second her brows clear and rise, her eyes deepen. She stands a bit straighter, and though her head lifts maybe only an inch, I see she has moved giant steps within, and she now observes me as through a kind of lens. In that second she dives the depth of the ocean it's taken her thirty years to plumb. One second takes her from Lise to Annie.

Lise is fun. But I suppose I live here because of Annie.

So you win, Annie. You drive a wedge into my silliness. Your old dog sits dutifully typing.

Hockey Night in Victoria

He might have left town anyway. But probably not. He could easily have taken some kind of job and stayed in Beau for a lifetime. Dull mystery that he was, he could not be bored then, by anything. He could have been bland legend, a shop clerk who for forty years never took a holiday. When he left town for good only months after his mother's death and Lise's flight, it was his tryout with the Black Hawks that got him on the train south.

But that last summer in Manitoba was coloured by what he'd learned at Alicia's bedside — a kind of perceptual hangover, much like the welling insight one rises with from an easy-chair after closing a strong book. For Vaughn, the easy-chair was Beauséjour, and the book was Alicia's doe-eyed death. During those summer months he was every day surprised to see in all people exactly what he'd seen first in his mother: that all people wanted something and could never quite get it, that there was an eternal war being waged between what a person would like to be and what he was, that a man's emotions were not the man so much as they were his ruler, and a merciless ruler at that, a king who wouldn't let anyone stay satisfied for long, who had a finger deep in everyone's gut, who twitched it steadily, and every once in a while, when conditions were right, gave that finger a cruel, flamboyant twirl.

Vaughn didn't think about these things. It was instead a simple act of seeing — simple because he couldn't help it. People had suddenly become caricatures. Their worry lines seemed extra black and active on their faces, their eyes followed the route of frantic insects, free of anything one might call will. You might say, "So what?", Annie, to hear that during that summer Vaughn learned exactly what wrinkles, frowns, and hunched-over posture meant, but consider this: how many people *really* read people well? Sure, they have a general belly-sense of people, they intuit the main differences between a hunched, growling old man and, say, an erect, bosom-proud matron. Most people hear the obvious tune a person's body plays, but how many pick out the small notes, the sharps, the flats? How many know that *that* frown shows a mind addicted to doubt, that *that* stoop, coupled with *those* hand gestures, signals a self-admitted sexual dupe? That *that* wrinkle, the new one linking all the others, reveals a newly born but final surrender to sadness? So Vaughn discovered wrinkles, and had he been capable of envy he likely would have envied those people who were so tide-worn with emotions that it wrinkled them up.

Though he had found a kind of key, Vaughn was still empty, Lise-less, with a dead stomach. Except when he played hockey.

All he saw of Chicago were three shabby blocks between the arena and what was called the Rookie Palace, a boarding-house where first-year hopefuls lodged. But his ever-greedy eyes were egged on by such newness: the buildings, the cars and delivery vans, the storefronts and signs, the textures of stone and slick paint, even the faces of bums. As eye-food, the bums were still best. Their worry-lines had become gargoyle-like, almost comical, abandoned by the rest of their hopeless face and released to hang loosely. Their eyes had given up watching the frantic insects, and instead held a steady stare, stunned dumb by the sight of something even quicker than bugs passing them by.

One bum — he had good posture, strangely enough — always said to him, "If *you* don't wanna drink, give me your money then." Vaughn gave him money more than once.

Near the arena was a bar called Mooly's which had all its windows painted black. Patrons at window tables had scratched various words through the paint, most of which were backwards when read from the street. Someone had got it right, though, and at night the inner lights shone yellow through a four-inch "OH BOY!" One evening Vaughn passed and saw a bored eye looking out through the dot in the exclamation. Hazel iris, like his.

Next to the rink was a bank with a stone lion over the door. The lion reminded Vaughn of the Hawks' coach, who stood at centre ice trying to sound just like the bank-lion looked. Like the lion, he appeared to have too many teeth. They didn't quite get in the way, but what were so many teeth good for here in Chicago?

The fact of pro training camp didn't excite him much, though his body always did love playing hockey again after a summer. The scenes he encountered in that dressing-room in Chicago, in 1945, were to recur each September for years. Veterans were for the most part aloof and stuck to themselves. But those veterans whose jobs were on the line, because of age or borderline talent, were the ones who laughed the most, and ribbed the rookies, trying to be nice guys. There was always a spot or two on a team for what were called "good team players", basically those who were best at jokes in the dressing-room and shouts on the bench.

The rookies had their own dressing-room. At first,

sitting down with the other rookies to put on skates, tape sticks, and all the rest, Vaughn had a sensation much like the one when he first entered a classroom: They're like me! He was wrong, of course, but the first impression was seductive: a roomful of unsmiling men exactly his age, who stayed quiet on the bench during scrimmages (were they watching their breath?) and equally silent and joyless when they scored their first scrimmage goals. Little by little, though, as these mirror-images of Vaughn made friends and reputations and got comfortable, their faces were ripped open by laughter and rage, and bent sour with curses. He saw too that their show of silence after scoring a goal was actually a show of strength, an "I do it all the time" stance, and that inside they were ripe plums of hope and pride. On the bench, after that big, silent goal, some of the plum juice would pump into their faces, and they couldn't squeeze back a quivering grin.

After two weeks, people told him he had the team made. Rookies would say this to each other to be polite, but other men around the rink (fiftyish, shiny suits, cigar chewers) were saying it too, and one of the newspapers had Vaughn pegged as one of the two rookies to make it. He read the articles over the Rookie Palace phone to his father, who called each night for his "camp report". Mr. Collin got very excited and stated that Vaughn needed help with his contract, that last year Garner had signed for peanuts, that Hawks' management were crooks, and that he was catching tomorrow's train to Chicago. But sometime during his train ride someone in an office made a phone call to another office in Toronto and Vaughn was traded. The coach with too many teeth called Vaughn to centre ice and said simply, "Traded to the Leafs, lad. You're lucky. Back to Canada." He looked wistful, and Vaughn realized that of course he was Canadian himself, maybe from the prairies too, and had no connection to that bank or its lion after all.

The Toronto Maple Leafs were a wartime powerhouse.

Vaughn Collin didn't have a chance. One rumour had it that the Leafs had worked a deal with the government, while another said that they simply had more than their lucky share of players excused from war, players with bad eyes, partial deafness, one leg shorter than the other. Whatever the reason, compared with the other five teams they had lost the fewest players to the war effort. The Leafs looked healthy enough to Vaughn. No elevated skate blades to compensate for short legs; no one wore glasses. They only kept him a day. He didn't once get to ply his trade on fabled Gardens ice. He was assigned to their second farm team in the Western League: Victoria. Mr. Collin, who was already on his way to Toronto, didn't bother chasing him to the West Coast.

Grungy, Vaughn stepped off the bus. He called the team owner for practice times, then found a hotel room. He chose the Empress because it was largest. He was too dumb to go elsewhere, even when the price of their cheapest room (the room's rococo was a good eye-meal) exhausted his expense money. Too stupid again to realize that the royal sum he'd handed over paid for his meals as well, Vaughn squandered more at the first restaurant he found. Sitting unprotected, save for knife and fork, at the plush restaurant window, under the steady gaze of his new landlord, the Pacific Ocean, he ate a very expensive *Atlantic* cod and chips (italics the menu's), his first taste of expatriate British snobbery. In the morning he found a rooming-house near the arena.

A month passed before Vaughn Collin thought to hang clothes in his bedroom closet, and this nod to stability came only when landlady Peen asked him one day if he "planned going somewhere fast?" after she kept stubbing her toe on the packed suitcase which lay at the foot of the bed she made each morning.

If Vaughn Collin had taken stock, if he'd turned his telescope eyes three-hundred-sixty degrees to sum up in a word his new home, the word would've been: pale. Pale colonial town, pale old people living in it. White, Victorian house which contained the pale room he slept in and the pale food he ate. Pale Mrs. Peen, landlady. Misty rain all winter, pale sun, sometimes, in summer. And what of that famous, awesome scenery? Vaughn would simply say that the prairies were good enough for his eyes — a poplar as good as a fir, wheat vista as good as the sea, cumulus clouds as good as the mountains. Better, in fact: poplar leaves turn yellow and fall; wheat fields are black, then green, then wavy gold, then a brushcut; prairie clouds swell and roil and sometimes blacken in anger, and fire bolts of fire. The West Coast didn't change much. Green needles, pacified water, washed rock. Pale rain.

Had Vaughn been a stock-taking seer, he might have nodded, yes, this was just the place for him to have his next bout with an emotion. It would be neither death-inspired nor love-inspired, but instead the most complicated, because subtle, emotion of them all: boredom. Though that would take years. Before this, some colourful and formative fruit would surface in the pale custard of Victoria life.

The Victoria Maple Leafs looked like the parent club, but besides the "Victoria" stitched into the blue and white jerseys, the players who wore them were slower, smaller, and less well-paid. The arena seated fewer than four thousand hockey fans.

Vaughn's making the team was not in question. Coach Haliburton pulled him aside as the first practice finished (Vaughn had scored twice in scrimmage). The handshake and smile told him that he'd been sent to bolster the team's defence, not compete with it. In one sentence he was given both his role on the team and the reason Toronto had demoted him: "We need your good wheels to get the puck out of our end (Vaughn's strong point), and — hell — we don't care if you fight or not (Vaughn's nonexistent point). We got enough tough boys." Which was true. There were plenty of players eager to do his fighting for him. Not to protect him, but rather to ease their blood. The Western League was the roughest hockey he'd seen, and that was saying something considering he came from the prairies, where big-shouldered kids were fierce to escape the farm.

Victoria had the toughest guy in the league — Buddy Carona. He had immense square hands and a tiny head that made his hands seem bigger still. Vaughn got his first glimpse of Carona's talents during the fifth game, against arch-rivals the Seattle Totems. The thing with Buddy was that everyone was afraid to fight him — ironically, the league's best fighter rarely fought. His few fights were long-awaited, and talked about weeks after the blood had been sealed under a fresh layer of ice.

A bench-clearing brawl erupted late in the Seattle game, with Buddy somewhere in the middle. He fought one guy and chased several more. Earlier a fan had spit on him through the screen, and now Buddy was letting himself go coolly berserk. The fighting went on and on, new scuffles breaking out when old ones ended. The rink was scattered with gloves and sticks. After twenty minutes the ref called the game and the timekeeper hit the buzzer. But the boys weren't finished business and the ploy didn't work. So officials sent the Zamboni out to start flooding. The driver, a babyish-looking man, steering it slowly along the boards, stopped to rev a warning in front of a group of wrestlers. Suddenly, Buddy Carona was beside the Zamboni, something was said, and Buddy lapel-dragged the driver from his seat and had him on his back, dealing him calm, precise punches.

"He coulda hurt someone" was Carona's plea in the dressing-room, and, incredibly, this same plea stood up in court.

In any case, Haliburton already knew Vaughn couldn't fight. The scouts had done their jobs. If you were a little tougher, the coach joked, we'd have to make you captain.

(Though Vaughn knew he'd have had to be not only tough but *popular.*) But rack up the points, the coach added, and you'll be in Toronto by Christmas.

But one evening, halfway through that first season, a bunch of young players, Vaughn included, had their futures smashed. A kid with a radio ran into the dressing-room with some news. The war had ended. Vaughn saw at least ten pairs of padded shoulders understand, then sag. Patriotic hockey players, some of them stars, were on their way home from Europe to strengthen the benches of all the teams in North America. (Vaughn's first thought: old faces would be back working Beauséjour fields. Bernard LaPierre would have competition in Winnipeg as a rookie barber.)

So Vaughn played for the Victoria Maple Leafs. It was an easy life to adapt to, minor pro hockey, even for those whose minds weren't as blindly open as twenty-year-old Vaughn Collin's.

"Better'n packin' a lunch pail to work." He heard that one often.

"Get summers off." At which time most limped home to the prairies or Ontario. Others stayed on the Island and sold cars. Georges Gingras, the goalie, spent summers commercial-fishing off Tofino. It was he who would teach Vaughn the way of the elusive coho.

"Damn road trips, though. *Damn.*" Vaughn saw teammates' eyes glaze over the moment they boarded the bus that would drag them the many miles to ride roughshod over the Bucaroos of Portland, to carve the Totems in Seattle, to shoo the Gulls in San Diego, to can the Canucks in Vancouver, to shoot down the Jets of Spokane, to train the Seals in San Francisco. (Mrs. Peen saved these headlines in a scrapbook.) On the road, games were but commas in the thousand-mile sentences which droned in and out of bus stations, freeways, bad motels, midnight truckstops, visitors' dressing-rooms which were too-small-on-purpose. Everybody hated road trips.

Except Collin. The bus window between Vancouver and San Diego was full of mountains, trees, snow, farms, rivers, palm trees. Or hailstorms, sports cars, speed traps, stalled cars, licence plates. Highway dividing lines changed with each border. Canada: white. Washington: yellow. Oregon: white-yellow. California: orange. Animals alive beside the road or flattened, on it. Farmers turning over fields. Strange crops, no wheat. When Vaughn was tired he tilted the seat and slept.

His teammates slept when they could, or talked, or read magazines. "Looked at" magazines — by the end of the trip the overhead racks were hung like laundry lines with pictures of half-naked girls stuck there with squares of white medical tape.

There was always a poker game at the back, which shot the front with curses or needlings of greedy glee. One trip during Vaughn's first fall, they needed a player because one of the regulars was back in Vic with his shoulder.

"Hey, Collin. You?" He'd never been asked before.

The rules were easy, and someone explained betting this way: when you think you have a good hand, bet. When you don't know, stay. When you think you don't, fold. It turned out Vaughn had a good head for odds, and on top of that was "lucky", whatever that meant. His real skill though, and the reason he won the money he did over the years that followed, was his ability to read players. These men didn't have many wrinkles to gauge, but they did have eyes that deepened when they saw treasure. It surprised Vaughn that neither the loud bluffer nor the one playing it cool with the full house realized how obvious he was. Vaughn watched a bettor closely: if he had the cards, he might tuck his chin slightly, widening his neck. His ears might blush. He might stiffen, and so would his breathing, just a little, just a bit. And, well, it was hard to explain, but the *air* around him would thicken. A bluffer might have the same tucked chin and wide neck, but his movements and breathing were *made* to look fluid, and the air was less thick than panicky with this act.

It usually took him twenty minutes to read a new player. Only one person did he ever find unreadable: Dog Merson. When Vaughn got to know him better he saw that everything he did — win, fight, or lose on the ice, or bet, call, or fold at cards — he did with slaphappy enjoyment.

Dog and he became friends. That is, of all his teammates over the years, Dog's acceptance was the closest to friendship that Vaughn would know. His loud colour worked on Vaughn like a magnet. What attraction Vaughn held for Dog isn't clear. At opposite ends of a personality gamut, they did share in common a freedom from convention. Dog Merson ignored style; Vaughn floundered in it. Dog was a careless firecracker and Vaughn was the quiet air around it.

Dog was the one who demanded Vaughn play cards each trip. He even named a game in Vaughn's honour, changing the name High Chicago to 'Bye Chicago. (Vaughn grinned to tell Dog he got the joke.) Dog's chuckling insistence that Vaughn play overruled the others' groans. Vaughn wasn't well-liked, for he added nothing fun to the table yet won money. Dog didn't fare badly either, relaxed in his unreadable good mood. He just didn't seem to care. His gleeful howls were loudest when Vaughn won a pot from him, as though Vaughn were his silent partner and they'd pulled a fast one on everybody.

Back in Victoria, between road trips, Vaughn often paid his rent with wads of ones and twos.

And, between road trips, Vaughn discovered how much time he had on his hands. He bought his first umbrella, and he walked. First he conquered the city, and got to know every sidewalk, fire hydrant, driveway. Within months he'd penetrated the surrounding bays and beaches, and found paths through Victoria's encroaching forest. Those enormous white logs lining the beach, those cavernous tree-root caves in the forest: *perfect* secret spots. He had so many questions tug him as he walked, but Lise, laughing and rich with answers, walked somewhere else.

After Christmas he was handed a letter at the arena. A Christmas card with a paragraph of scrawl:

"Merry Christmas! Doesn't it snow there at all? Hope your hockey is fine. Say hello to your father for me if you ever see him. Though he must hate me! Well. I live in Winnipeg again. Remember it? Or were you too small? B. and I might get married soon, we don't know. He got an excellent job at the meat packers. I teach reading to little Indians. They don't pay me yet, maybe next year. No good books to recommend — neither B. nor my job leaves me much time! Too bad Winnipeg doesn't have a team in your league. Love, Lise."

Vaughn wrote her back saying that hockey was fine, that no, there's no snow, that he hoped she was well. He knew how such letters were written. That spring she replied with another short note, with few changes except that now "B. had a good job at the railroad". Vaughn replied with a longer letter; she followed up with a longer one still. And so began their letters. Lise called them their "10% conversations", which is the percentage, she said, of reality conveyed by written words. Vaughn figured 10% seemed about right. For though he did manage to get a few questions across, he couldn't properly ask her the gist of adult personality, say, or God, or Bernard LaPierre in the bedroom.

But 10% of Lise was better than none. And her letters probably helped convince Mrs. Peen that Vaughn was no misfit-loner. After the letters started, Mrs. Peen became more perky in his presence. She'd hand him an envelope and announce in singsong, "One more from your special friend!"

Mrs. Peen grew to like Vaughn. After one year he even began confiding in her — in the winter of his second year he asked *her* about God. Two of his teammates were religious and brought the subject up at times and were very certain about something his father had once told him was an opinion. Mrs. Peen's answer was typical of her.

"God, the last time I saw him," she said, in her pious English accent, "was a one-hundred-foot-tall red jelly bean."

Vaughn laughed, it was a joke of course. Then she followed up this Peen reverence with Peen logic.

"He would strike most down for saying that, but He doesn't bother with atheists."

Mrs. Peen reminded Vaughn of the demanding matron of W.C. Fields films. At first look she appeared fat, but one saw her heaviness gathered in her bosom, shoulders, and jowls; her stomach, hips, and legs were almost slim. She wore her white hair short. Always black or navy, her dresses were cut to accentuate her figure, and the ever-present cameo brooch pinned above her left breast resembled a cream-coloured mollusc crawling uphill.

Vaughn had hockey and walking, and a third world opened up one evening when Mrs. Peen led him into the parlour to be introduced to her bridge club. Meeting three times a week, always at Mrs. Peen's, the club consisted of four other women in their sixties, three of whom were widows like Mrs. Peen. All the women were English, or at least still had their accents.

Mrs. Peen introduced Vaughn as the "handsome hockey hero", and ran down an exaggerated list of his exploits, adding that she didn't normally allow street brawlers into her home, but that in Canada this sort of thing was legal on ice and was in fact the sole test of manhood this fledgling culture possessed. Everyone said hello, a dipping of grey heads, and he was dismissed.

One evening Mrs. Peen caught Vaughn leaving for his walk and explained that Mrs. Mitton was sick and would he mind filling in at the table? And so he was taught a second card game.

Ushered into the parlour on his landlady's arm, he was introduced a second time. The women whispered to one another and giggled, and Vaughn was amazed to see how they remembered the mannerisms of girls one-quarter their age.

Something was wrong. Bridge was a game for four, and here he was, a fifth. A Mrs. Yearsley sat apart, perched straight-backed on a velvet ottoman. Perhaps Vaughn was staring at her, for Mrs. Peen explained.

"Mrs. Yearsley is the 'server' tonight, Mr. Collin. We take turns 'serving'."

"All of us except Mrs. Peen, sir," interjected Mrs. McGraith. "We thought it only fair that she be spared the chore as it's her invitation, and her home."

"It's only fair," Mrs. Yearsley agreed.

"Mrs. Peen is the hostess," said Mrs. Quartermain.

Mrs. Peen sat shuffling cards, erect.

Mrs. Yearsley did pour tea occasionally, and replenish the biscuit salver, but her main function was to talk. She talked incessantly, often answering her questions herself.

" . . . can you imagine her reply? She had the nerve to say to my face, her best customer's face, that since the price of dates doubled, well then it follows that the *fruit*cakes too . . . "

" . . . Mr. Anthony says it's a long flu, but it's a cancer . . . "

" . . . moving to Vancouver, the entire family. It makes you wonder. But I say Victoria is now free of a nest of *drinking* men. They're *burglars* . . . "

The other ladies mostly played on, taking tricks, sipping, and, their eyes not leaving their cards, nodding at the server's remarks. Mrs. Peen would sometimes ask her to expand on a story, or interrupt if a topic displeased her, and ask her to refill one of her guests' teacups.

Vaughn had not kept company with ladies before. In

Beauséjour, social life was dominated by the plain-speaking voices of men; here, surrounded by her women friends, Mrs. Peen seemed to have filled a spot normally held by a man. She reminded Vaughn of his father at a party. But a party the likes of which Beauséjour had never seen — this made him think of an Oscar Wilde play Lise once got him to act out with her. A snow crust of manners and fanciness covered the room's heart.

The following Wednesday Mrs. Ingram was sick and when Vaughn took her seat it was Mrs. Quartermain poised on the ottoman. He was fairly good at the game by that second evening, so he stayed alert to the way they drank tea and murmured "My, yes" and "I should say" to acknowledge Mrs. Quartermain's talk.

He had a game that Friday so he missed bridge. Mrs. Peen invited him again for Monday night, adding with a wink that now Mrs. Quartermain had taken ill. Over the weeks that followed he learned that a second rotation had started: after each lady took turns serving, she next time took turns "sick", thus offering a permanent place to the polite hockey hero. Mrs. Peen confided to Vaughn that he was the first novelty they'd had in years.

Vaughn learned other things about bridge. For one, Mrs. McGraith's serving nights always differed from others. She would begin her gameside chatter in the normal way, serving up the earfood. The only woman still married, every few minutes she would add an innocent, "and my Wallace agrees" or "so my Wallace heard". Soon she would start, almost slyly, a story exclusively about her Wallace. Her voice would rise and she would talk more and more quickly until, as if she knew what was coming from Mrs. Peen and wanted to squeeze in everything, her words became a torrent of *her Wallace.*

" — and so my Wallace says, if it weren't for his war-leg, he says, he'd be mending that fence in a minute. He says—"

"Mrs. McGraith," said Mrs. Peen.

" — and, he says, he would *be in that race to Vancouver* if only Romney would come down from Nanaimo *once,* he says, just *once* one weekend to help Wallace launch the — "

"Mrs. *McGraith.*"

" — but so it is even in the best of families, he says. I say my Wallace's family would *never* — "

"*Mrs. McGraith.* I would *like some tea.* My cup is quite *cold,* Mrs. McGraith." Eyes closed, cards and hands spread face down on the table, Mrs. Peen spoke loudly and steadily.

These outbursts of Mrs. Peen's were the only rude displays Vaughn ever witnessed at the card table, and Mrs. Peen was rude every time Mrs. McGraith served. Why Wallace got Mrs. Peen's dander up Vaughn didn't know. Perhaps he shone a tactless spotlight on the other ladies' widowhood. Perhaps mere mention of a husband was bragging here. But Mrs. Peen gave Vaughn the facts some weeks later: Mrs. McGraith's Wallace had been dead five years. While the other ladies allowed her insanity a lot of room, Mrs. Peen had decided to draw a line.

The third time Mrs. Peen interrupted poor Mrs. McGraith in Vaughn's presence, she waited until the lady had gone out to the kitchen before asking him if he would please finish the evening's serving. When informed of her dismissal Mrs. McGraith was silent, and took Vaughn's seat when he rose to take hers. The parlour took on the garish clarity of a public execution.

He'd been on the ottoman ten minutes and still Vaughn couldn't think of anything to say. He emptied Mrs. Mitton's ashtray and topped up the nut dish.

"Why not tell us about your hockey, Mr. Collin?" asked Mrs. Peen, not looking up from her cards.

In monotone, Vaughn listed recent wins and defeats.

"What about tactics, Mr. Collin? Tell us about *winning tactics.*"

Well, here Vaughn had on hand the theories of a half-dozen coaches, word for word. He began with the details of penalty-killing, then forechecking. Perhaps he got too technical. Several of the women coughed politely.

Mrs. McGraith's execution had been a mistake. Vaughn blushed, embarrassed, perhaps for the first time in his life. The feeling he felt was a new one: that he was inferior to everyone in the room, inferior to anyone who had any kind of social grace, who could say "hello" with flair. At that moment, people like Lise, Mrs. Peen, Dog Merson, and even Bernard LaPierre seemed like gods. Vaughn had always seen the gulf between them and him, but now he felt it. He had always known that he had no personality, but now, the cause of this card-game impasse, he ached for one.

Mrs. Peen was looking at him.

"Tell us about your Manitoba girlfriend, Mr. Collin."

"My Manitoba girlfriend . . . was our servant girl who ran away with a Métis. A Métis is half-French, half-Indian."

The table silence was absolute. Mrs. Quartermain stopped shuffling. Slouching Mrs. McGraith sat up.

But then Mrs. Peen laughed. A relieved laugh.

"Mr. Collin's *joking,* ladies!"

Mrs. Quartermain now caught Vaughn's joke too, and laughed, and lit a cigarette. Mrs. Dinghy giggled slightly, unconvinced, Mrs. Mitton smiled, nodding, and Mrs. McGraith resumed sulking.

"Yes? Your girlfriend lives with a runaway Indian?" Mrs. Peen's eyes sparkled.

"It's not as bad as I made it sound," Vaughn said. "My girlfriend is a half-breed too." This time, when the ladies laughed, Vaughn smiled. He told them about Bernard's ambition of becoming a barber. When he added, "but he might not succeed", and the table erupted with the heartiest laughter of the night, he saw that he had stumbled upon an undreamed-of achievement: humour. What he didn't know yet was that the humour he'd found was called "dry humour", which, when spiced with bigotry or sex, hit straight on the funnybone of the English prude.

He couldn't believe how hilarious he'd become. One memory led to another, and soon he was telling them how he used to read Victorian novels in rooms dug into the snow, and how he was *actually* a simpleton who would not have made it out of Grade One without his half-breed servant's help.

He'd been a diligent student of the ladies' mannerisms, and now that he had his chance he copied them well:

"If *only* you could have seen — "

"Mr. LaPierre was *such* the fool — "

Over the months that followed, when he told them how his mother "fled to her bedroom at the very *sight* of me", and how he'd "*skipped* two grades and failed *three*", and when he learned the art of exaggerating and even lying in the name of humour, he developed the trick of pausing, raising a steady pinky, and taking a slow sip from his teacup before delivering a wry clincher — "for I'd assumed her hump was some sort of ingenious *back*pack." And so while these women thought they were hearing the dry outrages of a comrade, they were in fact with their laughter confirming the absurdity of Vaughn Collin's life.

It's unclear where exactly it began, this desire of Vaughn's to be like someone else, to be *liked* at all, but there at the bridge games he first succeeded at it. Perhaps that's all that was needed: one dose of success and he was off chasing that firefly in the night.

Why does anyone want to be like someone else? One emulates, forms a personality which directs a lifetime. Vaughn was no different, except that what happens to everyone else in the cradle didn't happen to him till his twenties. And until now, like a baby, he'd never felt separate. On the contrary:

his eyes kept him full of the world. But now he was a leaf newly fallen from the tree. He suddenly cared about being alone.

Mrs. Peen and the other ladies were his first personality models. If they hadn't been so easy to copy he might not have become dissatisfied so soon. And because dissatisfaction craves heroes, he discovered that there were plenty around.

Dog Merson, for one.

Vaughn began in spurts. Copying Dog's wardrobe was a dead end, because its careless gaudiness needed Dog's charisma to keep it from being merely foolish. Through careful study Vaughn saw that the essence of Dog meant a laughing disdain of almost everything. At practices, games, and team parties Vaughn studied him; at night when there was no bridge game he practised grins, laughs, and slaps on the back, using his closet door, draped with a towel to muffle the noise. For the first time in his life he took up dressing-room rough talk, which, because Dog was a master of profanity, had suddenly become interesting. Vaughn saw how some players tried to swear but couldn't. The *fuck*s in any successful sentence had to have a certain rhythm to their placement, much like the metric stresses in a good Miltonic line.

The one time he forgot himself, after his swearing practice, and told Mrs. Peen that he had "a fuckin' game next Friday so fuck I can't play bridge," she slammed her door and left a note on his the next day informing him that it was his turn to be sick. He'd never been told to be sick before, and so he learned firsthand what he'd previously only observed — like fire and water, some personality types could not mix.

He began to notice odd looks his teammates sometimes gave him when he spoke. He never had talked much, but now when he did he understood that some of his words were glazed with bridge-club nuance. And if Oscar Wilde was laughable in normal society, he was something else again in a dressing-room full of scarred bodies. Once, between periods, when Vaughn witnessed his hand flip out into the dressing-room and he heard himself say, "I de*test* these San Diego bullies, I must say I *really* do," some teammates' faces told him they were trying to decide if they were looking at someone truly horrible.

So Vaughn began taking care to remember where he was and who he was with before taking on a personality. But it was easy to slip up, and it would get more complicated in years to come, when he began emulating a more cartwheeling folk. It was, of course, this impossible situation that led to his immense troubles, his breakdown, his tattoo — all of it.

But this oversteps the story of the middle years.

During that second Victoria year Vaughn wrote a letter to Lise, telling her the startling news that he had changed: "You'd be surprised at me and the way I can act. I've made friends. I often play cards with my landlady and her club, and I fit in very well. It's not the same as with you, but I can talk to them.

"When I think of myself now, I don't like the way I am anymore. So I'm changing. I *can* change."

Weeks later Vaughn got a letter back, and all it said was, "Guess what? I'm coming to visit!"

Several weeks after that, he was told someone was waiting for him outside the dressing-room. Her hair was shorter, her skin pale and tighter on her bones. Her dress was creased from the bus like an old bum's brow. But a beautiful smile, which Vaughn felt deep in his stomach.

"So. *Lise,*" Vaughn said, perhaps lisping. "How *are* you?"

Something twisted the corners of Lise's smile. So Vaughn tried something different.

"Fuckin' bus's a bitch to bag sleep on sittin' up, eh?"

Her smile disappeared completely. But they were together again.

March 15th

Scraped and cleaned the boat this morning, a labour of love. I was up at first light, a bit hung-over. After a day's typing nothing sounded better than a beer so, old but unwise, I braved the crazy beach rocks to the Tyee. I was unwiser still stumbling back in darkness, but my body was more fluid now and rolled with the rocks.

God, the pub twice in a few weeks. It's like the old danger-days. What's happening to me? Acting young and foolish.

Annie was in the pub too. We played our little game again, pretending we didn't see each other. She was with Mark and those others, anyway. They make me nervous, so I sat with some Moes and listened to them lie.

I've never been able to sleep in with a hangover. Self-ugly grit. That touch of thistle behind the eyes. I eschewed coffee and settled for a cold gulp of salt air. I wrestled the boat down its ramp and rowed a straight line out into the sound, rowed until my arms fought back. When I shipped the oars the boat stopped gliding immediately, heavy with its skirt of barnacles and weeds.

I rowed back to the beach. It's good to feel the drag of a fouled hull before cleaning it. Then seeing the froth in your wake when you take her out clean is the heart of delight, the reward of contrasts. Contrasts — the chill in your bones before your bed blankets warm them. Your weathered shack before you paint it up white as a beach bone. And so, says Annie, it's good to breathe in the spilled stench and perfume of your whole life before you gather yourself for a good death. Which is, I'm beginning to understand, this book's purpose. Not that I plan on dropping dead at the last period.

It took me an hour to do the hull. The smashed barnacles, their flesh like scrambled eggs; the ooze of seaweed; the creamy spawn of creatures unknown; the sea lice and stenchy krill: what a thickness of life I scraped off and killed. I let the hull dry, then rubbed in oil. Clouds were thinning as the sun rose over the black dome of Rat Island. I launched her once more, rowed hard to get my reward of froth.

Sunrises like today's move me to the kind of insanity I want. Trees and hills reflect in a mirror of morning water, all held by breathless clouds shot with the pink and orange of a new, indecisive sun.

Sometimes I see this, and I stare, and I swell with it. An urgency of colour and light. Music in a pink-orange key. The best music, never written. It's all a kind of silent command, the encoded riddle of life-death, a huge pointing finger, and I feel the light gather at and heat the dark pigment of my tattoo. I'm wide awake at once.

Sometimes this happens as I stand on the beach or in the sloppy bilge of my boat. Not really knowing what prayer is, I clasp my hands at my forehead and bow. Not knowing what the sun is, or what the terrible sweetness in front of me means, I bow to it, pagan. With the rawest heart I can. Sometimes my hair stands on end. The kind of insanity I try for.

Someone once said that the Earth doesn't turn on an axis, it turns on a spit. The sun sears us by day and nighttime the moon sucks our juice. Maybe it's true, maybe there is no benevolence. But give me my good sunrise and I'll keep bowing to the sun like a lover.

When I was done with my boat and my sunrise, I saw that Annie had been quietly in and out. She'd read my chapter. Her note:

"You exaggerate. You were actually pretty normal. The religion is only subtlety and its only two sins are laziness and fear. This book, any memory that affects you — if you cringe, go to the heart of it. Let it be bad.

"Yes I will drop by tomorrow with a jar of the onion pickles.

"A third sin: no sense of humour."

Lise Meets Oscar Wilde and Billy the Kid

They walked in rain to Lise's hotel. In letters they'd both complained about the frustrated urge to talk together again, but now, strangely, the rain and their footsteps fell loudly while they remained silent. And as they walked the streets Vaughn had come to know so well in two years, it was strange too how the pit-*thump* sound of Lise's limp made them seem only foreign again.

He took her hand, as always. She said she had five days to spend before returning to a new job. Junior librarian at the Winnipeg library.

"Well," Vaughn said. "The perfect job for you again."

"Not really. I have to work weekends. And the money's no good."

"You can read."

"I don't read much anymore."

Lise? Who used to read more than she slept? Vaughn asked why.

"Well, Bernard, he likes to do things . . . go downtown and things, and I go with him. He always laughs at me reading. He says books aren't . . . real. He's right."

They reached the SeaKing. They climbed the stairs to her room and made love then, for him the first time in two years, and the first time ever in a bed large enough for two. Their making love right away seemed so proper that he didn't think of Bernard LaPierre until after they'd finished. Vaughn knew what monogamy was, and sensed what jealousy meant. He looked at Lise beside him and pictured a phantom Bernard on top of her, arched in lover's fever.

"Would Bernard be mad at this?"

"Forget Bernard. Who cares?"

Vaughn didn't. More than two years had passed since

he'd touched Lise's impossibly rich skin. What Vaughn felt but could not say was that if a woman's skin is her sexual soul, then Lise was the most desirable woman on earth, all the skin on her body a smooth lip, an entrance to her soft mouth at one end and her magically soft vagina at the other.

There in the SeaKing, Vaughn was surprised how quickly his body remembered.

They spent hours lovemaking, and between times talked. He did most of the talking. Lise had him chatter on about his hockey, about his hero Dog Merson, about Mrs. Peen. She asked if he missed his mother, and he told her no. Beauséjour? No. His father? Well, Mr. Collin had been out to watch him play, twice, but neither time had Vaughn felt anything like an emotion pull his stomach.

On and on he talked, Lise looking content there beside him, stroking his hairless chest with a lazy finger. At times the finger would stop and Lise appeared to sleep, but whenever he fell silent she gave his chest a pinch to start him up again. Lise didn't talk much herself, and never mentioned Bernard by name. She described briefly the crummy rooms "we" had in Winnipeg, complaining about the lack of hot water, falling plaster, drunken landlord. She mentioned "our" habit of going to a beer parlour at night. Lise said she'd found the practice "somewhat foul" at first, but then had learned to enjoy the laughter, the rough talk and beer.

"Beer," she said, opening her eyes, "really makes me laugh. Some nights I can laugh at anything. Takes me three glasses to . . . Whyunt we go some time, eh? . . . " She eyed the shadowed ceiling, chuckling at some barroom scene.

For Vaughn beer parlours were impossible territory. He knew the purpose of beer parlours was to drink and socialize. Perhaps he could drink, he'd never tried, but he knew for sure he couldn't socialize. Beer parlours might as well have been the moon. But hearing now that Lise herself not only went to them but enjoyed them, he saw them in a new light. And didn't Dog Merson spend a lot of time in beer parlours?

Later, he nudged Lise and told her he couldn't sleep with her in the hotel all night. Mrs. Peen . . .

Lise argued, and Vaughn tried to explain how mad Mrs. Peen might be if he didn't come home all night, how he might be told to be sick again on bridge night.

"What?"

He ignored Lise's look. His duty to Mrs. Peen was like duty to parents. "I have to go home now."

When he stood to go, a look of fright lit up her eyes, one Vaughn had never seen in her before, the empty look some children have at bedtime.

"Hey but," she whispered, "can we be together during the day time . . . up here?"

"Yes."

"Good."

He felt proud of the way she said "good", prouder than the times Dog insisted he play poker at the back of the bus, prouder than the night his lying-humour made him the witty hero at Mrs. Peen's bridge table. He left the hotel with the pride of one body wanted by another — a clean, stomach pride that escaped the mess personality made.

They wrote more often. Lise became more intimate, never failing to mention the SeaKing, and his caresses. She complained about Winnipeg, her crummy room, and "his" general uselessness. She missed Vaughn terribly.

His three years in Victoria became four, then five. Vaughn wondered why Lise didn't visit more. He offered to go east, but Lise wrote a firm "no". Bernard, he reasoned, was the complication. Vaughn had turned twenty-five when Lise next visited, in 1950, and this time he was ready to show her how much he'd changed.

But Lise had changed more. She was drunk when he

picked her up at the depot. Drunk, tired, and mad at something. Vaughn had just left the bridge club (which had gotten more formal of late) and wore a suit and tie and neat brushcut. He led Lise to his newly polished, black Dodge. He held open the passenger door, something he rarely had a chance to do.

"Reg'lar G.I. Joe, eh? Ha!" Lise cackled, then fell sideways into the front seat.

She wore the dress she'd had on two years earlier, her hair was matted on one side, and her left arm was smeared with what looked like tar. Vaughn asked if she had fallen. She looked up at him, closed her eyes, and spoke as if reciting.

"Dunno where I slept, dunno where I drank, dunno."

"Oh." Vaughn didn't know what else to say.

"*Oh?* I slep' in Va'couver las' night, 'kay? Y'satisfied?"

He'd never seen her like this, so eager for a fight, not even in the old days, when his dumbness would drive her to distraction.

He drove her to a diner, ordered coffee, and insisted she go to the ladies' room to change. She dragged her suitcase with her, laughing, and reappeared in a faded blue dress which, though clean, was as rumpled as the one she'd taken off. A white slip hung three inches below the hem. Vaughn suggested she return to the washroom to fix this.

"*Easy,*" she said. Her breath had turned more sour since the ferry. "Jus' hack the bugger *off*. See?" Lise picked up a knife and, before Vaughn could stop her, slashed the shoulder straps and yanked the slip out from below. Then she raised her dress and, like a child, looked down giggling at her exposed pubic patch. Luckily they sat in a booth in an empty restaurant. He was grateful when in a few minutes Lise fell suddenly, head-lollingly tired. He drove her to the SeaKing, helped her up to her bed, and then drove home to his own.

They spent the entire next day in her hotel room. Vaughn said nothing about the previous night. In his eyes Lise still sat on her throne of age and experience — it never dawned on him to criticize. Getting up to visit the toilet down the hall, Lise stumbled working a leg into her dress, and she said, apologetically, "Oh, my, I drank a bit last night." Her empty eyes told him she had no recall.

Vaughn had a game that night, San Diego, and Lise was coming to watch, but first they dined at Mrs. Peen's. He'd spent a week afraid that the ladies would discover his special Winnipeg friend was indeed a runaway Métis. His trick would be ruined. It would be as if, after bringing down the house with jokes about his two-headed wife, the comedian suddenly reached behind the curtain and brought out a two-headed wife.

But Lise would pass. In midwinter her skin carried as bleached a pallor as the rest of them. She had no accent. In fact, her pretended British tearoom lisp ran rings around Vaughn's own. He shyly hinted that she use it tonight, but she only looked at him strangely. Still, she'd pass.

Mrs. Quartermain joined them at dinner and helped Mrs. Peen serve a Beef Wellington with mushroom-gravy potatoes. He watched the ladies closely. Their perusal of Lise was almost feverish, but he saw no suspicion.

Lise ate little. The table-talk centred around gardening, with both Mrs. Peen and Mrs. Quartermain anticipating great success with their flowerbeds come spring. They chatted about pests, fungus, the proper times to cut the blooms, and the best ways to arrange them for a variety of social occasions. Vaughn offered insights of his own, having helped his landlady tend her fuchsias and sweet williams for three springs running.

The ladies and he were quite witty. Mrs. Peen announced that the worry outweighed the joys of owning a large flowerbed, and that she was going to dig her bed under and plant in its place a sturdy laurel hedge! They laughed long and loud at that one, except for Lise, who was apparently no gardener. Though her table manners were otherwise passable, she sat for a long stretch playing with her uneaten food. Vaughn knew that this *faux pas* of hers would be discussed at the next card game he couldn't attend, but he wasn't going to worry now. Because here, one at each elbow, sat two of his three best friends. And his third friend waited in the wings — after the game his surprise for Lise was an evening in the beer parlour with Dog Merson and his teammates.

On the ride to the rink Lise stared out the closed Dodge window, quiet.

"Shy in front of Mrs. Peen?" Was it pride he was feeling from showing off to Lise how well he got on with his elderly friends?

"Shy? I was *bored*. They're snobs. They aren't funny, and neither were you."

"They're lonely old English ladies, they — "

"They aren't English."

"They aren't?"

"They're Canadian phonies."

But there were worse things than loving another culture, a grand culture, and taking on its accent. "There are worse things than loving anoth — "

"They're the living dead. You should move."

Vaughn recalled Lise's tucked face as the rest of them laughed at Mrs. Peen's hedge joke. It hadn't been Lise's shyness that he'd seen, but embarrassment. Lise: taskmaster! One dinner party and she was able to pass judgement on his life. His first friendships, his first leap for normalcy was a failure.

Though there was still Dog Merson.

After the game they were to gather at Sayers', the bar closest to the arena. Vaughn waited anxiously for the game to end — the bench was electric, his breath a bore. Teammates knew he had a girl in town, and some who hadn't said much to him in years suddenly had endless sexual cracks. The mocking started when Lane Hay, Vaughn's defence partner, announced, "So Collin's got a dame up there, eh?" Staring up at the dressing-room's sloped ceiling, staggered with the cement undersides of the arena's bleachers, he sniffed the air and pointed, "Ah, right there. I can smell her." Then to Vaughn, "Hey, *nice.*" Vaughn sensed that some of them were relieved to find out he was normal in that way, so eager were they to remind him what carnal bliss awaited him after the game. Buddy Carona winked at him from the corner, his look implying that he was lending Vaughn some of his manhood.

San Diego beat them that night, as expected. They were midway through a bad season. Making the playoffs was doubtful, as were the bonuses that went with it. Coach Haliburton's job on the line, he rode them with temper tantrums and extra practices. Attendance was down, the franchise itself was threatened. Every loss tightened the screws. But none of this was reason not to go for a beer.

Professionally sullen, the Victoria Maple Leafs, some with wives and girlfriends, filed into Sayers'. Vaughn had timed it wrong getting there early, his strategy clouded by impatience. If he'd followed Dog from the rink he could've sat next to him. Now, sitting with Lise in a ring of empty seats, he had to wait on luck. Dog ended up three tables away. He'd come in alone. Rumour had it that he and his wife were quits, but no one knew for sure. Teammates rarely talked about that sort of thing.

"More beer!"

The team's mood soon turned cynically sunny.

The pub was full of fans, the friendlier sorts milling about the tables introducing themselves, commenting on the team's woes, trading jokes, praising players for a bodycheck or goal.

"When you creamed number eighteen in the corner? Make 'em pay big for winnin', eh?"

"Yeah . . . " sighed Buddy Carona, who hated fans.

Players traded chairs to sit next to linemates they could safely whisper to about how rotten a coach Billy Haliburton had turned out to be. Wives and girlfriends congregated near the wall, talking among themselves. Vaughn didn't know what would've made him prouder: Lise here beside him or over with the other women, his own proper hockey wife. She seemed content where she was, at his side, talking with Georges Gingras, the goalie, both of them trying out rusty French, for him one of the rare occasions since leaving La Belle Province, for her the first time, perhaps, since her mother died. Then again, maybe she and Bernard spoke French sometimes.

Vaughn kept an eye on Dog. He was quiet after games as a rule and it took him an hour to unwind, gain colour.

"More beer!"

Not much else to do in these places, Vaughn saw, than drink beer. The place actually smelled of it, years of it. Drinking in Beauséjour he remembered to be different, always in someone's home, the adults helping themselves to what liquor they'd brought along, and the whole household, kids too, joining in on stories, singing, eating. Maybe a piano would snap things along. Here, though, nothing but jokes, puck talk and:

"More beer!"

Lise seemed at home. Vaughn admired her for this. He nursed his second beer while she looked to be on her fourth or fifth, and still as thirsty as his teammates. Dog was soon in full stride too, and started a beer-chugging contest with three others at his table. Vaughn elbowed Lise to watch.

"If Haliburton wants to work us twice a day," Dog said to no one in particular, "fuckin' booze farts'll push us."

They took turns, timed on a wristwatch. Dog went last. He took deep breaths, making a show of it. Hoist. Massive gulps. An empty mug, bang, on the table. Jack Reilly said five seconds, Bert Small said four, but either way Dog won. Vaughn made himself join in the victory whoop with Dog and the others, then elbowed Lise again to make sure she hadn't missed it. He turned to see her put her own full pint to her lips. Massive gulps. She set the empty down quietly. Vaughn hadn't counted, but it looked close. Faster maybe. Georges Gingras looked at the empty glass, then at Lise, then to the other tables.

"Hey Dog," he shouted, "here's one who — "

"No." Lise grabbed his arm.

Dog, busy with a waitress, hadn't heard anyway. Straining under the weight of her tray full of beer, she passed them down one at a time while Dog counted them off:

"You love me . . . love me not . . . love me . . . "

Vaughn nudged Lise to make sure she watched. The last beer the waitress handed down was a "not", and, in anguish well acted, he grabbed the girl's wrist. "Not *you* too!"

The waitress broke his hold and with a dead smile walked away. The men howled, Dog most of all.

"What was that about?" Lise asked Georges.

"Wife trouble. Marianne."

"What a surprise, eh?"

Jokes on Dog's marriage flew back and forth across tables.

"Well, *dogs* are made for kicking, eh?"

"Little pecker you got, girl *mouse*'d leave."

"Yeah, Dog," Vaughn found himself shouting — now was his chance — half at the crowd, half at Lise, "Marianne says you're like a fuckin' bee-bee in a damn boxcar!" He'd heard this joke before and knew it was good. But everyone laughed and talked so loud he couldn't tell who had heard. He looked quickly at Lise, who held his eye a moment, then shook her head and said, "Jesus." Had he been that daring?

"Yeah my baby's gone and lef' me," Dog Merson the black blues singer howled at the ceiling, then flung his arms out, Al Jolson now, to plead with the world, "Where she? Where mah baby? M' wife, m' life, m' hole, m' box, m' bucket?" He hung his head and wiped tears.

"Dave Merson!" Shirley Carona was standing, pointing

a finger at Dog's face.

"She isn't gone *yet,*" she shouted, "but you badmouth Marianne anymore in public and I'll see she hears about it."

"Shirley, come on, sit down." Buddy Carona leaned back awkwardly to put that huge hand on his wife's shoulder.

Dog waved her away and turned to study the waitress, who was coming with another tray. He bent over and rolled his pant legs up over his knees. By the time she arrived Dog had his chair pushed back, in her way, and his legs spread, exposed.

"Well," the girl said, professionally cheerful, leaning with difficulty to set down beer, "what have we here?"

"Knee injuries," said Dog. One of his knees did sport a purple half-moon from an old operation.

"Well good for you."

"No, good for *you*. My personal physician normally has the pleasure of massaging these. Tonight the pleasure is yours."

Teammates smirked but stifled their laughter. Dog was only half joking around. Lots of women like Dog's jokes.

Bent rigidly towards the scene, Lise watched.

"*Spill* it on him!" she shouted. Dog turned their way, his eyes as bright as Lise's own.

"So," Dog called out, "Collin's dark young lass doesn't like hairy legs."

"Got my own, pal," Lise shouted back, lifting a bent arm to flash her black bush of an armpit. "Like *these*, dickweed?"

"Hmm," offered George Gingras, "unshaved, in the French manner."

Lise was laughing savagely at her own joke, as were the players. Not Vaughn. There was nothing funny in it at all.

He whispered, tugging at her, "He's my friend."

"He's a jerk. I didn't hurt him."

"He's my friend."

Lise turned to him then and said softly so only he could

hear, "He doesn't give shits for you, Vaughn, know that?"

Noise grew louder as Dog climbed onto his table.

"I think Collin's *hole* wants to see the colour of my socks!"

"Show her the colour of your socks!"

"Your socks!"

"More beer!"

His pants rolled over his knees, Dog's socks were already visible. A green and yellow tartan. Perfect. Vaughn had guessed right tonight. All was ready. He elbowed Lise.

"Check these socks," he whispered.

"I see his damn socks," she snapped, glaring still at Dog, who turned slowly on the table making "nothing up my sleeves" gestures towards his legs.

"Not his socks, *mine,*" Vaughn said, nodding his head at his own feet. He had planned to unveil his surprise to Lise quietly, their little secret. It bothered him that all this noise and Lise's distraction forced him to yell his secret at her.

"Look!" He pulled her arm. But Lise wouldn't look; Dog was shouting again.

"These, lady, are the colour of my socks!" Dog pulled his trousers and underwear down the full length of his legs until the tops of his socks showed above the fallen clothing. Dog stood with arms raised in triumph, his legs stark white under the glare of his black pubic hair and rough-brown penis.

"*My* socks," Vaughn insisted, a little irritated with Dog, who normally left his underwear on when showing his socks. Vaughn pulled Lise's arm to break her glare and direct it at his own glory, his secretly purchased, meticulously laundered green and yellow tartans donned for this visit, this event, this girl. Lise finally glanced down, not at Vaughn's socks but at the zipper at the front of her dress.

"What *azzhole* wants to see the colour of my *Injun nipples?"*

He caught her just in time, wrestling her down. She was yelling at him and, to his amazement, he was yelling back.

At the moment he thought she might hit him, she shot up and ran, dodging tables so fast her limp hardly showed. Vaughn rose to follow. Over at the bar the manager calmly phoned the police. Dog, Vaughn knew, would stay. He had been arrested for bar pranks before. Vaughn saw the tables of teammates still roaring with laughter, and he stood for a moment, confused, not knowing whose side they were on, Lise's or Dog's. For that matter, whose side was he on? Before running off to find Lise he gave them a wave and a grin, not knowing what else to do. Because he did know that when you were having a fight with your woman you were supposed to smile to teammates, shrug your shoulders, maybe wink, acknowledge in a tricky little lie that though you didn't really need her your body did, and so you had to do what she wanted. Vaughn performed all of this in his shrug before leaving his first beer parlour.

Lise waited at the car. They drove without a word until the SeaKing where, not looking at him, Lise whispered drunkenly, bitterly, "Can't you do better than socks?"

He let her off and drove home to Mrs. Peen's.

In the morning, wearing a pink robe with a black hummingbird on the back, Lise stood staring at the floor, a fist to each temple. Never looking at Vaughn's face, she apologized for half an hour. She said she had no excuse for how she sometimes acted. She hated herself. She hated everyone in the world but him. She couldn't help hating Mrs. Peen and Dog Merson, but he had made them his friends and she should accept that. She'd acted horribly, she needed his forgiveness.

Vaughn had never seen her so formal.

"Well," he asked, playing the role of inquisitor, "what makes you so mad to begin with? What exact thing?"

Lise pondered. Vaughn could see she had an answer but not the right way to tell it.

"Lots of things," she said finally. "*Every*thing. I don't get along with . . . men . . . these days."

He nodded, helping her continue.

"Last night . . . this whole hockey business of yours. I hate it, always have, the boys who play, such pigs, so big on themselves." She looked up quickly. "You've always been free of that."

He nodded again.

"Bernard and his friends may be ignorant, and none of them have any money, but at least . . . at least they're not as bad. Treat their women better. Bit of respect." Lise paused, corrected herself. "Well, Bernard and them are pigs too, actually." She eyed the wall hard, focusing on something. "They're *pigs* all right."

"Why have you stayed with Bernard? Tell me." He proposed this quickly, for with Lise apologetic this long-tabooed subject was suddenly open. It did puzzle him. She, full of too many smart extras to even count, and him, a pimply dumb greaseball he could picture only in the dullest corner of his Beauséjour memory.

"He got me out of *Beau-sé-jour,*" Lise declared, pronouncing their town as if to explain what it was she hated in it. "No one else did. And I had to get away. No offence, but, I hated your father. That *house*. When your mother died so did my obligations. And here's Bernard with this truck." Lise looked up and smiled weakly.

"So why do you stay with him, still?"

Lise pondered again.

"You know. Habit. And — he's okay a lot of the time." Lise looked embarrassed now, and her fidgeting told him she was about to shirk his questions altogether.

"Those aren't good reasons," he told her, a judge now.

"Look, he treats me *okay*. And," she raised her eyebrows, "he knows I'm the best he can get. I never let him forget that." Her smile was stronger now.

"Still not good enough." He was enjoying this role,

though it made Lise look up fiercely.

"Okay, Vaughn. You win. Maybe he's the best *I* can get too, all right? I'm thirty-one, I'm not blonde, I'm not Monroe, all right?" Her nostrils flared. "And one thing Mr. LaPierre never lets *me* forget. I'm *Métis*. And so is he. And if you remember anything at all about Beauséjour, what it was like, you'll . . . you'll leave me alone on this."

Lise landed on the bed and held her head in her hands, not quite crying. Vaughn sat next to her and began to rub her back through her robe. Through the hummingbird. Its throat was embroidered with metallic red thread, as were its tiny eyes, which looked blind to anything but bright flowers.

"I forgive you," Vaughn said, not yet able to lose his role. He felt uneasy even pretending to judge her.

Eyes going sly, Lise turned her face up to him. "Look, I'm thirty-one, I don't have time to waste." She slipped under the covers and pulled him in beside her to start things going again.

That day and the one that followed, the last of her visit, Lise lapsed more and more into an anxious state, that frightened-girl look darting bird-like in her eyes. She murmured love words constantly, and clung to Vaughn harder with each passing hour as if he were waning, losing substance. In Beauséjour he had never understood her, and now he was no closer.

Lise's third visit came two years later, in 1952, and it opened the door to her more frequent, more horrid visits. In the meantime they kept writing letters, and otherwise his life changed, as lives do.

It seemed something in Lise's letters helped bring these changes about. More than ever Lise's letters gushed with romantic pleading, and he found himself praised to high heaven. He was the only "kind, innocent boy she knew".

Bernard was "a beast, a selfish dolt". Vaughn had the "incorruptible, pure heart of a true man".

Though he couldn't understand her feelings for him, perhaps now he started believing her gilded words. He'd always known his difference from others. Now, listening to Lise go on, he gathered that this difference was worth something.

Regardless of their cause, his new feelings about himself allowed him to broaden, to consider new vistas. First he took swimming lessons, finally a lifeguard certificate. A necessary step, he decided, living on an island. He began taking courses at the university. How many professional hockey players took English Literature courses at a university? He felt special sitting in class, flaunting stitches or black eyes to thin bookworms and their pale, library-sucked skin. He found his courses in British fiction interesting, for sometimes the professors' words echoed Beauséjour moments, afternoons in secret spots talking about heroes and heroines with a wide-eyed young Lise.

He stoked his remaining years in Victoria with many such courses, filling in an English degree with Psychology and Philosophy. But philosophy built castles with words, and psychology explained people with numbers. The few answers either gave him did nothing but spark more questions. (Vaughn had already suspected this trick of Knowledge.)

And perhaps he'd begun believing Lise that he was too good for Mrs. Peen and Dog Merson. Whatever the cause, break away he did. A gradual death, this parting of what he'd taken to be friendship. He pictured flowers that curl away to face out opposite ends of the window-box.

University meant less time for bridge, and Mrs. Peen felt snubbed. She wondered aloud how fair it was that special conditions were made for a member of the club who came only when he wanted. After this ploy failed to shame him back, she tried next the plea of a pitiful old-lady-soon-to-die, a pose that unnerves every young person on Earth. Not Vaughn, then.

"I suppose," she said, her voice quavering in a cliché of age, "we're old ladies who talk nonsense. Well, we won't be on Earth much longer to disturb anyone."

"I guess that's true," Vaughn agreed, his matter-of-factness coming less from sarcasm than from a still innocent heart and ignorant head.

He played bridge very rarely after this blunder. He felt no loss. Over the past year his landlady, her friends, and all they stood for had begun leaving an off-taste in his eyes. Their prim manners suddenly seemed puny in this land of gigantic Douglas fir, deep ocean, and gnashing wind. He had grown and they had not.

Dog Merson? Lise had been right. When Vaughn threw out his tartan socks, from that day on the fountain of Dog's personality began losing its height and sparkle. Vaughn still said "fuck" in the dressing-room, but everyone said "fuck" in the dressing-room.

But as Vaughn grew more uppity, he also grew more bored. Hockey a bore, university a bore, even Lise's praise became boring, and on the street no woman passed in whom he couldn't see in an instant the sameness that swung in the dressed machinery of her hips. Boredom. So bored he became, and so uppity after reading Lise's letters, that he began feeling a little superior to Lise herself. Who was she, after all?

She visited a number of times between 1953 and 1955, and each short reunion was more disastrous than the last.

In the fall of 1953 Lise seemed sober when he met her bus. But somehow, between climbing into his Dodge and climbing into the SeaKing bed, she'd managed to get herself drunk. During the drive he'd stopped briefly to drop off an essay but she wasn't alone for long. In bed he'd just started kissing her, "tickling" her Beauséjour-style, when she reached into her bag and waved the culprit in his face.

"Wan' some my hol'day bottle, Vaughn-Vaughn?"

Her "holiday bottle" was a half-empty quart of rye. Lise took down a good part of what was left. She convulsed, a short, controlled snap of the neck, then lay back and announced to the ceiling, "So *good* to get away."

She stopped Vaughn from taking off his pants.

"Let's just," she said sloppily, "let's just do it this way. Pants on." She took down his zipper. With a finger she simply moved her panties to the side.

Vaughn marvelled at this new trick of hers. He found he loved sex fully clothed — his dead fabric hitting her dead fabric framed with delicious intensity the target, warm and wet, the flesh. Oh, it was —

But halfway into their first lovemaking in two years, she fell asleep. A soft burp wiffed through her slack mouth. Vaughn didn't know what to do. He tried but couldn't wake her up. While it probably wasn't her first coupling in two years, Vaughn was eagerly aware that it was his, so he carried on.

It didn't surprise him much, Lise's fall from decency. For a year or so he'd noticed a pattern developing: the more self-assured he became, the more pathetic and debased grew Lise. During their trade-off of love letters, whenever he was late with his weekly letter to her (because of road trips and the like), he would receive a panic-stricken letter from Lise. She wondered if he'd forgotten her, if he no longer loved her; she accused him of infidelity (celibate Vaughn thought it quite a feat of cheek for drunken, common-law Lise to accuse him of infidelity, or anything else). It intrigued him that a mere delay in the mails could so completely yank a romantic rug out from under Lise's feet. Not out of sadism but rather in the interest of psychology did he give that rug an experimental tug.

He called it "the letter effect". Just as he'd witnessed

couples withhold affection, or even kindness, to make themselves wickedly more alluring, so he saw that this trick worked just as well long-distance. Purposely delaying his letters he gauged Lise's reaction to a week's delay, two weeks', a month. The longer he held back, the louder his predictable Lise would screech her need. He stopped the letter tests eventually. Not only were they cruel — Lise wasn't a lab-rat, Vaughn told himself — but they twice became embarrassing.

Mr. Collin, whose visits to his son were shy and brief, their one catalyst being endless hockey talk, was sitting at Mrs. Peen's one evening with Vaughn and his landlady, when Lise appeared in the flesh. Vaughn had gone almost two months without writing her. Mr. Collin, Vaughn, and Mrs. Peen were engaged in polite wit and tea, and a pleasant December dusk-light filtered in through the parlour windows. Mrs. Peen loved that light, she'd once confided to Vaughn, as it made her personality shine. At one point Vaughn looked up — and blinked, but there was no mistake — there was Lise hiding outside in the rose bushes. The skinny rose canes couldn't have camouflaged anyone, let alone someone wearing a red plastic raincoat, the kind kids wear. Lise's black hair was ruffled like a mad woman's. Vaughn could tell she wasn't sober.

When she saw he'd seen her, up she popped, waving. Careful not to shake his teacup, he scowled hard at her to go away. She gave him violent "c'mon" waves. Vaughn scowled harder, wagging his eyebrows fiercely up and down, as if to scour her off the landscape. It was out of the question that she interrupt just now, his father's first night there, his landlady's high-tea; even more out of the question to bring her in, drunk and looking mean. So he was relieved when Lise gave him the finger, stomped a rose cane into the ground, and stumbled off.

Later, after dropping his father at the Empress, Vaughn drove to the SeaKing, where Lise would be. But she wasn't.

She'd checked in that afternoon but only stayed an hour, said the old desk man. That same evening Vaughn wrote Lise a letter mentioning nothing about the window incident, making it seem like he'd written it the morning before. Within a week he had in his hands the most apologetic, imploring letter he'd ever had from her. She did call him a snob, but she apologized for thinking that way.

Another time, almost a year later, he'd been tardy with a letter, true, but this time a local postal strike was to blame. He had as proof of his loyal intentions a completed postcard — an emperor penguin from the San Diego Zoo — in his suitcase. But one night, just as they'd boarded the bus after a loss in Vancouver, he heard a commotion between the driver and someone in the parking lot. Between profane screams at the driver, a familiar voice called "Vaughn? Vaughn!" Players craned their necks to see and someone said, "*Collin's* girl," and, "Christ, *look* at her." On her love-lost way to Victoria, Lise had been waylaid in a Vancouver bar and, overhearing that the Victoria Maple Leafs were in town, had ventured out to find the arena.

Lise was yelling she wanted to ride to Victoria with him on the bus. A natural-enough request, reasonable even. There were empty seats. Vaughn almost argued on Lise's behalf. As he listened to Lise's yelling, and watched the trainer and bus driver try to pry her fingers from the door frame, he considered. This was a hockey team. Which, like a bridge club, could not tolerate outsiders, especially of the opposite sex. Bridge ladies may talk about men, but watch every facial tic at the table twitch into high tizzy the moment a living man penetrated their room. Or fishermen at sea — their communal thoughts pointing like a fleshy harpoon back to port. So it was with a hockey team, which no more wanted a woman sitting in its dressing-room or riding its bus than a gang of sailors wanted the flesh-and-blood object of their lust shipping out with them.

Vaughn didn't want Lise on the bus either, if the truth were known. You can hang out with a group for only so long before its thoughts are yours.

Vaughn walked Lise behind a cement pillar where, after enduring her brief tirade, he explained about the mail strike. He watched with wonder how her face took in this news and relaxed, a heart soothed to learn a dumb accident had done the damage, not another heart. Vaughn told Lise she could catch the last ferry if she hurried, and he gave her twenty dollars. When he got to Victoria he checked into the SeaKing and waited, and she came. At Vaughn's insistence, they did it pants on.

Vaughn last saw Lise in the summer of 1957. This visit took place only months before the beginning of her rebirth, or, in her way of telling, her "first death". His last encounter with the well-worn Lise occurred just when she had ripened, or "rotted just so".

As during the previous summer, after hockey season Vaughn had gone to work with Georges Gingras on the trawler he kept at Ucluelet. Fishing with Georges meant two weeks at sea with no break; endless days in rain, fog, or shocking heat; fretting at the malignancy of storms; standing knee-deep in salmon and slime if they were lucky, or, if they weren't, eternal gin rummy with a silent Georges.

Vaughn loved it. Fishing affected his stomach directly, and would for the rest of his life.

He discovered the joy of fishing to be an easy joy, the joy of the hunt, the harvest, the paycheque. But fishing was the best. A paycheque was a poor shadow of the gold, the meat, one should weigh in one's own hands. Farmers came close, but their joy was diluted, gradual as the growth of their fields. Hunters came closer, but animals were seen before they were shot. Fish, though, were from a hidden world. To fish was to lure and snatch gold from another realm entirely. Each fish a surprise, a nugget, shining, thick, alive. A gift that came out of night.

The previous summer Georges had seen Vaughn take to the work and in 1957 asked him on as a partner, to share in profit or loss, as the case may be. Vaughn did want to make money, but mostly wanted to snatch as much joy from the sea as he could between spring playoffs and fall training camp. They docked in Ucluelet to unload their catch and rest. Lise found them there.

She looked terrible. Even sober she seemed deranged, as though alcohol's tawny spider clung upside down in her skull still, spinning a confused web of a life. They spent Vaughn's shore time together, he sharing her web. In some ways he found this sober Lise more of a trial than the drunken one, when her boozy stupidity could simply be ignored. Now, though she was depressed, illogical, and best handled like a child, her occasional outbursts of Lise-of-old clarity kept Vaughn on guard.

For most of this last time together, Lise talked. They occupied a room in the Ucluelet Hotel, a room built entirely of cedar, which in July heat cloyed like a sauna. The room sat over the beer parlour, and the floorboards let in the shouting.

Vaughn sat in a chair in the room's centre. Lise circled.

"My *therapist,"* she said right off, emphasizing a word that was then a rarity, "demands that I confess everything to you."

It came out that Lise had had treatment at first for her alcohol problem, antisocial behaviour, and arrest record, and lately for her growing distress. Her first psychiatrist had been a Freudian, and her present counsellor a devotee of Jung. She had loathed the first man, a pompous old German who wrote all of Lise's problems off to her limp and, in Lise's words, "some kind of phantom phallus growing up out of a goddamn Winnipeg wheat field". She turned then to a Mr. Eintz, another German.

"There are four people I must confess to," Lise said, sombrely as a schoolgirl reciting verse. "I must confess to Bernard, who is my carefree child. To my father, in prayer, who is my invisible taskmaster. To the collective white man, who is my enemy. And to you. Mr. Eintz wasn't sure — at first — who you were."

Lise confessed many things, a few of which surprised Vaughn. Alcoholism. Sleeping with other men, with attempts to patch up things with Bernard. She confessed to periods of intense hatred of white people, then long bouts of hating Indians, for both races had gotten together one night to mix her blood. She confessed to hating most men, most of the time. Her try at homosexuality didn't shock him, perhaps because "lesbian" meant so little to him that he hadn't any means to judge it. And Lise seemed perfect for the part: she was smarter and in some ways more manly than any man Vaughn had known and, as for the sexual part, he saw Lise's skin to be universally appealing. An old ape would love her for her skin; so would a young bird.

Her confession of prostitution and time in jail did surprise him. Through tears, her eyes shone defiantly.

"For almost a year," Lise said talking rougher than he was used to, "I was a Portage Avenue regular. I walked the Métis block, one block from the full-bloods. Cops picked us up if they had nothing else to do." Lise spat on the floor. Sometimes, as though Vaughn himself were somehow to blame for any of this, she raised her voice.

"Hey, right, you like it 'pants on' eh? It's what we do in the fuckin' alley. You'd love Winnipeg." Lise sneered. "Hey — your name rhymes with *John*. Fuckin' funny, eh?"

Her sarcasm was lost on him. And eventually she would grow tired, and gentler.

"I wrote lots of letters to you from jail." She sobbed, and shut her eyes to squeeze out more tears. "It was the only time I was sober enough . . . *to write."* Typically, Lise ended such bouts by wailing and throwing herself on the bed to cry and sulk. Vaughn would leave then to consult with Georges, or have a beer. He was starting to like beer.

"That Lise, she's something, eh?" is all Georges said. Or the more general, "Women, eh?" He'd turn back to his boat to scrape something already smooth, or paint something already painted.

Vaughn would grin, shrug, nod his head. He could tell by Georges' eyes he was being polite, that he actually thought Lise a grand pain. But like all French he was descended from philosophers, and likely held deep in his heart that love tolerated all, even grand pains who tracked you down to fishing villages and commandeered your four days' rest. Love, *mon dieu.*

Vaughn wondered, what would impatient, cat-eyed Georges have thought if he told the truth, that he didn't love Lise at all? Because he didn't.

He often returned to his room to find her still on the bed, sometimes inert for hours. These silent periods begged something from him, some kind of advice. Perhaps she wanted a declaration of love, but he wouldn't lie. So advice it was, and though some of it was pretty stupid, who was to blame here?

"Why don't you move to the country?" he asked her, avoiding mention of Victoria.

"And *do what?* Jesus."

"Well, I *can't* see why you can't control your *drinking."* Vaughn thoughtfully poured out some tea for them, an act which often caused him to lapse into parlour idiom, and sometimes even made his pinky drift out into the rough cedar room. "You were *such* a reasonable sort before you started your *drinking."*

Lise jumped from the bed and put a finger in his face.

"You know nothing about being a woman, you know

nothing about being Métis, you know *nothing* about working shit-jobs for a living," Lise yelled, drowning out the ruckus that penetrated their floor. "You hang an English, snob, *ass*hole mask on your goddamn boring — *cowboy, puck*boy, *ass*hole-face — " She flung herself and her gibberish face-down onto the bed.

For an instant he wanted to tell Lise she was right. He wanted to ask her what she'd do if *she* had a boring soul which scared her with its pointlessness. But that instant passed, and instead of telling her the truth he turned his back on her and let indignation rise. Rich and self-righteous, almost *anger:* wasn't it ironic that she, a crippled, boozy, prostitute, should tell him, a healthy, polite, sportsman, how to behave? Like a wino lecturing a banker on the street.

"Cheap wine," concluded Lise while he straightened his tea things, his back still turned, "carries way less *bullshit* than your goddamn tea."

Four days of this. Georges was restless. The salmon, he knew in his bones, were running. Lying, he told Vaughn that he liked Lise, he admired her spirit. But he couldn't fathom their union. Vaughn was "a quiet man", while Lise was "a wild one that needed manners. You walk different roads. Time to go fishin', eh?"

So that afternoon, Lise and Vaughn sat facing each other, straddling a rhinoceros-wide drift log on Ucluelet beach. He told her he had to leave. Their bickering ceased then, borne away inland on the sea breeze.

"I've left Bernard for good," Lise said suddenly. "I haven't seen him in almost a year."

So, here she was, his childhood lover, split from her beau, his rival. Lise's silent invitation was louder than the surf.

"Perhaps that's for the best, yes," said Vaughn.

"Well — I should move in with you."

From her voice it seemed she was trying a return to her Beauséjour authority, that of a tutor telling her young dumb one what must be done. Her tone broke through to Vaughn's stomach, but only just.

"No."

"Why."

"Fantasy," he answered. It was the word that fit. Then he recited a phrase that had taken four days to get right, but a phrase that had thirty years of plodding thought behind it.

"Love," Vaughn pronounced, a little proudly, for he'd wanted to be rid of this word ever since a snow bedroom, "Love is an emotional wart on the honest, pointing finger of simple sex."

"No!" Lise shouted and bounced as if the log was bucking her. *"No!* Dr. Eintz says love *is* there! I've talked about you, I've told it all, more than I knew myself, he's said — "

Out of Lise's manic story he pieced together bits of theory this Eintz had injected into his helpless patient. How much Lise had bent it to fit her own need Vaughn couldn't tell, but it sounded so hopelessly romantic, so emotionally warty, he wondered if it had anything at all to do with a theory of this person Jung, or if it weren't yet another dreamy concoction of a prince-starved girl. Lise claimed, pounding her certainty into their log with her fist, that Vaughn was her Animus, she his Anima; that they were romantic magnets, "two halves of a bean-seed from the time we were born, and even before that"; that this was the reason for her addiction to him, an addiction that had caused her endless pain more deep than her bones.

"This," Lise lied, while tears coursed their honest stream down her cheeks, "is what we are." She held out her hands, then clasped them firmly.

"Lise. Look. *This* is what we are." He pointed first at her chest, then at his own, his slow-motion finger emphasizing one thing: distance.

Time was ripe. He swung his leg over the log to dismount, landed with the virile bounce of a cowboy. He kept walking.

"Vaughn-Vaughn!" Lise called out. Vaughn turned to her, watched her crying, squeezing the log with her legs. He shrugged, a salmon-are-waiting shrug. He smiled. Waved.

"*Be scared with me!*" Her voice broke. He kept walking.

"Call me *Annie!*" she cried. When he didn't turn around this time, he heard her little shrieks and sobs, and the murmurs of a young girl mired in dreams. "Please . . . just *call* me Annie. . . ."

Annie. The plea of an adolescent. He had outgrown her. Fated love, indeed. Annie, indeed.

The sun baked the beach, the incense of tidal decay giving hints of a rich sea beyond. Picking his foothold from log to log on the way back to the village, he spotted a pair of dragonflies coupled in sticky "love", fluttering helplessly among the logs. The one above, its tail arched and straining. These bugs and rhythmic waves and clockwork sun overhead joined to mock the silliness of Lise's fantasy, to outlaw it.

Fleeing to Europe, one year later, came as an easy decision.

In the dressing-room during fall training camp, Georges, sweating, head hanging, looking old and used, turned his heavy head to Vaughn. "My cousin, Raymond? The league he plays for in France? A team there wants another Canadian. The one they had broke an arm. Money's not too hot though, eh?"

Mrs. Peen also helped. She was in the kitchen preparing dinner and she looked immensely old, as old as something that had given up and begun to fall back into itself. She stood there in her faded pink "work dress", now two sizes too large for her, kneading catsup into a bowl of hamburger. She chattered inanely, her voice high and teasing and girlish. Vaughn saw an old lizard with a cartoon voice. Her flabby upper arms, hanging off the bones in pouches, bounced "thluck, thluck" as she worked on their dinner, that red burger she would put in the oven to cook as grey as herself. Victoria, he saw, was like that: it cooked everything grey. He'd been here, cooking, for fourteen years. He hadn't felt anything, not really, since his mother died. Except a growing boredom, and growing nausea. Mrs. Peen prattled on, kneading the meat as though nothing were wrong. *Thluck, thluck.*

His third reason to leave came in an envelope. In part, Lise's letter read: "Eintz was off base, he screwed me in more ways than one. I've met someone new. Ivan is actually more a teacher. I've changed. I'm coming. Be patient."

But she signed the letter "Annie". No changes *he* could see. Victoria is British Columbia's capital, and a passport was arranged quickly.

April 1st

I love mergansers and have been spending a quiet hour watching two of them preen and peck each other. Next to wood ducks mergansers are my favourite water birds. In sunlight, if they tilt their black heads you see they're really iridescent green. Thin orange beak and Woody-Woodpecker topknot — a goofy bird. They'll stand on one foot and with the other scratch their neck like a dog.

Another birdwatcher, Mark, one of the young guys who lives in the "community" down the beach, is hiding behind a rock with his pencils and paper. I watch his hand slashing, dusting, pausing. I don't like the guy. Fortyish. Ponytailed throwback whose look sparks bad memories. Apparently he sells his work.

Annie walked up the beach. When she got close and scattered the birds, Mark looked up angrily, then saw it was her. Both of them laughed like buddies. They talked, Annie flapping what looked to be my last chapter in the air to make a point.

"The group". That's what people call them. I don't know

what they call themselves, if anything. They fish, they garden, they craft, but they don't quite fit. They've been here a few years longer than me, since just before Ivan disappeared. I've heard there used to be more of them. When it sank in that Ivan was either dead or vamoosed, some of them left too. (Annie has since told me that leaving was the best thing Ivan could have done for any of them, herself included. Something about doing it alone.) Now there are only five of them, two men and three women. Actually, one of the women, Alison, is new. I hear she left a husband, who came after her once. She arrived maybe two years ago now, didn't know Ivan at all.

Whether they think of Annie as their teacher, I have no idea. I stay out of it. We nod, but I've never really talked to them. Annie visits them regularly, and — who knows — I could be a bit jealous of that.

Funny: though I've never talked with them I've seen them naked, a bunch of times. I'll be walking the beach and there they are, in swimming, or out, naked, drying in the sun. I pass, we nod uncomfortably, but I sense their discomfort is only for me. Once I said inanely, "Good day for swimmin', eh?" Breasts and hair and private parts, in public. But there's nothing at all lascivious about it, not like the scene I got to know on the Riviera, that lewd toplessness — women made up to the nines, with sunhat, sunglasses, jewellery, G-string, and chic little breasts. Here, the group's nudity has the aura of a health food store, and makes me feel uncool to be wearing clothes. Though when I last passed, the new one, Alison, did roll over onto her front. It made me like her.

Annie has just come and gone. We started our visit with an argument. It was likely my small jealousy attack that made me ask her when Mark planned to dunk that blond ponytail of his in happy-paint and write LOVE on the cliff face over the harbour.

She dropped my chapter onto my table. "Good," she said, "very nice. You caught her. Good old Lise." She paused, watching Mark from the window. "But Lise wasn't quite that stupid. And you weren't quite that cold."

"I guess we have our own versions."

"Nothing wrong with having some sympathy. Especially for yourself."

"I want to get at the guts of it."

"You can't let stuff go if you're still wrestling with it."

"That was my memory of me, and that was my memory of you."

"Of Lise. Nothing to do with me."

"Sure thing, Lise." I was smiling and Annie wasn't.

"No, I still *like* Lise. Wasn't very happy, but she was all right. The name 'Annie' is my tattoo. I feel like an idiot every time I hear it."

" — ?"

"Keeps me humble." Now she was smiling. "You saw it. You just wrote it down, for Christsakes. *Look* at her. 'Annie', Jesus."

"I never knew you didn't like it."

"So when you see that thing of yours in the mirror, don't cringe. Just compare yourself then and now. Be a good giant looking out over a garbage dump."

"A good giant."

"It's what range feels like. It's why you're writing this book."

France was a turning-point. A blooming of heart and eye. And France was where my life started gathering speed and garbage. The good giant William Blake called this *experience*. Mercy.

Two Friends and a Death

Pain, my heroin.

— Connor Peake

Georges Gingras's cousin had found Vaughn a player-coach position with Toulon, in the French Southern League. It was optimistic 1959. Vaughn was thirty-four and beginning his second career.

An angry-looking man named Roquebrun met him at the Toulon station. Vaughn still wasn't used to the shock that all people he would meet from now on were going to be French. Roquebrun was surprised too — they'd expected a Frenchman, a Québécois. Half of Vaughn's job was to coach, and how could an *Anglais* coach — Vaughn could see this thought squeezing M. Roquebrun's brow as they honked their way out of the station tumult — how could this new coach from the Fatherland of Hockey communicate winning tactics to his eager French team? Roquebrun decided to solve the problem by driving Vaughn downtown, where he pulled up to an imposing stone building. Stern, as though something were Vaughn's fault, he pointed at the sign surrounded by plaques of international flags: "Berlitz. Courses in French. Les Leçons d'Anglais." Roquebrun stabbed at the sign, enunciating one word per stab, "You, go, say, French."

Toulon's rink, and Vaughn's new apartment, were in the adjoining village of La Garde, so named because of its stark castle, which stood black and crumbling atop a central hill. Being driven for the first time past its foot, Vaughn heard a flock of French birds call out in accented tweets; he watched them drop off the battlements to soar off over the French fields, whose crop — artichokes — he could not identify. Roquebrun screeched around a corner onto a street Vaughn could not pronounce — d'Gnotes — and dropped Vaughn off at the door of his new home.

Toulon lay halfway between Marseilles and Nice. Lacking Nice's beaches it escaped being expensive and crowded, and having no industry it remained a quarter the size of Marseilles. Toulon's main function was to entertain the Allied sailors, merchant seamen, and fishermen who berthed there.

Near the docks lay the old city, a catacomb of cobbled streets. Doorways opened into the dim guts of bars, over which neon signs like The Manhattan, Bar Hong Kong, and La Billy the Kid distracted the eye from buildings so medieval that Vaughn expected on his first walk through to see Long John Silver guarding a gnarled alley, mumbling, "Should I kill the man? I wonder, has he any gold. . . . " Prostitutes lurked everywhere. This centre-city had been given the name "Cheecago" — from gangster movies. But this squat maze of urine-rank lanes was nothing like the Chicago Vaughn had known, if only briefly.

Vaughn's first foray into Cheecago he boldly entered the dark La Bar Nautique to have a beer. He had begun to acquire a taste, and wanted to sample the French version. In the bar all the lights were off and it was hard to see. The table was the size of Mrs. Peen's silver tea service. The seat was sticky. A ceiling fan clanked once every turn. An eel-thin girl glided over with his beer; he paid the steep two francs and gave the poor girl a tip.

"No teep," she said, and pushed the coins back.

"Pardon?"

"No *teep*. You buy me Chivas Regal, weesky."

Why should he buy a waitress a glass of whiskey?

"Why should I buy a — ?"

At his hesitation she spun away, moaning in disgust. He drank the good beer fast. Her mood, and that of this dark bar, tugged at his stomach. La Bar Nautique was like a secret spot of sadness.

In future he came downtown only to attend his French

lesson, treat himself to a saucy meal and, an athlete's dessert, a brisk walk along the docks.

He loved seeing the masts and rigging rise as he approached, loved the swampish tidal smell and cooler air. Rows of scows, yachts, old fishboats. And those French fishermen: their authentic wrinkles, turtlenecks, toques, salt-burned hands. Watching them unload crates of fish while wearily jabbering about a reef or storm or great school of fish (so he imagined their talk, not yet understanding much), he felt like a teammate of theirs. They knew the joy of fishing. And such exotic joy: shark, swordfish, octopus! But they misconstrued the way he admired their catch, and always tried to sell him some.

There was another reason he was drawn to the docks. Here beside the lapping water, where sunset's colours bounced off white hulls and riplets, everything gently grand, a carnival of brightness and mirrors, where even black became a colour — here he would stoop to place his hand in the Mediterranean and know that unbroken water led to Victoria and a similar dock. He could expand this fancy, a bit absurdly, and go farther, up against the current of a coastal river, up into the mountains to the dripping glaciers of the continental divide, balance a second, then down the eastern slope into a river which gradually gained size to spill wide onto the prairie and at last turn a slow and muddy corner right through Beauséjour. He'd never thought himself capable of anything like homesickness, so it never occurred to him to attach a name to the feelings that rose out of the Toulon water, up his arm, to swell in his chest.

Très bizarre, hockey *au sud de France*. Perhaps Vaughn should have expected it. It doesn't snow on the Riviera. Like cricket in Canada, hockey in Toulon was a misplaced sport.

He first walked into the dressing-room expecting what he was used to: a slightly smelly but functional room, a wall cubicle for each player. The team would be waiting a bit shyly for their new player-coach. Instead, pushing in the door marked "Vestiare "he found a small auditorium scattered with a chaos of benches at which sat all manner of men and boys, and little boys; street clothes strewn on the floor; mismatched hockey stockings and jerseys; the contorted angles and elbows of too many hockey players sitting, standing, bending; shrill little-boy laughter and the bark of men talking — all in one frightening French flurry. Vaughn had to watch his breath for a moment before he was calm enough to enter it.

M. Roquebrun appeared with a translator, a player named Papillon. They explained Vaughn's job. He was not only the new star defenceman for the Toulon Senior Team, and not only their coach, but also the director of the Toulon hockey program. He and eighty players were about to enjoy a practice together. No, he was told, no one gets "cut", for they all paid to play.

What, Vaughn asked, did eighty people do on the ice all at once?

"We divide up," Papillon said, "and the seniors give the young players *tips*." He seemed pleased using the word "tips".

"When does the senior team practise?"

"It does not."

"How does it get better?"

"We seniors are very highly skilled. I told you. We teach the young players — tips."

"Of first importance," Papillon nodded as he translated the shorter, pompous man's words exactly, "is to teach our young."

After watching that first farce — eighty padded players crowded like penquins on a small iceberg — Vaughn got the mess cleaned up in the end, scheduling an hour each to five age groups. God, to learn hockey you couldn't just stand around, couldn't just watch cute tips — you had to chase the puck with desperation, you had to do endless stops and starts and feel the wind blow your sweat dry.

With Papillon's help he worked up a small notebook of words to yell. Coaching words:

Keep your head up . . . *Ne collez pas vos yeux au puck.*

Always be moving . . . *Tachez de changer de position.*

Hustle . . . *Dépêchez-vous! Travaillez!*

Skate with your stomach . . . *Patinez avec votre estomac.*
He couldn't resist the last one, something he never could have mentioned in Canada. Revealing this secret to his new players gathered at centre ice to receive winning tactics, he saw a couple of heads nod. One of the things he learned to love about the French was their willingness to consider anything before returning to their self-certainty.

The seniors could skate well enough, in fact some had professional speed, but they lacked so much else. None could shoot with power, none had a gift for rough play, and Vaughn saw almost no evidence of puck sense — intuiting where the puck will go, which comes from countless childhood hours on backyard rinks.

One senior player, Franco Bonneville, an ageing Adonis type, played the closest to smart hockey that Vaughn saw, and patrolled the rink with a Caesar's bearing. The others admired his *macho* and for years he'd been the team's unofficial coach. Vaughn was later told Bonneville had laughed when "the first Canadian" broke his arm.

At the first practice Bonneville would not acknowledge Vaughn's presence. Perhaps he sensed correctly that nothing he did on the ice could impress the new Canadian. Indeed, Bonneville's first haughty glide around any rink in Canada would have gotten him beaten up by the likes of Buddy Carona, a quick lesson in *macho*. To make things worse, Vaughn accidentally insulted him before the second practice. Entering the Vestiare, he looked down to see Pillotto (Vaughn never did find out why, but some senior players went by one name only, like soccer's Pelé), a big-eared speedster, applying a pink bandaid to each nipple. Over in a corner, another player was doing the same thing. It was a joke, of course, a good old dressing-room prank. Vaughn knew how to point, and laugh richly with appreciation. But when he did, Bonneville leapt from his seat, red-faced, naked, gesturing with his hands something about the pain a jersey could inflict. "The *sweater* . . . it . . . *cuts,*" he explained, his face a big wince, his palm grating his nipple. So Bonneville was behind it.

Hockey was a game of sliced faces, busted noses, smashed teeth. Fuckin' bandaids?

Habit had built Vaughn some manly, Canadian pride. He knew how to roll his eyes. Putting on his own gear he could feel all eyes on him, watching what he did, or didn't do, to his nipples. From that day on no one used bandaids, and from that day on Bonneville was his enemy.

The games themselves were bizarre as well. What a shock to play in Nice, which had an outdoor rink ringed by palm trees. The ice was used primarily by wealthy figure-skaters, so before each game an old moustachioed gent had to stoop, walking backwards, and paint on temporary lines. Normally the paint is captured and protected under a layer of ice; these Nice lines were three-foot-wide blotches by the second period, and the refs had a guessing game calling offsides.

The arena in Avignon was an odd set-up as well. On a bankruptcy budget, it saved on electricity by using only a huge spotlight, aimed like a camera to follow the play. (The resulting dimness of light in the arena reminded Vaughn of that lantern-lit barn where the boy's foot had caught fire.) No spotlight can follow a puck passed sharply, tic-tac-toe; the light only served as a brilliant red herring, keeping everyone confused. Skating in and out of glare, it was like playing in a strobe. It was hard on the stomach, and goalies feared for their lives.

It took Vaughn time to adjust to the French version of

the game. No more could he relax into the safe comfort of rules. The referees were bad, skate sharpeners could not be trusted, timekeepers would cheat on home-team penalties. It took time and patience, but as usual Vaughn had plenty of both.

Just before Christmas he received two letters. The first was from his father. He asked how Vaughn was, and what the hockey was like. He said he hadn't been well, but that he'd be better soon. Next Christmas, if he could arrange it, he'd be over to visit and watch a few games. He asked if the French fans were as wild as at the Montreal Forum.

His father! Reading the letter, finishing up a half-bottle of *vin ordinaire,* Vaughn noticed the unmistakable swollen throat, a "heart in the throat", as books would have it. Lord, did he have to leave his *country* before he could find feelings for people? Why now, at age thirty-four?

The other letter was from Georges. Actually his was only a short note, and his envelope held a letter from Lise, with the explanation that when Lise wrote to him for Vaughn's address he thought it best to refuse and instead offer to send her letter himself. "That way," he wrote, "you can decide yourself if you want to reveal your hideout and have her chase you across the ocean."

But her letter didn't give Vaughn that impression at all. "Vaughn," she said, "I hope we're still talking. I have so much to tell you that's new. I'm embarrassed about what I became in your eyes. I have a lot of making up to do, but I'd rather just drop it. Let it go. I'd love it if you could forget the last ten of my years, and send me a nice, fresh letter. If not, well, I can't blame you. But too bad for both of us. Take care, cowboy. Love, Indian Annie."

Cowboy? Indian Annie? At least it looked like her cockeyed sense of humour was back. Tempting, but he wasn't going to encourage her by writing just yet.

In any case, he didn't want to think about Lise — Indian

Annie — now. In fact it became impossible. For the next year Vaughn Collin's life dropped several bombs in his lap.

Vaughn spent his ample free time shopping daily for food like a proper French housewife, sitting in the village square near gruff old men, and hiking the central hill with its castle ruin. Sometimes he'd cycle out to neighbouring villages on the old bicycle he bought, pumping through the rolling Midi hills, the earth cracked and yellow. Cycling, he'd nod shyly to old peasant women dressed in black. Mondays he bused into Toulon for French lessons. It was there he met Connor Peake.

He was a "new kid in class". He looked in his late teens. He sat slouched in the back row. He wasn't exactly ugly, but with his oily black hair, pointed features, and sloped forehead he reminded Vaughn of a reptile, or glowering fish. He had almost no neck. Connor Peake's eyes struck Vaughn the most — black, penetrating eyes which flicked constantly in search of movement, which was somehow funny since they themselves were the fastest objects in the room.

For courtesy and practice the teacher had them tell the newcomer their names and homes. Vaughn's classmates were mostly ethnics from Toulon. Vaughn said he was from Victoria, Canada.

Then the newcomer's turn. He looked undecided about something.

"Peake. Connor. Connor Peake."

"Oui?" the teacher prompted, "Vous habitez . . . ?"

Vaughn was instantly alert to his accent, which was so like Mrs. Peen's. And the name — did all Englishers have names like that?

"Monsieur?"

"*Earth.* J'habite on Earth."

Only one of Connor Peake's classmates laughed.

At class's end Vaughn heard him tell the teacher he'd

decided not to come back. As Vaughn made to exit, Connor reached out and touched his sleeve.

"You're Canadian. Might we talk? I need to talk. Go for a glass of Beaujolais?" He looked serious, if not a bit feverish, but at the same time his eyes had a glimmer which seemed to imply a hidden joke.

"Okay." Vaughn thought Beaujolais tasted like raisins. But this English teenager said he needed to talk.

They walked to the nearest café-bar, Le Up Shop. After initial pleasantries Vaughn asked him what the problem was, and Connor Peake looked startled.

"There's no problem." He smiled, understanding. "I just need 'to talk'. Literally."

They ordered their Beaujolais and Connor Peake talked. His eagerness to ramble about himself somewhat reminded Vaughn of the French enthusiasm for making love in public — to fondle, coo, and trade smacking kisses. Peake ranted on, sometimes so loudly that people stared.

He sipped his Beaujolais, wrinkled his nose like a rabbit, and pointed at it. Vaughn waited for a comment about the wine, but instead Peake said, "I was a child prodigy." Then laughed delightedly as Vaughn struggled with the gap. Peake loved to do that, Vaughn would learn, and the more mundane the situation the more bombastic the *non sequitur*.

He was eighteen, and a year ago his family had moved from London to — he shook his head at the absurdity — Nottingham, on the outskirts of Sherwood Forest.

"I mean, the name of their local is 'Friar Tuck's'. Do you understand my problem?" He paused, then smiled, surprised. "I *do* have a problem."

His parents were wealthy and full of plans for him. "My fathah, is a, solicitah." The look in his eyes left no doubt that his hatred of that world was complete. "They wanted me to be a happy prince. I just want to be a poet."

Vaughn had trouble picturing this dark, amphibious-looking boy as either prince or poet. But there was a story here that Lise might enjoy: the poet-frog-prince from Sherwood Forest. Europe was definitely more interesting than Canada.

Connor Peake announced that he had come here to "seek the stuff of poems". Then, looking away, he asked Vaughn, "So what do you want to be when you grow up?"

Vaughn was startled. Something flipped in his stomach. He sipped his Up Shop raisin-wine and considered. Was this Connor Peake a prodigy in truth? Was he wise? For Vaughn had the sense that Peake had seen through his surface blandness, through to his odd retardation, to the fact that he was still just a strange child, undeveloped and incapable of even the crudest passions. And from Peake's same question, a second truth dawned. What did Vaughn want to "be"? Perhaps Vaughn hadn't thought of it so simply before: one could become something other than what one was. It wasn't the same as copying.

Vaughn had no clue as to how to answer Connor Peake's question, but in any case Peake had gone back to the subject of himself.

"I want to be an alarm clock!" he shouted, pleased at this. He lifted his third glass of wine. "I want to yell, *Wake up*. If they stay bloody well asleep I'll *stab* them awake."

Why did Vaughn become addicted to Connor Peake? He'd never met anyone like him. In Canada teenagers chased girls or cars, or a spot on a hockey team, not "the stuff of poems". Peake had said he came from Earth. Vaughn had never heard anyone actually say they lived on Earth before. This was 1960, a decade before such profundities would become trite.

In Le Up Shop, Vaughn wondered aloud how poems, alarming or not, were going to wake society up. For that matter, was society asleep? Though he did have his own ideas about that: His mother. Lise. Not only fast asleep but dreaming vividly, relentlessly.

"Asleep? They're robots! *We're* robots!" cried Peake, a loud echo of his own thoughts. "Look, I quit French lessons tonight. Do you know why? I'll tell you why." He took a gulp. So did Vaughn. "Look. If you learn French, if you hang out with the natives, read your French newspaper every sleepy French morning — 'acclimatized', it's called, like it's a good thing — you get sucked up in the French sponge, no different than the old sponge. Might as well stay home. I want friction, man." Before Vaughn could respond, Peake added, "Look, do you know the Beats?"

"Beats."

"Beatniks, man. Beats. Poets, cats, crazy men."

Vaughn nodded. He'd seen pictures. He told Peake that he thought them a bit silly.

"Oh — well, hey — don't reject a movement by looking at the *followers*. The leaders are off somewhere seeking the stuff of poems. New York. San Francisco. The leaders don't even know they're the leaders. That's the point. They're *not* these sods playing bongos and wearing berets. They're the *cats,* not the copy-cats." Peake paused. "Dig?"

When Peake voiced these Americanisms, Negro expressions they sounded like, Vaughn couldn't help but see the young Englishman in white tennis togs, sprawling lawns behind him. But there were worse things than identifying with a culture and taking on its —

"They're *ripe,* man. They *see.*"

The Beats were going to liberate the popular spirit. They saw through the fetters of politics and morality. They would help the world flower. They began with themselves — physicians, healing themselves with laughter and apocalyptic words.

"So you walk into a roomful of *robotic* people," Peake summed up, "and you utter *joyous* incantations, *drunk* with truth. If they're not too far gone, they'll wake up."

"Why," Vaughn asked, "are you in Toulon? Especially if they're in New York?"

Peake, his eyes suddenly clear of rhapsody, looked at Vaughn.

"Because I'm not a copy-cat." He drained his wine crisply, set the glass down, then, pushing it with a finger, edged it off the table. The glass fell, broke, and Vaughn sat up straight.

"Because Toulon is nowhere," said Peake.

When he asked Vaughn about his own life Vaughn didn't say much. The details of his past bored him, and in truth he found it hard recalling how youth had been, exactly. He had a notion of a blank-slate purity that had become muddied somehow. He had since developed cares, like freckles on skin, or ripples on a lake. But bored. Maybe a little feverish too.

But Connor Peake called his life poetic! He thought it "wild" that he played hockey for a living, he claimed it was "poetic as *hell*" that here was Vaughn, an older bloke, alone, in a foreign country, in an unpopular town. Peake claimed they were kindred spirits.

"Well," said Vaughn. But the idea pleased him.

"It's even better you don't see it yourself. Flying over an ocean to play games with foreigners? *Small magic* in that, man. Danny Kaye!"

They ventured out into a lovely Riviera night, Peake never not talking, and walked to the young Englishman's apartment. At his doorstep Peake paused and seemed shy. Then he laughed.

"I kind of fixed it up." He threw open the door.

The apartment was one huge room, more warehouse than dwelling, but with sink, icebox, hotplate. The walls were covered with stolen signs: *Maria Grimal Fromage Roquefort, Perrier! Coca-Cola*. One wall held two Norman Rockwell posters, one of which showed a grandmother embarrassed because she'd poked her head in the bathroom to find a boy with his pants down. It had been doctored: now the old lady was surprised because the little boy had a bloody swastika on his bumcheek. In the other poster a smiling father carved Thanksgiving turkey for his smiling family, but it had been painted on as well: out of the turkey's cut breast sprayed a tide of blood, guts, and mean, wet little dwarves. This spray hit walls, windows, and guests, whose smiles became grotesque for this. Peake had taken the intestinal splatter off the painting itself, drawing it on his own wall and up onto his ceiling.

For furniture he had a battered card table, an overturned garbage can (these Peake dubbed his "study"), and a small mattress. Books, cushions lay scattered.

The room's strangest feature was its floor, which was covered completely with sheet metal. Some pieces were rusted and bent, others corrugated. When Vaughn stepped on it, it clanked.

Connor Peake saw Vaughn staring at his floor and he was pleased. He clanked over to the icebox, yelled at Vaughn to enter and sit, and returned with a fresh bottle of wine and a bowl of cold escargot.

"Look," he announced, sitting on the edge of the garbage can, "I'll tell you how I got this way."

Vaughn didn't know what "this way" meant. Again, Peake's eyes clashed fever and humour.

"Something happened to me." He talked rapidly. "I could've ended up a rich lawyer," he shrugged, "or any wank-off square you could come up with. But a year ago it was settled for me. Haven't been the same since." He had lowered his voice dramatically, and he paused to pop a cold snail into his mouth. He held it on his tongue before chewing. He looked Vaughn hard in the eye.

"Found it. Ultimate knowledge."

Vaughn's cup of wine stopped its ascent two inches from his mouth. His head tilted like a puppy's.

As Peake began talking he placed his palm on his thigh and started rubbing slowly up and down. He wore tight, bone-coloured pants, and there was a dark smudge where he rubbed. He rocked back and forth in time to his rubbing and talking.

"A bunch of us kids — we were eight or nine — we used to have this fort in the thicket." Peake's eyes were only serious now, and distant, seeing his old fort and his "thicket", whatever that was.

"One day we had this brilliant idea, raided a shed and came off with a lot of biscuit tins. We had paper and tape. We ran to our fort. And came up with these . . . *farts,* you see. Take down the pants and fart into a tin, seal her up fast. On labels we'd spell how it sounded: 'Phhttt' or 'Pweeeooo'." Peake laughed affectionately. "*Kids.* We'd fetch the tins off on forays into the lanes, open 'em up and shove 'em in girls' faces. Catch 'em skipping rope, catch 'em singing those songs, 'Queen Anne made a face, naughty knickers made of lace', that sort of wank, they deserved it, so, *bang,* a quick tin to the face. We were right little sods. Anyway, last year along I come, out on a nostalgic hike into the wilds of my childhood. I found the rotten old fort. Hello, some sealed biscuit tins. One was mine, I recognized the printing."

Connor Peake paused, caught Vaughn's eyes in his own, and then stated boldly, "I gained ultimate knowledge *smelling a ten-year-old fart.*"

Faht, is how he said it. Vaughn waited for Peake to laugh. He didn't. Vaughn took a sip of wine and settled in to listen politely. Peake saw his reaction.

"Let me *try* to explain." Peake talked extra-fast now. "Look, it all happened in one big, a big . . . *sharpness.* For years I've been trying to figure exactly what happened. And I see that within that big flash there *was* a progression. Stages. A, B, C."

Peake looked up from counting off on his fingers to make sure Vaughn was listening.

"Right: imagine being shot from a cannon, hurling

around the world and landing back on the same spot only one second later. It's only been a snap of the fingers in time, but you also know you've been — everywhere.

"Okay then: I had my nose in that jar. A timid sniff. Ugh — rotten smell! I pull back. Too late. The smell explodes. I am suddenly eight years old, at the kitchen table, forking into the braised cabbage sitting beside a chop. I am chewing. I feel cabbage go down, dissipate, digest. I feel it all — metabolism, shit, living fire. Then I am cooking the cabbage, earlier. *I am my mother*. Then, years earlier, I am breastfeeding myself. *My* nipple, and my lips. I am the *situation*."

Peake paused, breathing hard, staring at Vaughn. Vaughn stared back.

"This *gigantic instant*. I am born, *and* I'm in labour. Then I'm other people being born. I'm everybody. And dying. Eating. Everywhere. Part of it I'm eight years old, laughing at the funny sound comin' out my bum into a biscuit tin. Part of it I'm eighteen, snickering at me own foolishness, opening an old tin labelled 'Phhooot!' *All at the same time*. Time, it taught me, is our stupidity. There is no time."

Peake is on his feet now. He turned his back to Vaughn. He shrugged with a gesture of helplessness.

"At this point words are more ridiculous than they already are. There's this hurricane inside us, man, three hundred miles an hour, and, fuckin' bloody hell, we can't feel it."

Tired and dejected and drunk, Peake sat hunched on his garbage can. He took another gulp of wine.

"*I* haven't been able to, not since the tin." He reached angrily for the escargots. He tossed one at his mouth, underthrew but caught it with his front teeth. Thrusting his head forward like a dog at his dish, he got it back to his tongue.

Vaughn reclined on cushions. He swished wine in its cup.

"Well. So," said Connor Peake, "what do you think?"

Vaughn had given Peake not one facial tic. He really couldn't say what he thought. The young man's story made him recall times in his childhood, moments of especially clear vision. A stark tree. A frayed skate lace. His own fingers toying with a blanket thread. Maybe his mother's death bedside had been a small biscuit tin.

"I don't know," Vaughn said. "I just play hockey."

"Sure, man, sure. I'll bet," replied Peake, head cocked, seeing in the older man some mystery or spice Vaughn himself was confident wasn't there. That was one thing Connor Peake did with his eyes: he made Vaughn feel like an insider.

Peake sat quietly now, watching his feet. His sudden sadness gave a hint of what now seemed to be the truest thing about him. Vaughn thought of his father's sugarbeets, and how under those flamboyant leaves a glimpse of purple shoulder was all that could be seen of the five-pound beet swelling sadly in the ground below.

"Totality. Instantly *gone,*" said Vaughn's new friend. Peake's eyes searched the ceiling. He took a deep, sad breath. The notion struck the older man that it wasn't so much thought that separated humans from animals, but the affliction of yearning.

They spoke of small things for a while. Where to buy the best tomatoes. The brutish, thudding Midi accent. Peake finished another bottle of wine. He looked nearly asleep where he sat, but he kept softly talking. Suddenly he stood, laughing, pointing one finger straight up.

"But you know what it taught me?" he said excitedly, though they hadn't mentioned the subject for a while.

"I'll tell you. Look, it said to me, *nothing matters*. No *thing* matters. Be*cause* . . . " his voice fell to a hiss, "*everything* matters. It's even goddamn logical! Since everything matters, what difference does it make what we do? Doesn't fuckin' matter!" He looked around wildly, spilling wine, and swept his arm about to indicate the room. "Everything! Nothing!"

If Vaughn followed Peake's goddamn logic, he didn't do as well with what Peake said next, raging even more.

"We're talking *void,* man, and *believe* me, nothing matters. *Biff-bop-Krakow-zero*. If we're talking *all is one,* then *ergo post procter ego heck*. No — matter."

He stood over Vaughn, breathing hard. He weaved and blinked.

"Can't explain." He took a last gulp of wine and tossed the paper cup. "Have to sleep."

Vaughn was tired too. He got up.

"We didn't read poems. I talk too much," Peake said, making for his bed. He swept the books off it with his foot, then stooped to pick two up.

"Here," he mumbled, "borrow some books, okay?"

A book on Greek sculpture. The plays of Aeschylus.

"Beats're okay, man. But classics. Already *there.*" The last word exploded as he landed stomach-first on the bed.

Vaughn obediently took the books, clanked as softly as he could to the door, and let himself out.

Connor Peake. Vaughn knew he loved him right away.

His second French hockey season began, and he was up in the French Alps on a road trip with the Toulon Juniors when a telegram caught up to him. Two days before, his father had died. The funeral, so the sparse note read, was tomorrow. There was no chance to reach Winnipeg in time. Vaughn crammed the telegram in his pocket and a lid on the dark things swelling in his chest. For the next two days — coaching games, eating in restaurants with babbling Toulonaise teenagers — he felt like he had a dead father in his pocket and should be doing something about it. Vaughn searched the rinks for a man in a beaver hat who paced and clapped his gloved hands to keep warm.

Of the three bombs that fell on this year of Vaughn

Collin's life, one was Connor Peake, a kind of time-bomb who ticked and ticked. This second bomb, his father's death, fell fast. To Vaughn's deep surprise, he shattered.

Perhaps one reason he broke down so utterly was because he tried to sit on sorrow in the first place. He wasn't going to cry in front of the kids, or in front of the bus driver during the return trip, he *wasn't.* But when he walked into his dark, suddenly lonely apartment: He cried. He moaned. He wailed. He did this for days, and he thought he'd gone insane. What were these awful feelings for? Why this fire?

He learned that tears made a lens that forced you to see things.

What he endured in his La Garde apartment had no connection to years back when he saw into a mechanical, weak-minded mother and got in return a small jolt in the guts. No, when he walked into his rooms he felt his father's death horribly. He felt friendless, familyless. He felt as though his entire species had died off, that he was the last antelope on a wide prairie. Why bother to graze anymore, why roam? Even in the midst of this primordial sorrow his mind would tell itself in rational tones that his father had not known him; that their love was but a biological gimmick, the one that held together families of geese. This voice didn't help, of course. It was only a dry leaf spinning by his wet, sad antelope eyes, which were showing him things in the dark.

Funny about death though (the voice continued). The dead person had ceased to exist, or had slipped through some chink to a place the living can't see. In any case it's illogical for the survivors to be sad. The dead's troubles are likely over, yet the living flip and scream like prawns on a skillet until they exhaust themselves and settle into a small, sad death of their own, mourning.

Perhaps Vaughn became so insane with sorrow because sorrow itself was so new to him. Simply feeling it worked him up more, like panicking at one's own panic. Every glimpse into this new, Pandora's Box of emotions pried the creaky lid open wider. And once the Box is open. . . . For whatever reasons — maybe it was just all the wine he was drinking now — Vaughn Collin turned painfully human in Toulon.

Weeks, months passed, and his horror and sorrow turned to a dull but preoccupying ache. And funny (so says the voice, decades later) what grows out of death.

As he had Peake, Vaughn met Chantal de Tou in French class, when one night in walked a lithe, peach-haired new teacher of about twenty-five.

"Je suis Chantal," she said, with a slight lisp.

During the first lesson she seemed to Vaughn girlish and coy, with that confidence of knowing her own prettiness. Women like that tired him, for they thought they deserved the world. It tired him more that men tried to give them exactly that. A mindless lauding of a cute accident of birth, as blind to truth as the handing down of royalty.

The class, mostly men, loved her. They never worked harder, all for the reward of a tight smile and a widening of her eyes. So she prodded them on with the tapping stick of her beauty.

Though both she and the course were welcome diversions. His father was three months dead and he was still bleak, still shocked from the shock of it. His loneliness had grown with the days. Though he hadn't opened up much to Connor Peake during the crisis, Peake's company had helped — the blast from his mouth keeping him warm and dry — but now Peake was up in Paris on some poetic lark. Hockey, too, had lost something essential. Perhaps, Vaughn considered, it now lacked his father's approval. Also, because of the poor calibre of play, he'd taught himself to perform at half-speed, not wanting to appear a show-off. Now this habit had gone solid somehow: even when he wanted to he could no longer abandon himself to his stomach, and fly. So the game lost its joy, and whatever slim reason it had.

After several weeks of watching Chantal de Tou work the class, Vaughn began to notice how she treated him differently. Her eyes went wider when he answered correctly, her grin was more condescendingly sweet. She'd keep her eyes wide to hold his noncommittal stare, and drop her lips to a pout of sympathy and sadness. He had her figured out. She had eyes for him only because he was the one man who did not blush or toady up when his name was called.

But she was irrelevant to his pain. She was an actress and an ornament.

One stormy night in December, Chantal drew him aside after class. As if nervous, her smile suffered small spasms as she spoke. Jealous men gathered books and pretended not to listen to her proposition. With a good act of shyness Mlle. de Tou asked him to join her for coffee. Vaughn agreed. It gave him no pride. She would be a pretty waste of time.

They sipped coffee and she asked the usual questions: did he like France? Where was his home? They spoke English. She had a trained, old-fashioned accent which briefly took him back, absurdly, to Lise in snow caves telling him about Becky's dreams. Vaughn gave Chantal little back and talked in monotone, all the while searching the dark corners of Le Up Shop for a clue to the trick of happiness.

He noticed her eyeing him mischievously, and with her teasing classroom smile she said, "You never get excited. I find you very boring, you know?"

"Yes," he replied a bit snottily, "I've cultivated my boring side for years."

"Ah. Is that right?" she said, keeping her smile.

"When I was born I saw that life was too exciting. This won't do, I said. So I grabbed every boring moment I could. It was a battle, but I won." It just happened. He had stumbled into his bygone bridge-table humour. Half-truth, helped along by a cynical mood. He continued.

"Now everything is boring. My life is a dull lake under a grey sky."

"How very sad for you," said Chantal, playing along.

"I fool everybody. Especially women. They think I am Clark Kent, with Superman hiding under here." He tapped his chest. "They look at me and say, 'Still water runs deep.' No, mademoiselle. In and out, out and in, I am *pain de mie.*"

By now, Chantal was laughing. "The bread's middle! Yes! I think you are right!" She looked at him now with eyes that laughter had cleaned of any act. But was this a wider, better act?

"Do you know," she said, "in France is it *pas normal* for a woman to ask a man — and a foreigner — to such a place as this?" She gestured at the linoleum-souled bar as if it were an opium den. Connor Peake, Vaughn found himself thinking, would call her a lightweight.

He changed the subject, disturbed by her open seductiveness. Strangely, he did not want to forget his mourning. They talked for a while longer and then left Le Up Shop only to discover that they took the same bus home. Sitting there on the bench in a cold wind and drizzle, Chantal asked if he'd please sit close and put his arm around her, which he did. Why not. In France a touch meant nothing. They kissed their worst enemies on both cheeks and gave it not a thought.

They had a half-hour to wait. Surprising him, putting her mouth up almost into his ear so he could feel her breath, she softly asked him why he was so sad. He hesitated but, seeing no harm, told her about his father. He suspected his sadness had more to it than that, but he had no words.

"Ah!" she said, turning from him to proclaim with finality to the street, "so you are *very lonely.*"

They sat quietly then, his silence affirming what she had just said. She nudged in closer. Both of them stared at the lights reflecting off the sleek, black road. Chantal lapsed into a typically French, gay, schoolgirlish voice.

"So it is simple. You need love."

Vaughn sat there dully, not exactly shocked, for he had seen it coming. But why had she chosen him? She was almost beautiful. She could have anyone in the class. Perhaps it was because he was the oldest. Maybe because he seemed aloof, a challenge. Or maybe she was honest and did feel his loneliness and moved irresistibly towards it. Some women, he knew, were drawn to deprived men. He saw Lise's face loom up, but he easily blinked her away.

"I lied," Chantal said now, her soft voice again in his ear. "This is not my bus. I live in Toulon. But I would like to go ride home with you."

No question now. And he was still man enough to rise to her suggestion. He hadn't been with a woman since Lise, almost two years ago. Chantal: desirable, warm. Exotic in her French ways. But something fought his urge to abandon himself to what waited for them after a bus ride. His sorrow rose in his stomach like an old castle wall, and Chantal was but a bird singing outside. That was it! Was his need for sorrow bigger than his need for love? It couldn't be. It was sick.

Because he was connected to this woman. He was. Together, they sat in the exact middle of a wet Toulon night. Every time she pressed his shoulder with hers their nerves hit tinnily to course in a stream he could feel pool at his toes and the roots of his hair. An idea connected them too: lust hung between them as solid as a bottle of red wine standing unopened on a table.

The bus arrived in a roar and a splash. She turned to him just as he turned to her, and just before he kissed her to seal at least one night of shared fate, his fancy made him see her as another antelope trotting up out of the melodramatic darkness, a teasing smile of welcome on her face, her legs long and graceful, her bearing erect and proud, and her muscles as taut and eager as his. Boarding their bus, following her up, he fancied her lifting a stiff, short tail. He breathed in deep — as any antelope would, alone on a vast prairie with such a beauty.

April 15th

Sunlight needled its way through the burlap drapes this morning and made me say to myself, like a corny old bastard in a Norman Rockwell, "Well darn it, I'm goin' fishin'."

Once out there though, me rowing a bit to keep the bait active and attractive, I remembered why I haven't sport-fished much lately. It's not that it's boring: I can still sit hours waiting on the big strike. My hunter's joy still peaks when a salmon breaks water fifty yards out. But a dullness descends in fishing's aftermath. Perhaps it's simple guilt. Not so much when I tear the cold chain of guts from a salmon's belly, but when I first bonk its head. Not a lot of guilt, but it's there. I look down at my newly bonked fish. Was it worth it?

Sometimes I imagine I can sense — not see, sense — its fishy soul going out, easing from the cold flesh while the fins shudder in the bilge-water. Its mouth relaxes open.

A fish's nervous system and capacity for pain isn't much more than a grasshopper's, but it does feel pain. And I suspect that in the greater scheme a salmon shares my right to exist. It certainly *fights* like it does. So sometimes guilt hits when my hooked salmon rises beside the boat, tired but still fighting, sitting on its tail, head out of the water, shaking it wearily, knowing the hook's there and what must be done to free it, but just too tired. It can see me — it knows it's being pulled towards this tall demon from the upper world.

There's that Indian thing that says a hunter doesn't want to kill, but must for food. He prays to the deer god, and the next day he encounters the deer that was "arranged". He thanks it, shoots. And one of Annie's monk stories tells of this monk who is ordered to catch fish for the monastery.

But he is so full of compassion for the lives he must snuff that he can't bring himself to bait his hook or even drop it in the water. So there he sits, dangling a bare hook above the surface. The fish though, so taken with the monk's full heart, jump up one after another, gladly snagging themselves.

I caught nothing this morning. Maybe I should try some strategic compassion?

With my nets it's different. There's a distance in meeting the general, not the individual creature. I catch a load for sale, I haul the fish aboard fighting mad and aloof, and I bonk them while they're still surprised. There's no slow torture, no "sport", as we demons call it, from our end of the line.

So is it worth it? I know I'll sport-fish again, alert in a calm spring morning, alert for strikes . . .

Braising my winter bones in the rare sun I drifted in and out of thoughts about my years in France. My team, eagerly inept as a high-school orchestra. Chantal. Connor Peake. Annie jokes about those years as "our divorce". But it's sad, really, that I missed the best time of her life, her years of mystery, miracles. A stepped-on crocus bends back into the spring sun, grows despite the mud all over it. Rebirth, the stuff of fairy-tales — it does happen.

I look at her now and sometimes see only Lise. Then I catch sight — it's like a faint physical blow — of Annie.

Dipping a quiet oar, anticipating strikes, I thought of our "divorce" years and how our lives were shaped by who we chose to be with. Perhaps "chose" isn't the word. Perhaps I was incapable of choosing someone like Ivan; perhaps only gaudiness could attract me, like a crow. So, Connor Peake.

From what I've heard about Ivan, he would not be noticed at a party. Though women, says Annie, would draw round him without knowing it. He once told Annie, who since told me: Avoid extreme personalities. They are the whipped.

If I'd met him when I was thirty-five I probably wouldn't even have seen him. Annie was ready for Ivan's quiet steadiness, and I was ready for Connor Peake.

Boredom gets people addicted to all sorts of things. Drugs. Cleanliness. TV. Food. Fishing. It makes people go insane. It's made more than one tribe pick up its spears one bored morning and go to war.

Boredom, says Annie, is one of the hardest emotions to work with because it's so "small" and hard to see, yet it's deadly and as ubiquitous as gravity, droning on and on. It's an unspringy diving-board we try to do double-flips to escape from. God, look at any teenager.

Once I first tasted boredom it's followed me everywhere. Bella Combe is no exception. How bored have I been here? Bored enough to know that wood ducks spend an average of two hours feeding to one hour resting. Bored enough to know that, averaged over thousands of games, the median Las Vegas–style solitaire score is twenty-eight.

How, *how* is it possible that boredom exists in the first place? We are alive and don't know what this means, we're riding a ball of rock through space, while the greatest drama — what will happen to us in life, then death — stays unresolved, poignant. In the midst of *this* we get bored.

In all self-study Annie makes me reach my own conclusions, but in the case of boredom she's given hints, and says that boredom has less to do with laziness than with fear. That being bored is actually a state of being "stunned" with fear. I can feel this. In any case, in my dutiful study of boredom I've found that, ironically enough, embracing the minutest details of boredom might be boredom's only cure.

Connor Peake handled it a different way. When life got quieter, he got louder. He did see this in himself. Hung-over, momentarily apologetic, in the morning he might say, I guess I Peaked again last night.

And his way was catching. If I can say one true thing

about my young friend it's that in the time I was with him I wasn't bored. *Pas d'ennui avec lui.* Perhaps I was easily pleased. Perhaps I just absorbed his fear.

No salmon but it was still a good way to spend a morning. I gave up and threw my herringbait to the gulls, who screamed and fought over it. Flying rats, they have no ethics whatever. The boss gulls miss the food I throw because they're too busy screeching and pecking the smaller ones away. So the bait sinks, fades silver to white to grey, food now for crabs.

A difficult task, this one, to dream back to the early 1960s and try to get teenage Connor Peake right. Over the years his showmanship changed. I'll try to get him down as I first saw him, bright against the dark backdrop of my father's death. Peake the firecracker. Chantal the fire.

Adolescence on the Riviera

> *Sex interrogates civilization.*
>
> — Annie's aphorism

They became fast friends, calling each other "Peake" and "Collin" in the manner of English school chums. Collin rode Peake's wanton energy, and Peake carried the older man easily. They explored Cheecago. Sometimes Chantal joined them. She laughed at Peake's jokes and general oddness, and clung to Collin's foreign arm much as Collin clung to Peake's foreign ways. But Chantal taught most evenings. Between her teaching and Vaughn's hockey they were lucky to see each other more than one night a week.

Cheecago still repelled Collin; Peake loved it. Once when they passed the dungeon-like Bar Nautique and Vaughn told him what a dive it was, Peake insisted on going in.

The same mopey eel served their tiny table. The same ceiling fan clicked overhead. They sat in darkness near the toilet door and the smell of old urine. Vaughn announced that he found the atmosphere depressing.

"But why can't you dig *that?*" Peake said. "Now, *large* depression, like having your dad die, right?" He made his eyes wide in sympathy. "We can do without large depression. But this? *Small* depression. Sad old stories being told here. This bar," he concluded, brightening in the gloom, "beautiful as a burnt-out cathedral."

Peake was full of tales from a trip to Paris. He'd met amazing poets, he said, some true Beats. One, Midier Six his name was, composed the most outrageous work, and orated mostly to bums, *les clochards,* as he walked the alleys at night. He felt destined to become one of them. (Vaughn, recalling Lise's state, wanted to question the romance of this notion, but Peake talked non-stop.) Another poet, Gaston Bitchelieu, was writing a series of concrete poems in the shapes of hieroglyphs, the aim being to gain freedom from slavish ties to the alphabet.

"Bitch 'n' Six," Peake said, in love with their names as well, "man, we did some *talking.*"

He described a group of writers who met weekly to read, drink, and "talk about Heaven and Hell". Most of them were American, and several English, and one Canadian woman.

"Expatriates!" yelled Connor Peake, including Vaughn in this word with his shining romantic eyes.

They drank Bordeaux, the past summer's yield, just recently in town. Peake claimed he could taste in it the warm earth and gentle hills of its region. He also claimed he could taste the naïvety in lamb and the anger in rabbit. Vaughn had no reason to doubt him. Who was he to say, when it came to Connor Peake, what was imagination and what was not?

Their skinny waitress laid down their glasses with a slight sneer, it seemed to Vaughn. Only *les étrangers* drank wine apart from meals.

"I think I love her," Peake whispered as he watched the droop-haired, chicken-breasted woman mope away.

"You don't!" replied Vaughn, sounding British.

"Yes. Look at her. She's starving. It's Dickens. It would be like bringing a dead leaf back to life."

When she came with the next round he tipped her.

"No teep. You buy me Chivas Regal, and I sit and talk."

"Yes!" Peake exclaimed.

The waitress pulled a bottle from under the bar and poured herself a tiny glass. At their table she demanded the money before she sat. Vaughn could see her face was covered with a mist of fine freckles. Peake paid, smiling regally. Eight francs!

"Scuze," she said, set down her drink and left for the washroom.

Vaughn tasted it. Cheap whiskey, watered down. He told Peake, who watched his detective work with amusement.

"It's the rules, man. Watch, I'll ask her. She won't mind."

He was right, she didn't mind. Her name was Marie and, never smiling, she answered whatever Peake asked. Vaughn translated. Chantal was an excellent teacher.

Marie told him that a bar girl's job was to hustle drinks. Chivas only, and a girl got to keep half the money. She wasn't paid a cent for waitressing. The "Chivas" of hers was watered so the owner made more money. Marie related this news matter-of-factly.

"I admire the honesty of your deceit," Peake told her. Vaughn translated. Marie shrugged.

Peake claimed amazement that she was able to make her living this way. Marie explained.

"After a Chivas, I am allowed to love my customers."

Peake had more questions now. Did she support her parents? Did she like her work?

"Do you like yours?" she asked them both with a knowing boredom.

Peake told her he was a poet.

"Ah. I knew this, that you are rich. So you will buy me another Chivas, and we will talk more." She gulped the remains of her drink and smiled for the first time that night. Peake borrowed some money from his older friend.

Again she demanded payment before joining them. She suggested that the young poet might like more than just talk. Peake pondered comically as Marie ran down a list of prices.

"For this," she said, making a functional circle of her mouth and pressing a finger to her lower lip, "is six francs." Less than a drink! thought Vaughn.

"That is there in the back." She gestured to the black ass-end of the tavern. "But in my room, you pay ten. For one long night, is twenty-five."

Peake told her he couldn't leave his friend alone, so he'd take the first one.

"Ah. And there is a better first one. The better is twelve francs."

"Yes! The better one!"

"But tonight, I am very very busy. So tonight is fifteen." Marie made no attempt at good acting.

"The busy one then! Yes!"

Vaughn had to say something. It was his money Peake was losing.

"She's playing with you," he whispered sternly at Peake, though he sensed that somehow the reverse was true.

But Collin was ignored. With jaunty steps, like a child playing parade, Peake followed Marie's path to the gloom through which she'd disappeared. Then he turned back to yell, "How does Chantal play with you?" Those eyes of his.

Vaughn sat back, sipped, and lit one of his friend's Gauloises, "the cigarette of the people". Peake's remark had found a target.

Chantal and he were getting on well enough. Once he'd decided to bring her into his loneliness, he had tried to open his doors as best he could. But how far had she walked in? She persisted in first hesitating then "succumbing" at his bedside. He admitted he found it erotic, her playing innocent, predictable as it was.

Yes, he thought, she seemed so warm on the outside, warm as a plump, beautiful bird. But he could sense the actress behind her loving eyes.

In bed she taught him exotic games. But as they manoeuvred there on the mattress, the blankets flung off, unwelcome as skin that deadened touch, she never seemed truly caught up, never mindless in her loving, never abandoned as clumsy Lise had been. Teaching a new trick, Chantal was cool, patient, in class.

Though it was unfair to compare the only two lovers he had known, what a difference. Sturdy, limping Lise. Lithe Chantal, with all her shades of lipstick and the grace of the land that had invented romance. But there was another difference, one that grew more disturbing the more Vaughn thought about it: Lise, though confused, wanted to feed him. Chantal, it seemed, worked hardest at keeping him hungry.

He drained his wine glass. The answer was simple. They just needed more time. Chantal and he had to become better friends. Lise and he had been friends first. That was it.

Peake returned shamelessly wiping sweat from his forehead. He bounced less as he walked but still his impish smile. As he sat he exhaled, "Whoo!" and pretended to straighten a tie. It suddenly occurred to Vaughn that this young man might not have been with girls much.

He wasn't disgusted with him, though he wouldn't have bought a whore himself. Since Lise's confessions, the image of prostitutes rankled. Besides giving Peake a half-hearted fraternal leer, Vaughn didn't comment. They ordered more wine, this time delivered by an obese blonde, Molly, who stared only at Vaughn. At the bar, Marie pulled on a cigarette hard, as if to scour her insides with smoke.

"What did you mean, 'How does Chantal play with you'?" Vaughn asked, surprised at himself.

"C'mon mate. You know."

"No. I don't," Vaughn insisted. "Not really." He just wanted Peake's version of it. He got more than he expected.

"Well, cheers then." Peake spoke quietly. "She bosses you around so much. And face facts — she loves it." He paused. "And so might you."

Vaughn considered this. When out together Chantal demanded of him all the rites and services normally asked of a man. He would rise to hurry her drink along from a waiter, or search out a toothpick or napkin. Sometimes she had him follow and wait for her outside the ladies' room. He didn't mind doing these things, not at all. For all lovers' kindnesses were repaid in full.

"She gives me what I want, too."

"Man, enough said. None of my business. But you know what she calls you? According to Lucille" — Chantal's friend Lucille sometimes came along to make it a double date. Vaughn gathered she and Peake had slept together — "According to Lucille, Chantal calls you her 'big Canadian pull-toy'."

La Bar Nautique was waking up. At the back was a small stage, and behind a tiny drum kit a young drummer began to tap a rhythm on his snare. He appeared to be mongoloid, with curved ears, slack mouth, and overlarge head shaped like a green pepper.

Walking in stutter-step across the small dance floor, and dropping her shoulder to the beat, one of the bar girls did a twirl with her trayful of drinks and then delivered them, to laughter.

Big Canadian toy. Pull-toy. But who knew what she really meant by this? Third-hand news has usually shed its truth.

Vaughn said to Peake, "No big deal." He smiled without

feeling it.

"You're right!" Peake laughed, the kind of laugh that showed he wasn't telling all.

"Right: I know what it is. It's her father. I'll bet Daddy was in the Resistance, fought the Hun with a *baguette*. And when us lads came in and won it for them, and gave them wank-buckets of money to boot, old man Chantal hated us. Go ahead, ask her. Her resentment of you is sympathy for *him*. It's Freud, man. *Baguettes* galore."

"Right," Vaughn answered, Peake's Britishisms invading his speech more and more these days. The last thing he wanted to hear about was Freud. He'd had enough of that with Lise. "Annie".

"She doesn't 'resent' me," Vaughn insisted. "That's rubbish."

Peake sat chuckling to himself. Then became serious.

"One more thing Lucille told me. She told me you must never tell Chantal you love her. She said Chantal would keep you around as long as you never told her that." He smiled unsympathetically. "Small mystery, eh? It's called *French Woman,* man."

Yes, a mystery. Because any talk of love came solely from her end. He avoided the word, half due to that messiness with Lise and half because, though he gave Chantal all he was capable of giving, he didn't think that what he felt for her was called "love". He'd read in books: Earth shatters, oaths are sealed in lovers' blood, hearts soar to Heaven. Vaughn's didn't.

Peake could see his talk troubled him, but a mouth that couldn't stop compelled him to say more.

"Man, look: we all know everything. So do you. *Everything.*"

Vaughn could think of nothing to say. The topic had made him nervous. And Peake looked impatient with him. To both their relief, the bartender took control by flipping a wall switch.

The bar fell to a hush as it filled with red light. Heads turned to watch two musicians, one with accordion and the other with dented guitar, wade through layers of red cigarette smoke to the stage, where the big-headed drummer used a cymbal now — *tish* toomptoomp — to welcome them.

In the light Vaughn could see other customers, rats caught in a red dawn. Old sailors with black hands, tiny caps, vacant faces. A sick-skinny old man with a bulbous nose was bent asleep at his table, a dry fruit rind on a curbstone. The musicians tuned up and otherwise all was expectant. The red glow, steady drum beat and silent waiting gave the shabby bar a ritualistic, mystical air.

"This is . . . *wow!*" uttered Peake, transfixed now by the couples gathering on the dance floor. Money changed hands. "One franc, one dancing," a girl shouted in English at a foreign sailor. A huge man had Marie rigidly at arm's length, waiting for music, while a tiny, ancient tar chewed his gums and waited glassy-eyed with the big one, Molly. His head, Vaughn fancied, would fit perfectly between her breasts; and at the first cloying honks of the accordion that was where he put it.

With a "whoop!" Peake was up. He dug into his empty pocket, then dragged Vaughn's money off the table and searched for a girl to dance with.

Vaughn sipped wine and watched the band. The guitarist strummed with flair but was drowned out by the accordion and couldn't be heard at all. The young drummer pounded on as steadily as a machine. Vaughn saw the family likeness then. The accordionist father led them with nods and quick glances, his fingers running with spider-speed up and down the worn keys.

He could see Peake bobbing with his girl in a dark corner.

Vaughn envied him. Envy he was capable of now. Peake,

returned after several dances, manic and grinning. He downed his wine and signalled for more. When Molly came Vaughn put his hand over his glass. But then, seeing the flush-cheeked Peake welcome the wine with thirst and hunger both, and suspecting that in this hunger lay a clue to joy, Vaughn changed his mind. He lifted his hand off his glass and watched the ruby liquid trickle in.

And so they spent a night in La Bar Nautique. Peake infatuated with all that went on, his vigour began rubbing off on Vaughn. The smoke, the drummer a gargoyle in red haze, the sweetly sour music, the ceiling fan, the grotesque couples moving stiffly in and out of shadows; the old, wrecked men bold again with the bored prostitutes. Drinking it all in, Vaughn felt certain for a time that he did know everything.

At one point, Peake, his eyes on fire, brought his glass up for a toast. Then he threw his bead back and yelled.

"Yeah, ohhh . . . *butt* fuck, *tit* bang, *cheeter* hoop, *Ginsberg.*"

Vaughn started in his seat, spilling a bit of wine.

Peake grinned slyly and tossed off his wine.

"Sounds like a dactyl," Vaughn said, recovering, trying dry humour.

"Yeah? Fuck you. Here's a *pteradactyl.*" He threw his head back once more. "*Dog*-water, *bush*-beef, piss-egg-*jerky. First big nigger.*"

Vaughn quickly looked around. Heads turned their way, then back to their business. They heard worse here.

Peake was explaining. "Kind of poetry. Cleans the devils out. You try it."

Peake insisted. Vaughn took a self-conscious gulp of wine, a shallow breath, and worked up a hoarse kind of hiss.

"*Knock*wurst . . . garbage can . . . *Chantal* . . . *knock*ers!"

"Right," said Connor Peake, face falling. He turned from Vaughn to seek more exotic sights. "Spot on."

Months later, a perfect spring morning, Chantal and Vaughn were climbing the narrow road to the ruined castle of La Garde when he asked her to move in with him.

Good weather brought out the best in Chantal. He understood her beauty now, one brought out by its imperfections: her lips were a bit thin, and her hair tended to oiliness as, in the French manner, she often let her hair fall to its natural lubricated state, sleek as metal. But any thinness to her beauty was fleshed out by a rich animalness that hung around her.

Halfway up, they passed his favourite spot. In a partial crater an ancient stone house squatted against the black granite, and here lived the current groundskeeper. The crater floor was flat and damp and covered with the brightest green grass, kept closely cropped by two white goats tethered to pegs. A dozen geese, also white, waddled about the lawn foraging. A fairy-tale scene. The crater air held the charged stillness of caves.

They climbed another five minutes and reached the base of the castle tower. It was there he asked her.

"Vaughn, no, not now, I — " She wouldn't look at him. Then pointing, she said, "Oh, Vaughnie, get me that flower!"

He hesitated. That the flower lay closer to her than to him didn't bother him; it did bother him to be turned down and bossed around both within the space of two seconds.

He handed her the daisy, and asked why not. She pouted at the assaulted flower in her hand, not answering. Using a trick out of perhaps ten movies he'd seen, he reached out and brought her chin up with his crooked index finger. And what a true, Hollywood sight he beheld at arm's length: her fawn face and liquid eyes framed by castle stone and sprawling countryside vista, all bathed in a continental spring morning. The azure Mediterranean sparkled in the hazy distance. A butterfly should have landed on his Chantal's nose.

"Why not?"

"Oh, Vaughn, can't we just leave it as it is?"

No. "As it is" had compelled him to ask her to move in in the first place. "As it is" meant a lovers' impasse, a lack of depth and understanding.

For years he'd observed other couples, in Beauséjour, in Victoria, and now in France, and Vaughn conceded that Chantal and he had what some people called love. But to Vaughn — because he was still so new at it? — there seemed to be *an ocean* left to plumb, an ocean Chantal was choosing not to see. In bed, anywhere, he felt the need to give in completely, to open wide the old oak doors of his chest and press this yearning space against her, open chest to open chest, to have their secret selves flow in and out and mix. Sometimes he felt this so badly he shook with it. But Chantal withdrew from these moods of his and the loving looks he forced on her.

No, "as it is" wasn't enough. In fact, he sometimes wondered if his yearning had anything to do with Chantal at all, or whether he yearned for some potential she merely symbolized. But, no, she was more than that. Of course she was. Look at her. More time together, Vaughn decided, and Chantal would succumb to his need just as she had succumbed to his loneliness.

There was another problem he thought time would solve. As for sex, all he had to compare her with was Lise, earthy Lise, whose orgasms had come easily. Both of them just did what they did, and there was Lise laughing tiredly with what her body had just done. With Chantal, sex seemed perfect at first. Then too perfect. She was loud in bed, and her climax she'd announce in plaintive, piping cries. This always happened exactly when Vaughn reached his. At first he thought, what a fit! But then — as would happen at times — whenever he finished early, unexpectedly, Chantal would immediately reach a peak of her own. This knack of hers for instant ecstasy seemed odd. So he began testing her. He would pretend climax at unexpected times, giving no advance hint, and always Chantal sang out her clock-work crescendo. This lie of hers was selfless enough, but left Vaughn feeling hollow. Taking her to task one night, he told her how sorry he was she did not always orgasm.

"But of course I do! You don't hear me?" she said in a singsong. "Of course I do — you're a wonderful lover."

Strange, what she said last. Then he realized the implication. Her lack of pleasure was his fault, and she had to sing a lie to save his face.

But all this time could cure. What else but time was left? For he had done everything he could think of to bridge their gap. Lately he'd even been telling her that he loved her. And, good god — though his name was still Vaughn Hardy Collin, emotional dunce — perhaps he did.

His living-in suggestion had upset her. He followed her back down the hill. He watched the delicious machine of her rear. He could not see her hands but, one by one, petals appeared from under her feet as she picked apart her daisy. At the stone house the caretaker was outside with a pail, feeding the geese. He threw the hard pellets of grain with a violence not suited to the task, Vaughn thought. Then he saw the man was trying to hit the birds. Vaughn couldn't see his face. The geese raced to and fro, torn between their hunger for food and the sting of it.

Vaughn caught Chantal's shoulder and asked her to reconsider. He gave reasons. They would be together so much more. Hey, she wouldn't have rent to worry about. She could save, go to England again, take more courses. They could set up house, share food, toothpaste . . . The thought that he could do this with Chantal — try a chair there, then there; arrange favourite spices on the shelf; watch her fold his shirts against her chest — rimmed his eyes with tears and made his throat swell.

But again she refused. Why? he asked. Why? Why?

Her singsong. "Oh I am so busy with my teaching. And you always off with your hockey." She paused, a dip into sincerity. "What would I do at night, stuck out here in La Garde? Climb to this *château* in the dark? *Poff!*" She flung her hand angrily at the castle to wave it away, as if it were not stone but a trifle.

"Was your father in the Resistance?" Vaughn asked, then felt instantly foolish. Damn Peake.

"No, he was not. Why do you ask this?"

He shrugged stupidly.

"Oh, you. *Poff.*" She gave his face the same wave.

Before he knew it he was telling her he would quit hockey. His father had left him a little money, had he not? He could get a job, perhaps teach English, perhaps in the same school!

Chantal turned uphill to him, but kept her eyes on his chest.

"Vaughn-Vaughn, don't you see? I have other friends. It would be . . . *strange* for them to know I lived with a man."

" . . . friends?" He felt suddenly weak.

"Friends, Vaughn," she said. To the persistent flame in his eyes she added, "Men. *Yes,* men."

Of course. She often told him what she did nights they weren't together, casually mentioning a movie or restaurant, always with "people you don't know". Why had he assumed these people were women?

"Friends, oh." Hardly able to talk, he managed a gruff, "Like . . . me?"

"No, of course not, you fool," she answered, lightly. And in her singsong voice, "You are my only love."

"I . . . am . . . your . . . only . . . love," he repeated.

"Yes," she chirped, and turned to continue down the hill.

Vaughn stayed where he was. He closed his eyes.

"Then — marry me." No. He didn't want her that badly. But yes he did! Yes he did!

No matter, she refused him anyway, all the way down

the hill. When they reached the bottom she whirled around, flirting again. She played with his collar, cooed and whispered in his ear how none of that mattered, none of it mattered. In breathless baby-talk, she suggested they go to his room.

Yes. His room. But, god, how he wanted to break through that changeable face of hers, pierce her paradox of little girl and teacher, through to a heart she would not let him see. She kept him so hungry.

They spent a beautiful summer on the beach. Chantal had a month off and Vaughn had no duties of his own. Sometimes Peake joined them. It was clear he liked watching Chantal in her white bathing suit. So did Vaughn. But Peake burned easily, and got restless doing nothing, "lolling," as he put it, "like a tourist in the dirt". He'd been spending more time in Paris of late. He'd had a poem published in a Paris journal and now he felt apart from the scene.

Vaughn had bought a vehicle to take Chantal to and from the beach. An old postal van, olive green, a single-cylinder slowpoke that actually went *putt-putt* as it laboured along. Peake had selected it for him, claiming he was "ripe for something eccentric". Peake christened the van "Ferlinghetti".

Vaughn's teammate Papillon ran a small business on the beach, renting out sailing dinghies. Vaughn would take over sometimes. He loved the small mystery he became when a French tourist gave him a look and tried to figure out his strange accent. He felt like Bogart: a cool devil who had mastered the ins-and-outs of a foreign land. Few American tourists visited, preferring Nice or St. Tropez, but when they did, for the entertainment of Peake and Chantal, Vaughn pretended he was a Frenchman angry that they'd come to his country yet not speak its language. He'd huff and spit in a rancid pidgin English, "Rent baht one ho*wer*, five franc. Rent baht whole day, twenty franc. You CLEEN boat, haf*ter.*"

He could sail whenever he wanted. Deathly afraid of water, Chantal refused to go with him. So he would see her settled down with a book and then set off on his own, heading straight from shore until he reached the edge of the tidal silt where the water turned dark turquoise. He took down the sail to drift, letting the wavelets rock his little cradle. He'd dream, flying in one second from France to Victoria, from Mrs. Peen's parlour to his old Beauséjour bedroom, from a clunky Toulon hockey game to a hushed, twenty-below-zero face-off under a crisp Manitoba sky, every breath a quick, white puff. Sometimes he had an urge to drop a baited line in the water to see what strange candy-coloured creature he could entice from this water. The Mediterranean, sea of myth. Vaughn imagined only the most solitary fish inhabiting it. They would have human eyes.

One hot August day on the beach he opened Lise's latest letter. Like all of her recent ones it was preachy and dry.

"Dear Vaughn," it read, "It is said we are creatures of habit. But that wording sidesteps the dilemma: we are *prisoners* of habit. How to escape the prison. The odds are against us. But if we persist, we discover a fount of energy, a state of being, far beyond what we have ever known. But we must first give up our dreams and our ghosts. *Dammit,* Vaughn — good luck. Annie."

Lise's earlier letters had been less tiresome, a blend of "Why did you leave?" and "Ivan is helping me so much". Out of duty, every few months he'd jot her back the latest news. Her letters grew long, page after page of this Ivan's theories, which seemed to Vaughn like so much pain-born babble, a compendium of impossible stages and goals. At least as dream-like, he thought, than those same dreams she accused humanity of being stuck with.

In later letters Lise apologized for wordiness, saying she'd had too little knowledge of "Ivan's system" to explain it properly. Her attempts were premature, she said. So now she gave only short aphorisms like, "Knowledge lies inward, and will eventually consume the illusion of an outer world." She made no more mention of the Lise–Vaughn dilemma. She wrote less often.

Vaughn wrote more. He felt slightly irritated when the "I love you"s and the pleas for his return stopped. Who was this Ivan? Only after a year had passed and Lise's letters had fallen to the skeletal gist of Ivan's wisdom did he realize he had fallen prey to his own "letter effect". But he doubted she intended that.

He had new feelings for Lise. She did seem sober now, but a sobriety strange and tainted, encased as it was in those gothic letters. Letter effect or not, he began writing her long, rambling ones, his main reason for doing so not to hear about her new ladder to heaven but instead to describe his new hell: unrequited love for Chantal de Tou.

It felt good to spell it all out to Lise, imagining himself atop a lighthouse sending distress signals across the black Atlantic. In one letter, lying, but so thrilled to write the words, he told her Chantal and he were at last going to be married.

One hot day, squinting like a cave-fish caught in the sun, Peake raised his head from his beach towel and said in a way that included them all, *"Paris."* Vaughn glanced at Chantal. Why not? her bored look said.

They jumped into Ferlinghetti and within an hour were putt-putting north, three of them crammed in front like kids. Chantal was tweeting like a bird again, and Peake out of his mind, rifling through sheafs of poems at a loss to decide "what to read to the City of Paris". He had decided to do a public reading. Vaughn's duffel kit, Chantal's suitcase, and Peake's shopping bag bounced on an old mattress in back.

On their spin through Toulon, Peake made Vaughn stop by Cheecago and La Bar Nautique. He wanted to ask skinny

Marie to come.

"She's perfect for Paris," he said. "So sour."

It seemed he wanted someone on his arm the night of his performance. Vaughn was glad Marie wasn't at work yet. Prostitutes were just sad. He bought bread, cheese, pâté, wine. He let Peake take the wheel. Better now than later, after the wine got opened. Peake proved a conservative driver, Vaughn was surprised to see. His foot rode the pedal so lightly and he took such timid corners he seemed wary of arriving in Paris at all. He drove deep in thought, perhaps composing. Vaughn watched his preoccupied gaze. He looked to be driving from a tenth of his consciousness, while the rest of him hung painfully suspended, from the colossal meat-hook of art. If art was religion, Connor Peake aimed at sainthood. A piety so raw, an ambition that laughed at fame and sought but to climb onto the hot lap of his god. Vaughn envied his friend this passion.

They hoped to make Lyon by night. Chantal chided Vaughn for his slow vehicle but busied herself pointing out historical this and scandalous that. "You cannot see it but behind that hill are the baths where. . . ." She folded a newspaper on her lap to make little sandwiches. Occasionally she moved in front of Vaughn, her chest flattening on his, to offer up to Peake a knife-impaled piece of cheese.

"Ah . . . Ah?" she asked. Her knife bounced between his nose and chin.

"Mmm . . . Mmm," Peake replied, raising his eyebrows to tell her it was secure in his mouth, and good.

When the meal was over Chantal hummed while she carved shapes out of the block of cheese. Some of her art she nibbled distractedly, others she forced on the two men. Never a frugal sort, she threw the rest out the window. Vaughn didn't interfere. Tired and giddy, Chantal looked ready to bicker.

They opened wine and Vaughn took the wheel, Peake

insisting they do so all at once, and at top speed. It appealed to his sense of "contained chaos", as he put it. So he and Vaughn clambered over and under while Chantal, for background noise, pulled a cork.

They neared Lyon. Peake turned on the interior light to go through his poems. He read some aloud. One was written in Elizabethan dialect, a flowery affair about a young couple who on their wedding night were frightened by each other's genitals. It ended with a diatribe on lovers being too civilized.

"*Non*. Too, too juvenile," said Chantal, though she knew far less about poetry than Vaughn did. She gave Peake a look, and said, "An English hang-up, *non?*"

"Ah," said Peake, giving her a look back, "right then." He rolled down the window. He thrust out the faulty page, which rattled in his hand before he released it into the suck of the night.

"Connor! No!" Chantal laughed.

Peake looked down, pleased with himself.

He next read from a long poem which was painfully obscure. Meaningless, Vaughn wanted to say. A long version of one of his "cheeter-hoop" screams. Chantal said, "Hmmmm," and, *"C'est vachement drôle."*

"Let's have a go at this one then. Somewhat of an essay, with heart," Peake said. When describing his own writing he spoke formally, soberly. "About writing. It's called 'Words Are Stillborn Babies'."

He took a heartfelt pull of wine, a deep breath, and with sonorous voice launched into the first page:

> And when will these very words rear up from their crouch on this pallid sheet, rise full face to mine, stand and pig-face me as the dwarves of untruth they are: red-eyed mockeries, shaking flimsy beards, flapping fat tongues, making goo-goo noises and showering

> spit, squeezed with laughter at their newfound freedom. Words are lies, flung down dead by a naïve creator. Words hate us.

Peake looked up quickly from the page.

"Well? So far?" he asked.

"Good," Vaughn said, "it's good." A mountain out of a molehill. Words were words. The best part was Peake's theatrical voice. The English loved to — to exaggerate.

Chantal said she loved it. Which was fine. It made Vaughn glad. For Chantal to like his friend was important.

"But you must take my hand as you read," Chantal added. She held her limp hand over Peake's lap full of pages.

"She's got the spirit!" Peake laughed and took the hand. "Communion! Objective correlative!"

Vaughn pointed the wheel, drove. His eyes flicked to the lap, the hand. His neck was burning.

Peake had started up again, a deep droning:

> . . . only a matter of time. Didn't they stand up to haunt bigger fools? Didn't Shakespeare snap awake to the bad-echo of his words? Yes, and it happened this way: Willy finished his tea, returned to his study to begin his newest, and here's the sod Hamlet, mad for real, swaying bent-kneed on the writing table, dribbling pendulous penis o'er the fresh ink. Beside him Ophelia kneels, dog-end up, fish-mouthing suicidal vagina. . . .

She's got the spirit. Vaughn watched his knuckles, white on the wheel. He *would not* look at them holding hands. Chantal was the guilty one. Peake was a raving innocent.

"*Non,*" Chantal was saying. "It's not, I do not know, 'poetic' enough, I don't think."

He's got plenty more just as bad, Vaughn wanted to say.

What had come over him? He was on a summertime lark with his two best friends, and his guts were ablaze.

Downtown Lyon. Vaughn waited for Peake's pause then butted in to ask if they should find hotel rooms. Rooms, plural.

"No! Paris!" A direct command from someone out of control. Peake was part of the bouncing van now. Fuelled with wine, he would not stop. North to Paris.

> . . . there are only things in the end, no words to catch a man who, even now, acts. He is an old man, wearing an old suit and a grey hat pulled suspiciously low on his forehead. He faces the brick wall of a rowhouse. No moon, no sun. He holds a fresh lemon. He's come from the cricket pitch, jealous of the bowler he has seen. He looks around. No one there. He strides, stretches, throws. SPLUT! Twenty feet away, a mouse scurries for cover. The man has already walked away. The lemon, its broken lipless mouth, begins to pale . . .

They reached Paris in the middle of the night, Vaughn still hording his ribcage full of jealousy, Peake drunk and sloppy, Chantal irritated with them both. They got rooms at a ratty hotel Peake claimed to love.

Vaughn and Chantal woke at ten, their moods shaped by a short sleep on a narrow bed. Peake was not in his room, so they went in search of breakfast. At a sidewalk bistro they settled into a Parisian morning.

Vaughn couldn't help but brighten at the sights. Birds in black branches, European birds, which really sang; artists at easels; beggars whose eyes were burning fuses and whose clothes looked designed to startle. Their pain seemed stagy; they looked to be having a good time. Fifty feet away, the Seine, a slow-moving mirror, whispered history.

"Won't it be fun seeing Connor read tonight?" Vaughn asked Chantal. She was on her third coffee but had eaten only the end horn off her croissant. She didn't answer.

"He's bloody amazing, don't you think?" he added, wanting to break through to her and borrowing Peake's colour to do it.

"Yes, he is a nice toy, *non*?"

Vaughn turned to stare at the river. *Toy*.

The writer's group met in a basement café, La Boule de Neige. The three of them joined Bitch and Six at a table. Gaston Bitchelieu, thirtyish, had wild hair, trampy looks, and cast a wry look over the whole affair. He gave Vaughn untrusting glances, spoke only to Peake or Midier Six, and otherwise jotted on a notepad. The older Six, on the other hand, was friendly and rambled non-stop. Between him and Peake the table's chatter never died. Six looked something like George Washington, though his face had pulled into French lines. He treated the table to a bottle of cognac.

The crowd shared a lot in common, Vaughn saw, as homogeneous as a hockey team. They all had an edgy manner, a pre-game fever in the eyes. They even wore a kind of uniform: dark clothes, turtlenecks, greasy long hair. Some sported berets, others sunglasses, and a few had sandals. Beatniks. Even Peake had dressed for the event, wearing all black, and dirty old tennis shoes.

Vaughn knew his short hair, camel V-neck, oxfords, and white summer pants were somehow *gauche* here, and not only Bitchelieu gave furtive, assessing stares. His athlete's build perhaps. Maybe he looked like police, *un flic*. Whatever they were doing here looked illegal just by the way they were doing it.

Chantal also had dressed well, and Vaughn was glad. No one could doubt they were linked.

A thin young man took a chair up front and began to play a flute. Following no beat a toe could tap to, he blew only low, haunting tones interrupted now and then with high-pitched noodlings. No pattern, everything a surprise. When Chantal said "Poff" to it, Peake leaned over to whisper something, and Chantal settled in and listened.

Vaughn smelled sweet, bitter smoke wafting behind them.

"Maree-huana," Midier Six told him brightly, seeing his curious look.

"Pot?" Peake sat up straight. His nose twitched and he took it in like a rodent.

Midier asked if they wanted some. Vaughn shrugged, Chantal poffed it away. Peake begged off sadly because he was getting ready to read. Midier collared a friend for some anyway, and he and Bitchelieu shared the tiny cigarette. Chantal took turns too, but after her third drag she began to cough, and with a disgusted face waved the rest away. Soon both men were jabbering too fast for Vaughn to understand. Chantal became bright-eyed and alert. She looked around as though at a brand-new room.

"Connor! I'm on the cloud!" she exclaimed. A little bug-eyed, she tugged on Peake's sleeve. Vaughn sat up. Why was she telling this to Peake and not to him?

"Well cheers. I'm on the cognac," he said to her, raising his glass half-heartedly, his head still down in his poems. Chantal burst into delighted laughter at his joke. Her eyes, watching Peake, Vaughn recognized from a classroom of two years ago. Chantal rose and circled the table to sit next to the poet.

"And still you cannot decide your poems?" she said into his ear, her thin lips protruding and prehensile as a giraffe's. Vaughn wanted to whack them.

The first of three poets to read that night took the spotlight and began. A tubby man with white, white skin and shaved head, he read quickly, whispering, at the end shouting. The crowd gave him its attention. Vaughn gulped cognac.

At the applause he leapt up, searched a dark hallway and found a grotto-washroom where he splashed his face with water. That felt better. What was the matter with him, anyway?

He returned to witness Chantal at her little-girl finest. Peake stood with poems in hand while she draped her white silk scarf around his neck. Her face looked six years old.

"*Tiens!*" she lisped, "And so you will be the greatest poet." She kissed him on the cheek. Scarf tucked, Spitfire pilot Connor Peake steadied himself, said, "Right then," and strode for the stage.

Vaughn sat carefully. Bitch and Six were holding hands over the table. Seeing Vaughn, Bitchelieu quickly withdrew his hand.

On stage Peake looked not at all nervous. He briefly surveyed the room, then broke into one of his yells.

"Hello. Salut. Ma fat mama, ton dumb papa!"

He apologized for having to read in English. The crowd didn't care. Vaughn heard whispers: "So young."

Midier Six leaned over to Vaughn. He asked if he would please translate his young friend's words. The old man was visibly excited. Vaughn shrugged.

Peake began with what he'd read in the van. Vaughn found himself telling Midier Six that beginning writers often wrote about themselves writing. At this Chantal whirled around to glare at him, then snapped back to listen.

" . . . for didn't they stand up to haunt bigger fools?. . ."

No matter that she'd heard. For the time being he was amazed how he could change his anger to pleasure by getting half of Peake's words wrong on purpose.

" . . . that sod Hamlet, mad for real . . . "

Peake's "manifesto" earned rich applause at the end. Very polite crowd, Vaughn thought. Then Peake began a long poem, written that day, he announced, as a lover's tribute to

Paris. Vaughn's eyes burned the back of Chantal's head.

Well into the poem, Six had to shyly remind Vaughn he'd promised to translate. Vaughn sighed, began to listen half-heartedly. He burped some cognac and the fumes burned his eyes. He voiced every second line or so for this goofy old man, only peripherally aware that Six was the first homosexual he'd ever met. The old guy's mouth was too moist, he noticed.

> Yes, seagulls on the Seine.
> A city seining:
> Tattered men and sticks, Babar, balloons,
> Baudelaire, but in colour . . .

Puns, tricks, *shit.*

> . . . wine breath and grape thought,
> fecal poems edge, bank
> a river in Paris . . .

Pretending he's a poet.

> . . . Small Parisians skip, superb
> nasal squeaks and toots in my ears . . .

This stuff's *bad.*

Vaughn didn't realize he'd shouted this until heads turned. Bitch and Six looked up. Chantal stared in disbelief. He stared back, then stood up and stammered, "We're going. Now. Toulon. Tonight." He pronounced "Toulon" through his nose, like a Frenchman. Chantal poffed him and turned back to Connor Peake, who smiled and pointed at Vaughn, shouting, "Yes! Poetry war!"

Vaughn pushed through this dark Beatnik dressing-room, putting a shoulder into any player in his way. He didn't know this game or like it. Peake began again, his loud words

> . . . you run alone, beside a dead river,
> under a glaring sunlight eye . . .

following Vaughn into the cool evening air, all the way to the next block and beyond.

What happened next perhaps needs no telling, because it is an old and worn portrait of pain. Though indeed it is fresh each time. In any case, it completes the record of Vaughn Collin's baptism. The day a sour old man came to sit on his shoulders, where even today he belches bitter pepper breath into Vaughn's face, keeping at bay any lingering innocence.

Vaughn headed for the heart of the city. It was midnight but Paris was still up. Students, lovers, beggars. Tourists gazing, charmed, into each derelict alley. Many drunks. All these loud, gesturing French. Actors, artistes, a city full of leading men and ladies, one grand *cinéma de Paris*.

He began to cool down as the cognac began to wear off. The echo of his own act — childishly leaping up and running away — gradually seeped through his rage. He thought of Connor Peake, and felt badly for deserting him on his big night.

But Chantal. Her, he hated. And, of course, loved. She was so beautiful when she forgot herself, absorbed in a book, or asleep. Or at a poetry reading. Striding amid this midnight city's gay details, Vaughn could see only the art of her thighs, insistent under that light summer dress. The mesmerizing lines of her breasts. Her girlishness, which set her body up like forbidden fruit. Walking, he could feel her body in the pit of his stomach. He felt this to be proof that his love for her was nothing less than a matter of survival, identical to a need for food. And what was wrong with that? Any culture, any book, all of history called love good.

Hungry, Vaughn turned midstep, took a different, faster route back. One mile along he trespassed through a colony of hobos, *clochards,* twenty of them spread out on sidewalks and in doorway nooks. Most appeared asleep, though a few looked dead. Thick, matted hair. It was hard to tell where the crusted cloth of a shirt ended and the thick dirt of skin began. A clutch of them lay over a subway grate bathing in warm exhaust. Some lay in pools of some kind of liquid. The block smelled.

Nothing of this could penetrate the earthy joy of holding Chantal's body in his stomach. It was true: love overcame all.

At one-thirty he reached La Boule de Neige and found it empty. He ran to their hotel and found both rooms empty as well. They'd obviously gone somewhere to celebrate, the whole batch of them. They would be drunk, happy, teasing Connor Peake with sage winks and grand fellowship. What better place for reconciliation? In the City of Love, Vaughn would be greeted as love's prodigal son. Love conquered all.

He decided to get his van and search. The alley where Ferlinghetti was parked was dark and silent. Nearing the van he stopped, hearing noises. Sleep sounds from an overhanging flat. He drew closer. Then the sounds again, this time unmistakable.

"Oh? Oh? Oh?"

Chantal's piping climax.

"Oh? Oh? . . . Oh! Oh! Oh!"

Vaughn stopped dead, spun round to run, stopped, spun round again. This meant that Connor Peake was finishing too, right now, and it was awful because you couldn't hear him. He was a reptile, he had the toad clamp on beautiful Chantal. Vaughn had a brick in his hand. His ears' inward roaring shut out all devilish sounds, and he didn't hear the smash of the brick through the van's back window.

He ran then, crazy-legging it in and out of alleys, gripped

now by an absurd fear of getting caught. And as if there were still secrets. He ran and ran until, somewhere in the darkest part of the City of Love, he jumped into a taxi. He was crying freely. He couldn't see the driver's face. The driver didn't ask directions, he just drove. Maybe he'd seen this French movie before.

Not caring where the taxi took him, Vaughn sat doubled up over his arms to stifle the hot metal his guts had become. He could feel the blood rush behind his eyes and thud under the fillings of his teeth. For a second he forgot where he was, and wondered if his father had just died. No. *Chantal.*

He swore then and there, in the taxi — gritting his teeth so his pounding monster heart would not blow his fillings through the roof of his mouth — that anything, a bored, dead, staring life, *anything* was better than this.

May 2nd

A sparkling night in the pub last night. I rarely go but when I do it's always the same faces, boozing away. But last night the room found an edge and the laughter, though still helped by booze, was good-hearted and child-like.

Annie and I almost never spend an evening in public. Together. A pair.

I see her around of course. She hangs out — even gets a bit drunk it looks like — with the seediest, dumbest fishermen and natives. At such times she's loose, laughing, probably trading dirty jokes. Never chiding or instructing. Peculiar, because if anyone in the world needs advice it's these Tyee losers. I admit I get bothered by it. I want more of this undemanding Annie.

Last night's occasion was May Day, her birthday. One of my first Beauséjour memories is Lise bouncing around our house, full of herself, chanting, "May Day is *my* day."

At my place, I waited till she finished my last chapter,

then greeted her from behind with a handful of drooping crocuses and asked her out on an official date, which in Bella Combe means a Skookum burger and Bella Koolaids at the Tyee.

"I'd love to," Annie said. She gave me a teenager's promiscuous smile and topped it off by shyly toeing the carpet. For an old lady she can still do it.

At the pub she proposed a toast — we raised two Bella Koolaids. I believe they were named after Jonestown. Roy has his own humour. They comprise a capful of everclear mixed in soda and the fruit syrup of your choice. I drank cassis, and Annie elderberry, a pun, I think, for her birthday.

"To Chantal de Tou," she said, with only a slight smile, "and the wonder that is woman." We gulped.

I raised what was left of mine. "To Bernard LaPierre and the mystery that is man." We gulped again. I pulled out my wallet, bait for Roy, who was at my side in a flash.

We sipped the fruity alcohol and chewed burgers dripping sauce that hid the taste of long-frozen meat. We decided the Tyee needed new food. Something indigenous, something tourists would talk about back in the city. Bear burgers. Bambi stew. Booboo soup.

"You made her a bit of a caricature, eh?" Annie offered after a while. She's often gentle with me at first.

"Nope. That was her. Chantal de Tou."

"Why not give her a black hat. Describe her cackling and twisting her greasy moustache — "

"Right."

" — as she tied you to the railway tracks."

"Good idea. I'll put that in."

"All her fault. Right."

"It was." I wanted praise here. Or sympathy. I'd just conjured up and written down a lot of old hurt.

"The thing is, you're painting yourself innocent. You weren't that stupid then. You're way off."

"So I'm stupid now."

"Okay, let's drop it." She paused. I could see she couldn't drop it herself. "You made Connor Peake a stiff little jerk too."

"I loved him then, I hate him now. Getting my digs in."

"Well why not, eh?" Gentle with me again. She added softly, "Your life opens up in the next bit, doesn't it?"

"I guess," I whispered back. She knows what comes next means much more old pain.

"Stick with it."

"But as they say: if you remember it, you weren't there. It's a bit of a blur." Which is maybe a blessing.

A Monday night, we shared the Tyee with no one save a table of quiet natives and two Moe brothers, anchored like anemones to their corner of the bar. The Moes must have sensed our private party because they didn't join us.

I lifted my glass again. "To fifty years of . . . love." Annie followed my tease, answering with, "To a jilted antelope. Who might just get lucky tonight."

Again the tart's smile and inclined head, and again I'm struck by Annie's bag of tricks. Sometimes I see myself as the straight man to her whims of personality.

It doesn't matter. Our main difference, and what does matter, is that Annie is usually awake and I am usually not. I daydream, I lose myself in tides of mud. A brain too full and fancy for its own good. I toss and turn with demons that fill me up and demons that drain me dry.

I remember an event soon after I arrived at Bella Combe. We were hiking Turtle Boy Lake. Annie was talking about discipline, her impossible doctrine of "no rules but wakefulness". As she went on, almost teacherly, I was wondering if she practised what she preached. She'd been strict lately, ascetic to the hilt — no unnecessary talking, a weird diet, days spent alone — and I thought, if these weren't "rules" she was following, what were they? I couldn't help but see her fervour as coming both from an allegiance to dead Ivan and from a reaction to her Winnipeg life. Hadn't she in fact fallen into the trap of one who's fled the bad world and lies swaddled in dogma, habit, belief? Discipline her buffer against the scary world out there?

She talked and I thought, and we came across a group of naked kids playing Tarzan on a knotted rope overhanging the lake. Seeing us, two adults, they looked suddenly sad. A pre-slap look. They covered themselves with their hands. Still talking to me, Annie eyed them.

" . . . so it doesn't matter what you *do* as long as you have disciplined *eyes*, and they stay on the path, which in fact could lead *anywhere* — "

In two steps Annie had kicked off her shorts and thrown her sweater down. She ran, limping madly, at the rope, grabbed hold and flew out over the water, rotating once, kicking, a ridiculous naked witch. She let go but seemed to pause, airborne, facing the kids. Copying their morose faces, she gave them a sober "hello" in Tsimshian before crashing sideways into the lake.

The kids laughed quietly, in their way. I could do nothing but stand still and watch Annie's splash, a kind of bull's-eye, widen in rings and take command of the lake. I knew her leap was meant more for me. Still nervous and damaged from my arrival at Bella Combe, I didn't like it when anyone moved fast.

Of course I've seen much since Turtle Boy Lake. *Can* she in fact influence the weather? But I follow her advice and focus instead on what's close, what's right at hand. Sometimes she gives me nudges: that time when she turned the salmon on my cleaning plank, grabbed into the slit and pulled out, then swallowed, two slabs of bleeding roe. She seemed to make a point of not chewing, not breaking the eggs in her mouth. When she met my eye, something in her look told me her body had a hidden use for those eggs, and that the eggs were all for it.

Annie raises her glass. "Here's to . . . nothing at all!"

We set down two more empties, I looked Roy over and pulled out a crumpled ten, worn and softer than suede.

I'd been telling her how I'd never in my life had a nightmare until the night after hearing Chantal with Connor Peake. It was the first of many, and they were always the same. Chantal and I would be at a party. I'd look up and she'd be gone. I'd ask if anyone had seen her. They'd exchange glances. My search would have that awful panic, through halls and rooms. Then at a door I'd hear her laughter. I'd open it and see the other man. Her naked body always looked more beautiful than it ever had before. I'd wake up, and the horror of my dream would fall full weight into my European morning.

Funny, but as this dream recurred over time and I began even while dreaming to know its pattern, the horror at the end never died down. It was as though jealousy had its own lust for itself, and had to be satisfied each night with a hellish orgasm.

Another odd angle of those dreams was the type of man I'd find her with. They were always deformed and unable to talk properly, managing only grunts and guffaws as they prodded my Chantal's smoothness. Often their deformities centred in their penis. One man, all soapy in a bathtub with my love, had a penis three feet long but slim as a thumb. Another had one made of translucent candy, green with a red head.

"You can't believe how I hated women for a while," I told her when our next Bella Koolaid came. "I was actually thanking Chantal for showing me what women were. She'd shown me women were *black worms* in the apple of humanity."

"And you're over that now."

"Well, yeah. I am."

Annie sat smirking, but her eyes were careful.

Chantal had got to me, sure. In France my post-dream fury kept me pinned to the bed composing theories about women. They infected men with a disease, the onset of which rendered a man weak and stupid enough to misconstrue a serious illness and call it "love". Sex was to love as vomiting to the flu, temporary gushing relief. "Chantal!" I would moan aloud in my bed, using the French accent I knew all anguished lovers did, "Thank you, Chantal, for letting me see these things!"

"Vaughn," Annie interrupted, "you're not alone."

She looked me in the eye.

"Dreams are bad, okay. I'm not saying your pain wasn't real. But dreams are more fixable . . . than" — she paused, swallowed — "than cars full of teenage boys, shouting. Than hating customers but needing one so you can eat. Or drink. Having an address in your purse for the cops because half the time you won't be able to tell them where you live." She was glaring at me and I straightened. I couldn't see even a ghost of humour in her eyes.

"Some men pay ten dollars and think they have licence to beat you up. Being beaten up? Bad. Being beaten up by a man who thinks he's earned it, who's not even that mad? *That* is bad. You think you hated women. But Vaughn, the worst part was that I put myself there. That was my nightmare, and Jesus Christ — I was awake."

She laughed. "I had a gallon of gut-bile to every pint of yours, boy." She was smiling at me, happy as a clam.

"It's nice you can laugh about it." I don't think I was being sarcastic.

"I can because I'm outta there."

I thought of her phrase, the good giant. There she was, across from me. Surveying the garbage dump.

"So," I asked, "how did you manage to not hate Ivan

when you met? It was on the street wasn't it?"

"Good question," she said. From her buckskin wallet she eased out a piece of paper, folded once. This she laid carefully, still folded, between us.

"I met him on the street during a hard snow. He didn't look like a customer, he didn't look like a cop. I didn't know what he looked like. He looked forty — he was sixty — but he had child-like eyes. He wore no hat, and snow had collected on his bald head. He walked so smoothly. I got the funny feeling he liked the snow there, a kind of blanket. He began telling me strange little jokes. I could tell he was no joker. In fact the jokes were meaningless. In fact the words didn't matter somehow. Just a kind of comfort. Maybe it was like someone making sympathy sounds to a dog. Then when he asked my name and address — another normal asshole, I thought. But I gave him the address. I needed money. When I got home I found this pinned to my door."

With a finger Annie slid the paper at me. I opened it and read.

> The red rose is shut and the bird is sober.
> You are a slave to the child killer.
> A lame emperor has said
> Your time is tied, your stones are set.
> Softly, Annie, ask
> That the best in your song
> May loosen knots of terror.

I pushed the poem back and Annie secured it in her wallet.

"Since then I've hated only once, and only for a moment." Annie pushed an ice cube with her finger to stir the juice and alcohol. "Ivan and I spent fifteen years together and he left one morning without a word." She paused, thinking. "His last little joke. Last little message."

Then Annie raised her glass and smiled the saddest smile I've ever seen.

"To Ivan."

The Connoisseur of Sport

> *Within my darkness I slowly explore*
> *The hollow half light with hesitant cane,*
> *I who always imagined Paradise*
> *To be a sort of library.*
>
> — Borges

He couldn't stay in France.

Hockey gave him no pleasure. Watching the sloppy French amateurs nauseated him. He smoked now — Gauloises — and had let himself get out of shape. So Vaughn quit hockey for good, after Christmas of 1962, and got a basement apartment. Having arranged with brother Hugh to send him portions of his small inheritance, he didn't need a job if he lived cheaply. A loaf cost a dime, a litre of red a quarter. Vaughn turned thirty-eight.

After quitting hockey his mood got worse. He'd never quit anything before and it felt like a dereliction of duty, compounding his everyday bitterness. Mornings he'd look out into the always ideal Riviera weather to behold instead a sky, as he remembered his middle-namesake once describing it, "that was ashy and furtive, as though associated with crime". Thomas Hardy's words suited him well these days.

He had to get out of France, but somehow it took months to pack up. He didn't fix the van's back window, not until he ran into snow in the mountains, and even then he only taped it over with a *Herald Tribune*. Nor did he remove the mattress. It was a perfectly good one, said a rational voice, so there it stayed to be hauled around, in the back of the van and in the back of his thoughts, a cancerous cargo. When he slept on it he awoke not replenished but poisoned, as though his veins ran with ink.

He drove east to Monaco before the thought of Italy made him turn around. Then north to the Alps, where manicured hills and dessertish chalets seemed perverse, as though they hid blood in a birthday cake. About to cross the English Channel, he pictured an islandful of Peens and Peakes. Where and how would he exit France? For he had to. Because they were everywhere: prim women clicking along in high heels, busy shopping, picking at the ends of *baguettes* which stuck obscenely from their bags. The way they kissed their fellow shoppers' cheeks, all cute faces and smooch sounds. France swarmed with these women, hot effigies of a Madame Chantal Collin.

But he couldn't cross the borders that framed her face, her beautiful face. Changeless now and ideal, it had an eternal beauty, like something cleanly dead, after the decay is over: bone pearly as porcelain, or the perfect arc of a burnt-black candle wick.

He told himself he was no longer mad at Connor Peake. A letter from him, full of honourable schoolboy apology, found its way to Vaughn and helped him pull the dagger of blame out of Peake's neck. Peake was leaving for "another nowhere nothing place, Canada". He called Chantal "a Gestapo agent for the daughters of selfishness", but Vaughn thought this went too far. Chantal was just another mindless player. Vaughn's bitterness was aimed at the game itself.

One day, looking around Perpignan, eyeing the Spanish border, he realized how bitter he was. He was cutting across a hospital grounds, a clean park-like scene, gardens and walnut trees. Nurses in crisp whites stepped past well-groomed families dutifully visiting. At the edge of the grounds a wooden gate, slightly ajar, opened onto a lumberyard. Passing this gate Vaughn sensed movement and turned to see a grubby man about his age. He slowly kneaded a half-limp penis, pointing it out the gap in the gate at a group of starched, squeaky-clean nurses. He wore an unmistakable expression. Nothing in it of pleasure, or even lust. Only bitterness. Seeing he was spotted he pointed himself at Vaughn now, sneering with new enthusiasm and showing canine teeth. In earlier days Vaughn would have hurried by, mystified, in the end writing off another human mystery. Now? He'd seen a comrade.

But Vaughn finally escaped France, began to wander Europe, and did so for five years. There is no story there, no thread to link events nor crisis to weight them. Though he had small adventures all over. He walked the dikes of Denmark and Holland. In England he drank black beer and stood at poets' tombs, where he thought of literature, and Lise, and wept, stupidly, no real reason. He could do that now — silly crying — at the drop of a hat, but it felt not much different from gossip. He rented a villa for pennies in Greece where he had a tipsy affair with retsina and gazed drunkenly out over an ancient blue sea and stark hills and tried to hear the golden tread of those old gods. In Spain he stumbled through a dalliance with a German girl who was blonde and a bit plump and too good-natured to really rouse him. He witnessed a Peake-like character piss off the tower in Pisa and get hauled away laughing in Italian handcuffs. He sold Ferlinghetti and took a boat to Egypt and the pyramids, and got far enough south to catch dysentery in the Sudan.

He eluded both lovers and heroes. The main story lies hidden in the lost days. In the drone of weeks and months passing, Vaughn couldn't see clearly at all. Though he tried — cathedrals, bars, new food, tongues, cultures — nothing much registered. It was as though his keen Beauséjour senses were smothered under a bruise.

Annie's one-sentence postcards found him in Athens, in Valencia, in Amsterdam. He read them and laughed the bitter but desperate laugh of a schoolboy who opens a set of exam questions which mean absolutely nothing. In Brindisi he read, "To Be is to acknowledge pain, not hide from it." In Madrid, "If the wine is harsh, become the wine." He mocked Annie with his bridge-club voice accented with Peake irony: Superb. *Very* bloody useful. *Wish* you were here.

He craved friends but eyed all with suspicion, a kicked dog. It was funny, though, during these years, how he relaxed into grubbiness, longer hair and dark, formless clothes. As though Peake and those Beatniks had bested him in some vague war and now by joining their ranks he duly acknowledged that. He smoked hashish and nodded his head to jazz in Copenhagen; in Soho he wiggled with droves of teens to Beatles, Kinks, and Who. He found a pair of peach bell-bottoms in an alley. His hair grew longer by itself. He turned forty in a huge fluorescent cafeteria in Essen, Germany. That is, his body turned forty. He had all the symptoms of a pimply-faced boy, ripe to follow anything, anyone, *out.*

No decision made him go back. It was as if his imagination simply expanded enough to allow a trip called "going home". Home? He went straight to Victoria, and that first day walked with his head down past Mrs. Peen's, feeling too guilty to knock and see if she was alive. He hitched to Ucluelet and got a job on a trawler. The waves were as he remembered; so were the fish. But he was different. No joy seeing a salmon break water. He wrote to Hughie, then hitched to Manitoba.

Beauséjour. He found himself in a backwards farm town. Square buildings, square people. More colour in the ghosts: the school and rink had shrunk but still stood. And there were certain charmed ditches, basins between tree roots, and paths leading off to damp secluded spots, small indentations in the land, and Vaughn's memory.

He spent an evening with Hugh the prosperous lawyer. Vaughn had five teenage nieces and nephews, and meeting them tickled up an odd new fear. He saw in their faces his true home: a mindless domain of genes. He was glad to leave the roomful of staring hazel eyes and look-alike meaty noses. Hugh promised he'd do the necessary tricks to get Vaughn's share of their father's money to him in one lump sum. But with the children still in the room he told him, holding Vaughn's eye, that he would "damn well deduct lawyer's fees".

Why did he choose Vancouver? Manitoba was out, and it wasn't just the family. The prairie sky was too demanding, too wide. The mind ended up crushed. And Victoria was out too, it was small now, provincial after all those capital cities in Europe. Vancouver was between the two. He rented the smallest house in Lynn Valley and planted two trees, tokens for staying put. He went to most of the Western League Canucks' home games. Watching younger men do his old job.

He needed to work now, at least a little. He cleaned himself up, got a job behind a hotel desk for a year, then switched to selling fishing equipment. Alarmed at his flabbing body, he did a month of morning push-ups, got back a big chest, and became a lifeguard at the YMCA. They valued his age, and what they saw to be stability. The chlorine bleached his hair and hurt his eyes. Giving swimming lessons only made him hate anyone afraid of water. He quit the day he hesitated before pulling a water-gulping boy out of the deep end.

He changed jobs each fall, the start of what would have been a new hockey season. He got on with a logging crew in Cypress Bowl. Choking logs was deadly work, and this very quality gave the chokermen the closeness of a hockey team. They called the bosses "pussies", the machine operators "armchairs".

In 1969 he took an office job in the advertising department of Eatons, where he wrote copy for newspaper ads. He'd write this: Thirty-point Helios bold, *Save 40%.* Ten-point Helvetica light, *Save now on brand-name quality, leather-look*

Naugahyde tilt rocker! Latest frontroom fashion stands everyday wear and tear! In Tan and Black. While they last! Save now!

It beat getting pinned by logs. The ads were honest deceit, as Peake would have said, and those who didn't understand this deserved the over-expensive toys, hammers, diamond rings.

Vaughn's co-workers were of a species, middle-class go-getters. He learned how to join their cafeteria chatter, and watched *F Troop* and *My Favorite Martian* so he could contribute. But no one attracted him. One month into the job he noticed Rob Mac, a janitor who kept to himself, and who sometimes giggled pushing his broom. Or sometimes just stood there with it, staring at nothing with lively eyes. He looked twenty, a handsome face. He always wore a baseball cap.

Once, working late, everyone else gone, in the men's room Vaughn surprised Rob Mac standing on a sink with one arm out the window. He'd snapped his head around at Vaughn's entrance, and a strand of hair escaped the cap and settled on his shoulder. Rob Mac looked frightened, his smile a plaintive reflex. Vaughn smelled the marijuana smoke as the young man brought his empty hand in. "I was — "

"Hey," Vaughn said, "it's okay." He paused at a cubicle door. "Sometimes smoke it myself." Disappearing into his stall he gave the young man the half-grin of cohorts. Vaughn could perform that look well. Snappy.

"Aw, well shit."

Vaughn heard him scramble to look out the window, search, assess smoulder time and chance of salvage, then sigh.

"You could have had some."

Vaughn had only smoked it a bit in Copenhagen. He couldn't imagine doing so in a bathroom, at work. It would be like drinking whiskey on the bench during a game.

Mac and Vaughn ate lunch together a few times over the next several weeks. They weren't particularly drawn to each other. It was a case of the two loners finally drifting together in a school cafeteria. Like Vaughn he was biding time there, aping conventions and keeping his true self under his hat. He lived in North Vancouver too, he said, in Deep Cove.

One Friday Mac mentioned a North Van bar, the Coach House, where he and his friends went on weekends.

"Pile along sometime," Mac said. "You can always leave."

One Friday evening Vaughn piled along. He didn't leave. It's perhaps tragic how many years must pass before one can see which innocent Friday-afternoon decisions were the life-shapers, were entrances to tunnels so large one could not see the walls, or one's confinement.

At the bar Mac pointed to a corner table. "Our spot," he said. A group of young men: long hair, jeans, casual riffraff. Nothing too — Vaughn stood up straight, his body reacting before his mind could. God, look who it — Going bald, his receding hair seemed to thrust his face forward, making him look even more like a lizard. He was (Vaughn made a quick calculation) twenty-seven. Sitting off to the side of the pack, he looked a little shy, like he was trying to get a word in. Connor Peake.

Peake saw Vaughn, did a double-take, looked again. Vaughn gave a curt dip of the head.

"Peake."

"My word," Peake whispered softly. He looked afraid. Not so much of Vaughn, but of the possible weight of such coincidence. He recovered and smiled, nodded. "Danny Kaye. Small magic."

Heads turned to size Vaughn up. A huge unshaven man wearing a jean jacket let his gaze linger, some kind of shapeless challenge. Vaughn was wearing a suit.

Vaughn took a chair. He surprised himself by selecting a chair two away from Peake rather than right beside him, as if to say that it wasn't so extraordinary that they'd met. His choice of seat felt like power, something new. He and Peake talked quietly. Vaughn did most of the talking for once. His travelling, his work. Peake said all he was doing was "playing".

The unspoken subject made everything they did say transparent. Several times Peake faltered in the middle of a sentence, tripping over the shared lie. Vaughn realized he was letting his old friend dangle, and this felt like power too.

"How's your crazy Annie friend?" Peake asked.

"Still up the coast here somewhere. She's getting silent in her old age. I wonder about her a bit."

"Right."

Another pause. Connor Peake with nothing to say, amazing.

"So," Peake said, "what are you up to, tonight?"

Vaughn said he'd planned on the Canucks game but —

"Lads!" Peake yelled at the rest of them. "Who's not seen a live hockey match? Bubbles night at the arena — gladiators, man."

A few groans, others ignored him, but the big greaser looked at the ceiling and thought. He bounced in an unsmiling chuckle.

"That," he announced, his voice deep as his chest, and professorial, "sounds appropriately fucked up."

The plan was to race back to "the house", where they'd eat and "pick up the bubbles". Vaughn was invited to dinner. In the parking lot he squeezed into the back space of an old Triumph. Rob Mac's long hair whipped his face as they hit speed. Vaughn loosened his tie.

Mac turned and shouted at him, marvelling over coincidence and this tiny world they lived in. He asked questions about France, about Connor Peake there. He yelled that they all shared a house in Deep Cove. Actually it was Peake's house, and he let whoever wanted to live there free.

"He's got money somewhere," Mac shouted, hinting at mystery.

"Parents," Vaughn shouted back, hinting at dependence.

"Well it's an okay place. Conman has these ideas and he tries to take control, but, you know, we put up."

Conman Peake. Vaughn liked these guys. "What are bubbles?"

Mac told him LSD.

Right, okay. Lucy in the Sky with Diamonds. Bubbles night at the arena. Well. Vaughn took his tie off and put it in his pocket.

At the house an impish guy wearing wire glasses and whose name Vaughn learned was Benny did a jerky dance in front of the stove while he fried up a dozen pork chops in three frying pans. Extremely non-dinner music thudded the walls and rattled dishes.

Peake took Vaughn on a tour. Though this was Vaughn's first look at a house like this, it contained what he came to discover were the Late Sixties symbols of bachelor good housekeeping: walls covered with posters and flags, a barber chair and dismembered mannequin, some scared-looking plants, macramé, a couple of dusty jars of dried beans in the kitchen. Mostly, lots of bare space, bare plywood floors, nothing left on a ledge where an elbow might knock it. The house had a feel of having been cleared for action.

"We keep it sparse. For our sock-hops," Peake said.

In a corner a gutted TV–cum–puppet theatre sat chest-level on two stools, homemade puppets on the floor underneath. One appeared to be a tattooed breast, another a crude Hitler, another a wax blob with three doll arms sticking from it. One had a plastic submarine for a head. Puppet playthings were scattered about: a crucifix, a scalpel, a squirt gun.

Double doors opened into what would have been the dining-room. Peake flicked on the lights and announced, "The Rimbaud Room."

Vaughn eased his face into a room completely splattered with paint, rags, and what looked like porridge. Layers of graffiti shouted from every square inch of wall. The lone window was broken and boarded up, as were several holes kicked in the plaster. No furniture. A single thick rope, knotted once at the bottom, hung from a hook on the ceiling.

"You can do anything in this room except kill people," Peake said.

Passing them by, the big one, Bob Cumming, stage-whispered to Vaughn, "He's a proud laddiebuck, isn't he?"

Peake mumbled a fuck-off, and Cumming wandered humming into the kitchen.

Peake's bedroom was surprisingly orderly. Neutral colours. Clothes folded over chair backs. A wall of books. An aquarium with healthy-looking fish.

"What do you wear to hockey games?" Peake was digging in a drawer.

"Clothes."

Vaughn had used this dry one before and knew it was decent. Though he still wasn't concerned with impressing his old friend. He settled on the foot of Conman's bed and looked around. Nothing special, though the far wall had a picture of the pointing Uncle Sam, under which someone had printed: GOD'S BAD BREATH.

His bare back to Vaughn, Peake asked, "Look, did you get my letter?"

"Yup."

"You didn't write back. I mean, I can't say I blame you."

"Yeah, well."

Vaughn was about to say he'd felt too embarrassed. For that was what he'd felt. Chantal he'd been able to cleanly hate but the Peake part of it embarrassed him. How someone unrelated to their friendship had so easily ended it.

They looked each other in the eye for the first time that evening. Peake's gaze was still charmed with irony. But quieter now. He brought up a hand and put it around Vaughn's neck. Fingers graced his spine while the thumb tip rode his

Adam's apple lightly. Peake's eyes rimmed with tears. He looked confused. Vaughn had never seen Peake look like this before.

Vaughn knew his young friend was trying to apologize. He'd forgiven Peake long ago. What he felt instead was a sudden strength. Peake was not the leader in his own home. Nor was he the man Vaughn had once thought he was. There was something new rising here between them. It was power, and it was Vaughn's.

"Sorry about that brick," Vaughn said, his voice powered by benevolence.

"Well hell then, mate," Peake pulled a shirt over his head and laughed, relieved, "sorry about that *fuck*."

They packed into Benny Powys' windowless bread truck. Because of his suit Vaughn was offered a front seat but declined, choosing to flop on the greasy cushions with the others in the back. He undid the top two buttons of his shirt.

He watched this group of young unknowns. Some of them still gave him quick looks. In the eddies of chatter he noticed, as he had in every dressing-room, a shared voice and wit. Here he heard the same "Ya know" and "I mean", and a kind of snorted snicker they all used, even Peake. Everyone up and at 'em for Friday, for bubbles night. Except Peake himself, who simply turned and smiled at Vaughn from time to time from his spot beside the wheel well. Someone would crack a good one, the van would erupt, and Peake would grin and catch his eye as if to say, "These lads, eh?"

Vaughn began to notice the big one, Bob Cumming, lounging in the back corner studying a little magnetic chessboard. His authority lurked underskin somewhere. He no longer looked mean, but he clearly had no time for trifles. If there was a leader to this group it was him.

The hockey game was strange from the beginning. Vaughn's new companions kept him more entertained, in any case more nervous, than the game itself. Heads turned when they walked in and found seats.

No one was a hockey fan except Vaughn, with the possible exception of Cumming, who watched intently and said nothing. Peake worked hard to build Vaughn up in front of his friends.

"Look, Vaughn used to *play* in this league," he reminded them, tilting the word "play" to suggest that even while employed by the league Vaughn had at the same time been above it. The others looked a little tentative sitting there, as if they sat in the lair of a known monster. Peake prodded Vaughn for subtleties of the game, and after a while some of the others did too, Mike Evers in particular, a quiet, nervous boy, the youngest. He appeared the most disturbed by Vaughn's presence.

When a player fell, or a fight began, some of the group let loose a mock cheer. Dads in their hockey jackets spun to eye them and out of the corners of their mouths whispered lethal warnings to their sons. Not many hippies came to hockey games and — Dads' suspicions confirmed — when they did they came to laugh.

They took the LSD between the second and third periods, Vaughn gulping his little pill as casually as the others, Peake winking at him as he did so. The Copenhagen hash had made Vaughn see things in a tangy kind of detail. His imagination had even taken modest flight. He expected "bubbles" to be a dose of the same. More convenient if anything. A pill.

Then, an odd thing. In all his years of hockey he'd never lost a tooth, lucky for any player in the pre-shield days, especially a defenceman. With ten minutes left in the game, just before he began to feel the drug's effects, an errant puck caught him laughing at one of Benny Powys' jokes. Vaughn lost half a bicuspid. The St. John's Ambulance boy thumbed a cotton ball between his lip and bleeding gum and told him to see a dentist for a cap. For some reason — and this may be too convenient a symbol for this stage in Vaughn Collin's life — that tooth stayed chipped for years. More than once he would use the joke that he was trying to grow it back.

Right about then the LSD came on: a foreboding flip in the stomach, and all colours contrasting extremely. The ice surface got too white to look at. Then, god, what an avalanche of eye-food: thudding body-check at centre ice; a Canucks' break-out; neat pass; diving red San Diego defenceman; clever feint and backhand shot; bulge in the net; leaping white left-winger; cheering arena full of crazy multicoloured arms. All in five seconds, such swirl and shatter! Vaughn suddenly saw why fans were fans and, sitting back and shaking his head, he was stunned to discover after all this time the secret of hockey fandom: they were actually experts, connoisseurs of these fantastic sights.

A face-off. With the drop of the puck and the crowd's new silence the arena seemed to darken and Vaughn's stomach suffered a yawning, ominous twist. The scramble of bodies now looked ridiculous: men with little-boy brushcuts, ridiculous uniforms, and contrived steel feet on an ice floor, their faces desperate, teeth gritted so hard their neck cords might snap. Blind to life's enormity, men chased a puck.

He heard Bob Cumming, sounding awed and even a little scared, wonder to no one in particular, "A carnival of crude motives, man."

In this darker light Vaughn noticed the fans again. Physically unable to compete on ice, they cheered, elbowed each other, booed, yelled at the ref. They'd paid money to be second-hand insane. Unable to be insane enough themselves, they paid others to do it for them. Idiots, losers. While he watched, horrified, on every face an inner ugliness bloomed a matching physical deformity.

Then, again suddenly, as if from a panoramic viewpoint, he saw himself watching the game, saw himself and the game and the arena in the city, saw vividly the puny role the game played in the affairs of the planet, but how large and ludicrous a role it had played in his life.

He must have shown all this on his face. Or perhaps it was nothing new to see things this way at ten o'clock on bubbles night. He heard a snort-snicker and turned to see Peake watching him with eyes that said, "Welcome to *our* game."

Though the Canucks tied it with five minutes to go they left then, which relieved Vaughn as much as it seemed to everyone else. Peake steered him to sit in the front seat this time, "for the view", and Vaughn saw instantly what he meant. Everything — his hands, the dashboard, other cars outside, the strings of street lights as seen from the top of the hill they began descending, to the chorus of screams from the back — all were showing themselves off with a gaudy flair he'd not noticed before, flair that came from within the object, nothing to do with some drug he'd taken. Car bumpers grew metallic cartoon teeth and growled — but were no more scary than Popeye's Bluto, so full of spinach was Vaughn. Pedestrians were clowns, nuns, assassins. They slowed for a police car, and Vaughn laughed at this like he'd never laughed before. They were driving! And there were rules! What was driving, anyway? There was sort of a puck to it all but it was invisible. Why not just stop, get out, sit on the curb and laugh!

"How we doin' there, Benny-enny-enny?" Cumming asked from the back.

"No probs," Powys reported, the hint of a shake in his voice, grateful to have been asked. "The Grand Canyon opened up back there, but we floated over. *Hey*! We just hit a baby! No, sorry, no, we didn't. Sorry. My tires *are* babies."

Tentative groans from the back. And Benny looked like he had scared himself with his own joke. Vaughn saw how his new friends managed a courageous kind of humour on top of a potential for actual terror.

Panic and wonder. Powys turned on the radio and now and then spun the tuner. The music and the ads, all funny. Vaughn could see each type of music and its role in the spectrum of human noise. Country music dumbly honest, old Huck Finn missin' his baby. Rock music was drums and lust and money. An elevator-music station gave them a jovial string version of "Baby Elephant Walk", and the van went silent. Cumming whispered, "Daddy's music." The playful tune, ominous because so playful. A candied euphemism for cancer, chaos, bad men in high places. A van-load of people, silent to "Baby Elephant Walk", actually frightened for a moment by this musical syrup. But to Vaughn it felt good, this brotherhood of fear, this quiet banding together against a sinister song.

His chipped tooth-nerves hurt at each intake of air. Since the accident he'd been holding his lip over it for protection, but now, grinning wide at nothing, he didn't care. The pain was still sharp, but this new world had framed it and hung it in this bright gallery along with everything else.

Vaughn noticed Powys glance his way, turn again to see the road, then jerk back to him again, surprised, a classic double take. He burst into incredulous laughter. Between coughs and laughs he squeezed out, "An *old* guy . . . *in a suit*." He had to pull over.

Now Vaughn was the centre of attention, everyone arcing his neck to see him and howl. He heard Peake shouting, "See? He's great!" Vaughn found himself laughing hysterically too. Why not? He was unbearably funny. He was old, his body was completely different. He had some grey hair, and slashing wrinkles. Funnier still, his old body had worn a business suit to bubbles night.

They made it over the bridge to North Vancouver and someone suggested they could improve themselves with a cherries jubilee sundae, so they drove to the Whitespot. Food right then felt like nonsense, but they had to do something. People went out Friday evenings and did things. Dined, for instance. At the restaurant he followed them out of the van. Things were getting wilder. His field of vision had become a telescoping, hinged pattern, sectioned into previously hidden but utterly logical planes. He had multiple, insect sight, he thought, then stopped thinking. He pressed himself against the van to keep from spinning off into the sky. The dusty metal was cool to the cheek. And then (laughter!) he felt the vehicle as a huge growth hanging off the side of his face, a wart so unreasonable he'd had to install wheels and an engine to get his face around town. No, stop thinking that, he wasn't attached, it wasn't true.

What was true was he was in a parking lot, of a restaurant; yes, he could walk, something remembered how. His joints had little brains of their own. He didn't make it all the way in but got trapped in the little glass room with the pay phone and cigarette machine. He stopped, turned around, then around again, laughing his head off, a bumpkin deranged by the unexpected colour of his deb county fair.

There was Connor Peake peering at him through glass, making faces, but also checking up. A gentle man, really. Looking past Peake he could see a group of meteor-eyed friends getting into county-fair trouble. Nervous Mike Evers staring at his cherries jubilee as if they were the glistening intestines of Satan. Big Bill Cumming in speechless awe of a baby propped and coy in the booth across from him. Vandal Benny Powys with two bent forks hanging from his glasses. Giggling Rob Mac afraid beneath the note pad of a bored waitress, unable to order under such pressure. A busboy double-palmed his way through a swinging door, probably seeking a manager to manage these men who bent silverware and ogled infants and clearly had no idea how to dine.

Vaughn, watching from his little glass room. Trapped. But not really. He could go farther in, or he could leave. Which one? Colourful sequins of portent framed his vision. He flicked his eyes right and left to try to see them but they stayed to the edges. He sensed, though, these sequins to be hundreds of images of his own face, each a different face he might use to work the future. Hundreds of possible faces, flickering, a range of metallic tones, all shiny, seductive, possible.

He bubbled with laughter. That's all he could do.

May 5th

Oh, the "Itchycoo Park" of it all.

Sorry to go on about a hysterical suburban acid trip, Annie, but you missed all that. And though I can't snare an old hurricane with words, I'll never forget that first time. If I could recall my birth I'd stick both events in the same bronze-bootie corner of my memory. Though LSD is maybe one of the bullets that got me in the end, I still revere it. Chemical pirate that makes you walk the rational plank. I almost shake, recalling. I do shake.

Here in Bella Combe I've learned to take surer steps. I built this little house with good wood, good muscles, good hammer and nails. Things that last. Right?

You've told me how Ivan would no-no all drugs, yet you say his leaping into the chasm never stopped. But we had daring too. Give us that much.

Anyway. Recalling the Late Sixties kindles powerful nostalgia — I know this stereotypes me. We've talked of this before. You called it the Charlie Manson peace parade. You're maybe more right than wrong.

Because of my age I could straddle the famous generation gap. I had a good view: the tide gathering, swollen with youth's effervescence — a kind of antigravity — then crashing like a wave on the beach. The beach-front property owners saw it coming. They heard its peculiar roar, feared the coming damage, eyed the secret calligraphies it carved in the sand, mocked the silly foam, tsk'd at the blasted jetsam it left behind.

Many said the wave was nothing but a bunch of brats who could only whine and take from the hand that et cetera. People my age made the mistake of confiding in me. I could see they really wanted to scream. Parents trying to make their kids in their own image woke up one day to find kids holding radioactive secrets from them, then slouching off to the alleys of druggy revolution. I watched the boxed minds of my generation mourn but mostly hate its spawn of mutant sons.

It was like we were up on waterskis for the first time, hordes of us, going faster and faster, a siren howl of psychedelic engines overpowering the lake, all of us checking out each other's first-time-up body and grin. Swimmers had to duck-dive or get keel-burned. Yahoo! We thought we'd invented waterskis.

"Hippies" were an invention of *Life Magazine*. I mean, could one person do all this: learn yoga, rage over Vietnam, care if Paul was the walrus, trade in the Chev for a VW van, abandon parents, learn guitar, grow marijuana at the commune, stink and steal and use needles, join an alternative theatre, read *Das Kapital*, become a Mátala cave-dweller, discover health food, smash your guitar on stage, have indiscriminate sex, become a pacifist, juggle in public, astral travel, bomb a building, throw the *I Ching*, shame drivers with peace signs while hitch-hiking, wear fake army fatigues, meditate on Tantric deities, chain yourself to a federal fence, join the women's movement, trek Nepal, grow organic corn, drop acid in an isolation tank?

Young sheep had a new barnyard of trends. But the heart of it, Annie, I think the heart was good. It was suddenly right to see the world, not just one country. It was suddenly right to see your life, not just a job. Men didn't have to be the

Fonz and women didn't have to be Annette Funicello. Crack the cement, grow the flower. Christian vigour, Buddhist eyes. Good stuff, eh?

But what were my friends up to? The Deep Cove guys. Well, they started by rejecting politics, because that was just rules. They rejected Donovan and granola and Dan'l Boone look-alikes, and the bug-eyed folk on a fast-food spiritual quest. They hated all style. In fact they fled all ideas, for in this lay freedom. Because long hair was such an issue, by 1970 some had shaved their heads, forecasting a trend ten years down the road. Bob Cumming, Mr. Opposite himself, wore old black horn-rim glasses and polo shirts.

Me, I'd never had style so I fit right in. Looking at us, no one had a clue what we were, what we stood for. In fact, we didn't stand for anything, except freedom from any stance. Rationality itself was seen as a bad habit.

In one sense we were visionary. If the peace-and-love era was a golden age, like all golden ages it was doomed to decadence. We skipped a stage and got right to the decadence part.

Decadence has a logic. It is a balancing act between supreme pleasure and its necessary partner, supreme pain. It has a purpose, it's what Rimbaud tried: burn off the mundane mind and trust that what survives is pure. We tried that too. I reached heights of — heights of — I can't seem to remem —

I'm joking. Half-joking.

What about Connor Peake? I exaggerate, but like some Mongol warlord Peake had ransacked my village, stolen my woman, used her and discarded her. Could any peasant boy not respect such power? And then try to beat it?

Annie, I see now that in one sense my whole story is about power. Since I had none of my own, I was always drawn to whoever I saw was the least controlled by others. Lise, Bert Flute, Dog Merson, Connor Peake. Now the whole Deep

Cove gang. I think Bob Cumming was my next target, though my pursuit had gotten subtler. Because he was subtler.

But the hearth-stone warmth of comradeship. In Deep Cove I discovered it. Our group had a homey side we knew never had to be mentioned. Whispers beside a four-in-the-morning campfire. Flopped in a cabin in the woods, so wasted we could say only "Bleep, phoom," but be perfectly understood. Sharing root fun but also root helplessness, those big questions which defied us all.

I can supply only fractions. I moved into the Covehouse. From then on I have no sense of month-to-month or even year-to-year. One summer I broke my foot. I owned an Austin and two Beetles but I can't recall what car followed what. Random events break through. Images of sex. My favourite coffee mug. Epiphanies on drugs, heights of — I'll try to remember. I recall lolling around the Covehouse on a Saturday in my brown velour bathrobe, butting cigarettes into an almost-empty wine bottle, flipping the TV on, settling into cartoons, too lazy to get up and change channels. There were no zappers then.

An easy life. We made our own danger.

Here is a document of Vaughn Collin's adolescence. His friends were half his age, and he adored them. They owned the youngest part of him, his feelings.

The Birthday Party

> *Go against grain. Drugs not wasted time.*
>
> — Bob Cumming

Deep Cove is a small bay lying under Mount Seymour, ten miles from Vancouver up Indian Arm. Technically a fiord, Indian Arm is walled by two ridges of mountains. On top of one of these mountains, Indian Arm looks like a huge ditch. In the afternoon, at the height of its brightness, the sun edges behind peaks. In a ditch one never sees a sunrise or a sunset.

Imagine a pod of friends on a beach after swimming. A mismatched group, by appearances. One of them has an older body than the others, could be their father. A chipped tooth he hides with his upper lip, making his smile come too late and seem considered, which, in fact, it is. The friends are starting to shiver. Quick movements, tiny hard male nipples. A summer afternoon, and while the rest of the world lounges in the sun, these friends, in tune to the coming darkness, search for other things to do.

They know there's something behind the peacefulness. Picture a dark bay with a main street leading down to it like a stem into an apple. A collar of houses on the water. Except for an occasional dog, and a car starting and then chugging up the road, there is no noise. Black, clear water domes, swells out of itself. Coloured boats sit on this black mirror like sharp chips embedded in a bubble. From one of them, a tinny radio plays an old song, half-heard.

Obviously, such stillness holds an imminent trick.

The group set out along the beach route, the path a low tide had left beneath waterfront houses. Seven pairs of feet crunched barnacles. It was likely the day's beer that made Mike Evers start calling a "hup, two, three" march, and because none in this group was afraid to be idiotic, they fell in and marched. Like children, but tall and devious and drunk. Barnacle-smashing rhythms.

As usual, Collin watched them carefully. First walked the youngest, Evers, red hair, the nervous face and bugging eyes of one who still knew right and wrong. The group's Jekyll and Hyde, he was shy until high, and then of all of them he could go the farthest out. Next came Connor Peake, poet, a Brit whose accent gave him the air of transience and exotic knowledge. He wanted to lead these men, but his most poetic of commands were ignored. Next walked handsome Rob Mac, Marxist janitor, wrench in the gears of the corporate panzer. He didn't speak much, but his eyes' censorship could nudge the group's direction. Behind him marched Bob Cumming, quieter still than Mac, yet perhaps standing tallest in the gentle pecking order of friends. His nickname was The Sandman, said behind his back with respect, though Collin had no idea what it implied. Then Benny Powys, short, with fixed smile, laugh lines and crow's feet all framed by his afro head of hair. Never offstage, a laughy gnat. Next was Jim "Johnny" Carson, Powys' best friend and straight man.

Last came a marching kink, a clean-cut greying man who resembled Ward Cleaver to the group's collective Eddie Haskell more than he knew. He often wore a suit, rumpled and tattered now, because he knew they liked him to. The sight of him gave their gang an almost frightening twist, an outlaw cast. Chipped tooth, facial scars, eyes that gave you nothing but their own question. They called him Ward, Coot, Mica, Death, but nicknames never stuck. His eyes and the tilt of his face revealed a mind off-key, like a background oboe note gone flat. Collin himself looked powerless to get in tune.

Unlike ne'er-do-wells in the city, this group's den of iniquity was the forest. Their Sally-Ann couch a ring of stumps, their cockroaches raccoons. LSD nights had given their forest a luminous edge. To them, everything here seemed somehow conscious. The rocks, the shrubs, the path-roots seemed aware of themselves; above, the blue framed by the clearing-edge trees showed us that Heaven was waiting; the patterned waves, and perfect arrangement of logs and boulders at the high-water mark. On still nights the trees had a near-absurd vigour. It was in the trees especially.

"Hep, toowp, threep, fo'." Mike Evers remembering some movie. The houses came to an end, a small park lawn was crossed, and they were in the trees. To give adventure its due they ignored the trails and pushed into the thickest mess. A feel of desperation was sought in fighting uneven ground. Boxing at branches, making their own trails, soon the commandos were far from the hearing of houses, necessary should things become Lion Birth at the Zoo. Like last week when they attacked and destroyed Benny Powys' car, parked back up on the road. Sticks, logs — *wham, wham* — they danced on the roof, down the hood, the trunk, kicked out the windows, Powys himself the rabid instigator, so no guilt. Perfect him climbing into his car at dawn, a calm "g'night" and driving the old shoe away. This afternoon the windshield glass still glittered in the gravel when they passed it.

After reaching The Circle, a clearing with fire-pit and ring of stumps, they stood around, smoking, no one able to sit down. Collin saw in his friends' bodies the blood-energy of booze and in their faces the eye-spark of dope. He could see their impatience, beggars waiting for grace, waiting for the good waterfall to stagger them, not quite drown them, fill them to the brim.

Connor Peake had his head thrown back, transfixed on the cedar branches black against the dusk's royal-purple wisdom. He looked like he might shout at it. Vaughn understood that his Britishness was Peake's only glory here. They never tired of his cockney-in-a-bar, or his Liverpudlian Ringo hitting on Yoko behind John's back. "Yoke? Wan' a bit of a lay-down then?" "Reechard. Only when you understand my AAIIIIEEEEEEEEEEEE."

They started passing a jug of wine around.

"Why not just suck this through a straw and hyperventilate, get it over with." Evers' guilt.

Cummings and Mac rooted for firewood beyond the rim of The Circle. Others pulled bits of paper from pockets and wallets to jam under the pile. Soon flame tongued through gaps in the heap, and gusts of smoke began to follow the devil around.

"Maybe we should have eaten or something. I feel a

bit . . . you know, too soon."

"The store. Weenies."

"Chipmunkabob."

Several pairs of eyes searched the bush at their backs, as if for something edible.

"Red Meat! Red Meat!" Mike Evers tried to get a chant going, which died with himself, much too early in the evening. Group embarrassment for rhythmless young Mike.

"Lotsa pets just past those trees . . . O, dog over an open fire . . . Little Lisa's crispy puppy, eyes popping." Peake. His nightfall brain an ebony snail that would slime your face tirelessly.

"Jesus!" yelled Jim Johnny Carson, bored. "We need some women. Let's just go to the bar for once. Christ." Johnny sometimes forgot the simple beauty of nature, and needed chairs and other people to look at.

"Easy now Johnny." Cumming, as if soothing a horse.

But, women. Not many women hung with the group anymore, no core members at all. They used to live at the house from time to time, but rarely for long. Why weren't some of their species here tonight? Collin didn't know, they simply weren't here, they were Where Women Were. To find one you had to dress differently, you had to adjust an inner lens, and go seeking.

When Collin first came to Deep Cove they came. They zeroed in on the Covehouse: high school girls out for trouble, college women out for fun, working women out to play. Connor Peake, gracious landlord and drunken love poet, walked the slow walk of a man whose lust was sated, wore the ragged, swollen look of having sponged too much pleasure. He could now be enticed only by fillets of rarest antelope, or imported, underripe, sassy figs. "Women," Nero-eyed Peake said once, "are almost selfish as me."

Collin had his share of warm nights too. Women had been such a problem before, but now he would lie in bed beside one, amazed at how easy it all was if not taken seriously. He was an older man, prized by some. His age and bumbling, oblique bearing made him the oddest hippy for miles around, status for those for whom odd was in. A one-night kink, like sliding an ornate bone through the nose. Seeing underneath their urges, Collin suspected he'd solved or started more than one father complex in young heads.

The time he and Peake made love with two women in the same bedroom. Communal noises. Peake had leaned over and whispered, "Listen to me." They'd had amphetamine at the bar, and though Collin did his duty he was not much aroused. So he listened. Peake began groaning, clearly playing. UUGH. WHO. UGH! WON. AHHH! TH. AHHH? HOCKEY. OOWW! DOCKEY. UNNG. GAMEY. GODGOD. WAMEY? For Collin's sake. And Collin felt good, so in tune with this friend who gave his attention not to the woman he was now exploding into, but instead to him, his best friend and playmate once more.

The forest was cooling, and overhead the night rolled by after its own purpose, ignoring them, a wheelbarrow over dumb ants. The wine finished, Carson and Cummings went up the trail towards the shopping centre for more, threatening to return with tequila. And sombreros, rifles, and those bullet-belt things. Mike Evers had remembered it was his birthday today. There would be gestures.

At the clearing they talked without reason as hash oil was syringed onto cigarette ends. A quick smoke and then adventures were constructed. Trees were scaled and pissed from. Hideous and coo-coo animal noises from the bushes, while real bears slept a tense sleep and Indian spirits murmured sad love to them and caressed them behind the ears.

Collin had found his place. From this sacred clearing he could feel nature soaking in through the pores of his skin, a gift. Ten miles down the road lay Vancouver, the swarm, the madness. The mad nest. Revolving restaurants spinning in the sky, centrifugal force pressing people's faces, full of sirloin, against the windows, what a view. Disco palaces hopping with bouncing bodies bounding for their partners' furry glop, oh show me something new. In one hundred years they would all be dead, and there will have been no reason for any of it. And in Deep Cove the Indian spirits would caress the necks of high-rise janitors sleeping off their gin in the boiler room. But the Cove itself would still be deep, and black and pregnant at night, with tiny silver fish, or maybe only mud eels now, hiding in the depths to wait out the madness.

Connor Peake was whispering these ideas into Collin's ear. They were off walking, ambling a path, waiting for the wine or whatever to come. Maybe food. Yes Peake wanted food he did. The older man had his head tilted towards his friend's mouth, from which things tumbled.

"Thinkin' of leaving. It's gotten a bit, it's gotten a bit, dunno."

"What has?"

"I dunno, maybe a few o' the lads," he said, the cockney coming out as it would when he was actually being serious, "a few o' the lads, including meself, I dunno, might be a bit, I dunno, chemically no longer all that independent."

"You think?"

"An' I'm not getting laid enough."

"Right."

"An' I haven't written a poem in years. An' yer all ugly."

"I thought you 'did' them. Poems."

"Right, right."

"So do one."

"You're right. I'm just too eager, that's what it is. Gotta relax. Relax and, and do one."

Looking at Collin, who was smiling encouragement, Peake cocked his head, eyes glassy and wild in the moonlight. He whispered, "Or maybe it's your turn. A Weird Thing."

Collin first heard about Weird Things from Peake, a private lecture. Peake had seen the art in action when in Europe he met an Australian Limp-Faller. Limp-Fallers had developed the talent of falling, off their feet, off barstools, and even balconies, purely limp. Part of the art was then to lie inert, not breathing. Legendary Limp-Fallers included one who had played dead for five minutes with a broken arm under him, caused by limp-falling off a staircase after a fellow artist limp-punched him. One Irish Faller reportedly limp-dropped two storeys, played dead for the screaming shoppers, and walked away from it. And there was the Group Limp-Fall of Brisbane, where a dozen Fallers gathered in a crowed pub, raised their pints in toast, took down their beer, and then performed a Simultaneous Fall of Instant Death. A dozen dead on the floor and a crowd finding itself with poisonous beer halfway down its throat. Art.

The people cry exhibitionism, ego-*chanteur!* No, said Peake. To paint your body blue, except hands and face, and go about your normal day, paint hidden under clothes, found the spirit of the art. You could go public or private with a Weird Thing. It definitely had nothing to do with self-promotion. Nothing to do with the race of the purportedly weird, that gut-turning horde of show-offs with its similar-looking original hats and airs of superior detachment. No, Peake had more respect for the goggle-eyed shrimp who stayed home building radios. No pretence. It was better to be simply normal. As long as you saw that it was necessary now and again to take a swan-dive into the void.

The outward Thing was not its essence. Pulling down one's pants in a bar is at face value slapstick, but in the hands of a master it could be art. Finger to the wind, a master gauges all factors and then maybe acts, maybe not. The bar would have to be full of college drunks and the pseudo-weird, those inclined to pull their pants down unartfully. All things gauged, the master acts: he enters invisibly, has a calm glass of something dry, stands and pulls down his pants. There must be no odour of a joke. His bending at the waist shows graceful strength, like drawing the Zen bow; his rising is the release of the arrow of liberation. His face reveals a pure absence of desire for laughter or praise. He might Prolong the Act Indefinitely, which means no movement of any kind until someone does something to him. Or he might scream (Forced Insanity), urinate without using his hands (Dirtying Their Picnic), or shit on his legs (Holding Hands with a Running God) — a highly advanced technique, the rumoured result of which is enlightenment or death.

Peake, talking, at least half-serious.

They switched paths to head back to the clearing. The night had fallen blacker now, clouds having moved in to nudge the moon's face off. They tripped on roots and caught their sleeves on thorns.

So, thought Collin, they needed a Weird Thing. He recalled some from the past, a few of which he'd been in on. Small ones: the time they went to a nice restaurant each with a prawn tail protruding from one nostril. The time they took toilet plungers to a concert — Fleetwood Mac opened for Jethro Tull — and gang-phoompa'd anyone who deserved it. But these were planned, and too silly, and everyone except Peake was embarrassed from the getgo. Better ones just happened out of thin air. The time Bob Cumming ate a live housefly and then phoned Ottawa, incredibly got Trudeau's new wife of one week — Maggie — on the phone and told her all about it and she listened. Bigger ones: jumping cliffs in Lynn Canyon while tripping on a blind mix of chemistry. Driving a mountain pass to Long Beach in a car with no brakes, using the inner rockface to slow down, scraping all paint off one side and flattening two tires in the process. And lord, the time Powys made off with the severed foot while the rest of them helped out at the fatal car crash they'd come upon, then the balance-the-foot-on-your-head dancing back in the Rimbaud Room before packing it up to send, with apologies, to the hospital. A friend had phoned that they'd made the news. Not that they cared what the aliens thought.

What ideas could Collin himself come up with? He knew that opportunities were ripe for him to take the lead. An odd life had seen him through all those dull years to a kind of vanguard. His friends. People were afraid of what they did. These were men who looked up to no one. Buddy Caronas of popular culture. He was part of an élite. Was it possible? Collin? Yes.

Vaughn studied now the back of his young friend's head as they walked. Peake's bald patch glowed a bit in the moonlight, and Collin imagined a brain in there bubbling at the edges, delicious with contradiction, fillet fried in spit.

Yes. Collin. In the fearless vanguard. Life had denied him long enough.

They broke into the clearing to find their friends huddled in the firelight over two bottles of tequila and a small brown bag.

Already worried because he knew what this meant and how he would feel tomorrow, Mike Evers mumbled, "Cumming got some peyote."

"Happy birthday," said Cumming. Sandman.

The first bottle was half done and into it Cumming was shoving broken peyote buttons. There were far too many for the seven of them to reasonably take. Tilting the bottle of swelling buttons at Peake and Collin, Cumming said, "We've been waiting for you."

In lieu of a lemon, along with the bottle they passed a dug-up, dirty white stick to chew, a fern root that tasted of strong licorice.

Their eyes glazing more red with fire with each pass of the button-bottle, root dirt outlining their teeth and smearing their clothes, these men could look no more like bad-movie Mexicans if they'd tried.

"Brain cells. Line 'em up," whispered dirt-mouth Mike Evers, "mow 'em down."

Round and round. Mushy buttons fished out on a hooked twig and eaten. They took half-breaths and looked inside themselves for what was coming.

Powys and Carson plunged beachward into the bush, going swimming they bragged. Evers and Mac began juggling two chunks of spinning wood between them, and did very well, thought Collin, considering. You didn't need to practise, or be in an arena, he decided, head lolling like a rear-window ceramic dog, to be a great athlete. Mac, handsome giggling squirrel, plucked a flaming brand from the fire and twirled it at his partner, who considered the surprise gift's approach for one second before letting it fly past his head and hiss on into the trees. Cumming sat silently wondering at the function of his fingernails. Peake sang himself off a log. Over their heads, the stars had become drenched in irony. Or perhaps they had always been that way; the heavens had simply clarified. Hidden new constellations became clear as well, funny and sympathetic ones that winked in time with their merest remark or gesture, so obvious in their friendship that their most amazing feature was that they hadn't been noticed before.

Powys and Carson burst back into firelight, hair wet, laughing, claiming ecstasy. They threw themselves on the ground to demonstrate. They had been lying on the beach with their heads, not their bodies, in the water, pretending: screaming into their bubbles, arms pounding spastic swim strokes into the gravel. A man out late walking his dog came upon them like this, considered his options, and ran. "Come on, Tammy, come on girl!"

"It's name was Timmy," said Powys.

"No, he said 'Tammy'."

"Or," Powys actually looked serious, "or Jimmeny."

"Oh yeah?" A dumb voice out of the shadows. Peake. "You so . . . you so *baa. Baa.* Baaad *Arab.* ARAB! We *BAD ARAB.*"

They turned to study him. Peake had taken a careless route tonight. He watched them back like a bull who had taken seven swords and is near death, eyes almost shut. He was ignored.

"What's the funniest thing in the world?" someone asked.

"Rock. No. Carrots. *Carrots.*" Powys.

"Plynxth." Peake again, his slobber sizzling in the fire.

"Sleeping with your mouth open." Mac. "I mean, you're unconscious with your m — "

"*Plynxth.* Wankin' fuckoffs."

"Killing yourself, because you're tired of hell." Cumming.

"Needing pussy." Carson.

"Me." Collin, but no one seemed to hear.

"*This is a waste of time!*" Carson. "We need WOMEN."

"Bicycle treat!" Powys, echoing imp.

"Let's just go." Carson now rising, severely disruptive.

"Well, what time is it?" Evers. "And who'd, you know, drive? Or call a, you know, a thing, a cab . . . "

Cumming had left the clearing and, when he shouted, he was halfway up a tree.

"I, want, woo*maaan.*"

The mournful call of an old man, an old Italian farmer, who hadn't talked in twenty years, Fellini's *Roma.* Cumming was mocking, and yet the yell was coarse and gravelly and heartfelt, from the groin and the heart.

"I, want, wooo*maaaaan.*"

Lodged in mid-branches, Cumming leaned into it, a treed moose in rut: taught, bellowing. His roar broke apart, it retched with yearning. It was perfect, they all plunged in.

"I, WANT, WOOOM*AAAAAAAAN.*"

They pulsed, they heaved with the chant. The peyote

decided to leap in then too, flooding their stage of desire with light. Collin watched Rob Mac pounding the ground with a caveman's club, grunting as he struck the planet's crust. Collin watched Benny Powys whimper and reach his tiny unrequited arms towards the forest, to all the coy creatures living in it. Jim Johnny Carson kicked at the fire, sending up a tree of living angel bits. Mike Evers was taking off his clothes with gaa-gaa movements. Connor Peake lay on his back, almost gone but screaming sloppily into the air, the tree trunk beside him leaning at him and undulating its shadowy pelvis, helping his descent.

"I, WANT, WOOOOM*AAAAAAAN*."

Collin stared at the ground between his feet, then deeply into it, down past roots and soil to where scorpions walked and clicked their tails. He stared in further and suddenly, somehow logically, he saw Lise. Annie. Woman. That's right, Annie was woman. Where was she? Where was Bella Combe anyhow? Could she even imagine this world of his? Could he ever explain it to her? Maybe someday. This was not just a frenzy of fools. They sought a bigger mind than the one they owned. They had to erase theirs first. There droned a pure night over and around them, and they were aware of it. It squeezed the gut and bonneted the skull. Nor had they forgotten the stars that hung over them, seeds of irony, clues to purpose. But entertainment too. And Vaughn Collin sat amazed, as always, at his friends' talent: they were in awe of the night and stars, and yet they juiced every drop of laughing elixir. Both at once. Lunatic boys at play, yet blessed by a holy night. What talent.

Captain Cumming had descended his crow's-nest to join his pirates. He sat beside the woozy Peake, who'd quaffed too much grog amidst these waves, and who was trying to get out of his clothes for some reason. He'd got his pants to his ankles but then quit and sat staring at the fire, with seaman Vaughn Collin trying to talk him back to dry land, perhaps pleading a little. Cumming looked at Collin, then at Peake, then laughed. He brought up his big leg, encased at its end in a running shoe, and with the toe of this shoe the Sandman nudged Peake under the jaw. Peake teetered gently back, fell into the dirt, into private hallucinations, passing out. Collin looked at Peake, then at Cumming, who was up now with the rest of them, dancing, whooping, glowing with firelight and, no effort at all, what talent, casting giant black replicas of himself up onto the surrounding wall of trees. They laughed the shuddering laugh of hippos, the reedy laughs of weasels, the silent laughs of tricksters. They spun, tottered, fell, rose from ashes. One, naked Mike Evers, came hopping towards Vaughn. Eyes bugging, mouth slack, face dangerously red, Evers made the noises of a man whose stomach had been shot out. A glowing chunk of peyote mixed with dirt and vomit stuck to his lower lip. Evers was smiling, happy at last.

"I, WANT, WOOOO, *MAAAAAAAAAAAN.*"

Waking in the dawn, looking up, Collin thought it must be about six o'clock. He'd slept a few hours. Deep Cove seemed wide awake still. Always watching. The sun rising over the ridge was painful to see. The mist was already thinning on the water. Funny how, in the morning, the water looked so innocent, a sleeping baby sister. Tiny fish tickled her mirror skin.

One chirping bird, then an answer, then ten at once. Collin saw that Peake had left sometime in the night. He started his own stagger down the trail, battered Ward Cleaver going home from work. He hoped he wouldn't scare any early joggers. He wouldn't want a mirror today, no. His other friends lay back in the clearing, soaking up dew, curled up for warmth, rat pups in a pink dawn. There was nothing to yearn for yet, it was morning, everything calm.

The morning with its hidden trick. Because it was telling

Collin that there was nothing in the world to get worried about, ever.

May 24th

Can't tell if that was accurate, if it revealed much. I doubt the heart of friendship can be conveyed to an outsider, friendship being by function a private land. I was wary of showing Annie these Deep Cove pages. She's sitting with them now on the beach, sitting there in all that tranquillity reading all that noise. I've never coughed up this part of my past to her, not really. Writing it was almost . . . fun. How memory can find an old mood. Almost dangerous. Which is maybe — which is maybe why I'm doing this.

She's going off up the mountain again apparently. For a longer time this time. Not telling me, either.

I learned of her plans in the bar. (I'm turning into a regular socialite these days. Annie is pleased.) The news didn't come from her mouth but someone else's, and damn if I wasn't hit with a "the lover is the last to know" twinge in the gut.

I was at the urinal when old August Bob came in and took his wide-legged stance next to me. So confident was his posture that I fell to philosophy about the way men pee in public, how revealing it is. Some take the farthest urinal; some cringe up into one, hiding. Some, lots actually, can't pee in public at all. Mike Evers couldn't; he'd lock himself in a cubicle and flush constantly for noise.

Anyway, standing way back, August Bob started his confident stream. Wearing shorts, I felt his rebound spatter coldly on my legs.

I yelled "Yikes, hey!" and stepped back.

August Bob, eightyish, squat, weaved a bit then aimed down. But I stayed back.

"Get some goddamn clothes, boy."

When I first got here I fell into reverse prejudice: all natives were noble, obliquely wise, and hard done by. I'd mistake silence for mysterious knowledge. I'd fear them a bit and toady up. I remember, early on, watching in quiet respect as Betty Jack poked deer droppings with her foot and announced, "Gonna be cold summer." We baked that summer and, after learning that such predictions were often wrong, I began to see natives for the fallible, normal people they are. (I think Hollywood made a generation of them feel they are expert trackers by birthright.) I also learned that the ones who do in fact read nature don't tell you anything unless you ask the right questions.

August Bob would be admired anywhere. He drinks a lot, but. He's got brilliant eyes, and his smile you wouldn't know was a smile unless you knew him. The first time I saw him drunk I felt let down. Annie said, well, he'd be out of touch with his family if he didn't drink. I didn't buy this, so she added something odd, saying that, though he drank cheap wine, if a giant came along and squeezed him over a glass you'd get a good brandy.

Zipping up, Bob said to me, "So Annie, she off, eh?" From his eyes it was clear Annie owned a spot in his heart too.

"Oh?"

"Bought ten pound a' jerk from me. Five pound salmon, three pound deer, two pound bear." He proudly showed me with his hands the size of each package of dried meat.

"So where's she off to?"

He shrugged then pointed inland through the bathroom wall.

"Long ways. Big time. That much meat, maybe Alberta." Bob the joker. "Or she takin' somebody wid her, eh?"

When she got back from reading my pages on the beach I asked her about her trip. I'd intended to appear casually uninterested. I think what came out was:

"You're going on a long trip you didn't tell me about. Why not?"

She didn't seem curious how I knew. Instead, she considered the pages in her hand, reading something from their weight, or lack of it.

"I wanted to surprise you."

"When do you figure on — ?"

She lifted the pages. "When you're done."

So this meant I was going with her?

"Is it, is it far? I don't know if I can walk up hill for any length of — "

She smacked the chapter on the table. "Your style changed completely." If her intention was to change the subject, it worked.

"It did?"

"Still have quite a link to these boys, eh?"

"I. . . . Sure. I mean, that's the point of this, right? To go deep, get inside, you know . . . "

"You're stuck here. You enjoyed writing this part."

"Well I guess I did."

"No, it's good. Get into it. Putty on a window."

"What?"

"Putty stuck to your window. Spit in it, get your fingers in there, get it sticky again. Won't come off if it's dry."

"Is this like smelling your own shit? That one?" I was being facetious, perhaps, and Annie didn't respond.

"Well what if it sticks to me?"

She didn't answer.

"I need a break." Up a mountain.

"There is no break. Here, there, anywhere."

I turned to the window. The morning calm and gentle light contradicted her. I couldn't imagine anywhere out there being as bad as inside this cabin, sitting in a chair chasing ghosts.

"*Finish* it. What a day that'll be — like finishing your own ship, the *Vaughn Hardy Collin,* your own doggy-face on the prow. You can sail anywhere when it's done. Joy! *Finish* it."

We drank our tea and chatted about surface things. Lovers (why not use this word once and for all?) can do this endlessly, ignoring and sitting on their deeper questions like chairs.

Annie spoke of her last several days. She'd attended a birth at Bella Coola where she delivered a stillborn. She described the cord around the neck, the blue face, the parents' numbness then understanding. Gnashing of teeth.

"I've had DT babies and I had a boy with no arms. But never dead. It felt like *my* luck. But that's pretty self-centred, eh?"

"So now a long trip."

Annie didn't respond.

I watched her face. I saw pain there, sparking her muscles, making her eyes fire up. I often forget she's a student too. What kind of crisis is she riding? I know Annie better than anyone alive and yet there is a weight in her heart I can't even begin to help her lift.

She looked impatient to go, and got up, but stopped, having a thought, one that made her smile.

"What."

She thought a moment more, and laughed to herself.

"What."

"Oh I dunno. Just your life. How funny it is. How — how 'emblematic'. *Un tableau vivant.*"

"How funny it is?"

"It's like you're this portrait of the decades. A symbol of the times. It's probably just in the writing, I dunno."

"I am a portrait of the decades? I sort of don't think so."

"Look at you: this pre-war innocence, this post-war naïve confidence, the sixties smash-up. Now reassessing everything." She points at me in mock drama. "You're North America. You're a portrait of the century."

"I was easily influenced by what was around me."

"Right. I guess that's it."

She was going through my kitchen drawer. She put one of my two forks in her pocket, waved at me, then left.

At first I was only a poor copy of my friends, but in the end I did attain them.

We tried to keep things wild. We broke most of the habits humans build to shelter themselves from wildness. (Annie, I'm already at it, glorifying these boys some more. Embarrassment you call "the back door to insight". So, I'll glorify them, I'll writhe in embarrassment.)

But wildmen grow tired. Most do, anyway. One, who had been living life backwards, getting younger and younger as his body aged, never did get tired. And so he became captain at last. Captain of a team of one.

Weird Things

> *You come back tomorrow, tell me again*
> *you wanna ruin your life. An' it'll cost*
> *you triple.*
>
> — Marilda the tattoo artist

Collin was happy.

He loved Covehouse life. He had learned a lot about a lot of things. The days lurched and whispered and pinwheeled by. They never plodded. Perhaps years went by as well, but Collin had no sense of them unless reminded at some New Year's thingamabob, or unless he found himself in a store buying a sweater because he'd been kind of cold or something lately, and, right, summer was over again — it gets colder when that happens.

He was also content these days to be sharing his bedroom with a woman. From Montreal, Leona had been travelling for years on whims when she stumbled on a Covehouse party. She liked her drugs "organic" and was disdainful of alcohol, a common stance. When Collin nodded in agreement, saying, "After the bar closes and the acid or whatever kicks in, I tend to abstain from alcohol myself," she laughed, then saw he was serious, then gave him an assessing look. Leona slept beside Collin that night, and in the morning stayed put. Leona turned twenty-six the day after Collin turned forty-nine.

She had a California look, minus the tan. Blonde, blue eyes, healthy shoulders. She would have been striking if not for what she did to her face, squeezing it into a pained wonderment. Her eyes quizzed to a squint, her lips pursed, and even in sleep when she did release the scrunch of her brow it was clear to Collin that those wrinkles were there for good.

"A bird aimed at the horizon" is how Cumming summed her up, and maybe he was right. She talked always of the future. If she sat in a comfortable chair she would sit on its edge. Even sex gathered worry to her face and scrunched it tighter. (He couldn't help but compare: Lise, a homely glutton. Chantal, beautiful liar. And Leona, orgasm squeezed by doubt.) Would she leave soon? Well, it didn't matter if she did, for things were done this way these days, transience was the deal, and he was proud to be a part of all this freedom.

The others liked her. Though no one paid rent, Leona did more than her share of work as if to pay for her keep. Peake said she balanced the yang of the house with her yin — so the idea went, perhaps another way of saying the men liked having a woman around. She was everyone's friend, but she slept with Collin. He didn't know exactly why.

Sometimes with Leona and sometimes with the others Collin spent aimless summer days walking Mount Seymour trails or in winter drizzle the streets of Gastown or Kits to nod heads with folks and more often than not flip them the quarter they needed. He did beer and Frisbee on the beach, he took in bands in the woods or the bar, he trekked to Long Beach or the Kootenays. A perfect midweek evening meant a few mushrooms and a good wine on the gentle rocks of Lighthouse Park.

At one point Collin suggested they head up the coast to a place called Bella Combe. He had a crazy old friend there, he explained, who lived in a driftwood cabin with a beach for a front yard, just right for campfires and midnight screaming. The idea seemed like a go. Peake, for one, wanted to meet this mysterious Annie.

Collin was surprised when his chatty letter north was answered with a blunt, "No, Vaughn. Don't come. A."

For money he still wrote ads for the department store, but he did it part-time now, at home. He often put on his suit anyway, half because he knew the others still got a kick out of it, but half also because in truth it put him in the frame of mind, propping his head up to give birth to crisp words. Other days he would help frizzy Benny Powys make his monster men: "The Famous Fetish Figures of Doctor Benway" read the sign on the portable booth which he set up at craft fairs and concerts. Powys had found in a deceased aunt's attic a set of moulds for making plaster nativity scenes, and one exacto-knife job later the moulds no longer formed up a Mary or a wise man but instead a woman with claws and hunchback, or an evil man with horns and Vandyke beard. The old, robed prophet now had a headband and guitar, and was Powys' best-seller after the sheep with black bra and panties. He and Collin would smoke a joint and spend a quiet morning enamelling eyeballs and teeth.

Basically, Collin still waited most of all for those wonderful times when all his friends would gather and play. Nothing had changed in his life for several years now. Except, perhaps, that he had grown more and more passionate.

Collin? Passionate? About what?

About everything. His enthusiasm never died. It was almost as though the ebbing vitality of his friends funnelled into him, was almost as though their spent furies had to be kept awake by his constant spending. Any drizzly Tuesday evening, should one of the stumps he sat with propose a tired "Anyone wanna, I dunno, a movie — "

"Yes!" Vaughn Collin could be counted on to exclaim. Then he would stand, knowing that this and only this might move them to stand as well. "Let's go, lads!"

He could also be counted on, strangely, to cry at the movie. Or, later, at the bar, when an old song came on, any old Beatles thing, or even more so something from the war era, Swing it was called, some song no one else had even heard of, and which Vaughn himself couldn't recall having particularly liked. Or he'd cry hardest, laughing at the same time, later in Cates Park when something like friendship was declared, everyone nostalgic on wine. For a time he was introduced to newcomers as the weeping hobo. The tattered suit, he reckoned.

" — and maybe after the movie we can hit the b — "

"Yes!"

You can't blame rats for deserting a plague-bound city, and you can maybe only laugh at the one rodent too dumb to leave. So maybe this is a funny story.

He was too enthusiastic to see that things had changed. Joni Mitchell's Mátala caves had long been filled with human shit and patrolled by Greek undercover cops. The drug of choice was anything easy on the ego — downers, cocaine, white wine. By now the truly concerned had fled to the land to build log caves and farm the dirt and never be heard from again by city brothers and sisters who were themselves mutating anew in a broth of disco music, church weddings, and real estate.

But what brought Collin trouble was not the death of a movement but rather the death of youth itself. He had never seen youth die before, not really. He didn't know that each ant takes but one turn under the magnifying glass of youth — to have its bum seared, then leap and shout out a quick philosophy of right and wrong — but escapes the hot eye after its brief time to move on into age, quieter now. That was law. Collin could read wrinkles and shrugs, but he had no inkling of law, of how the tread of years wears on the spirit, leaving its edges smooth. Was it Collin's fault he'd spent his Victoria years with men in their thirties who continued to play a boy's game?

If he'd only been able he would have seen that his beloved lunatics were winding down while he was speeding up. He didn't notice the young plague rats gnawing the walls, looking for exits.

He could have seen signs in the Covehouse changing. Its cedar-shake siding had never been painted, and had the grey, weathered nobility of a Haida longhouse — so Peake insisted to any neighbour who complained about property values. And neither, Peake informed these neighbours, did the Haida cut their grass. And that was no upside-down bashed motorcycle, that was a metal sculpture. And we choose to newspaper over the broken front window because you sods keep staring in at us. The noose in the tree? That noose predates our arrival.

The changes to the Covehouse did not occur all at once, but now the shakes bore a tasteful blue stain, the lawn was generally cut (after the neighbours paid a company to scythe down the brush and saplings), and it seems late one night Peake himself had sneaked glass into the window.

So gradual were the changes in his friends too that perhaps Collin's enthusiasm should not be blamed for blinding him to the fact that these exalted bohemians, forever head-above the glue of labour, of matrimony, of consensus reality even, were no longer so free. Jobs, it seems everybody had one now, with the exception of Peake. Mac was head custodian at the department store. Powys organized the craft guild's consignments throughout the region. Cumming was almost done a PhD and taught courses. Carson had taken the real-estate exam and had actually sold two houses. Evers was a sunburnt and hung-over apprentice landscaper. Leona began working day-care for minimum wage because she decided she needed a car.

And one by one they were moving out. Some, to women. (And Carson — it seemed to no one but Collin's surprise — came out of the closet. Best pal Powys' shocked disapproval made Carson roll his eyes and tsk at him like a disappointed mother. Benny, tell the truth, he said, and Benny left the room.)

Inside this fixed-up, emptying blue house, parties lasted "evenings" instead of weekends, or weeks. Sometimes, at a planned potluck-dinner affair, the air above the matching place settings thick with garlic and coriander, Collin would catch Powys and Cumming trading a look of melancholy recognition that something was wrong with this picture. Uninspired table talk often turned nostalgic.

"Remember the time Powys took that chicken leg — "

"God that's right — "

"Stuck it in his fly? Raw skin dangling like — Pointing it — what was her name? Gale?"

" — this white, this warty white thing hanging out, this chewed scrotum, I mean it was — "

Powys sits back smiling like a grandad at his old antics.

"I mean thanks, she was hot for me, she basically ran out the door. Gloria."

Laughing explanations for those who hadn't been there, and nostalgia interrupts again.

"Remember that chicken we took camping? Up past Squamish — "

"Alice Lake! Alice Lake!"

" — we found it thawed and it was pretty bad and we played — "

"*Who* just stuck it in the trunk like that?"

" — chicken soccer! That's right!"

By midnight on such evenings, unsmiling Evers would be trying to lure people into the Rimbaud Room to smash things, and when no one followed and after they'd gone he would smash things alone. Or sometimes just Collin would join him in this, or in a prank outside, but with just him and Evers it lacked the good feel of teamwork.

A drizzly morning in November, Collin stood in the middle of the living-room, blinking, wondering how this new day would go. Leona entered in her robe. Somewhat rare these days, someone new was curled asleep on the couch. In pain on the floor, Mike Evers sat smoking, staring at the TV with the sound off. That's right, Leona seemed to remember, there'd been a party. She grabbed her temples, felt the residue of last night's poisons, shook her head.

"God, but we abuse ourselves."

Evers nodded, vacantly agreeing. Collin didn't think things were so bad. For one, Peake had cleaned the mess up sometime in the night and the house looked quite nifty. Ready for more, in fact.

Bacon smell wafted in from the kitchen and seemed to catch Evers sideways on the cheek.

"What's with this, what's with this constant *food* shit?" He squinted and turned towards the sizzling sound. He lurched up, shaking his head, and went out the front door, leaving it open, going home. He had his own place, though he still used the Covehouse couch a lot.

At this Leona joined Peake, taking a break from his cleaning and cooking, out on the back steps for fresh air and herbal tea. Collin was alone with the guy sleeping on the couch.

His friends just weren't coming around as much. Even weekends — rumour had it that Cumming and his new wife sat in front of a TV. They had a kid coming, but still. And Jim Johnny Carson had stumbled with a small nervous breakdown, Carson himself wasn't sure why, but as a precaution he had quit all fun except the odd beer. And Powys, Powys just seemed sort of quiet and embarrassed these days.

The guy on the couch stirred, coughed painfully. Dodic, that was his name. One of Dodic's eyes was sort of stuck open and Collin could see a metallic slice of eyeball. Dodic, Evers' friend from Toronto, bumped into him at the bar last week. At last call he'd insisted on an impossibly huge last round, sort of the brag of a rookie-drinker, like Toronto could guzzle beer and Vancouver couldn't. Then Peake hosing Dodic's vomit off the side of his car later, kind of funny. Except Dodic didn't laugh, nor did he leave. Almost a week now.

Dodic was short, and handsome in a downtown way. If the light shifted even slightly you saw the weasel in him. His sneer grew with time. Vancouver's ways he'd identified as a lack of drive, which to Dodic meant name-dropping and lying. He claimed to know what "Manson *really* did," but was sworn to secrecy by some U.S. lawyer. It would hit the fan, believe me. I can't say a word, he said to women whenever he could. He gleefully insulted anyone in the house for their placidity, and whenever he got insulted back he'd effect a startle, smile, and say, "I love it." His name was pronounced an exasperated "*Do*dic". (After meeting him, Cumming summed him up simply: "A doe with a dick.") It got so bad in the house that whenever Dodic came in the rest of them would stiffen like the elderly, and glare at nothing.

One night in the midst of a small gathering Dodic had dumped a small black pistol out of an oil-stained sock. He began sighting at light fixtures and plants. "Pu*kow*, pu*kow*," he mouthed the little-kid sounds and showed with a flip of his hand how the gun would recoil.

"Hey," said Collin, shyly, understanding that it was a real gun. "Neat. Let's all — "

"The fuck's that, *Do*dic?" Mac, the next to find words.

"Just thought I'd get the little heater out and clean it while — "

"TAKE THAT FUCKING GERM OUT OF THIS HOUSE." Holding a spatula, Peake stood at the portal to his kitchen. His clearly yelled command, most of all its noble enunciation, later earned him Cumming's accolade for a "great, in fact superb, mother imitation", and with gunslinger Dodic off sneering somewhere downtown, Peake cooked up a batch of Mother's Ceremonial Pink Porridge for the Rimbaud Room. It was the first time they'd thrown ceremonial porridge for maybe years. The irony — that it had taken the destructive force of a Dodic to rekindle Covehouse camaraderie for a night — was lost on Collin.

And Dodic worked as a harmonizer only the once. When Cumming next came over, tired and proud of his four-day-old girl, Emily, whom he summed up as "a creature who lives on milk and has sky-blue skin", Dodic's only comment was to leer and ask if he'd tasted any of the stuff himself. It was so off-key no one could say anything, and Cumming appeared to dismiss both the Covehouse and his own past when he left soon after.

Why didn't they just kick Dodic out? Peake called him "lingering shoe shit", but Dodic only smiled and said, "I like that, people trying to say what they think." Peake could only silently rearrange some furniture. Unwritten protocol said it was Evers' job to evict his friend, but even Evers was avoiding the place these days. Cops had been coming by more and more lately, and a spy car had taken to parking down the street. Mike had been dealing a bit on the side. The cops had come to the door once and asked for him by name, and after a few dumb questions one had turned back to give him an "I'll get you for selling poison to kids" look. So Evers imagined it.

What did Collin do in response to these sad changes? Picture a modest skyrocket compared with Peake's burrowing mole, or a high teeter to Cumming's totter. In one sense, Collin had become his own man. Somehow he had learned how to whoop on his own. Searching for livelier pastures, he now knew other places to party, both in the Cove and in town. The crowds were even younger than his Cove friends, and this was fine, they had more zip.

He'd learned exactly what would break them up. Again, his gift for dry humour. He understood how his suit thrilled these young folks because they hated everything it stood for. His English-butler routine added spice to any kitchen scene; by squaring his shoulders and sticking his chin out he did a great "Chuck Connors as The Rifleman" in dance crowds; at midnight he'd be Ward Cleaver playing air guitar to Blue Oyster Cult or blowing Ornette Coleman's frenetic riffs. He kept his dress carefully bumbly, his greying hair trimmed. It seemed that none other than Vaughn Collin was getting famous in party circles as North Van's Strangest Man.

He'd also begun instigating his own Weird Things. Small ones at first. At his insistence a few guys went sky-diving. They went to a Canucks' game and he did a fair Limp-Fall while the usher checked their stubs. He did another solo prank at work, and got himself fired. Occasionally borrowing Mac's master key to go in after hours to deliver his ad copy on time, he realized that he now had access to ads after the proofreader had proofed them. He began by altering a few Dollar-Forty-Nine Day liners. *Flea shampoo, for clean fleas* $1.49. *Bra special, sizes small to wow* $1.49, etc. The next time, more ambitious, he changed a headline: over the picture of a sofa, a two-inch-tall SAVE! became SAVAGE!

They had a good giggle over the next day's *Vancouver*

Sun, and now every week or so the Covehouse would await its paper with extra glee.

Though the savage chesterfield had a strangely solid customer response, questions were asked. The bosses assumed anarchist prankster vermin in the *Sun*'s union printing shop, Collin wasn't suspected for months, and it took a hired Pinkerton dick to catch him red-handed in the proofer's room. The ads had been coming non-stop. In the spring of 1976 the store advertised for sale bisexual alligators, the Queen of England, Hitler Wear, and a facial cream guaranteed fatal.

But Collin had his eyes aimed at more than small Weird Things.

It was Connor Peake himself who had become the main source of Covehouse tension. More so than jobs, women, cops, or even *Do*dic.

He had grown quieter and spent more time in his room. Often Collin found him just sitting there.

"So. What's up?" was the closest Collin could get to asking him what was wrong.

"I dunno. Nothin'" was the closest Peake came to explaining.

For Peake to stop a party was unheard of. He'd never minded noise, rarely strayed from the source of it in fact. But one night they witnessed a first. Dodic had rented a TV for the house. Peake hated TV, and maybe that explained half of it. But Powys got a kick out of old movies, and Collin had to admit he liked catching *Hockey Night in Canada*. On this particular night everyone's attention was snagged by a Japanese horror movie. A guy in a warty plastic suit waving his arms and stomping a dollhouse Tokyo made for plenty of hoots and giggles, and perhaps it was Benny Powys' stoned donkey brays which broke the landlord's back. Heading off to bed earlier, Peake had warned them with a sour "I have a cold," followed by a door slam. Now he reappeared, sweating and pale. He squatted in front of the TV, facing the viewers. His face gathered to a pinch and he sneezed. Still in his squat, a bit of wet yellow on his lip, he waited several seconds before saying, "I have a *cold*. Turn this off and *shut up*." It would've been a decent Weird Thing if he hadn't been serious.

Several weeks later Peake did try to explain to Collin what was wrong. It was Friday night, and while Peake sank heavily into the couch, tooling a bare toe in a pile of books on the floor, Collin perched restlessly, slapping his knee and bouncing his foot. When Leona came round to fill their wine glasses Peake put his hand over his and slowly shook his head. He couldn't seem to find words for his exact problem. He would pause constantly and sigh.

"I don't know, man. So much . . . wasted time. I don't know what it is. Bored, I guess." Peake scratched at his crotch.

Bored? thought Collin. How could a man like Connor Peake be bored, ever, here? They had done so much! All that perfect recklessness in the Rimbaud Room: dragging girls in to threaten them with purple poster paint, scaring them a bit before letting yourself be painted purple by a laughing girl.

Peake sighed. "You're talking the same old wank. What's happened lately? Tell me."

Collin could think of nothing convincing. In a way it was true. Though he himself had been trying to get things going again. He'd had a couple of ideas. Weird Things. One was to line the Covehouse roof with cannons. He'd even priced the chicken wire and papier-mâché. But when he suggested it everyone had just sat there. "They'll get rained on and melt," someone said, and changed the subject.

"It's not simple," Peake was saying. "I mean, it's dangerous to *do* anything. You decide to do something and then you're stuck in it. And, I mean, *time* is — " He groped for words. "*Time* is an asshole skeet-shooting the days as fast as he can pull the trigger, man."

Collin nodded his head. True, time was awastin'.

"So I'm torn between something and nothing, and both are dangerous." Peake paused. "I think I'm feeling my years . . . not so young now, you know."

The older man heard no hint of irony in these words as he nodded his grey head in agreement, but that was okay. Everyone had a right to contemplate the cruel passing of time. But Peake's complaint seeded Collin's idea for the party. Peake would be turning thirty in a few weeks.

"You were lucky, to stay unstuck," Peake said, giving him an odd look, just the hint of a sneer. "Man, you escaped *biology*."

That made Collin feel proud.

But he came up with nothing to ease his friend's problem, and as weeks passed he watched Peake drift into greyer moods. He wanted to grab him by the collar and scold: look, you're young, smart, you have money. Some people are born with no arms, some support blind mothers, some are dying of starvation with flies in their eyes. But Collin could sense that this argument did not apply. Something floating around in this modern world said Peake had a right to an abstract dilemma.

"A good Weird Thing, that's what we need," Peake announced at breakfast one day. He sounded freshly buoyant, but as he did dishes his chatter over the kitchen sink was sarcastic.

"But what? I could get married, right? Or buy a race car?" He laughed. "Or I could join the Peace Corps. Yes, my, wouldn't that be weird. A 'servant of man'. One might catch, one might catch *altruism*." He winced and wriggled his wet fingers distastefully.

He was still embarrassed over what Collin had caught him doing that morning. Not thinking him in, Collin had entered Peake's room to find him sitting on his bed in a lotus posture, a strained tranquillity on his face. Collin had apologized and wheeled to go.

"Vaughn — ?"

Collin stopped. Peake's voice sounding strangely far away, a kind of ventriloquism, but worried. "Vaughn? Can this be our secret?"

And later that day while Collin was taking a bath Peake came in to use the toilet. His back to Collin, his stream tinkling in the bowl, Peake's voice echoed off the porcelain.

"It's not like I'm convinced about this meditation stuff, understand."

"Well it's probably a good — "

"No," Peake spun around to him, then turned back to the bowl for the final spurts. "I mean . . . (tinkle) . . . who wouldn't see God . . . (tinkle) . . . after lying all night . . . (tinkle) . . . on nails?" He zipped up and faced Collin. "I'm just keeping possibilities open. Testing *systems*. I'm *not* sucking some archaic fucking *lux mundi*. I mean, you know *me*." He said this last bit sort of hopefully, it sounded like. He sat on the toilet lid.

"From what I've heard," Collin offered, "meditation can be quite wild — "

"No. Hey — makes me sick, right?" Peake waited for Collin to nod. "But then I stop and think, is it the religion or the believers make me sick? I figure, even if believers are ridiculous, maybe there's a system out there that's good, that does clarify things." Peake pointed at Collin. "But I doubt it." Peake stood to leave. "But it's, it's one reason for all the cleaning. You've noticed how I've, I've been sort of cleaning things? Keeping things in order?"

"Yeah. I've been worried."

"Well it's part of it. The idea is that your surroundings are a reflection of your mind. No different than mind, actually. A vast mind *includes* it all. That."

"Ah. Right."

"And I think it might be, you know, I think it's the next big thing. I really do."

"It's sort of been around a while already."

"Not just talking about it. I mean really doing it."

"Ah."

Collin studied his friend. His sloped brow glistened with sweat and his eyes moved quickly but looked dull. Religion? Collin felt a vague disappointment. He'd thought turning thirty would've sparked his friend's sense of absurdity rather than this hackneyed depression.

"I mean, why write anything? Why even do anything? The idea is to 'be'."

It was more than clear to Collin that a new Weird Thing was needed to help his friend, who was now not only bored but boring. Collin decided it was up to him. And not just to help a friend. Here was his big chance.

After leaving the Hastings Street parlour he drove around town for an hour waiting for the pinpricks of blood to bead and dry. He couldn't stop grinning, and his forehead stung with the salt of his sweat. At each stoplight he stared into the rearview mirror. He mopped and dabbed with his handkerchief, careful not to start new bleeding, too excited to think. Amazingly, as promised, no ink seeped out. There for good.

On the way to the Cove he stopped at the fish shop for a pound of prawns and revelled at the shock of the Chinese lady who wouldn't look at him again as she pulled his money across the wet counter. Still sweating and stinging, Collin found the Covehouse street so crowded he had to park blocks away, but he was delighted that so many had turned up for Peake's birthday barbecue. He went around back, slipped into his room, and put on tennis shorts, sneakers and clean white T-shirt. Simple, clinical chic — a perfect foil for his stark ornament.

Joining the party, Collin decided he would say nothing at all. Over the years he'd learned a few things about how to be attractive. A vain woman scratches her own beauty; a silent man is a mysterious man, and mystery is a lure; an act of bravery loses its heart if bragged about. Et cetera. He would say nothing. His exclamation mark could do the talking.

Leona met Collin in the kitchen, "tsk-tsked" at his forehead, asked him what kind of wine he wanted but otherwise left him alone all night. Peake himself looked subdued, or like he was waiting for something — something that had no chance of occurring at this party. But he did give Collin and his forehead a thumbs-up sign, smiled, and nodded.

The party was Vaughn's doing. Making calls, he'd announced Peake's Thirtieth and First Annual Covehouse Reunion. Get the original boys, and whoever else had been in on the scene, back together again. He'd added that "it's gonna be great, like the old days."

But it wasn't. Collin had expected that others would put a bit of oomph into it; instead, people just showed up as if for any other summer barbecue, a bottle of wine in one hand and a brown package of meat in the other. Cursed "dinner parties", so much more civilized than plain old parties. All that food, buffering the booze and making you tired. He should have started it at midnight, he should have sent out invitations written in blood, he should have demanded that disguises be worn. Because this was tragic. Cumming didn't even show. And Powys, great with women unless he was courting them, had a date and sat there in humourless hell. Once, Collin saw him shake his head and say to the bored woman at his side, "Reunion things, they're worse than New Year's."

So Collin simply declared to himself, "I've turned the party into a cartoon, and no one knows it." He drenched his prawns in black bean sauce, popped them on the grill, and sipped wine. Lots of young people were there, both new friends and strangers, who grinned up at his prankster forehead. Others played it cool and didn't react at all. Jim Johnny Carson noticed the exclamation mark while in the middle of nodding hello, and then he simply looked away. Carson had always been timid with Weird Things, and since the breakdown, well, it had been hard.

But Mike Evers was still game. After dinner, already drunk, he noticed Collin for the first time and asked him eagerly where the black paint was.

"I don't have any black paint" was Collin's carefully mysterious reply, but Evers missed the cartoon hint, and forgot all about face paint after putting on Peake's old German army helmet with its ring of bright yellow happy faces.

So no one had discovered the fact of the tattoo. Good. He would stay silent. He was now a master, was he not?

Collin spent the night exalting. His tattoo was an open secret that made him both invisible and invincible. Nothing could touch him. So it didn't matter that Mike Evers' cartoon father came unexpectedly to tell Mike the police had been looking for him, then saw his drunken helmeted son and yelled at him in front of everyone to "Take that trash off!"

Nor did it matter that Mr. Evers stared at Collin with utter hatred. For it could only be hilarious, couldn't it, that while these two men were the same age, even looked and dressed a bit alike, one was outraged and the other was joyous? Mr. Evers eyed Collin for a monster, a Walt Whitman provocateur. Collin could only grin at Mr. Evers, this obverse cartoon of himself, this picture of what easily might have been. He wanted to ask him if he knew his little boy ate drugs like candy, turned red and bleated like a sheep in the Rimbaud Room? Did he know Mike's little pal Dodic carried a black pistol in a sock? Did he know what a man with a tattooed face might *do* at a barbecue?

Mr. Evers left, but the cartoon did not stop. For now Leona

ran towards him, mouth agape, hands pressed to her cheeks.

"Vaughn, I'm *sorry*," she moaned. "I just *forgot*. Someone named Annie called this afternoon for you. She's visiting from out of town."

Collin nodded to his cartoon girlfriend while his cartoon stomach fell at the sound of that name. It had been a year since she had refused his visit in a letter. Well, why not, Annie, come right on in, join the show. Isn't it fitting that the first time she called in so many years he was sitting in a tattoo parlour changing his life? But you were too late to stop him Annie, if that was your intention.

"She left a number where she'd be till six. Oh Vaughn I just forgot!"

Nine now. It didn't matter. Not even her name or his falling stomach could dent the power he felt building.

"She wanted to tell you someone named Ivan died and she was in town arranging things. She sounded very nice. I said I didn't know when you'd be back — and then I just forgot!" Leona looked about to cry.

"Doesn't matter Leona. And I never did come back."

No one seemed to hear this last bit, so busy were they all falling asleep.

Leona found out first.

It had been a dull party. Except near the end when enough people were drunk enough to follow Mike Evers' chant in Peake's honour, "Peakey thirty, nearly dead! Peakey thirty, nearly dead!" and started to break glasses in the fireplace. And there stood much older Vaughn Collin, chanting youth's view of age but feeling regal with the certainty that age had nothing to do with anything. Wasn't he himself proof of this? Recognition would come when they found out. What a grand Weirdness he was giving his friends! He had taken it farther than any of them. He shook with this thought. He was a hidden hero, the clown prince of the New Age.

Peake went to bed, thirty and drunk. Evers and Dodic played a game of Indian poker in the kitchen. Collin and Leona lay on the living-room floor. She had a thing for sex in semi-private; Collin had noticed her sharper lust when a turned corner was all that separated them from other people. Now she straddled his naked stomach as he lay half asleep, worn out by the weight of his secret. He was just awake enough to hear her whisper "I want a normal guy tonight," as she licked her finger and rubbed it on his forehead. He felt her finger rub the perfect little circle then shoot up the four-inch shaft. She sighed, got up, and returned with a rag dipped in what smelled like vodka. She rubbed again, softly at first and then very hard. And one can only imagine her face as she ceased rubbing and stared down in disbelief at this man who grinned now in half-sleep; as she understood that tiny scabs and a layer of skin covered a depth of black pigment.

After a long pause she rose. Collin fell asleep smiling.

In the morning, Collin lay in bed for some luxurious stretching. Neither a hangover nor the fact that Leona had fled could dent his day. Her clothes had vanished and her side of the bed — he reached over with a hand like they did in the movies — was unslept in. Well, so. A man — Collin rose to see it in the mirror — must live by his art, must he not?

He dressed to sounds of an argument in the kitchen. From the hall he saw a pale Connor Peake being confronted by Bob Cumming, hands on hips. Mike Evers sat glumly at the table.

"I'm *not* the guy's keeper," Peake was saying, plea in his voice. "Am I supposed to *predict* every stupid little thing he —"

"You mean '*weird* thing'?" Cumming snorted.

"I didn't encourage it, all right?"

"He gets himself fired trying to impress you, now he — "

"It's not just me — Gimme a break, eh?"

Collin was beside the fridge, smiling. He coughed. Heads turned. Eyes x-rayed his forehead. So Leona had told.

"So it's true," declared Bill Cummings.

"Jesus *Christ*, Vaughn," moaned Mike Evers.

Peake looked out the window at the sky.

"What's for breakfast?" Collin stooped and opened the fridge. He'd kept his smile, which was hard because something wasn't very right. In fact Bob Cumming grabbed him hard by the arm. His neck was red, but his voice low and gentle.

"One thing. Did *he* tell you to do this?" Cumming flicked his head at Peake.

"Well, no, it was my idea." Collin's smile trembled now, threatening to fall. All last night he'd imagined that when discovered he'd first undergo a rain of laughter and backslaps, then would come pleas for the wild details — the smelly lady, her ink gun, the two greasers in for tattoos who left at the sight of him. Somehow none of this was happening this morning.

"Look," Peake said to Cumming as if Collin wasn't there. "Maybe it's not such a big deal. I mean, they can dig them out, right? And a red scar is better than a black, you know" — he wiggled his index finger at Collin's head — "thing, mark. It could be worse." He turned smiling to Vaughn. "Right?"

What was this about having it dug out?

"And tell me, Cumming, what's *wrong* with tattooing your face?" demanded Peake, more confident now. "I mean, we're all going to die, right?"

"*All going to die, right?*" Cumming mocked back.

"I'm just defending his point of, you know — "

"He *has* no point of view. Isn't that clear? Are you a moron?"

Peake looked out his window.

"Maybe," whispered Mike Evers, "maybe Peake's right,

we're not responsible. Vaughn's his own man."

They turned to examine Collin and see if this statement could be true. He sucked it up and smiled for them. He'd obviously caught them by surprise. They were in shock. He kept smiling. He didn't know what else to do.

"You know Leona left?" asked Cumming.

Collin nodded, and held his smile. Cumming sighed.

"None of us really know you, Vaughn," he said softly. "Even Peake admits that." Eyes turned to Peake, who shrugged but stayed with his window. "I mean, I'm not saying we don't *like* you. You always — you're always nice. But I'll be honest. It's about time." He looked sharply at Peake. "We never knew why you hung out with us to begin with. Or why you stay."

Collin looked over to Peake, who didn't look back. At the table Mike Evers toyed with a cigarette butt, using a pencil as a hockey stick. Cumming fell to silence now too, the kind that said some kind of truth was out and was being allowed to grow solid.

Dodic came in. He was living here now. He had on a dirty robe and nothing else and, trying to make comic the fact of another hangover, he held his head and took short thudding footsteps. When he saw Collin he hooted, ran up to see his forehead, then punched him like a jock on the shoulder.

"Hey! You did! Right on!" To Vaughn, Dodic sounded hauntingly like the Peake of old. Dodic said to the others out of the side of his face, "Shoulda been a comma," and winked, and laughed, and didn't stop laughing until he was back in his room.

June 2nd

This morning in bed, when I went up on my elbow to look out the window and check the weather, I startled: not six feet away a doe was finishing off my snow peas. Her head was up and her bright eye was on me, her jaw frozen in half-munch. She'd seen me too.

My heart had leapt, scared. Scared of a doe? No — shocked by something *alive*. There I lay, cloudy. There it stood, alert. That is the point: an alert doe is keener, smarter than a half-asleep man, shockingly so. The animal's eyes, brilliantly wary.

I moved to see her better and *crash* she was into the trees. This sudden explosion of deer shocked me anew.

But on I plod, another all-day chit-chat with myself, a devilish fog, surely. What life will I see next, what wild eyes? A tourist, a child, a salmon, a doe. I am saying that I am effectively dead, in clouds, that any reminder of the fact of shared life is a boost. That to be comfortable in this journey is to be dead in it, that every moment has its startling doe in the garden if I can just stay awake.

All day long my infernal chit-chat has been going on about something other than deer eyes. Or even, perhaps, the real. I suppose since they play such a role in this part of my story, all day I've been thinking about hallucinations.

I want to sort the whole thing out. All of it: omens, portents. Signs that, against all reason, *do* appear. Luck. Coincidence. All that which tickles science with its maddening feather, and which at the same time gives the public its nest of superstition.

I think I understand why a shaman might abandon a day's rites at the sudden croak of a raven. Why a hermit's mood might rise as a wind shifts. Why a shadow on the axe handle might make a wood chopper take the day off to sit in his cabin musing on those who, alone in the bush, died of a simple gash.

I understand but can't explain. Nor could the shaman, hermit, or chopper I suspect. Ask a scientist about basic intuition and he'll say "fantasy". Persist and he'll get technical about partial memory and statistical probability. Bring up the wilder concepts of luck and magic and spirits and, if the scientist's face doesn't rip from the supercilious launch of his brows, he'll go to the lab and prove you an idiot. For he will have proof. But I think I've seen evidence he may have missed.

Small-fry coincidence: I remember in Vancouver I had a little romance with pedestrian streetlights. They would always say "Walk" just as I arrived and stepped off the curb. I made nothing of this pact I had with streetlights other than to treat it as a cosy game. But I never hesitated, and for months I didn't have to stop for a light to change. Then one day I remember my stomach felt wrong, there was a tilt to the air — and the light I approached stayed "Don't Walk". Since that day, lights have been hit or miss.

If that episode means anything I don't have a clue what. But to take it up a notch: the first time I saw a spirit, and didn't know what to call it, was in Toulon. Chantal and I were in a butcher shop, an old place with none of today's glass and steel, but chopping blocks and quartered beasts hanging from hooks. The air smelled of blood — dull, sweet, nauseating. It seemed this smell was a key. There was a deeper layer to it: I couldn't see them, or even smell them really, but I could certainly feel them: the collected spirit of dead cattle, lambs, rabbit. A couple of centuries' worth. Here in this awful spectral pungency stood Chantal, prim, finicky, instructing the butcher to pare a slice of veal off the pink slab that lay there blindly brooding, her cute voice denying the undeniable spirit of death in the room, reminding me of the euphemistic Mrs. Peen when she excused herself to "go to the kitchen" when in fact she sought the toilet.

In any case, that *charcuterie* air was rich with something other than what I was simply smelling. It felt like a shocked fatality. Perhaps it was just a sensitivity on my part to the adrenaline in the animal the instant it was killed — I am not ruling out any chemical, scientific explanation to this notion of "spirit". Whatever it was, I sensed a presence I'd never felt before. Eating my veal that night I felt honest and alert to what I chewed. Meat-eating had been given a kind of depth.

Up another notch: I'd been here almost a year before Annie suggested the spirits of trees. Hung-over from the fog and drugs of Deep Cove I expected something colourful, an old oak sporting a cartoon face, Tolkien stuff. But the spirits of trees, being so obvious, took a while to see. We were walking at dawn and came upon three scotch fir standing darkly against a silver sunrise. We stopped at the scene and Annie, mischievous, asked me if I could describe their spirits.

"Well, that one's weak, pathetic," I said. "The middle one is content, kind of fat. That one's noble. The elder brother."

"Don't personify." She was shaking her head, apparently serious now. "It's more subtle."

I tried but could think of nothing else to say about them. I told her I couldn't find words.

"Well now that we're beyond words," she said, back to playful, "look again."

She said it was nothing hidden. She suggested I relax and not think, and look past the edge of the tree and in doing so "brush" the tree's character. I tried this, and it seemed I could more clearly sense their minutiae of shape. And the faint, individual urgency which arose as a sum of these details. A subtle distress in the arc of branches towards the sun. A gentle pain of growth. The more I relaxed the better I saw.

"In fact," Annie continued, in an unusually long burst of instruction, "a tree's spirit is nothing other than its essential form. You cut off a branch, you change its spirit. I used to think it was just your basic aesthetics. Our sense of it. But that's too much weight on the viewer. It's more a 'gesture'. A 'living gesture'."

I looked at the three trees, considering. Then, almost startling, I turned to eye the boulder I was leaning on. It was head-high, roughly grey, cut heavy with shadows in the sunrise. In essence "as solid as a rock", it was propping me up, and shared the beach with me.

"Rocks? A 'living gesture'?"

"I think that's sort of the situation, yes."

As I relaxed and became more adept I saw that everything had its "spirit". Seaweed, salmon, the sun. Molasses, manure. A corner grocery store has one, a row of bean cans does too, and so does every can. The spirit of a hockey rink, the spirit in ice, the spirit in her eyes.

The living gesture. The world does talk. Some say the boundaries of schizophrenia are crossed when the world starts talking to *you*.

Hi there.

Up another notch, to hallucination. I think there are two basic kinds. One is a sort of shift, an exaggeration of ordinarily there. You're staring into someone's blue eyes and they move into blue-green, then electric green, and the experience is one of realizing they have always been this colour and you simply hadn't seen it before. (A fundamental trait of hallucination is that it is seen and felt as truth.) These shifts can be fun, God having become a caricaturist: Hey, Jane's pug nose is suddenly incredibly puggy — it's going up, up, it's going going gone right up, back into her face, it's concave now, *a concave pug nose pugging backwards up into her brain*. It can get extreme like that, but it's still a shift, an exaggeration. Tall gets taller, colours become fiery with themselves, sadness is tragedy.

The second kind of hallucination takes us up yet another notch. What about when there's no apparent connection between the normal world and the hallucination? Sometimes these were dismissible, when on some pill I could lay blame for anything uncomfortable. If I saw that my hair was in fact a gang of slim aliens who sucked out my thoughts, I could usually realize, after not too much effort at clear thinking, that the drug was lying to me.

But I couldn't explain away all I saw. One day, Peake and I were very high, lying on our backs on a knoll up Indian Arm. I saw this: small puffs of cloud rode the breeze and whenever a cloud attempted to pass in front of the sun it burst apart geometrically, just like a kaleidoscope, then was gone. Once, when a larger-than-normal cloud touched and exploded in its astonished pattern of colour, Peake gasped and said, "*Nice* one." I agreed, then my stomach flipped in a kind of cosmic double-take as I realized we were hallucinating the same thing. We confirmed this by describing what we saw as new clouds fleeced up and exploded. Purple diamonds? *Yes!* With yellow edges? *Yes! Exactly!*

How could we both be seeing what wasn't happening? What was real now?

I remember Deep Cove life in general getting weirder about this time. Nothing too outrageous, though Carson did start hearing his "voices". Mostly it was little, inconsequential omens. (A funny pattern attacked Peake. Within the space of two days he was urinated on four times: first for no reason by a dog on the beach, next by a monkey at a party, then he drenched his own feet by accident, and finally Benny Powys, drunk and just too crazy for a tent to contain, pissed up and down Peake's sleeping length as though watering a trough of geraniums.) Mostly it was the link that had no business linking. Someone I'd be thinking of would phone. A certain song on the radio at an auspicious time. Synchronicity. The weather generously accommodating, or purposely not. The very air had become charged not only with meaning, but meaning for *me*. Solipsism. How had Peake and I both seen what hadn't happened? The only explanation was that I had created the event. I had created the scene, the hallucination, the drug, and I had created Connor Peake too.

Solipsism explains basically everything. It also provides

a supreme cure for the shaky ego. Where it leads is schizophrenia, a sickly form of egomania.

Hi there.

Maybe in Bella Combe signs are different. Friends are fewer here, life less complicated. No roads, no noise, no rangle-jangle city. Where the weave is simplest, maybe its patterns are clearer. Am I on to something, Annie?

The time you changed the weather I thought I'd gone crazy again. Anyone who says, "There is no magic, only science," then proceeds to turn a gale in on itself is playing with epistemological fire and for the sake of public sanity had better watch what company she keeps.

I'd been in Bella Combe a year. Remember? To help my integration into the community you suggested that I catch some salmon for the next day's village fair. A wind looked likely, and even now a black line grew on the horizon. But you said, "Oh, who knows, get your nets anyway." I humoured you, thinking I'd do a set close in, maybe fluke a coho or two before it hit, and I'd come ashore amid dangerous waves, a martyr.

When I returned with my gear I saw you sitting, sitting hard, concentrating. You looked like an energized stump. Approaching on quiet sand, I heard you whisper a firm, "Okay." I don't know why but I looked up. The black line on the horizon was gone.

"What did — ?" I asked.

You were mad I'd seen, remember? You wouldn't answer. You tried to push the boat out before all was ready. But I wouldn't budge.

"I suppose I changed the sky," you finally admitted.

"How?"

Still mad at yourself, you turned away. I stood and waited.

You sighed after a minute and gave in. "I suppose I changed my *dream* of the sky. To tell the truth I don't really know what I did. And since I don't completely get it myself I don't want to talk about it."

I stared at you, then at the sky, and asked the obvious.

"But you changed *my* sky too."

"Well, you're in my dream."

"So then . . . you're part of mine?"

"But I *did* something to my dream. Yours just happens to you."

You probably saw the look in my eyes, how embroiled this made me, taking me up to craziness and rage and glory again. Is this what you saw?

"I'm probably nuts," you said. "Nothing really happened. Maybe I just somehow knew the wind wouldn't come in the first place."

That's all you'd say, case closed. It's been closed for years. So I don't know what I saw, or if I saw.

I was so pissed off at first. It was like *Bewitched*, and you played both roles: you were nose-wiggling Samantha making cars and jewels, and you were also Darrin, stupid and sincere: "No magic, Sam. It's wrong."

I was mad because I was wondering if you could dream away my tattoo.

The tattoo lady did a good job. The black has gone a bit purple but has hardly faded. Unless I scrunch my worry lines, the dime-sized circle is perfectly round. The shaft tapers up from narrow to wider, like a tear drop travelling up my brow, like I'm never not moving at a hundred miles an hour.

Even if this life is one large dream, some things do go solid in it. My tattoo is the hard cause of so much. I *am* a marked man.

It's funny, getting used to embarrassment. It does burn something away, lets you see some things clearer. For instance: Dodic was right, a comma would have been better. Dodic was more subtle than me. I made a ten-year-old's choice.

Why haven't I just had it gouged out of my head? That's

a good question. Over the years a central, a crucial question. A nice red mottled scar on my forehead — I would no longer be a tattoo man but a burn victim perhaps, in any case someone nobler. So why not? Well, getting it dug out would mean going to the city, it would mean renting a place and waiting for the operation, it would mean waiting rooms and doctors and talking and —

Funny, Annie, how you've never suggested I have it out.

And it's been a useful scapegoat. Quasimodo, crying, twists to see his hump in the mirror. He gives it a loving lick.

The Box

Just him and Peake now in the Covehouse. The chicken-shits, none of them came around anymore. He hardly even saw Peake, Peake up in a sniffy English panic every morning and out the door on some ten-speed health craze or fit of self-betterment, God the guy was scared all of a sudden. Was it turning thirty? Amazing how a calendar — numbered boxes, the ultimate anal invention — could square up what used to be a fine and crazy brain.

He'd wanted to cheer Peake up on his birthday, sure, but he knew now that his act had been basically selfish, a bouquet to the birth of his own wild self. And look what destiny, in 1975, had left him: a perfectly open world. All tradition had been smashed and broken. Hippydom itself was flabbergasted and splintered into twenty factions. No one could agree even on music anymore, these days you heard anything from banjo to disco. Clothes, lifestyles, philosophies: no one had a clue what was hip now. Fantastic! Collin, for the first time, found himself in a world of equals.

Equals? No, not exactly.

If Collin could have thought coherently he might have asked this question: What's worse on a hung-over Sunday morning, to find that in a kid's game of dare you have disfigured yourself for life, or to realize that your favourite treasure, friendship, was all along nothing but an empty toy box? Instinct helped him avoid the question altogether, for either answer would have crushed him. He did ask the question, What's wrong here? But the obvious answer, "I have made a mistake", didn't arise. Not at all. Instead, deciding he was seeing clearly for the first time in a long time, the answer he arrived at was: these chicken-shits had no balls to begin with. Equals? No way.

Amazing to everyone but him, the tattoo gave Collin the brassiest pride.

He began to take solo jaunts downtown, where he might hit a bar, maybe bob heads and talk with the street youngsters who beamed to see an old guy as crazy and cool as they were themselves. He laughed, he hooted. More of anything! He threw mud-wads at Chevrolet billboards, he waggled his great wild forehead at scared bankers and hockey coaches running by. Kiss or piss on everything. Burn it, noogy it, it didn't matter, just make it move. It didn't matter that migrating-bird Leona had flown, and it didn't matter that scaredy-cat Jim Johnny Carson had finally let himself flip and be locked up till proven sane at Crease Clinic, it didn't matter that the only audience left for Cumming's growls of judgement was the baby whose diapers he changed, and it didn't matter that nervous Mike Evers had gotten busted at last, or that Powys was engaged to be married and had lost his sense of humour as easily as a ring of keys. It didn't even matter that Connor Peake was for all purposes dead, because this genius who'd started it all had passed Vaughn Collin the torch.

Such was Vaughn's accelerating dream, the stuff of religious conversion. Collin, lacking a church, had found inky baptism in the Union Tattoo Parlour, coming away from his place of worship with visual proof of a lifelong commitment to a sacred black joke.

A joke no one else quite seemed to get. This fact really didn't sink in till Squamish.

Getting up at five-thirty in the morning, pulling on freezing workboots and clothes stiff from a week's fir sap and dirt, he stubbed out his smoke, caught a glimpse of himself in the mirror on the way out the door, and asked his face a few questions.

How'd you end up *here*? "Squamish." Jesus, the name alone. And *logging*. Sweat, bugs, morons giving orders. It was hard to figure out, or even remember, the years leading up to this Squamish business. A bit of excess, just a bit, oh my. That was one reason to come here, that's right, to get away from all the stuff. The booze, the booze, and coke wasn't so pure and easy as people first thought. Christ, the money. Not that it's a concern at the time, but it sure spends your money for you.

Grey hair and a face tattoo had combined to make gainful employment a tad harder to come by. No one seemed to party in the woods anymore and he lacked funds with which to hit the nightspots. Though this was maybe just as well. Not that he was getting tired — never. His audience had gotten tired. It had been fun at first, in the discos. It cracked him up, getting his hair styled, buying the John Travolta gear — the shiny shirt, the platform shoes — and hitting the dance floor, seeing the teeny boppers' first take, the novelty of an old straight geezer in their midst, then their fear when he turned on them fast with a forehead waggle. But then they all got tired, Vancouver was not big, he'd outraged the whole city in no time flat. Some bouncers got so tired they barred him.

Half the world saw how stupid disco was and went punk, a contrary but sane reaction, Collin reasoned. In fact he and the Cove boys — and anyone with spirit, from Kerouac to Keith Moon — had always had a punky place way back of the brain, and it felt almost nostalgic to be in a rented warehouse smashed on bourbon and up front bashin' heads not three feet from the red running shoes of the lead singer swearing distortion into the mike. Vaughn got an earring, then a nose ring, then an eyebrow safety-pin, the first one around — maybe he started that fad. Some of the young shaved lads, thinking he was just old or crazy, wouldn't bash chests with him with proper gusto until he drove them hard unilaterally a few times and got their anger up. He still had his hockey balance and hardly ever went down. But even the punks got tired.

He lowered his standards and dressed up a notch and tried a few fern bars, but it was boring beyond belief in those, no one would meet his eye, they were all escapees from the wilderness, all bureaucrats-in-training, white-wine drinkers, and it depressed him mightily when he bumped into Benny Powys one night and the closest Powys came to acknowledging what they'd been through together was a kind of genial but careful politeness.

Money, why did something like money have to go and become a problem? Though Peake was still good for the odd endless loan, the wank-off ended up going back to Sherwood Forest to attend the death of a parent or some such and didn't come back. Then with no warning the house was sold out from under him and Dodic, who sometimes crashed there with some starving street girl he'd lured back.

He might have been able to do some job thing "out of his home" if he'd had a home. Welfare afforded an apartment, but no play money. Loans from Cumming and the rest dried up fast. And in the midst of this came the news that nervous Mike Evers had killed himself in jail. Jesus, how scared can you get?

It was clear that Collin was the only one of them left with any jam for the freedom they all used to declare.

The tattoo was great, *great* for cadging drinks, and getting invited once in a while to a back-alley dope circle, but Collin could see it wasn't getting proper respect, not at all. He tried explaining the facts of life to the odd kid whose eyes were brighter than most, hinting at the art of it, trying not to slur as he dropped names like McLuhan and Warhol, asking the kid if he understood how an exclamation mark by itself was the medium and the message. Hey: Do you understand the purity of surprise itself? Can't you fucking see — ? Sometimes he'd grow kingly and unforgiving and his bright-eyed audience would blink, tiring.

How could he help but be unforgiving, living on the street? Since rent money was better spent on night-fun, that's where he had to live. He landed the occasional bed, until his host or girl got tired of him and his kingly bearing. It was bloody hard on the street though, the cement the cold the dirt the rain, especially winter, when he'd migrate to Stanley Park, a little shelter he made there. But it was hard in general being an artist under these conditions. He was sick a lot, his nose and eyebrow punctures red and infected, burning to the touch. He saw it was the city itself that had killed everyone, the city put a lid on your head and dressed you like a worker ant and turned you to its will.

But Squamish. He'd found himself in Dodic's car, driving north. Out of the city. Squamish — wild name, good stuff. A job? Well, maybe for a while. Maybe save a bit — get a few more tattoos! Dodic didn't laugh at this. Dodic the only Cove guy (odd thinking of Dodic as a Cove guy) who'd been friendly in a while. Odder still to be in his debt, to be depending on a *Do*dic for your salvation . . .

He'd gotten here in Dodic's car, coughing and shivering hot and cold in the back seat. It was the nicest bed he'd had in a while. He'd cried, of course, and enjoyed how it threw Dodic into a panic, making him look in the rearview every few seconds at first, and then not at all.

But hard work eased a mind, even gave crumbs of satisfaction. If there was any place besides an asylum where a man with a tattooed face could escape notice and breathe a bit, it was a west-coast logging camp. If you did your work and made no trouble they let you be. Here's the kind of place it was: once after a few beers the owner of Squamish Timber had ordered a small mountain be given a Mohawk, and the crew was a month into the shave before a tree planter found out and called Victoria.

Collin was a chokerman, the worst job of all. But between each choke set — a frantic minute's crawl over and under crazy-fallen logs, dragging a steel cable "thick as a good dick" — was a minute of idleness while the logs were hauled off and unhitched. Catching their breath, chokermen were forced by sudden silence to think on things. The nature of chokermen's thoughts? The usual, the heaven of next weekend, or how each passing clump of minutes meant another buck in the wallet. Or danger — this camp had averaged a death a year — or lunch waiting in a bag. Some chokermen, one in particular, had looks on their faces indicating thoughts that curled off on angles that couldn't be talked about.

A huge vessel of beauty, the Squamish Valley can probably be seen from space. It is rimmed by five glaciers, two of which, depending on the time of day, glow turquoise at their centres. Eagles hang in a sky so blue it threatens violet. But the floor of the valley where Collin stood thinking was none other than a slaughterhouse, a kind of vegetable abattoir, and the turpentine smell of sap — tree blood — sat thick and sharp in the air, a testimony to the shocked death of noble, healthy, ninety-year-old trees. The smell burned a newcomer's nostrils, and even after it was gotten used to it kept one dizzy. It was hard to look up from this smell, or from the miles of bleeding trees, clanking machinery, and men who pissed where they stood.

Once shift was over there wasn't much to do. They had a rec shack with dented pool table, dart game, and koolaid dispenser. Outside was a "volleyball court" — someone had stolen an Indian's net from downriver and strung it across two poles. A chainsaw-made baseball bat lay muddy on the ground because someone named Clarkie had hit the only ball all the way to the river and it was now long gone, and still going, out to sea, Clarkie's infinite home run. Twice a week a bad movie was shown in the cookhouse but, afraid of getting anyone riled up over female skin, the company ran old cowboy and gangster shows. Gunfights and car tires squealing on gravel.

It was a dry camp. One hint of booze and you were gone, no question. No gambling either. Desperate for distractions, some loggers tried hikes, but that was a busman's holiday — why stomp bush for free? One guy spent hours tying trout flies. One quiet forty-year-old finished his high school by mail. A mechanic had trained himself to sleep whenever he wasn't at meals or on the job. Two young chokermen, Chuck and Dale, or "Chip and Dale" as they were called, grew marijuana on the fireweed slopes.

The men kept their distance from the tattoo man. Not knowing what he'd say or do, they didn't seem anxious to find out. But Chip and Dale asked him to play pool, a version of cutthroat called "dent" where, after sinking the eightball, you had to feather the cue ball so that it stopped in the table's main dent. It seemed no one else would play it with them. The glaciers and towering trees had made Collin feel full of noble juice and independent for a time, but soon he was bored. So he played dent. Then he was invited to visit "the plantation".

He had to carry two jugs of water on the mile hike in. God he had let himself get out of shape. Or maybe it was age, who knows. Chip and Dale, bringing up the rear, were nervous, bursting with questions. Collin caught whispers of an unbelievably stupid argument: "There's no way he's a cop, asshole." "Maybe he's straight, never even smokes." "Yeah right. *Look* at him."

They looked about twenty-five. Both utterly lacked charisma. They shared a nasty humour and a love of breaking things, and were forever insulting each other, the kind of best friends who called each other asshole, but not smiling. The "smart one", Chip had a babyish body and was constantly sarcastic. Tall Dale wore glasses and a soulless, icy look even when he was giggling at some remark of Chip's. He tried to copy his short friend's wit but couldn't, so he giggled. For a tall man he had a disproportionately small head.

"Like, okay, how'd you get the tattoo?" asked Dale. Collin had stopped to rest, and Dale could keep it in no longer.

"Ink, asshole," said Chip. Dale giggled.

"A kind of joke," offered Collin.

"An' you lost, right?" said Chip. Dale giggled.

"It wasn't a practical joke. It still *is* a joke, see?" Collin scrunched his brow up and down, which made the period open and close like a little mouth. But Collin knew they wouldn't understand.

"So wadja do, wadja do before this?"

Collin supposed Dale meant work. It was all these people here talked about. "I was in advertising." When he saw Chip and Dale share a smirk at this, he began to sweat. They were humouring him. He heard himself say, "Actually, I mean before that I was mainly a hockey — you know — a professional hockey player."

The boys stood up straighter trying not to laugh. They were having a good old time now. Collin began to shake slightly. The ragged feeling came on hard. He hoped he wouldn't cry.

Here they were, grunted Dale. A sudden smell of rot, then Collin saw the bear's head, impaled on a pole. From the mouth hung a bluish tongue, dried to leather. The eyes were gone. A wasp flew out of an ear.

"A-bear-a-year-keeps-our-pot-plants-here," Chip said. Dale's tired giggle indicated he heard that one a lot.

"Basically," Chip said, "we only need a head when plants're small, keep deer 'n' shit away. Don't need a new one till next year." To ease Collin's disappointment at this, he added, "You can come. We knock 'em out of a tree, up close. Twelve gauge." His tone took for granted that anyone who'd ended up in the Squamish Valley would enjoy shooting a treed bear, hacking its head off and ramming it on a pole. Collin grunted vaguely.

They had five hundred plants scattered in the fireweed. They only had to worry in late fall when the marijuana darkened and grew taller and could maybe be spotted from the air. Dale argued that they had search planes in California, and was Collin aware that the FBI ran the Mounties? But they wouldn't get caught, said Chip. A guy was coming in a month to take it to Vancouver. An old packing crate, almost as tall as Chip, sat beside the bear-pole. One of its sides was smashed in. Collin stared at it.

"He even planted it," Dale said. "Alls we do is grow it."

"The sun grows it, asshole," Chip said, not unkindly. "Alls we do is *guard* it."

"The fuck's this then?" Dale hoisted his water bucket and shook it, slopping water on himself.

"Lots of *money* growing out here," said Chip, sagely surveying the plot. "Both of us got cars with it last year. *His*" — he put an elbow in Dale's ribs — "is a lemon."

"Eat me," said Dale, not smiling.

Collin, eyeing the box, wasn't listening.

Choke-set. Grunt. Heave. Dead blackflies squashed to your face. God this was hard. Logs winched off. Catch your breath. Rest, daydream. He began to daydream about Annie. He could hear her voice, a clanging bell. How close she had always been in a certain way, even in recent years, how much her presence up north had ridden on his shoulder, keeping him vaguely comfortable. Strange, wasn't it, how she'd phoned the very day he tattooed his face?

Yet hadn't she turned down his visits? Maybe that was why, as he stood in this murdered, topsy forest, he had begun thinking of her. Didn't love-rule number one say that the harder to get she played, the harder she rode your brain?

His third week in the Squamish Valley he wrote Annie a letter. Too bad they'd missed each other, he wrote, and too bad about Ivan. "But the living have to keep living, don't we?" he added, giving her back some mild Ivan-style wisdom. "But just imagine seeing each other again! How we've both changed. I bet I've changed more — I promise you won't recognize me." He refused to acknowledge what he felt rising under his desire to show himself off to her — it was a deeper, frightened need, that of a boy who's played brave for too long and wants to be held, and told what to do.

If there was a last straw, a final nudge, Collin wasn't aware of it. It may well have been the morning he tailed Chip and Dale to the cookhouse and overheard the words "hockey" and "Bobby Orr, let's call him 'Bobby'" and "like he can be our mascot". They saw him and clammed up but giggled in the breakfast line, turning from time to time to ask mock-polite questions.

Shuffling along in line, humbly receiving food on his plate, Collin realized that somehow, as in a comic nightmare, he had fallen below these two in the human pecking order.

Reminders of his failure began landing around him in log-sized crashes. What was wrong with people, how could they snub the man who was the walking holy book of dry humour? Look at him: a man with an exclamation mark being shy with the arrogant Greek cook. Look: a man with an exclamation mark, shaving. Look at him nod to the boss then drag a chain under a log, Jesus that's funny. There he is playing "dent". The tattoo made everything he did surreal, didn't it? Wasn't everything he did a Weird Thing? So why was no one laughing? Why was everyone so serious? Everyone was going to die, why not have fun? Why not tattoo the shit out of yourself?

And glimpses — why now? — of that merciless Covehouse kitchen.

we never knew why you hung out with us to begin with

He was a *Do*dic; older, politer, but a *Do*dic all the same. They had been too shy to tell him to his face.

or why you stay

He'd found the acute eyes of his boyhood as the kitchen had waited quietly in pain. There he was, fifty, but with a ten-year-old Vaughn's clarity he'd seen he was with people he could never understand. In his silent stare he suffered the old sensation of people breathing, their constricting lungs, their moist bags forcing air in and out of twinned nostrils, the soft terrible noise of this, a wheezing disharmony in the kitchen.

Abandoned by his friends, abandoned now by a camp of fools, humoured by two crummy boys who disgusted him. He didn't need to be here and yet here he was, work, work, hard work. So easy to lose yourself in work and forget any purpose you'd ever had. Lord, a man is so easily satisfied. And because of that, so easily damned.

He'd go and visit Annie, the one who understood. He'd written her, hadn't he? Yes, and he'd go to her. He'd keep his pride, he wouldn't run, he'd simply go. He could cheer her up and be cheered himself.

But, for whatever reasons, the panic began. It was the panic of a body that feels it is disintegrating. That the panic arose in his body is fitting, or perhaps even funny: like a small-town secret, his insanity had been clear to everyone for years, and now even his own body knew about it. But Vaughn himself was the last to know.

The calm first weeks in Squamish were just a delay, as when a baby falls and hits the floor and sits stunned before its lungs can let go that first wail.

It was a hot afternoon in mid-September. He had showered, and looked forward to dinner as he always did. Steak night. No matter what the state of his life, Vaughn could always please his body and eyes with a good meal. He walked across the field towards the cookhouse. In mid-pace he stopped. He just stopped. There was no reason for stopping, but in the stopping, terror surged through him. He threw his head back in a gasp and in doing so saw the two horses, in the trees, not ten feet away. They were connected to his panic and moved in it, with it — two jet-black horses, copulating, tossing their manes in wild, ecstatic arcs. He could hear the wet noises of penetration and suck. Their eyes were bright and on him.

The blow of panic left him feeling hot. He stood where he'd stopped. The horses were gone. He was breathless, stunned. He thought of taking a step, but it frightened him. Then horrified him. Panic.

Simply, Vaughn could not move his feet. With immense effort he tilted his head to look down. The grass. For the first time in his life he saw how it churned, its churning was so obvious, as it sucked greedily in all ways at once, sucking wet stuff out of the ground, sucking in light from the sun. All it could do was suck, churning non-stop in greed, its lone purpose sex and the ambitious swelling of its seeds. Greedily, like the two black horses. They'd been beautiful horses, yes, with those grand tossing manes, but their beauty had been solely to attract one to the other and then they were two ugly creatures glued, wild-eyed and jerking stiffly.

Behind him and overhead, Collin could feel the suck of

greedy trees. The surface of the planet was churning.

What to do in the midst of such *trying*? Standing there, Collin felt in his stomach the truth that if he took a step in any direction he would condemn himself for ever. He must move, but where? If he moved one inch towards the cookhouse, he was one inch farther from the bunkhouse. Irreversibly. If he moved an inch towards the bunkhouse he was that inch farther from the cookhouse. Irreversibly. Any movement cancelled out an infinity of other movements. Irreversibly. What Collin saw, standing in the horrible, magnified heat, was that every second of life wanted a decision from him. There was no turning away. Time was dying a high-speed, one-way death, demanding Collin come with him. Where? Terror pushed through Collin's body.

If he took a step, or thought a thought, was there any guarantee it was the right step, the right thought? Anything he did condemned him to a future he might not want. He wanted no more unhappiness. *Don't,* his stomach roared in the heat, *don't make a mistake.*

But there were no rules! The world did not care what foot he moved. What Vaughn realized and suffered with in the diamond-clear light was that the world had never been on his side. The grass wanted him out of the way of its sun. The horses were not his friends. Neither was the future his friend. Nor an enemy. The future was here, that's all, demanding a decision from a leg which could not move out of fear. His eyes no longer knew where they dare look.

Don't make a mistake. No more mistakes.

Somehow he made it to his bunk and sat on it. He didn't move. Nor did he move to turn on his light when it got too dark to see, and he didn't move the next morning when the foreman pounded on his door.

"Sick," Vaughn managed to croak.

The first-aid man told him to stay in bed for two days. He ate the soup they brought because if he didn't they might ask questions and he didn't dare make a mistake like that. Sleep scared him. Thought, if he thought of it, terrified him, because how could he know if a thought he had was the right one? Each thought entered an irreversible labyrinth, so to even think — He flicked his eyes to the window just once — the stars framed there were too bright, too demanding. He began to cry, a kind of plea, but the stars wouldn't stop, and then the crying scared him more than not crying, so he stopped.

Somehow, after a few days, he found himself back at work. Fatigue had grown to a heavy fog, and he'd forgotten exactly what had happened. What's wrong with me? he'd wonder, sipping coffee with the others in the crew cab. But as he stepped out into the morning light, where crows hacked dry vomit noises at him from their bleacher seats in the trees, he'd wake again into horrible clarity. His breath would catch and he'd tiptoe the precipice of fear, as every new second crushed the one that came before.

Make no mistakes.

One night after Collin had missed another day of work, Chip and Dale paid a call. They chattered pointlessly and nosed about his room before Chip whispered to the bedridden man, "You on some bum drugs or something?"

Flu.

Drugs, if only it was that simple. He'd done his share, certainly, and maybe an undefiled mind would be less prone to his particular "flu". Even though hospitals were full of those who'd found drug-induced hells, he knew he wasn't one. Because he knew now what the problem was. He couldn't yet see its face, but he could smell its breath. He knew it had to do with luck. Or, more serious, grace. He'd been dropped from a great height, released by the talons of some huge sympathetic eagle — the eagle of luck — and he'd landed on the floor of this magnifying valley. What had caused him to fall in the first place was the arrow-in-the-eye insight that there was no height, no eagle at all. No luck. No grace. No sympathy. He had been riding a beneficent dream.

What are you going to do? Why are you shaking, wasting time? But don't make another mistake. Collin, don't —

The worst moments came by surprise. One day, just as the loader horn blew lunch break, he lifted his head and breathed deeply, as if trying to gain health, and when he opened his eyes the billowed clouds above were shifting in obscene sexual postures. He couldn't make out everything — the clouds hid the worst of it behind their puffy façade — but he knew what was going on. The clouds were juvenile and filthy: dirty bouncing puppy games.

Then the obvious insanity of this vision scared him, and this fear opened the door to more of the same: the living trees edging the cut were abuzz with sex, their one urge being to strain to be taller in the sun so as to flourish and sprawl and spread more pollen. Breathing hard, panic growing, Collin made the mistake of closing his eyes. Now his feet felt the undulations of the valley itself, entire mountain sides joining deep underground, excited where they met at a fissure, jostling for position. His eyes squeezed shut, Vaughn Collin's stomach became the jealous fulcrum for grinding rock slabs, miles in size. The sex of mountains. The infidelity of the Earth's crust.

Bad flu, he told them. Time off in Vancouver? they asked. *No*. No. He didn't need it. He'd just rest here in bed and get better. He pulled his hardhat down lower. His hair didn't cover half of his forehead yet, his damned forehead — amazing how slow hair grows when it's watched second by second. Just rest. He'd be okay. (He was going to see Annie, was he not? Not run, just go. Now, just rest.)

A few days later Collin again felt improved. More stable. Fear had fallen to a kind of anger at himself. He could think along certain lines without being electrocuted. In bed, he stretched, considering his plight.

"It's beyond me," he said aloud, to the ceiling. Feeling better still, a little reckless even, he tried a shy grin. Still no panic. The room stayed steady, his stomach calm. Deciding then that this disease of his could be played with, he shot past stability and tested his old flair.

"I'm a mad man!" he told the ceiling. He grinned.

His thoughts found the face of a man he and his Deep Cove pals had met at Long Beach. An older man, Collin's age, with wild white hair. The man seemed to want to be Uriah Heep — he wore a tattered greatcoat and gloves with the fingers scissored off. He walked with a slight hop, and talked like this: "I live with the wee beasties of the sand, fleas they be, and talk to thee angels at eventide, and mornings I dig in the sand round my hut to see no one's left no *skillentons* there." The one other time Collin had heard "skeletons" pronounced that way was in *Tess*. Though his friends regarded the man as a living joke, "gothic fun" as Cumming put it, Vaughn had felt in a way attached to him.

Lying in bed, he wondered whether that would-be Heep hadn't given him a taste of his own future. Surprisingly, the thought lifted his mood. For didn't Heep walk in a private smiling world all his own, dishing out nothing but fun, a mad joy, to those he met? And Vaughn would never get *that* mad. So there was still a place for him. By god, he'd win this thing. He *was* special. He'd escaped biology.

Vaughn went to the mirror and clipped his front locks back, framing the exclamation mark perfectly. He admired himself. Maybe it *was* just the flu. Walking across the field to the cookhouse, he stopped, smiled, stamped hard on the spot where he'd had his first attack. He spun around and looked for horses. Nothing. He smiled.

In the cookhouse he grabbed a tray, slid it to the salad tank and forked a pile to his plate. He added dollops of French.

The hall was full and Collin could feel the eyes boring into him from the side. His plan was to turn and give them a brow-wrinkle surprise. Time to show them his art.

He turned. He wasn't sure, but when he turned he might have screamed. He did drop the bowl of soup the Greek had just handed him. What he saw was this: Each logger's face was a bubbling sac. The eyes were horrifying. Tunnels of a sort, what they let Collin see inside each man was something once alive but almost dead now, a place of dulled intelligence, the colour of the wall of a moth's cocoon. Only their faces moved, the sac bubbling with random emotions. The urge for food dominated each sac for now, turning the room a little red, for it was steak night. The massed bubbling clicks of steak being chewed. The chewing sacs turned and watched in unison as Vaughn held his breath and stepped carefully for the door.

He missed more days of work. Chip and Dale visited again.

"It's not like we got an in with the boss or nothin'" — Chuck snickered, trying to brighten a man whose mind had vacuumed even the possibility of light — "but word has it layoffs are close." He paused, trying to read Collin's face. "Holidays are done. All seniority's back." He paused again. "Y'know if you don't climb out of bed you're gone."

Collin had never seen the young wank so self-important. Fired? As if the job meant sour owl shit in the first place. Squamish! As if jobs like this weren't a nickel a dozen.

But were they? Maybe Chip, not so dumb, was thinking all along what Collin only thought of now — a marked man, tilted in the head, an outcast in a camp of outcasts — where *would* he go if fired?

"So unless you're feeling real shits," piped in Dale as they left, pointing at him like a teacher, "I'd get my butt out of bed."

Fired. To the horror that kept him pinned to the bed was added the weight of a larger, more shadowy problem, one of living somewhere and feeding himself. He envisioned Uriah Heep scratching the sand for fleas, and didn't smile this time.

That same afternoon Annie's magical timing poked through Collin's hell in the form of a letter. His problem was solved. Nothing was wrong, never had been, what was this fuss? Annie had answered his letter. He'd go and see Annie. Not run, just go.

Her four pages were mostly still about Ivan.

"Ivan was a man who . . . "

" . . . so I can't begin to explain what he gave me . . . "

" . . . body wasn't found but . . . no money, though to his grandchildren and friends around the world he left a coin, or a gem, or a poem . . . "

He flipped past the Ivan stuff. In the last paragraph he found it, words about him, about him coming.

> It's still not a good time for you to come here, Vaughn. Ivan left me a lot to assimilate. It's hard to explain the nature of our work. Suffice to say you sounded upset in your letter and I don't have the extra energy to take that on right now. One more thing, and I hope you take this in its proper spirit. It has both to do with our past, and with your present motive for seeing me. It is this: you haven't earned it yet.
>
> Annie.

Collin found himself at the window. With a controlled thrust he forced it open, poked his head out and looked up. Nothing there. Nothing but empty evening air which, hostile with frost, hurt a man's eyes.

"What about your fuckin' *pay*cheque?"

Idiot Dale was shouting. The lid was still off and Collin could hear him well enough.

"Spend it," Collin said evenly. Anger kept him strong enough to be cocky.

"Can't cash *your* cheque," yelled Dale.

"Send it to me then."

"*Where?*"

"There." Collin rapped his knuckles on the underside of the wooden lid just as Chip lowered it into place. The last light on Collin's face caught the beads of sweat, the tentative grin and determined jaw. He shook a bit, like Peter O'Toole at a film's climax, barely able to contain inner demons.

Chip and Dale banged in the nails. Then, silence. Darkness. Wonderful.

"*How* ya spell it?" Chip was shouting now, sounding dull and muffled. "Bella-*what*? *Ass*hole here smudged the magic marker."

"Combe. C-O-M-B-E. Bella Combe."

Since her letter, anger had not let Collin rest. That first evening he wandered the camp's periphery, then into the forest trails, where at one point he stumbled nose to nose on a black bear which he chased away by screaming, running at it like a creature afraid of nothing on earth.

Back in camp he wandered in and out of buildings, finally ending up in the machine shop, where he curled up like a sick cat on a pile of fire hoses to sleep. Next morning it was Chip and Dale who roused him.

"Made it out of bed, eh?" sneered Dale, hiding his shock at finding Collin inside a coil of hose. He elbowed Chip. "'Cause it's steak night probbly."

Chip and Dale had come snooping for crates to use to pack their pot. After a few nervous jokes they continued their search. Collin watched. And when he saw the stacks of wooden packing crates, saw the size of one in particular, he knew what to do.

He didn't take much. Afraid of the tattoo man from the start, the Greek cook asked no questions as he passed loaves of bread, chicken legs, cheese, a cherry pie, and a jug of juice out the back door of the cookhouse. Collin found a gallon jar and filled it with water. Then empty jars for urine and plastic bags to shit in. Toilet paper. Cigarettes.

The chair had been hardest, but Chip finally found a straight-backed one behind the rec shack. After screwing it to the box wall they cut two seat-belts out of the oldest pickup and stapled them to the chair, one for his lap, the other for his chest. Chip and Dale were missing breakfast but this tattoo guy who thought he was Bobby Orr was into something too wild to miss. They drilled air holes. Collin worked them hard. His anger would not let him stop. Chip gave him a *Playboy*, saying, "Bet you want this," and tossed it in while Dale giggled. Collin kept working.

Then he was nailed in and it was dark and, though the two boys persisted, he would not answer their questions or silly knocks. After a while they went away. Then the truck came and he was loaded, and soon he was moving down the twisting valley floor, the smell of gravel and dust coming in his air holes.

Not once did Collin realize that this was only the second time he'd deliberately gone against the wishes of another. In both cases against Annie. Once leaving her, once returning.

Time to go and see her, because the bitch said he couldn't. To Annie, because she deserved it, she needed it, shake up her wise ways, show her what the wild world really was, put a tattooed bee in her bonnet. To Annie, because *she* had finally earned *him*.

Life in the box went well at first. The novelty kept him alert, happy even. He could read, with difficulty, if he held the book up to an air hole. He made himself cheese sandwiches in darkness, proud how his fingers had eyes of their own. He filled half a urine jar, sealing it tight. Smoking, he nozzled his lips to exhale through a hole. He took cat naps, and on waking tried to guess from the curves where he was on the road south to Vancouver. He tried reading, a copy of the *Iliad* borrowed from Peake in earlier days. Unable to keep the small print steady enough, he switched to Chuck's *Playboy*. From out of nowhere came an old feeling, adolescent, lust rising in a private place. He hesitated, but then — why not? Wasn't this box the perfect secret spot? A dank den, protected.

He woke to jolts of stop-and-go city traffic. He tightened his belts. Soon the truck stopped for good, and amidst the whirr of forklifts and shouting men he had to hold his bottles steady as the box was lifted, run down a ramp and stacked. He spent two days, maybe longer, in a place so silent it must have been a warehouse.

The box still felt good. Lord, but hadn't he stumbled onto something here? Strapped in, safe, not a care in a small, small world. Maybe that was the secret, to keep your world tiny, entertained, shut in. Maybe those suburban TV couples had the secret after all. And his box-life even had a clear purpose: he was going to Annie. Perfection, this box, nothing less than a womb.

He woke stiff from a long sleep. The box was jostled and lifted. Onto another truck. He traced a mental map: by truck to the north of Vancouver Island, then by boat up the coast. No roads in or out except the big one, the Pacific.

The trip north began. Collin felt a quick burst of elation. North, out of an old world that had served him badly, that had led him to a present that was just not his fault. This trip wasn't a retreat but a fresh, brave step. He lit a cigarette, inhaled deeply, stretched out a leg cramp. He had to shit badly, for he'd been avoiding it. The first time, even though he'd burned a whole pack of matches, it had taken an hour for the stink to fade. But he unhitched his belts, found toilet paper, plastic bag, and twist tie. He was halfway through his chore when the truck lurched badly, making him stumble out of his squat, drop the half-loaded bag and hit his shoulder hard on the wall.

He cleaned up the mess as well as he could. But an awful sharpness to the lingering smell told him he'd gotten some on his clothes. He searched and cleaned some more, cursed the acid smell that refused to fade, then gave up and lit a cigarette.

In the flash, Collin saw.

"Damn!" he yelled, and punched the crate wall, breaking a knuckle, smashing the skin. *"Damn! Damn!"*

What he'd seen had squashed his mood as quick as a swatter a fly. His nice box, his perfect womb, had in one fast twist of vision been seen for what it was really: a container holding the whole of Vaughn Collin. And what was a Vaughn Collin? An old, filthy man, doubled over with cramps, chain smoking, sitting in ashes, reek and shit. A ludicrous tattoo. Was he anything more than that? No, there was nothing of him outside the box; all he was was here. Nothing but: a bad mind, cramped bones, shit smell, broken knuckle and blood. And where was this gargoyle going? In a box, to see good Annie, who didn't want to see him. What lie was he perpetuating now? And, ohh, *damn*, it was all beginning again, the waves of diamond terror, the paralysis, the first of endless seconds leading off into . . . another mistake. A huge mistake that stank. *He* was the mistake. Collin yelled and struck the wall again, and though the pain frightened him he struck it again. For it frightened him more when the box didn't break.

The *Queen Charlotte*, a coastal freighter too small for open ocean but too large for anywhere else, drew in its lines and pulled out of Port Hardy, a box lashed to the stern deck and covered with an orange tarp. Sunset, calm seas. The seagulls lining the rails could hear nothing over the droning of the diesels except, coming from the orange tarp, faint but very strange whistlings, hoots, belly-laughs, wailing. The gulls didn't want to get too close to that box of demons.

When the onrush of madness ceased, Collin swore he'd get a grip. He had to. He came up with a plan. One, no more yelling. To get caught in this box, tattooed and smelling of shit, caught by a gang of rough seamen, was unthinkable.

Two, he'd get pure. Cleanse himself. Through abstinence and discipline he'd earn Annie. He'd start now.

Tapping his feet in the dark, he found and then stomped on his cigarettes. Smash, crump, the packs buckled and tore, tobacco spreading like sawdust on the floor. Next, his feet found the *Playboy*, and working the soles of his sneakers on the breasty gloss he ripped away page after page. And there, the *Iliad*, why not? — fighting, swords, warriors' macho, what had the book done for the world? Faster, he ripped at that book too.

A renewed waft of shit-smell rose. God, he'd ripped open a bag. Damn! He kicked his feet into the tobacco and pages to clean them when, *crack*, he broke one urine bottle against another.

Collin stilled his body. He sat for a moment and then began to shake, and then to cry. It wasn't working! Purity, there could be no purity, all was *contortion*.

No, he'd try again. He had to. Shit a problem? Well, he wouldn't eat. Urine? He wouldn't drink. That decision made, he closed his eyes. He wouldn't see. He wouldn't smell either — feeling with his hands, he found what he wanted and then stuffed his nostrils with the butts of two cigarettes. He'd earn her, he'd be pure and he'd earn her. He'd earn her and *they could be scared together*.

Collin reached down and again searched the floor of his

littered, ridiculous, hyperbolic box. And found some. He'd never felt shit before. It could have been butter. He brought up his hand, slow with the poise of ritual, and anointed his forehead slowly and thoroughly, covering his tattoo with extra care, adding hell onto hell.

So it went. Collin fell in and out of madness. But never really out of it. His periods of clearer thought were, ironically, the worst times because only then was he awake to his pain. So he'd fall again, lost to a body folded and strapped like boneless meat to a chair, lost to a mind swept by tides of memories, voices, hallucinations. A stampede of inner beasts filled the box entirely, bouncing off its walls like trapped monkeys, like fighting dogs, like any mind's parts let loose and fallen to war. Just as so narrow a thing as war will reveal nature's whole range, so Collin's cramped box became impossibly vast.

Chantal stood before him.

Here she comes. I don't want her here.

She undresses, holding his eye. He doesn't want her, she isn't really there. He tightens both belts and closes his eyes.

Go away.

From the stink at his feet, Peake rises, mischievous. He lubricates his head with sweat from his palms and pushes himself to the hilt of his shoulders up inside Chantal. He spews words into her, you can see the lumps of alphabet rushing under her skin. Chantal throws her head back. This time, a real orgasm.

Stop now. Ridiculous. I'm in a box. Just a joke I'm playing. Backfired. But still to see Annie. I'll find a doctor there, get some pills for this.

"Pills! You want pills Vaughnie?" Here was Bert Flute, painted up in carnival colours, two pills taped to his nipples. No, it was Bonneville, that Toulon player, licking peyote and rubbing it on his nipples. No, it was . . . This was almost funny. He could conjure anyone he wanted.

This is not funny. Conjuring is part of the problem is part of the craziness, just shut up. I need sleep. I haven't been sleeping enough. Breathe slow and sleep. Breathe. Sleep.

But awake. Alone now. There is a strange light. Here on the floor lies his mother's skirt. Her robin's egg blue skirt. Glowing. And, who? Yes, here is his father, the man of law, his father reduced to the law of fathers and sons. Crying. His father, crying into his mother's glowing skirt. Father is wearing hockey equipment. He is very small. He is actually just a boy.

God I've thrown up on myself. A storm. I can hear the wind. It has blown some tarp aside and light is coming in through a hole. So there is no glowing skirt. It's real light, coming in a hole. Real light. Light at the end of the tunnel. But why should light give any reason to hope? How does anything out there have anything to do with hope?

If there's no light at the end of the tunnel, then no truisms are true. That's the key. Avoid truisms. Avoid anything anyone tells you. The fact they can say it means it can't be true. Stay free of facts. Certainty is mental illness.

I am here. This is a fact.

"I'll give you the facts." Connor Peake takes a facing chair and straps himself in. Eyes reptilian in the darkness.

I don't want to hear him.

Yes you do. Here's the one fact: the world is new each moment. That's all there is. Why not be on the edge, help it expand, push at walls with elbows and spit. Be a parade!

Why should I believe you?

There are no rules. Fact is, we're free. Paint your pets purple. Pull out your teeth. Burn the Buddha. Horse poonts, cat snaps.

You're really smart.

Good. It is sacred that you mock me.

Why should I believe you?

"Doesn't it make sense?"

No.

You don't even have to do much. You have your chair. Sit in it and watch the multifoliate rose . . . explode.

I hate what I see.

The rose's beauty is strange, I agree.

I hate myself.

That too is part of the rose. Sit and watch.

You might be lying.

I might be. That's part of the rose.

Then there's no hope. It makes me want to kill myself.

Kill yourself. It's part of the rose. One more dying petal. Die. The rose does not care about anything. That's the nature of this one very regal lady.

Evers did. God, Mike killed himself, he's gone.

Impressive, eh? Maybe he won. We were all impressed.

He didn't win. He was afraid.

Well you can do it right. You'd win then, that's for sure.

How to do it. Die.

"How can I die?" asks a man surrounded by glass. Maybe you broke those jars for a reason.

Wait. The boat has stopped. I'm docked. It's over.

Maybe you broke that glass for a reason.

It's over. They're hoisting me. I'll be out of this box.

Will you? When you're standing there contained under clouds, will your box stink any less? It's even worse out there. Maybe you have that piece of glass in your hand for a reason.

No. I'm on the dock. Annie will be here to let me out.

Have you forgotten she doesn't want you? I thought you came to chastise. What happened to your big joke? One more Weird Thing. Can you bear the sweetness of the slice?

Yes, now they're through prying nails, now the lid comes up and in comes the light, sharp as this razor of glass and . . . Ah! . . .

with the blood of the rose red and sweet I'll bathe this stink in the blood of roses, I'll stand and show myself and see her — there she is, Annie, Lise — I'll aim at her the red sneer of creation.

The *Queen Charlotte* was on schedule. Standing on the wharf in the fading light, watching the freighter round the point, August Bob and offspring waited for their new Kenmore stove, Becky Charlie her water heater, and one Moe brother his Warner reduction gear and case of rye.

Annie Delacourt was just finishing her job sweeping tourist dirt out of a Tyee room when in ran a boy with what in Bella Combe is huge news: something for you, from the city, on the wharf.

She was tired. She put away her things and started down. Though she arrived at the dock too late to give the villagers permission to open the box (Why wait? they decided. Why not do old Annie a favour?), she did arrive in time to see what came of it.

When most of the nails were out, and when they'd begun prying the lid and lifting it, they jumped away at the hand they saw helping from within. They caught the reek and stepped back farther.

The lid came up quickly now. Then, more slowly, a wincing man. He jerked as his long-bent knees popped straight, and he gave a little scream at this.

The creature they encountered was none other than a man who had grown up backwards, a baby now, who cried at anything, a bubble in the back of his throat, a ripple in his underwear, a baby, a baby, a shattered sloppy baby. One villager claimed he had the eyes of the devil. But most agreed that he was pale, and pained by light. He had a brief, ugly, salt and pepper beard, pebbled with dry vomit. What looked like black mud on his face had cracked away from worry lines to show his one clear feature: an exclamation mark.

The creature was bleeding from one wrist, which he held

out to them. For help? No, he looked not at all pleading. His eyes flashed an infantile defiance, and more cruelty than humour. He aimed his wrist like a gun first at one onlooker, then another, as though he searched for one face in particular. Though he squeezed it and hit it, it still failed to shoot. When he found the face he wanted, and when all the wrist would do was dribble a bit down the box's wall he gave up and began to whimper like the poor baby he was.

Though it's been years now I remember the creosote smell as I lay on the wharf, my head in her lap. To think of the sight she saw, looking down! My hair, my face, my self-sick eyes. I lay shivering on the weak ice of my life, under Annie's hard calm.

"Well," she said quietly, "now what have *we* been through?"

Her teasing me, right at that moment, startled the hell out of me. Perhaps it saved me from more years of self-pity. In any case, she had defined the terms of our new beginning then and there.

Annie stared down on me. I could feel her love, there was no doubting it, but she wouldn't quite let me have it, wouldn't let me take it within, where I could let it warm me, bathe me, put me to sleep.

I soon found out that was precisely not her purpose.

June 9th

And so, at fifty-five, I came to this place.

I may have exaggerated, but so what. I got the flavour, I got the heart of it. I know because I shook to write it. I know because I cried. And I haven't cried in months and months.

Here I am. Bella Combe, this beach, this cabin — how can this be said? — has been on the surface serene and calming.

But its placidity *works* on you. Something insidious here. The calm sets a person up to see that mind is a child which makes up its own terrors. The calm makes one scramble, grope for roots, until one discovers that roots — toeholds we think must be there if only because we feel we need them — simply do not exist.

I can say that the calm makes the obvious — obvious.

Bella Combe: tedious curse, undeserved blessing.

But here in Bella Combe, and here in my story, I have caught up with myself. Quietly falling into age. Is there any point in describing my life here? Should I keep going? Who am I writing this for now? Because you know the rest, Annie. You know it as well as I do.

She came this morning returning my chapter. She placed it gently on my table as if not to jostle the sick man in it. She smiled, nodded at it, said, *Boy* you were a mess. She joked, saying I was a mess no longer and she took full credit for that.

I kept quiet through all this. She added that it looked like I'd kept my sad sense of humour in the writing of it, and that that was the best thing of all.

I said I was glad she liked it.

She looked at me, took in my tone. There was something weighty in the air, something to do with her, not me, not my book, and she knew that I knew it.

"So," she asked, "are you finished?"

"I don't know. Am I?"

"That's completely up to you." She paused, and I don't think she was being funny. "Always has been."

I decided to say nothing. I would think about this. About being finished. Was there anything left to look at? Was I finished looking?

"When you're done," Annie said, "I have a gift for you."

Her casual tone did a weak job pretending that this gift

would be a normal gift: a bottle of brandy, a book, even my Evinrude back. No, it was something of magnitude, something having to do with me.

"I hope you like it."

At the edge of a huge seriousness, her sly curl of smile.

The loon again. Jerry Lewis, I call him. Lewis the loon. I can't see him under this new moon but he sounds close. Between calls I hear him splashing, can picture him beating his wings while standing on the water, like his feet were held by underwater chains. He's been yelling for an hour — not in his sad clarinet double-note but his maniac's warble.

Something's up. Annie makes me nervous. New moons always make me nervous. Maybe it's just that outside it's dark, and not even the animals can see.

Lewis. What a noise. He showed up last year and he's been doing his clown act out in front of my porch since then. Funny: I keep expecting something to kill him. Cut him off in mid-warble, sudden *GAK* of surprise and strangulation, Jerry's goofy routine getting the big hook. Likely my whimsy is connected to the time years back when Annie and I heard the death screams of a water bird, a loon we decided, just outside. Surprised in its sleep. Surprised us in our sleep too. Squeezed in bed together, rare for her to stay.

"Can come at any time, eh?" Annie'd whispered. She used no cheap drama, but because we were in the dark the effect was eerie. "Even if we think we're ready for it, when we leave this joint it'll be a surprise."

She often called life on earth "this joint".

I used to think her morbid. She approaches death in many ways, but what she says amounts to this: if some state of being persists after death, ironically the instant of death may be the one important moment of our lives.

I asked her what was the use of dwelling on death, and she accused me of putting words in her mouth.

"Not 'dwell'," she said. "The word's 'prepare'. It means living the richest life possible."

Something like that. I suppose I'm on about this right now because of the feeling I have. Because she looks like she's preparing for something.

And because the last thing she said today, leaving, and the way she looked saying it, put my hair on end. After telling me that when I finished my book she had a big gift for me, she added a joke that wasn't a joke. At the door, something monstrous in her eyes. That sly curled smile. Maybe a tear in her eye — but that might just be me, remembering wrong, wanting a tear from her.

What she said was about my book, but her eyes told me it was also about something else.

What she said was, "Endings are so sad."

Annie?

Medical Love

> *To evolve, you must enter the corridor of madness. Once in, the far end is the only exit. To travel the corridor you need a guide, one who has survived the journey. But there is no guarantee your guide is not still in the corridor himself. Mad, or worse.*

— One of Ivan's notes, and something I still think about when you tell me things, Annie.

She had him carried to a room at the Tyee, where she stripped him and washed him. Her hands were strong and never stopped.

He fell asleep in a sitting position, on his side, and woke up the same way many hours later.

Annie sat at the bed's foot, reading. She wore industrial eyeglasses, the kind with the plastic side-skirts. When she met his eye she looked tired and a little bored.

"Lise . . . " Vaughn started to say, but stopped, shocked at the croak of his voice. "I'm sorry . . . I'll just get up and. . . ."

"I'll try to help you," she said matter-of-factly.

"I'll try to help myself," he croaked. It seemed the right thing to say. And maybe he could. Here he was in the middle of nowhere. Nothing could hurt him here. He was wrong of course, but for the moment — peace.

With an almost playful look, Annie nodded to his face, his tattoo, acknowledging it for the first time.

"That's quite something," she said.

"Probably should have been a comma," he told her, feeling a bit confident, almost smiling himself.

Annie's smile was instantly gone.

"I wasn't congratulating you. I was summing up what life can do, eh?"

"This is Ivan's old place. He built it."

The one-room cabin's central feature was its wood stove. Hugging the periphery were a bed, cedar chest, table, bookshelves, and a cupboard for utensils and jars. The room's attitude was one of spartan cleanliness. All the wood, from furniture to countertop, showed the dull sheen of use. Ferns grew from pots at each window. The yard was full of such ferns, and the effect was that the cabin was not shut to the forest.

Annie said, "You take the bed." She slapped the mattress as she walked by it.

He told her the floor was fine. He wouldn't hear of —

"Vaughn," she said, "for the time being please do as I say. I have some plans for you. You won't understand some things, but just do them. For one week, just do what I say. After that you can do what you want. Deal?"

He nodded, sat on the bed. His mind hardly worked. Thoughts survived mere moments before drowning in dull panic and fog. "Doing what she said for one week" sounded perfect. As for "her plans" for him, he hardly cared.

In the morning, after a breakfast of trout and bannock, Annie led him on a mile-long hike down the beach. He spotted, in the distance, an object on the sand. Fear rose out of seeing even the vague shape, before he understood what it was. As they drew nearer his fear was confirmed. She had led him to his box.

"No one'll come by so don't worry about people," she said. Vaughn eyed the box as though it were a growling animal. Its lid was festooned with postage tags, and *Bella Combe, British Columbia* inked in Chip's childish scrawl.

"Today you get back in your box," Annie said.

"Well, I . . . *No.* I — "

"Please just do it."

Trembling, he looked out at the sea. It was calm, but he feared he might vomit.

"Vaughn. It's important I don't explain. It'll ruin it." She paused. "Okay?"

He'd never had much pride. And perhaps a case can be made for absolute pridelessness. In any event, the Vaughn Collin who was to follow a strange woman's words and climb back into his crate of horror had no pride left whatsoever.

He gave Annie the faintest nod.

"I'll explain this much. This is some of the hair of the dog that bit you." She did a parody of a sing-song nurse: "Every time we're in a dark place we can't be going crazy, now can we?"

"No."

"When things go bad, try to stay aware of your breathing."

He climbed in. Annie pounded a couple of nails in with a rock. She yelled that she'd return in several hours. He settled into the chair. He took a slow, deliberate breath.

The box had been sprayed out. But a smell remained, almost an odour to the dim light itself. The box was so familiar it made his Bella Combe interlude seem only a dream. The Tyee bed, the coastal air, Annie's hands — had they been hallucination as well? Of course not. He ran his palm along the fabric of his new jeans. He killed his doubts by smacking his knee.

But roiling confusion and hallucinations began anew, try as he might to defuse them by watching his breathing. He tried to convince himself of the simple fact that he sat in a wooden box surrounded by rocks, sea, and mountains, but this fact was too precariously thin, and inner vivid seething rose easily to puncture it. At one point he thought he was back on deck and could feel the sea's toss and roll.

On it went, with brief intervals of clarity. Halfway into the morning he came upon a plan. By inviting hallucination, by creating as many images as possible, he would exhaust them. Since lightning could not strike the same place twice, he would eliminate all possible sites. Of course the plan failed, but it did produce some entertainment. One was a long string of visions. There was a bag of nuts on his lap. He took one out, walnut-size but hairy like a coconut. After some difficulty he broke it apart and found inside the tiniest elephant, carved in ivory, radiating a white glow. Though it was no larger than a thumbnail, the work was so delicate he could see the end-hairs of its tail. He broke open another nut. This one hid a tiny machine, dark metal, made of countless moving parts, tight as clockwork. Another nut held a miniature hockey rink, lit bright white as if viewed from above at night. Tiny forms chased a puck too small to see. Another nut showed nothing at first, but in a nightmarish surprise a kind of mush that smelled of fish began oozing out in throbs, as though pushed by a heartbeat. Another nut let loose a quick, pale brown bird, which flew into the darkness, circling his ears. And so on.

He slept some of the time. Dreams were hard to distinguish from waking visions. When not in a fantasy, he was horribly bored.

BOOM.

Suddenly the box roared as if it were a cannon going off. Collin almost fell off his chair.

BOOM.

Again the box quaked. Collin half-stood and pounded at the lid with his palms.

"Stay put," came Annie's muffled shout.

He hesitated. He tried peering out an airhole but could only see distant sand and clouds. He strapped himself in, his heart speeding.

He passed the next minute completely alert. Nothing could interrupt the attention he aimed at the outside world. Was it a bear?

BOOM.

Now he knew. He'd heard footsteps come and go. Annie was pounding on the box with some kind of club.

He sat and waited for the next one, smiling. Then, a subtle fear. He hadn't seen Annie for many years. Who knew what this Ivan had done to her? Fear-bred fantasies began to well in his stomach.

BOOM.

Again he was jarred alert. This continued into the afternoon. With each roar and rock he'd snap awake. He'd wait for the next blow, for the other shoe to drop, yet when it did it was always a surprise. It seemed she timed her blows randomly. Once he was struck five or six times in a minute; then he spent an alert hour in silence.

Her surprises kept him at the ready; always, so to speak, in the box itself. What dreams he did slip into died a loud death, the deeper the dream the ruder the awakening. He grew to notice the contrast between dream and simple wakefulness. One was syrupy fog while the other was crystal, holding the potential of lightning.

Finally the lid came up. He wanted only to hike home

and collapse, but Annie, conducting him with an almost ritualistic air, had him take up her club and smash the box lid to splinters. They carried it back for kindling.

So Annie's plans for him were revealed. He spent the second day in a lean-to woodshed behind the cabin. Annie had painted the inner boards with ugly, spider-like blotches. The third day he sat in a cage of loosely woven saplings. And so on, each day another kind of box. He spent day four in a hole in the ground, with no lid, where he experienced the dim, hopeful life of a mole. Day six, the last of his trial, he stayed in the cabin itself, feeling oddly pleased, and content enough just to sit there, listen to gulls, watch his breath from time to time, and otherwise let his eyes be absorbed in the swirling woodgrains of the burl-carved table.

It was November, and Vaughn understood early on that nothing much happens in Bella Combe in November. It was a good guess that the rest of the year wasn't much different. Sitting at a window in Ivan's cabin, or hiking shyly to Vedder's general store for supplies (Vedder was gruff, never talked, and never looked at you, so Vaughn felt okay there), he saw that to live in Bella Combe was to live in isolation. Contained under clouds, walled by mountains. But at least this box was a large one.

Yet he was quickly in a quandary. What to do now? He felt harshly tender all over as though recovering from a recent burn.

For several days he did what he could to postpone any grand decisions. He chopped wood, split shingles for a corner of the roof, began the new outhouse (its pit had been his fourth box) and generally aspired to be helpful — trying hard for the illusion that he'd come to Bella Combe simply to visit and lend a needed hand. Evenings he spent getting reacquainted with the daughter of a Métis maid.

She had aged, but aged well, as do eagles and elk, which look stronger even though they probably aren't. Deepset wrinkles revealed extremes of laughter and pain, but her main feature was the tranquillity which relaxed all the muscles of her face. Her flesh was still firm on the stocky frame. She still had Lise's skin, which reminded Vaughn of tawny pudding.

One night Annie forced his hand.

A gale had blown all day. Waves pounded themselves to pieces on the rocks while a low canopy of clouds raced and tumbled and broke apart on the hills. In the zone of grace between sea and clouds, ragged strings of geese fled south, honking but hardly heard above the wind.

After dinner they drank wine and talked about midwifery. From miles around people paid to have Annie come and stay and wait for the baby. This, plus work at the Tyee, had been her living here. She told him that, during her street life in Winnipeg, she had not only delivered babies for her friends but also performed abortions.

"Did a doctor's work for no pay. But I got to know girl parts like no one else." Annie kept a playful eye on Vaughn even as she tilted her head back to drain the wine. "I was the best lover any girl ever wrestled. Put a bag over my head they were in heaven, eh?"

Annie's plunges to raunchiness startled him. She had grown such a range. Time and again he saw her move from the Elizabethan coyness of young Lise to the alley-wise sneer. Or from humble host, from nostalgic friend, to a teacher with box-clubbing ice in her eyes. This last Annie he felt the least at ease with.

She finished her wine, and her face changed.

"So. What are you going to do?"

"When?" Nervous as a lying boy.

"Now. Tomorrow. The rest of your life."

Though he'd been stifling thoughts of his future the best he could, it seemed some part of him had been working things out as though behind his back.

"I want to stay here."

Annie had an answer ready too.

"Why should I let you?"

Though this hurt, he was ready for it. She had a right to say no to her years here being invaded by the likes of him.

"And what would you do?"

Again, to his surprise, he already knew.

"I know how to fish."

"Where will you live?"

"I'm going to build a cabin like this one." He added that he'd build it up the beach where she'd put his box.

Annie sat a moment, something on her mind. Unnoticed by him until now, the wind had fallen completely. He looked out the window at the lack of noise, saw that the moon found a hole in the clouds. It was full, signalling some kind of completion.

"That's all fine. But I have a proposal." She watched him closely and didn't hide that she was weighing his instability and choosing words to suit.

"I can't stop you from staying here. And whether or not you accept my proposal we can still be friends. I don't want to dangle friendship as a reward."

Vaughn nodded, warily, wondering at this "proposal".

"I have work to do. I don't have much time. So we can be friends" — she pronounced the word to stress "merely" friends — "or we can be something more. Completely up to you. But I propose a commitment. A kind of marriage."

Perhaps his eyes flooded with romance, for Annie became stern.

"A marriage with conditions. Severe conditions. Should I go on?"

"I have to say yes or no tonight?"

She nodded. "Should I go on?"

"Okay."

First she had him admit that he was in pain. He admitted it, it was a fact. Then she asked if he accepted that he had something to learn from her. He accepted this too, as quickly as he would have forty years ago in Beauséjour.

He was to commit himself to five years in Bella Combe. He did. Next he had to make "three vows to three teachers". The first vow was to "trust his own goodness". Next he vowed to "trust the sanity of heaven and earth". Annie suggested he take a minute with each vow, and make a silent promise to uphold it. Stricken now with the fever of commitment, he felt let down by this lack of ceremony. He recalled Peake injecting oysters with food blue colouring, plopping them into fat glasses of whiskey and, to background strains of "Rule Britannia", the boys downing them while vowing "to remain children".

Vaughn closed his eyes and promised, and did it well. The plain optimism of these vows bolstered his heart.

The third vow proved more difficult. He was to "trust in the sanity of Annie Delacourt". He did trust her sanity, that was not the question. The peculiar nature of the vow was hinted at by the way Annie tilted her head and narrowed her eyes as she proposed it.

"Do you mean I have to do everything you say?" he asked. The image of Annie and him hand in hand had dissolved.

"That depends on the depth of your vow." Her manner was almost sly.

Vaughn responded by simply going silent and making his vow. They lifted their wine in a silent toast to seal all three.

Little did he know what was in store. Little did he know that Annie would grow wild and mysterious to his eyes and that he would come to fiercely love her and also hate her; that under her tutelage he would find himself sitting "watching his breath" on stumps hour after hour in rain, snow, or moonless night. He had no idea she would have him fast for a month, then gorge on meat; no idea that a year of sexual abstinence would be followed by masturbating five times a day. "Pay attention," she would say over and over, until he grew sick of it, sick of her, his trust tried to the utmost.

She would always slap his comfort away. Like the time she had him clean her beach. They'd been strolling the shoreline fronting her cabin when she turned to him suddenly and told him to "clean my beach". Of boulders, rocks, and little rocks. The beach was huge. Her voice had suggested a whim, nothing more. Vaughn refused. His cabin was almost finished. Winter was close. Her request was ridiculous and he told her so.

"Okay," she said, as simple as that. She even smiled, subtle, not unfriendly. He panicked, of course, and began cleaning her beach and continued for the next five weeks. Snow fell on the floor of his unfinished cabin and he hated her.

Or the time she spit in his face. He'd been given someone's spiked boots, climber's belt, and a topped-tree, thirty feet high, to sit upon. "Find your best eye" was all she told him. He sat on that treetop every morning for a month. It was an ugly part of the forest. He sat and sat and tried not to hate her for the agonies he suffered. Watching thoughts, emotions, scenery, whatever, he would identify the seer of these things. But then came the question, What sees *that*? What sees that which sees? He would settle down anew and find that eye too, but then, what had seen *that*? And so on, his mind an infinitude of hair-splitting, of mirrors. A dog chasing its tail, needless madness atop a ludicrous tree. Then the day she climbed up with lunch, an old lady with spiked boots, leaning back into her belt, her head at the level of his waist. He was desperate. Viewing her from between his knees, barely civil, he hissed:

"*What sees finally?*"

"Shut up." She handed him a sandwich.

"I quit."

Her face shot forward and she spit in his face, a gob on the forehead, warm then cold then dribbling down. He rocked back, almost toppling, shocked. As he wiped himself she told him: "Your best eye was there the second after I spit. Because *you* weren't."

She climbed down, and shouted up, "Searchin' for God ain't for *suckholes*, eh?"

Aha, he thought, having never heard her use the word "God" before. But then, from her face, he saw she was only kidding.

Or the time one hot summer day they sat drinking in the Tyee when she announced she had a surprise for him arriving that day by freighter from Vancouver. Meeting the boat, they watched a man-sized wooden crate dangle down to the dock by crane.

"Here he is," Annie said, solemnly. A wooden crate. Collin's hair stood on end. He lost his ground for a moment, envisioning nothing definite, but something alive in there, somebody dangerous, from the past come to get him, it was Peake it was Leona it was Dodic it was Lise it was *him*. "Fuck you!" he shouted and raised the crowbar to strike it but Annie stopped him, took the bar, and opened it herself to reveal his new Evinrude outboard. When his embarrassment passed, when they had the motor clamped to the transom of Ivan's old dory and were roaring over the perfect glass of the bay, chasing gulls, they took off their clothes. At twenty miles per hour he named his loud, mindless engine "Peake" and Annie held her blouse up in the wind like a flag.

Vowing, he'd had no idea of all this as he put down his glass of wine. Annie's little smile throughout told him she might not even be serious. But she was solemn now. He sensed his five years had already begun. Indeed, when she next spoke her voice was pregnant with the tone he'd hear more and more from that evening on. It reminded him of quiet French horns. She sat erect in her chair.

"In our marriage," she said, "you might not see my love. I might seem distant. I might *seem* distant."

She got up and stood behind him. "Look out the window," she whispered.

He did, and saw clouds churning past the ripe moon. He could hear the wind again. What had the Winnipeg streets, what had life done to this woman?

"Can't see me now, can you."

"No."

"It will be like this," she said, and he felt the warmth of her breath on the back of his neck.

June 21

What am I doing in this chair. I'm finished I'm not finished.

The weight of her keeps me in the present. The pull of her keeps me watching out the window.

Something's up. Four days since she came by. It's not my life I'm looking at now, it's hers.

June 22

It took me years, but this morning I visited their cabin. Mark was there with the others. Tim, Joanne, Glenda. Alison.

Outside, their place is shacky, weatherbeaten. They used found logs. But this crude husk hid a surprising inside, which was spacious, with a clean, studious air. Wine-brown and cool. Loaded bookshelves. One wall was hung with musical instruments, handmade-looking, well-used. Other walls held da Vinci prints and Mark's wildlife studies, some showing a Leonardo-like interest in anatomy.

I counted three curtained-off bedrooms. Three women, two men. I wondered who was the odd female out. Assuming it worked that way. I guessed it wasn't the plump Joanne, who brought me tea. Maybe it's shy, black-haired Alison, the newcomer. Late thirties, maybe forty. What has she left behind? She looked the most unsettled in the presence of a strange man. Strange in both senses. Visiting, seeing her, I felt like a young man out on the town. What odd thoughts we have at odd times.

Odd times. Yesterday's note in Vedder's store, pinned glaring to the board, in Annie's scrawl. *IT'S AT MARK'S*. No "to Vaughn", no "from Annie", but I knew who it was for, who it was from, and what it was about.

They looked surprised I'd come. I suppose they consider me a hermit, or misanthrope, some combination of those.

I took tea, then did an extraordinary thing. Plucking off my toque and placing it on my knee, I revealed my forehead to them. I removed the toque with grace. I wasn't sure why but I felt at home. There hung in the air a suggestion that pretence be cut, and in taking off my toque I was merely complying. They regarded my face with no embarrassment but something more like deference. I sensed their gratitude for my gesture. It's not like they didn't know.

"Did Annie leave something for me here? There was this note, this note in Vedder's."

"It's here." Alison went to a shelf and brought me a heavy package. She smiled handing it over. "Actually it's been sitting here for months."

"What is it?" I held it to my ear and shook it, joking.

"We didn't peek," said Glenda. She was tall and muscular, violently drying her hair with a towel. Patches of wet T-shirt clung to her back.

The wrapping was grocery-bag brown paper, stuck with black squares of electrician's tape. I sat with it on my lap, wondering what to do.

"Blow out the candles and make a wish," Glenda said as she went to the kitchen. I looked at her and smiled, though no one else did. Maybe she was never not snide.

I peeled back some tape. Lifted the wrapper. It was a three-inch-thick sheath of paper. Typed on Annie's old typewriter, now mine. I recognized the typeface instantly; it was like looking at my own book.

The first page began:

> Dear Ivan:
>
> I'm not looking forward to this and I don't know where to begin. So I'll begin at the beginning. I was born in Beauséjour, Manitoba, and my father died the same day, I suppose celebrating. My mother and I lived with

"What is it?" Mark asked.

Annie had asked me to write one just as Ivan had asked her. This was Annie's book. I was about to tell Mark this when my stomach understood something, and fell. I asked Mark a question instead.

"When . . . when Ivan left, did he leave after Annie finished writing a book, a journal, for him?"

My stomach fell farther as Mark nodded casually.

"Don't know *if* that's why he left, but that was more or less the timing. Why?"

Glenda returned from the kitchen. "Must of been a great book."

"Did you — did any of you write a book for her? For Annie?"

Mark looked at the others, shook his head.

But Alison had been watching me, and the look in her face perhaps mirrored my own.

She whispered, "Why?"

"Well, I did. I wrote a book. And I just finished it."

And endings are sad.

After some argument, Mark and Glenda — who claimed she recalled Annie saying where she was going — decided they would search for her and find out one way or the other. The argument concerned whether or not she wanted to be found. If she was on a week-long hike or gone for good, either way would she want someone looking for her?

This having been said, I started feeling a little foolish. If I'd misread the whole thing, if she was only off on a hike after all, I'd feel like a hysterical idiot when I next saw her. Or if she had gone for good, and because of me was found, wouldn't I have betrayed her?

Not that anyone was at all convinced she'd left. Perhaps they humoured me. Tim argued that she was just not that corny, that pat.

"What's the big deal? Somebody writes his big life *story* down, why would — " Realizing he was insulting me he turned to me and added, "You know what I mean."

"I do."

"Well who knows what Vaughn meant to her?" This, after a silence, from Alison. I'd gathered by now that Annie had told them as little about me as she had me about them.

"Well, she did speak of leaving." Mark hadn't said much throughout. "And mentioned you when she did." He nodded, remembering, and the others went still. I think it was here they decided something was up.

"She said something like," Mark searched for her words, "something like, 'When I leave this joint, save my chair for the guy up the beach'." Mark looked at them while they all looked at me. "Or, 'He might want to take my chair', something like that."

"We have these weekly discussions," Alison was telling me. "They're sort of, I don't know, formal."

I was looking around, stupidly, at the actual chairs. Maybe they did have their own chairs to sit in, who knows. I wondered if hers was, figuratively speaking, the big one.

When she leaves this joint . . . Jesus.

"Some of us," I found myself saying, "need some formality. It helps us respect, and remember."

"We'll just find her and find out," Mark said cheerily now. "Not that she'll tell us anything." He winked at me. His blond hair tied back, his high cheekbones and icy eyes reminded me of a Nordic warrior, but a warrior interested in the flight of wrens.

"I'm in the mood for a stroll anyway," Glenda shouted over the rain that was suddenly loud on the roof. She unloaded a bag on the floor. Dehydrated food. A pair of walkie-talkies. Tim and she began to load packs. They laced on boots and I saw they planned to leave immediately.

Lunch first. I accepted sandwiches and coffee. I felt okay here, in no hurry. I did feel respected, an elder of sorts. They were going to hike miles in the rain because I'd had a thought.

After eating, a map was spread on the table, a grid drawn on it and the squares numbered. Glenda went outside to test the walkie-talkies.

Tim asked from inside, "Found her yet? Over."

"On the beach," came Glenda's crackling reply. "Suntanning. Real ugly. Over."

"Stop it. Over."

This time they did smile a little, sad smiles. I knew I was seeing Annie's friends.

As gear was shouldered to a balance, I sensed in the cool bustle her steady hand. This roomful of bodies felt contained, vaguely guided. Nestlings under a wild brown swan.

Dear Annie:

I'm finished now. Finished with me. I'll talk to you.

This morning, after my "dream", I turned to your Bella Combe journal. It's— Endless pain. The occasional diamond. I wish you'd let me have it sooner. I flip through. You say:

> Up Portage Ave, the glass buildings, I see in the windows all the people making the same big mistake. Critical bitch. Then I step on a dead bird. Killing the killed. Beyond a properly given gift, there is no better thing than a symbol.

Symbols, signs. There's one huge thing I don't get. Are symbols messages we give to ourselves? Reminders, like string tied to a finger, of truths we know? Or *can* messages come from outside, the multifoliate rose playing games with itself, petal to petal?

I need to know because of my dream last night. Have I been shown the symbol of my fear, or are you dead?

I'll just talk to you here, Annie.

I want to recall a day a few years ago. I want to see it again clearly. It has to do with losing myself, it has to do with symbols, and with magic. It has to do with seeing you for the first time.

Five years I'd lived in Bella Combe. It was my day of graduation from my three vows. You and I hiked to an alpine meadow with sleeping bags and bottle of brandy. It was a sunny day, a day of prizes. Do you remember? I walked happy and hard. Ferns at our knees, young eagles resting way up on the wind. A smell of hot, sapping trees.

"Who are you?" I asked.

"Your mother your lover your sister your maid."

This little camping trip was my graduation prize. Part of it was your offer to answer any question I had, and I'd been asking questions all day, gorging myself. For five years you'd kept pretty quiet, and I'd been sitting on stumps. You did have answers, some of which were obvious. When I asked you why you made me clean your beach, you said simply that you'd been cleaning mine for years.

"Those three vows." They'd never once been mentioned. "Did you take them with Ivan?"

"I made those up. Not bad, eh?" Seeing I was about to get mad, you added, more seriously, "Some of us need some formality to help us respect, and remember."

We reached a sunny knoll and sat on a bed of gold moss to eat lunch. Dried salmon and bannock, west-coast fishes and loaves.

"What is magic?" I asked as I chewed my miraculous sandwich.

"God, what isn't?"

"No I know, but, c'mon, what is?"

In your hiking boots, logger shirt, sweat pants, and hair-in-a-bun you looked more fool than magician. You stopped chewing.

"All right," you said. "I'll show you magic."

With slow, ritualistic movements you reached into your pack. Your face on high serious. Having fun with me, I see now. You withdrew a burnished bronze plate that doubled as a mirror and, handing it to me, said, "Look."

I hesitated. You made me nervous. I expected big things from that mirror. Would I see the holy face, or the chattering skull, of my soul? Would I panic and be flung spinning into hell? You had ways I didn't comprehend. That gale. The objects which appeared on your doorstep some mornings. Your weird luck.

"Look."

I took a breath and looked. In the plate was a man. The bronze gave his image a timeless cast, like a face in an old daguerreotype. The man had an exclamation mark on his forehead. Given what he'd been through, he hadn't aged so badly. The eyes searched for something not there.

"Well?" I asked. "Yes?"

"Well what."

"Magic?"

"There it is."

"My face? I look only — normal."

"Aha!" you laughed, girlish. "Should have seen yourself five years ago, eh?" You took a great bite of sandwich and tilted your head back, chewing and grinning at the sky. "Should have seen yourself *fifty* years ago."

What happened next was a little odd. We've never discussed it before, am I right?

It's not that I wasn't grateful. I was grateful for the bit of magic I'd just seen in your plate, grateful for some kind of sanity. But today was my graduation. I felt sanctified under a spring sun. And, Annie, you have said that when we ride the crest of our best awareness the world is a shrine, and anything we do is sacred.

"I want more," I said. Sacred greed.

"What?"

Perhaps I just felt mischievous. Sacred mischief. Or perhaps I'd been caught by the heat that hung coiled and sacred in the trees, causing twigs to swell, the air to thicken, *fulla fock*.

I grabbed your shoulder and pulled you down. Do you remember? We wrestled and laughed. You stopped laughing when you saw this was for real, when I yanked at the elastic of your sweat pants and said, *I'm going to show you a time machine*.

"*Vaughn* — We — " But that's all you could say, because I caught you that time, didn't I? You were neither Lise nor Annie but caught in between. You hadn't had sex for years. Did your teacher role rear up and panic? I had a power over you, I had a wedge for the soft centre of your indecision. You ever see a doe in rut? The hard-breathing stag sidesteps closer. Once touched, her hind legs lock on her, spread apart without her wanting them to be. In her face you see a bisected spirit.

I got your pants down to your ankles and one booted

foot out. I drew my pants to my knees. I recall how I had to work on you. Do you remember how clumsy we were, how uneven the ground? You were breathing hard now. We tried out contours on the mossy rock, and found one. I looked down on you. I paused to taste the moment. On our bed of sun-warmed moss and brown pine needles we made love slowly. Do you remember those dry, spiky needles only an inch away from where we were wet and joined? Were you aware of them too?

Though we lay in no secret spot but high on an open hill, exposed to the sky and its demanding eye, we did find the magic of a time machine. There you were, your same good skin. Lise. I could smell your sex, your scent hadn't changed. Smell, the hint of a soul. I realized then that you, that everything about you, was my only secret spot.

We finished, almost together, our sacred dumb bodies somehow remembering what to do. I smiled down and you smiled up, shy with each other.

"Was that magic?" I asked, still mischievous.

"Yes."

I grew soft inside you, but I would not withdraw. It was my graduation day, I had power and I wouldn't lose this prize easily. You'd given me my inch and I was going for the mile.

"I want more," I said.

"More?"

"Magic. Show me something real, and tell me how you did it," I said, still on top and inside you.

Again you pondered me. Again your face changed.

"Okay, Vaughn."

It was the first time you showed me your eyes.

More days go by. Annie, have you left? Annie, are you just off on a big camping trip? Annie, are you dead?

The dream said you were dead. I sprang awake. Annie,

dead. I sat straight up. Black horrors lurched about the cabin.

This morning I rowed the shoreline, scanning the high-water mark for fire logs, pretending that life does go on. I could think of nothing but life without Annie. Never in my life have I felt so sane and yet at the same time so empty. I spotted a good log, rowed in, and stepped out into a foot of water. Instead of walking to shore I turned and walked into deeper water. Not knowing why, I waded waist deep. Again you're right, there is no point in figuring things out. Except for one thing: why survive? Why survive at all?

I turned and faced the shore. I looked at my right wrist and its tiny scar. Why survive? I imagined cutting my wrist again, with a shell. Laying the cut arm to the water gently, the waves nudging my back, I'd watch a stream of red drift from me, spread to the beach. A washed pink would reach the sand.

How noble to simply relax into being part of the food chain. Clams would filter the best of my blood, shit out the devils. Clams dug up by Mom and Dad and little-daughter tourist. That evening a nice chowder. Daughter keeps in the good, poops out the devils. But not all the devils: in the morning Mom screams, a clam-coloured ! showing faintly on daughter's forehead . . .

Humour helped me out of the water. I wrestled the log out and towed it home, where I began to cut and split it. Why survive? The question wouldn't leave me. I stacked the blocks (why?), sat down and pulled out an apple (why?), which I chewed. This business, I thought, recalling the words of my father, will take some doing.

I've never had a dream like it. So clear, it seemed like another species. Clear as life. It hasn't faded.

In it I watch Mark and the others carry you up the beach. They stop at my place, my doorstep, deposit you on the porch. Clear, scientific, frightening. Your eyes were gone, your nose swollen. Death's overdone smile. As always, you have a message for me: *Your face soon,* Vaughn-Vaughn, *your face soon.*

Your skin is smooth, but because it is swollen up from within, vital underneath with the weird glow of that which lives on death. Body wreckers, transformers, they who do Shiva's dance. Your body's last lesson is to show me the fallacy of physical death. The liveliness under the skin speaks only of exchange, not death but an odd iridescent life, busy in its own world. It whispers the pre-birth of a phoenix, and the start, even, of a rainbow — but only because, even with death, I am a romantic fool.

I visit their house. They are of the same mind as me.

If you're dead, I wonder what course your dying took. Was it crackling and thunderous, your fists tearing at branches and shrubs? Or was death the sigh of a silk scarf falling from a crystal globe? I need you dying in strength. I think of my dream and ask you again what kind of symbol did I see? I have to know if your death was flawed or perfect. Are you as deliberate as I've grown to believe? Can you blame me that I have to know whether your teachings are true. Because I am in your footsteps. It's up to you whether or not my story has a happy ending.

You haven't read the end of me. I have lots more to tell you. You, the one person I've found to whom I can open the doors of my chest. Here I am, a fool, who in my life's nick of time came to live in quarantine with the one person I know who escaped the waking sleep.

I know you think I'm being romantic and corny but I can say whatever I want. I am free to rave now, to rhapsodize, for who is listening?

You baffled me out of my hyperbolic box, you bored me out of my slapstick life. My life is no longer cheap. Neither is my story. I have a good story now.

But you leave me with nothing but the symbol of your leaving.

What to do now? Alone, like you warned me. Here I am.

I wonder what I've achieved, really. I have periods of peace. Bell chimes, even, of certainty. My explosion the day we made love on the knoll and you opened your eyes for me. It was like seeing into a vast aquarium, a charged, perfect colourlessness that went forever. I think I knew everything then. I lay on top of you, Annie, but you watched me from below and above and behind. I relaxed in this hierarchy of sacred selves, I sensed the gentle accord of angels.

A second later I was normal again. Perhaps someone like me can achieve nothing more than normal.

But near the end of your book I find talk of a fourth vow. (If you made up the first three, what is this doing here?) If I understand right it is a necessary step. And if I understand right it is unattainable. Can something be both necessary and unattainable?

You say:

> I hated people. Everyone lied and it was too hard a sight. I lied too, and hated myself most of all. But when I began to see why we lie, it became impossible to hate.

You say:

> It is the love-urge of a dog. Intelligent people find this hard. Intelligence doesn't exclude this love, but leans on it cruelly.

You say:

> The Fourth Vow comes of itself, an eagle in your

empty heart, and when it comes you simply love as
if the world has become your body.

I'm reminded of the time you whispered to me that the final job of a lover is to give away even his *luck*. I can feel yours now, a breath behind my neck. That this might be my imagination makes it nonetheless true. I feel your luck outside tonight, I feel it in the paper of your journal here at my elbow. I feel it in the wood of this table. You are in its grain and you feel the weight of my arms.

Is it so absurd to think that the attitude of the living can help the quest of the dead? Annie, is there anything I can do to help you? I like to think you no longer limp. If I give you my luck will you stay with me? *I give you my luck.*

Because you've given me your eyes. This morning I went outside to piss. I was still stricken by seeing your body but I had to piss, as I will tomorrow and the day after that. I pissed and, while I shook the last drops out, shaking my penis like a fat rubber band, I realized I'd never given this familiar act my best eyes. There I was, sad old man with a cartoon head shaking his dumb rubber thumb. A drop flew, it landed on the back of my wrist, impaled on a hair. I looked closer. The sun was on it, a yellow prism bead. In it a magnified hair, and skin a mysterious green. I rolled my wrist, but there the drip stayed, defying gravity, kept perfectly round by the laws which govern little drips. I let it dry there.

And still with your eyes I lift my gaze to an improbable world, one that smiles a snake's smile and shines with god-wild light, yet sings the good corny music of a babbling brook, the sound of a world being tickled to death.

You've taught me, Annie. I ride the body of time like a running horse, and as I ride I fly a kite of small joy high above me. The kite is tied to a string that is anchored to a hook through my heart. For that is the way it is. You've taught me. I'll sit on my stump. Go to bed, rise, eat. Fish. Little things. It is here the knot unties. Maybe I'll go bother Alison. What do you think of that?

DATE DUE